Tainted Money

Tainted Money

James Kelly

To order additional copies of this book, contact:
Xlibris
1-888-795-4274
www.Xlibris.com
Orders@Xlibris.com
789627

Tainted Money   The End started here.

I left the architect's office at 6:30 on a Friday in March 1977. I was hoping to get out of there by 4:30 and beat the traffic, but he purposed to replace the exterior back wooden stairs with wrought iron or ornamental iron so we went over the plans and cost. I told him I would run it passed Mrs. Mace and see what she says. I then headed directly to Mary Mace's Union Street flats in Pacific Heights with the architect's plans for a roof garden and all the paper work for her construction permits and his plan to replace the back exterior stairs. She owned three flats all identical almost two thousand square feet each with three bedrooms two baths and a bath and bed room in back of the kitchen for a maid's quarters. I pulled up and parked in her driveway next to the other two garages on the side street. I was on the side of the house which sloped from the back of the house to the front of the south side of Union Street. The back of the building was a half story shorter than the front so the car was listing sideways towards the Bay. This was normal because of the hills in San Francisco and the crowded neighborhood the parking was catchers catch can. The apartment house was box shaped stucco affair with over hanging parapets covering the top of the soffits in Spanish tile with the windows placed symmetrically from the first floor to the second and third floor giving it a Mediterranean look. The entrance was recessed four feet and approximately in the center of the building on Union Street. The front door was painted forest green with the entire center panel glass which gave you a perfect view of the small, but smartly decorated foyer and the bottom steps of the stair case as it turned up through the ceiling to a landing on the second floor. I caught the first floor tenant leaving and I grabbed the outer door before it closed which saved me from having to play tag on the intercom with Mary. I was in a hurry so I bounded up the two and a half flights of stairs then stopped to catch my breath on the landing in front of her door. I suddenly had a peculiarly ominous feeling. It was her front door; it was ajar and that was not normal. I tentatively pushed the door open to a familiar dark slate floor. It was a wide hallway about eight feet with period sconces opposite each other illuminating soft shaded alabaster walls. As I stepped in I pushed an umbrella stand to the side and called out Mary's name; there was no response so I walked down the short hall to the living room. There were two couches apposing one and other the furthest one against the large window looking out into the Bay directly at Alcatraz and the back of the other facing me; I zeroed in on the back of someone's head sitting in the couch closest to me. I called out Mary's name again and again no response. The feeling of Deja vu was over whelming as I turned around the corner of the couch I saw Mary staring at me with blank eyes that were beginning to get opaque and with blood still seeping from her chest. For reasons I couldn't explain I started to feel numb; I had a problem bringing this to reality I seemed to be someone else I ignored the body and began to take in the murder scene. Her flat was still sparsely furnished in one glance I saw that her Aunt's figurine of Umbrella Boy was missing from the mantle it was a very expensive Hummel. I recognized her china set on the coffee table it was an heirloom inherited from her Aunt; there were two cups, a sugar bowl and creamer but only the cup in front of Mary was half drunk and the other was still full and untouched. It was apparent to me there were bullet wounds in her chest and from the position of the body and the way she was dressed she must have known the murderer and was completely surprised. She was wearing light brown slakes, Cordovan loafers and a man tailored pale yellow shirt now stained in blood. She looked exactly like Allen which made me shiver. I came to my senses then backed away from the scene retraced my steps and went to the down stairs neighbor and called the police then my wife who at first said nothing to this news than after a long moment of silence asked how long would I be. I told her I didn't know.

I went down to the entrance lobby to wait for the police. When the patrol car pulled up I opened the front door and met the first officer and explained I was the one who called the police and told him the body was on the top floor. The first officer told his partner to take my statement while he checked out the top floor. A second cruiser pulled up behind the first patrol car as I was giving my statement when a totally absurd thought struck me that the officer taking my statement was writing in the same little note book that all San Francisco policeman used and wondered if they were issued it. When I finished my statement I told the officer I was going to sit in my car and to let me know when I could go. I decided to just lean against my car and watch the fog roll in across the bay and try to clear my brain of all that has happened in the last few years that would try a man's sanity. The two officers that came last circled the building and one climbed the back wooden stairs which were attached to the outside of the building so I could follow his progress. As I was watching the policeman climb the stairs I thought of the architect's plan to replace them with iron. I was snapped out of my thoughts when I heard my name from the opposite direction I turned to see Detective Oscar Norman walking towards me. We greeted each other and the first thing the Detective said was, "This looks like a gruesome replay of her husband's murder".

"I know I couldn't help but think of the irony of me finding both bodies".

"Medwin's talking to the maid who lives and works on the second floor; she saw a man that she recognized as a frequent visitor at Mrs. Mace's Flat that fits the description of Allen's old roommate Jean Le Beau. She saw him leaving in a hurry going down the back stairs within minutes after she thought she heard two loud cracking sounds from Mrs. Mace's apartment. This is sounding more and more like her husband's murder especially if he has an air tight alibi". Medwin, Oscar's partner came down the back staircase and ambled over to me and Oscar then told us he called the Precinct to pick up Le Beau at his apartment for questioning. Oscar looked questionably at Medwin then asked, "Le Beau is that his real name or just a stage name like Allen had"?

"What do you mean a stage name he wasn't in the theatre it was the name of his boutique; and it happened to be his real name he's a French Canadian originally from Quebec. Unlike some people I know who change their name to sound more American".

"Medwin why don't you bite my ass"?

"Touchy, touchy let's not be thin shinned; tell Mr. Kerry your real name and see if he agrees with me you should be proud of your family name".

"We go round and round on this I changed my family's name because it was a tongue twister it had nothing to do with proud or not proud".

At this point I had to ask, "What was your family's name".

"Normotinescue it's pronounced "Nor-motin-esque" it's Romanian; my parents were from a little town no one ever heard of; they spent the last year of the war on a German farm as labors curtesy of the Romanian Government and a year in a Displaced Person camp after the War. We left for the States and never looked back so to me changing the family name was a natural; any other questions"? I realized it was a hot button issue between Oscar and Medwin and realizing Oscar's age he was probably either born on the German Farm or in that D.P. Camp; so I opted-out. I asked if they were done with me so I could leave and Medwin told me to wait and he would see if the lab boys were done upstairs so they could give me a paraffin test then I could leave, but of course, you know the drill by now we'll need a formal statement down town probably tomorrow. I went upstairs they performed the test and I left for home. By the time I got there the baby was in bed and Anne was at the kitchen table drinking coffee. I kissed her on the cheek, but it was more of an air kiss and she asked if I was hungry. I sort of lifted my eye brows and asked if there was any cognac left. She told me one bottle, but I better get it because it's hidden my father has been helping himself to the case so I hid the survivor. I had to snicker at her caustic humor then asked if she had eaten. She sort of frowned and told me she really wasn't hungry. She came back from the pantry with a bottle of cognac. While I opened it she got a glass for me from the cupboard. I poured myself a drink and said why don't we go to the living room and relax. After we sat I blurted out, "What a chain of events I can't help feeling this was Mary's destiny she kept flirting with the wrong people all her life". Anne didn't answer she pick up her coffee then realized she couldn't drink it then tried to say something but got choked up and returned to the kitchen. I continued to stare out the bay window at the street below. I heard a familiar clanging of the cable car bell and the humming vibration of the towing cables under the street and felt myself slip into my revere. In that instant I saw Mary standing in front of their open apartment door in her negligée with the back light silhouetting her body. In the next instant I saw John pointing and gesticulating with a cigar between his fingers from behind his desk; then back to when it all started.

Chapter 1

1969 I arrived in San Francisco to visit an old friend from my childhood in New York. We had planned a ski trip to Lake Tahoe and when I returned to San Francisco I never left. I gravitated back into the construction trades as a carpenter intending to just try out living in San Francisco for a year because it reminded me of little old New York when I was kid, but then I met Anne Marie Montalvo a local girl and we were married with in eight months. I myself was of average height about 5foot 10inches and 180 pounds with light brown hair and green eyes and as Irish as patty pig. My bride was a perfect opposite; she was Mediterranean Italian with black hair and deep brown almond shaped eyes all framed in by clear alabaster skin. I won over my Mother-in-law with my knowledge and love of Italian food and my Father-in-law,

"Because I had strong hands of a working man".

Time line 1973; I had been buying houses in need of repair bringing them up to code and selling them. One of the houses I sold to an expatriate, but a long-time San Franciscan Tom Valance a famous photograph with societal and political connections. This would take my life into a direction I could have never imagined.

Tom had introduced me to another ex-New Yorker John Mace; a greying red headed blue eyed Irishman an inch or two taller than six feet in a hand-tailored Ferragamo suit. He told me he was a mortgage broker and was relocating back to San Francisco and starting up a one man office. He said he was impressed with my remodel of Tom Valance's house and he thought we could do business. He invited me to dinner to discuss further business; we met at Le Mason a very expensive French restaurant; I thought the choice of the restaurant was to impress me and it did. I thought he wanted to discuss remodeling his house or apartment to my surprise he offered me a job in mortgage brokering. I felt obligated to tell Mace I knew next to nothing about mortgages and finance other than single family housing on the most basic level. Mace just smiled then he told me I had all the basics and what he had in mind was accumulating properties for income and managing them for the long haul. I need someone like you to bring them up to code and you can use someone like me to finance them; I think we're a good match. And one more thing there's not much to mortgage brokering I could teach you in a matter of a few months. I have to tell you up front I just finished serving eighteen months in Lompoc on a dispute with the government over taxes; I've been told I have paid my debt to society and I'm starting all over. I hope you don't judge me too quickly and give my offer serious thought because I think we would make a good partnership. I was quiet and was fiddling with the salt shaker with my eyes roaming the room when John asked if I had any questions. "Yeah what's Lompoc"? John's steely face replied, "It's a Federal Correctional Center down south". The rest of the dinner was spent on John reliving some New York nostalgia, but what John was reliving was way out of my league. I told Mace his offer caught me by surprised, but I would give him an answer by the end of the week and it was nearing ten o'clock so we said good night and I headed home.

We lived in a house on Hyde Street that Anne had inherited from her grandmother so I drove down Van Ness turned right at North point and another right on Hyde then up the hill to the middle of the block and avoided a cable car coming down Hyde by making a right turn into Bergen Alley. The Alley was cobble stoned, narrow and slippery with room for only one car at a time it ended in a small parking area with two covered parking spaces in the back of our house. I opened the back door and passed through the pantry and laundry room combo into the kitchen where Anne was waiting for me with a two cup expresso, the Italian chicken soup.

"So how did it go"?

"Interesting, but not what I expected".

"What'd you mean"?

"It wasn't about a remodel job at all he offered me a job as a mortgage broker".

Anne was quiet for a moment and when she was about to ask the obvious question when I said, "Let's sleep on it and we can talk about it in the morning". That didn't work the questions started as soon as I hit the pillow.

After talking it over with Anne the following morning she thought it would be a good idea to ask Tom Valance how much he knows about John. I agreed but decide to meet John Mace and discuss the offer further so I called him and made an appointment. His office was on Bush Street a few blocks up from Montgomery. The office was on the second floor of a four story building with only a single elevator so I walked up found the door marked U.S. Brokerage and entered. The receptionist greeted me by name and a smiling hello. She was an extremely attractive woman in her late thirties or early forties and even in her sitting position it was obvious she had a body to match. She told me John was expecting me and to go right in. His office was small with an opened window overlooking Bush Street inviting the street noise. John came from behind his desk and said come on we're late and hustled me out the door and down Bush heading for Montgomery Street. He was telling me they had to meet with the manager of the old Bank of America building at 300 Montgomery Street to finalize their new office layout. I had to quicken my step to stay up with John's long strides; it was the first time I had been in the refurbished building and I didn't like the main entrance. John remarked he liked the airiness and the clean modern look, but I thought the old Art Deco with all the Carrara Marble fit the building's 1920's stile. We took the elevator to the fourth floor and as we stepped off were met by a man named Alex Neuhaus, the building manager. John introduced me as his associate and building contractor. I glanced quizzically at John but got no response. He took us to a series of small offices that were being remodeled into larger more spacious offices. Most of the partition walls were removed and a plywood table with plans on them was in the center of the middle room; as Alex was trying to explain the progress John kept interrupting him with the question, "When will it be done"? I looked over the plans and got a good idea of the office layout that's when John asked for my opinion. I thought John was more interested in engaging me in the office remodel then really my opinion so I kept my opinion short and to the point and all the while John kept looking at his watch. He suddenly blurted out they had a luncheon meeting and they were running late so we left Mister Neuhaus a little frustrated carefully rolling up the new office plans. John herded me to the elevator telling me we had a business meeting at the new Bank of America building across the street. As soon as the elevator started to move I told John I hoped I hadn't misled him and that I was not a licensed contractor. "You didn't mislead me I knew that". As we were leaving the Old Bank of America I looked up across Montgomery Street at the mammoth black frontage fifty two stories dominating down town San Francisco; I was fighting the feeling of intimidation, but followed John straight across the street while dodging traffic. When we entered the lobby I was a stride or two behind him and tried not to be obvious about quickening my step. We took a series of express elevator to the restaurant on the fifty something floor. The maître-de was standing at his lectern head down concentrating on a reservation list and without lifting his head said, "If you don't have a reservation give me a minute and I'll see what I can do". John just continued walking with me in tow passed the maître-de to a table at the window. The maître-de recovered dropped his pencil and took off in pursuit of John and me; he caught up with us just as we were about to sit and started to explain that the table was reserved. John continued to sit and turned to the maître-de and told him they were meeting Mister Richard Somers and he being a member of the Bankers Club I'm sure he made reservations. The maître-de's sniffy attitude sweetened a bit but he felt compelled to say that Mister Somers table was in the Banker's Club a more quiet area of the restaurant. As all this was going on I saw a gentlemen heading directly at us with a look of exasperation; I just knew it was Mister Somers. He was a little taller than average with greying hair and dressed in a blue conservative business suit. When he was a step or two from the table he said, "Arthur this will be fine we'll have lunch here if it is O.K. just switch my table reservation over to here". "Certainly Mister Somers I'll make the change immediately". I was still standing when Somers extended his hand and introduced him-self I shook his hand and in return introduced myself as Jim Kerry. We both sat and John's surly manner with the maître-de disappeared into a smile and said, "What's new Dick"?

"I have to ask you why you have to antagonize maître-des, bank vice-presidents or anyone else that you think is putting on airs".

"What's the problem you're a big mucky muck around here I'm doing your job for you; you should be putting some of these people in their place".

"I thought you got over that knee jerk reaction of being a kid from the street attitude? Just to let you know all us big mucky mucks are held to the club rules and I'm sure to hear about this".

"I got your point so let's get to business; did you go through the loan package from Blackstone Corp."?

"Yes and I see Johnny Peresci's name as president, but I didn't see his father's or his brother-in-law's names has there been some family troubles"?

"No not at all the father and brother–in-law retired, Johnny has taken over the land development business".

"I don't know if that is good or bad the last land development he did it almost went belly up they were saved by the explosion in the Real Estate market".

"Come on Dick you know this business is always a matter of timing. The family has been land banking for years they just got this property incorporated into the City and rezoned it from agriculture to residential development they own the property free and clear. What'd you say about an interest rate of one over prime"?

"I'd be saying more like three over prime".

"Come on Dick we can do better than that".

"When you say we is that the regal we or the editorial we"?

I was trying to follow the conversation but most of the jargon was foreign I was at a loss so I sat and tried to look competent, but I would glance now and then at Mister Somers. He was a handsome man in a rugged sort of way until he began talking. His mouth would lose its serious curve and turn into a Dutch uncle smile; his penetrating grey eyes would begin to squint in a harbinger of what was on this mind. I liked him immediately. As the two were talking I found myself starring at the cars coming and going on the Bay Bridge ramps the view from the fiftieth floor miniaturized everything. There seemed to be a break in the conversation and Dick asked me what my thoughts were? In a quiet panic I turned to Dick and said, "I'm sorry I was just spaced out looking at the approach to the bridge and the ramp reminded me of final approach of a runway".

Suddenly Dick looked deep in thought John glanced at Dick then shrugged at me in a questioning manner I just returned John's shrug.

Dick looked up at me and asked, "Did you fly in the military"?

"No I got my ticket as a civilian just a single engine land and half panel".

"Half panel what's that"?

"I don't know my instructor used the term for basic instrument flying".

Dick mused, "It is odd what will come back to you out of the blue, literally, your remark about the ramp on the bridge brought me back to my first solo landing at Fort Rucker, but I washed out on multi-engine and wound up a navigator in the Eighth Air Force in England".

"Were you involved in the Schweinfurt raids"?

"I like your terminology involved, but no that was the XVI Bomber Group I was in the 4th BomberWing of the 96th Bomber Group we went to Regensburg for the Messerschmitt factory". Just then a waiter discretely cleared his throat and asked if we decided on the lunch menu. When the waiter left with their order John said, "Let's get back to business".

Dick apparently over his nostalgic trip said, "By the way if the land is free and clear why don't they go to a local bank or savings and loan for their finance".

"You know Johnny he doesn't feel comfortable dealing with banks".

"What are you talking about his cousin owns the Union Commercial Bank".

John huffed, "Yeah, well that's one of the reasons".

Dick started laughing then stopped caught his breath and started laughing again and asked, "What's going on in that family".

John looked annoyed as lunch arrived, but waited until the lunch was served then said, "Look Dick this is a money maker we can split the commissions and we're talking a land loan then a land improvement loan then a construction loan three concurrent loans".

"I'll have to look at the property".

"Great Jim can drive you down tomorrow".

Chapter 2

I parked in the back of the house and entered through kitchen where my mother-in-law was cooking dinner. Little Gina was seated in her high chair toying with some dry cereal. She was dressed all in blue and I knew my mother-in-law dressed her because she said it made her eyes more blue and her curly black hair even blacker. I was heading over to her highchair when my mother-in-law asked how my day was.

I replied, "Not bad". She said I looked snappy in my sports jacket and tie, but she thought I looked better in my work clothes. I thought I better change the subject before it started an argument so I asked what smelled so good. Crab Ciappino and we need bread two loaves and maybe a spinach pie for dessert; go to Macaluso's Bakery they're the best.

"Did you call Anne at work she can pick up the bread on her way home"?

"She's running around so I'm asking you; you could be there and back in a couple of minutes".

"I'm interested in where you get your concept of time; Macaluso's is all the way down Columbus this time of day it's at least twenty minutes each way".

"Your exaggerating you could be there and back in two shakes of a Lambs tail".

"I'll tell you what I'll stir the pot and you go to the Bakery and I'll count the number of shakes of the Lamb's tail".

"This time of day it's a man's job to go to the bakery".

"Then why didn't you call Anne earlier when you knew she was at the shop and ask her to pick up the bread on her way home that time of day it could be a women's job to pick up the bread".

"Are you going to pick up the bread or not"?

Before I could answer they heard Anne's car going through the alley and before they could resume their banter Anne walked through the door with two loaves of bread under her arm and cake box balanced on the palm of her hand. I got up and took the bread from under her arm and put it on the kitchen counter. I kissed her on the cheek and whisper you saved the day. Her mother peeked in the box and said ricotta pie then Anne said no it's cheese cake; her mother shrugged and said, "Same thing". Anne gave me the look not to say anything and I knew it would only start another round with my mother-in-law. Anne picked up little Gina and we headed for the front room. We walked down the hall passed two bedrooms and bath to our favorite room the living room overlooking Hyde Street. This time of year the late afternoon sun shone through the green tinted water glass of the bay window causing imagined droplets on the beige carpet to move and change shape.

The front of the house facing Hyde Street started right at the side walk with the bay window hanging over the street; the entrance to the basement apartment was directly under the bay window and a twelve step entrance to the main floor to the left on the down side of the slopping street that was typical when the houses were built in the 1920s.

Anne sat with the baby in her lap while I stood at the window watching distorted shapes pass below. Anne asked, "What's the verdict; you going to take the job or not"?

"We had lunch today with another broker an important one he belongs to the Banker's Club; John volunteered me to drive him to the East Bay to look at a land development project".

"So this means you're interested right"?

"I didn't get a chance to ask Tom what he knows about John Mace but I'd like to see where this goes". The conversation ended with the call from the kitchen that dinner was ready.

In the morning I drove down Avila Street in the Marina found the address and parked my truck. The building was of Spanish motif with arched entrance and an iron gate with a line of mail boxes with intercoms attached. I pushed the button marked Mace and a woman's voice answered and I announced my-self and the woman said, "Come on up 2nd floor 2F then buzzed me in". I glanced back at the apartment number on the mail box on impulse to confirm the apartment number then bounded up the stairs to the 2nd floor and there John's receptionist was waiting for me at the open door. My momentum slowed as I walked toward her one reason she was wearing a sheer night gown and the light from the apartment was behind her accentuating her well-formed body. The closer I got the better looking she got with no makeup and her hair pulled back in a ponytail. I made a conscience effort not to let his eyes roam, but it didn't work. When I got to the door I asked if John was ready she chuckled and said, "He's having breakfast by the way I'm Mary John's wife and temporary receptionist". She motioned to come in and told me he was in the dining room down the hall to the left. As I walked down the hall I could feel her eyeing me all the way to the dining room. John was at the head of the table just finishing his breakfast when he looked up and said, "Good timing do you want any coffee"?

"No I had my quota for the day".

"I've got to change my tie I dropped something on it".

He yelled for Mary to get him a clean tie and then started to lay out my day with Dick Somers. Fifteen minutes later Mary entered the dining room dressed for work and a clean tie for John. John all most sneered when he said, "I won't wear this rag so get me one of my ties". Mary seemed unperturbed and in an even voice said, "It's a power tie I got at Allen's Boutique". "That's another reason I won't wear this rag;

That fag owes me ten thousand bucks I lent him on your say so because he's such a good friend of yours and I'm not going to extend the loan".

At this point I was getting uncomfortable so I told John I would wait for them down stairs. John told me to park my truck because I was going to use the Cadillac to drive Dick to the East Bay. I said fine I parked my truck in a ticket free area and went back and leaned against the car until they came down and John was wearing Mary's tie.

Dick was waiting in front of 300 Montgomery in the loading zone dressed minus his suit and tie in favor of a swearer and slacks. When I pulled up Dick put out his cigarette and opened the back door to put his attaché case on the floor then got into the front seat and pointed to the East Bay Bridge and said, "Advance to the gang plank". I laughed at the expression and headed for the bridge. After some maneuvering and Dick's directions we were on the 680 heading for Union City when Dick asked me how long I knew John. I told him I met John through a friend here in San Francisco just a few weeks ago. After a pause he said,

"Then you didn't know him back in New York".

"No I doubt I would have known John back in New York we were in different leagues". He paused again then asked, "How much do you know about John"? I was getting an uneasy feeling not so much from the questions but from the way Dick was asking them. Now it was my turn to pause then asked Dick if there was something I should know. "No I'm sorry I didn't mean to sound like I was probing it's just you both have the same New York accent". I replied that I didn't realize that, but thought there was more to Dick's questions then his answers.

Dick again took over with his directions and we left the freeway went through the southern end of the City to a construction trailer on a piece of property that looked like a part of a farm. As they were pulling in next to the trailer the door opened and a guy in very clean work clothes stepped down and headed for our car. He obviously knew Dick they shook hands and Dick introduced the man to me as Johnny Peresci the builder and developer of this piece of property. Johnny extended his hand in a macho grip and I found my-self in an eye ball to eye ball confrontation tightening our grips until Johnny leased his grip and smiled. Johnny turned to Dick and told him he could give him a tour of the property to be developed, but Dick said no let's see what you got on the drawing board. As they went to the trailer I was trying to figure out this guy Peresci he was a head shorter than me average build with a broad face and thinning black hair probably in his forties and has an ego problem. Dick was asking for a list of subcontractors and material suppliers and especially the excavating company he was using. Johnny seemed to be fairly organized he found everything Dick asked for without too much confusion, but kept mentioning the land was free of any loans and all permits have been filed and approved and we're ready to go. Dick went over the plot plans and copies of the permits then rolled them up and put them in with the loan package then told Johnny he would see what he could do and he would keep in touch; at that point we left. They were no more than ten minutes away when Dick mused out loud, "Something is wrong". I glanced over at Dick and asked, "What".

"I don't know but something isn't right the question I have is why doesn't Johnny go to a bank or savings and loan for the financing and eliminate our commission there must be a reason".

"We could stop at the building department while we're here and see what we can find out". I replied.

We went to the counter of the building department and Dick asked a young lady if she could help them with information for a development by the Blackstone Corp. While Dick was talking to the young lady I went to the Planning department and found a knowledgeable clerk who worked on the rezoning of the Blackstone property and was very informative; we talked for twenty minutes. When I found Dick he was leaning against the car; he had a smirk on his face when he said, "You found something out didn't you"?

"I certainly did the Blackstone development is being held up by the Water Conservation Committee. It seems the supervisors of this fair community are adapting the recommendations of the State Drought Report and are holding up the issuance of any water meters until they can figure out what the water availability will be now and the future".

"How long will that be"?

"No one knows, but if the Politian's are involved nothing will be resolved until their election and then maybe not".

Dick was smiling when he said, "The young lady at the permit counter told me all permits have been issued subject to the water meter availability and Blackstone is near the top, but all issuance of meters has been put on hold; I think Mister Peresci could have mentioned that".

The ride back Dick was very chatty he gave me a history of the Peresci family he told me Johnny's father and his father's brother bought farm land all through the area and over the years broke up large parcels into smaller parcels and sold them off. They built custom houses and that got them into small housing developments, of course, they took their children into the business; that's when the rift between the two bothers started.

Johnny's father bought out his brother and stayed in the land development business while his brother went into the banking business.

"It appears both fathers are retired and their sons have taken over their respective businesses; Johnny the land development and his cousin Phil the Union Commercial Bank down the road in Fremont.

I dropped Dick at his office and headed for John's office. When I opened the door I could hear John on the phone but Mary was missing. John yelled from his office to come in; I peeked around the door jam and John waved me in. I started for a chair as John hung up the phone, but before I could sit John bellowed, "What the hell did you say to Johnny Peresci"? I froze not knowing how to react then stood up straight and asked, "What do you mean".

"He says you torpedoed the whole deal".

"I don't know what he's talking about I didn't say more than two words to him".

"Not to him to Dick; why did you take him to the Union City Planning Department "?

"It was Dick that smelled a rat he wanted to know why Johnny didn't go directly to a bank and as far as Johnny is concerned he's an idiot with an ego problem; if you put any weight in what he says you'll look like an idiot". John was turning red and about to say something to me when Mary sang from the outer office, "I'm-m-m back". John's eyes shifted to the wall as if he could see through it to the main office he was now seething, "You told me you were going to lunch that was four hours ago".

"Yeah well I had to do some shopping".

"I told you those letters were important they have to get out in this afternoon mail".

"There's plenty of time I can type these two in five minutes and the mail doesn't go out until five". Gradually John's color was returning he reached for his ever present cigar and said, "You got to learn to stick to the game plan".

"What game plan? You told me to drive Dick to Union City if you didn't want me to help Dick you should have told me".

"Yeah well those water meters could nix the deal and if you didn't drag Dick to the Planning Office who knows we might have found someone to fund the deal".

I was still standing looking down at John and in that instant I realized John knew all along about the water meters. John pushed back in his chair and coyly said, "That's the game plan".

Mary typed and mailed the letters then I drove them to their apartment switched to my truck and drove home.

The next morning was Saturday and if nothing was on my work schedule I would sleep in. I awoke to the muffled sound of voices coming from the kitchen as my mind adjusted I recognized my father-in-law's voice. I dressed and wandered into the kitchen for my morning coffee. Anne was feeding the baby and her mother was at the stove making breakfast. Carl my father-in-law was reading the sport section looked up smiled a hello and went back reading the paper.

Anne's mother asked if I would like breakfast.

I said, "Yeah sure".

"We have some left over spinach frittata I could worm it up with a couple of eggs".

"That sounds good and with a couple of poach eggs".

"I already have a frying pan heated up for fried eggs".

"I like poached eggs with spinach you know like Florentine".

"Florentine, what do you think this is a restaurant I've been at this stove all morning now you want me to boil water for your poached eggs"?

Carl leaned over and whispered, "Take the fried eggs it's less aggravating".

Anne saved the day when she told her mother to sit down and have her coffee and she would make the poached eggs. On her way to the stove the phone rang she grabbed the receiver off of the wall phone and said hello. She turned and starred at me with a Mona Lisa smile and talked as if it was me she was talking to, "Yes she's fine getting bigger every day well thank you, yeah he's right here she handed the phone to me and said, "It's John".

"What's up chief"?

"About yesterday, no offence taken you said your piece and I said mine. Yeah; you were right it clears the air". When I was listening to John you could hear a pin drop in the kitchen they all listened to me say yes and sure a number of times and ended with why not and then finally O.K. and hung up. Everyone looked at me for an explanation, but I starred at Anne and with a twitching smile said, "You want to go to Las Vegas"?

For what was left of the morning I was peppered with question I couldn't answer; then finally I told them John has an important deal at the Tropicana and we have to be there on the ground running Monday morning. Mary's making reservation at the Hotel and flight arrangements she'll call back this afternoon with all the information.

Anne's mother asked if they were taking the baby and Anne said, "Not if you'll take her for a week or maybe ten days".

"What kind of a cockamamie deal is this you go off and leave the baby on the spur of the moment because some guy has business in Las Vegas"?

"Just answer the question will you take the baby for a week or not"?

"You got some nerve telling me it's a take it or leave it offer".

"Its O.K. mom we'll make other arrangements".

"What other arrangements you're not taking the baby to Las Vegas are you"?

"Maybe I want to check out some professional baby sitters and call Madeline to see if she can help".

"Madeline, she's too old to keep up with little Gina, she'll probably tell everyone I wouldn't take care of little Gina". I was watching Carl standing behind Anne's mother with a smile on his face watching Anne manipulate her mother; I could see her play her mother like an old violin and realized there was a lesson in all this. Her mother had a few more complaints about being taken advantage of, but eventually agreed to take care of little Gina if she could stay at our house. That settled Anne started packing then realized she didn't know how long they would be in Las Vegas so she called Mary. When she got off the phone she told me it was for a week and we'll be staying at the Tropicana and we leave Sunday afternoon with the Valance's. We left with Tom and Nancy Valance at 3 o'clock from San Francisco

Airport and were in our rooms at the Tropicana by 5 o'clock. Mary left word not to make dinner reservation because they were all having dinner at Lam's Restaurant at Caesar's at 8 o'clock and to meet at the cab stand at 7:30. Anne and Nancy were on the phone for an hour discussing what to wear when Anne got off the phone I said, "Why don't you wear that sleek black job that you can't even wear under wear with; she smirked and said yeah that's the only dress I have and don't be a smart ass I wear sheer black undies. "Yeah but no bra and I could help you get dressed".

"Yeah sure then we'll never get to dinner. Do you think I need a bra"? "Not at all you don't need one so enjoy the looks". They met Tom and Nancy at the cab stand a little after 7 o'clock and Nancy was also dressed to the teeth and told them they could walk to Caesar's in ten minutes, but I'm sure Mary wants to make a grand entrance. Anne and I had never been to Las Vegas so Tom and Nancy volunteered to be our unofficial guide through the maze of lights and all the glitz. John showed up with a new cigar in his mouth and in a thousand dollar suit, but it was Mary that stopped traffic she was in a revealing retro 1920's flapper out fit with a cloche that was topped off with multi colored pin feathers. Tom told John they were going to walk and they would meet at the steps to the Casino. Anne and I were gawking at the casino spectacle of flashing lights robotic people at the slot machines and animated people at the gaming tables.

We were there fifteen minutes before John and Mary showed up, but Mary got her grand entrance and we were off to the restaurant. John told the maître-de they were with the Kusterson party and were taken to the V.I.P. section of the restaurant that was elevated two or three feet above the main floor where you could be seen, and overlook the ordinary people. We were all jockeying for table chairs when a tall prematurely grey haired man in a Hawaiian flowered shirt approached John and introduced him-self as Dale Kusterson. John greeted him and then introduced everyone around the table and offered him a seat with a hand gesture. He apologized and said something came up just minutes ago that needed his immediate attention, but we would get together before you all leave. I was closest to John and could hear Kusterson tell him there was a meeting tomorrow at 9 A.M. in the casino office. John said he'd be there and Kusterson left. Dinner was elegant, rich and unrushed when we finished John headed for the casino Mary said she was meeting an old friend so the Valance's took the Kerry's for a tour of Caesars. We wandered through the rotunda passed the shops until the girls disappeared into an expensive woman boutique when they came out Anne was laughing and Nancy looked dead serious. We continued down to the Forum in time to see the Roman Statues come alive at a very impressive show. At that point Tom said he had a feeling the 21 table was calling him and Nancy said she wanted to play a slot or two so we wondered off by ourselves. I saw a sign for the stage door deli and told Anne that's where we're going tomorrow for lunch. I asked Anne what was so funny when you were coming out of that boutique. Anne giggled and told me when they were looking at dresses Nancy looked at the price tag and announced we have to leave; I asked why, she said because she could feel her charge cards starting the quiver.

I told Tom I'd meet him for breakfast in the morning while the girls slept in. I caught up with him playing Keno in the coffee shop. I said good morning but Tom looked mesmerized by the Keno tope board. I repeated good morning and Tom told me to hold on because he thought he had a winner; then yelled god dam it I only needed one more number. "I'm sorry Jim I got carried away good morning".

"I'm sorry I brought you bad luck".

"No such thing it's all in the stars you're destine to win or not it's got nothing to do with luck". I wasn't sure Tom was serious or not, but I asked how was his destiny at the black jack table last night.

"Same as this Keno I needed one more number; he smiled broadly then said last night winning was not in my destiny. I actually quit after an hour and went for coffee and ran into Mary and her friend and before you ask it was a she; Mary use to dance with her here in Vegas".

"Mary worked here in Vegas"?

"Oh yeah, that's how John met her about twelve years ago she was in the chores line in a show".

"Her friend can't be still dancing I would imagine she is about Mary's age". Tom looked at me with an accusing grin which prompted me to back tract on my statement, "Of course, if she looks anything like Mary and is in the same shape she could be still dancing". Tom suppressed a laugh and said, "Good recovery I'll have to tell Mary what you said but her friend is not aging as well".

I turned red with embarrassment and quickly replied, "Don't you dare".

"Why not"? She would be thrilled by your remarks about her shape".

"Yeah well maybe but I'm not sure how John would take it".

"I wouldn't worry too much what John thinks he has a myopic view of the world; business is everything what the people around him do is either ignored or he is oblivious to. He told me some things in conversation about the marriage counseling they're going through and it sounded more like therapy most of the content I wouldn't tell a priest".

I wanted to change the subject so I asked Tom if he knew what we were doing here at the Tropicana since John hasn't told me what kind of business they're supposed to be doing.

"Kusterson is trying to buy the Tropicana and needs financing and I'm sure John is one of the sources he's exploring; I'm here to do a photo layout and I expect you're here to do an appraisal for a financial package".

"You must be wrong I'm not an appraiser".

"John thinks you're a diamond in the rough and he's going to polish your many facets". I realized the waitress was standing a foot or so from the table waiting for my order so I ordered a roll and coffee and right behind her was the Kino girl with her nasal mantra "Keno". I finished my coffee and left Tom playing Keno and returned to our room. When I entered Anne was at the window in my dress shirt it was limp and damp taking perfectly to the contours of her body. She glanced briefly over her shoulder and commented it's a mesmerizing view. In my best "Duke Wayne" voice I said, "What are you doing in my shirt woman"?

"I had nothing to put on when I got out of the shower so if you want it back you'll have to take it off of me". That accounted for their absence at lunch and their unanswered phone calls.

Chapter 3

When I got out of the shower Anne was on the phone with Nancy I heard the tail end of the conversation and it was about an early dinner.

They suggested the Stage Door Deli and I was all for it; they hadn't heard from John and assumed he was still at the business meeting and Mary was with her friend. Later that evening we found John at the craps table, but Mary was still among the missing. John wasn't hard to find he was cheering on someone at his table and could be heard fifty yards away. Tom begged off and went straight for the 21 tables and the girls stopped at the nickel slots. John saw me coming and raised a finger to signal me to wait. Everyone around the table was staring at the woman with the dice someone yelled all bets down and she through the dice in seconds there was a collective groan with John's being the loudest. He picked up his chips and tossed one to the croupier then took me by the forearm and said, "Come on I'll buy you a beer". We went over to a table in front of a lounge bar and ordered two beers. The show was hours away so the bar was almost empty. We got comfortable and John explained the reason they were in Las Vegas and more importantly why at the Tropicana; it was an almost rehash of what Tom had told me. I stopped him and tried to explain I didn't think I was experienced enough to appraise a casino or for that matter anything in Las Vegas. John kept plowing ahead he told me he would sent me to a real estate broker here in town that would give him all the casino comps and even the latest building costs so is all you have to do is assemble all the facts and come up with a number.

I was lost and in a defensive tone and told John Anne was the one who compiled the comparative prices for me in San Francisco real estate; she use to work in real estate before she went to work for her father.

"That's even better take her with you we'll put her on the books and she can make a little money while she's here; just keep in mind Kusterson is footing the bill so don't be shy about spending money. I rented you a car it will be here tomorrow at ten. The real estate guy's name is Morgan I'll give you his phone number and address so call him he's expecting your call and meet him tomorrow. We'll all meet for breakfast at the coffee shop at 9 o'clock ".

When Anne and me got to the coffee shop a little before nine Tom and Nancy were playing Keno and John was arguing with Mary about some clothes she bought; we slid into the both next to Mary and she greeted us with a big hello and wanted to know how we liked Vegas so far?

We offered a few comments then John took over the conversation with business; he laid out what everyone's job would be and then said to me he had one favor if I would do for him to day. "Of course, what is it"?

"I'd like you to deliver a letter and pick up an envelope from a guy named Guy Corsey he owns the Feline Follies Casino in old town". Before I could answer Nancy let out a gasp and Tom stone faced stared at the Keno tope board. John turned to Nancy and asked if she was O.K. she replied it was the coffee it was too hot. John looked at Nancy a second longer than necessary and said,

"Make sure you check the temperature before you drink it". I felt obligated to say yes and John thanked me and Keno dominated the rest of breakfast. It was nearing ten o'clock and Anne told me they better get going. John smiled at Anne then said, "I love eager employees and handed me the envelope". As John said the car was waiting for us and to emphasize John's comment to spare no expense the rental car was a Cadillac. I drover and Anne gave directions and in twenty minutes we were at the Real Estate Office of Raymond Morgan. He had a full package of comps plus a map of the casino's locations. When Anne glanced through the papers she was surprised that there were the casino's annual reports and three years gross earnings. Morgan seemed to be preoccupied so we said our good buys and left. Anne directed me straight to the Feline Follies Casino; I maneuvered through the parking lot and entered through a side entrance. Anne told me to take care of business and she'd be right here at this slot machine next to the entrance. I found the office and asked for Mister Guy Corsey. I realized John must have called ahead because they called me by name and told me to take a seat Mister Corsey will be right with me. I didn't have time to get comfortable when a short bull like man in a Viavanti suit opened his door and motioned with a wave for me to come in. Corsey extended his hand and introduced him-self while still holding on to the door and said, "I believe you have a letter for me".

I cocked my head and said, "I have a letter for Mister Corsey could I see your driver's license"?

"What are you a lawyer you're in my place who else could I be"?

I didn't know quite how to answer because the guy didn't look Irish so I said nothing and just stared at him. He looked exasperated but dug out his wallet and handed me his license. I looked at the license without changing my expression and without looking up and said, "The name on this license reads Guytano Corsenti". He snatched his license back with a, "Yeah, Yeah Corsey's my stage name O.K. are you going to give me the letter or not"? I gave him the letter and he gave me an envelope with a comment that there was no mistaken you work for Mace. I left Corsey's office and picked up Anne at her slot machine. While I was driving back to the Tropicana Anne was looking over the envelope and told me I better ask John what's in this envelope. John was in a meeting all day so it wasn't until evening that I caught up with him; I gave him the envelope and asked John if he could tell him what was in it?

"Sure I.O.U.'s Guy held on to these while I was in Lompoc this town doesn't respect anyone who doesn't pay their debts; he's a standup guy he didn't tell anyone and waited until I got out and was able to pay him". "I hope you don't mind me asking, but the whole incident with this Corsey or Corsenti unnerved me especially the driver's license names not matching".

"Unnerved you; Guy called me in a panic after you left to make sure you weren't a cop so I asked him why did he do something wrong? I had to laugh when he just hung up on me".

Everyone seemed to go their own way for the rest of the week with me and Anne exploring every hotel and casino they could fit in before they left for home.

When we got back to San Francisco I took a day to organize my personal business when Mary called letting me know the new office was finished and the phones and furniture are being delivered tomorrow. She told me John was going to be in the East Bay all day and if I could give her a hand arranging the new office. I got there at 9 o'clock and the door was locked so I knocked and listened at the door for a minute and thought I heard someone so I knocked a little harder when the door opened there was a young man who looked familiar. He said, "You must be Jim I'm Allen a friend of Mary she'll be back in a few minutes she just went to the manager's office for extra keys for the office". We shook hands and I asked, "What's the schedule do you know"?

"No I don't and I'm not sure Mary does they're all scheduled for morning delivery so let's hope they're all on time".

As Allen was talking I noticed a slight effeminate lisp and I realized the reason he look familiar was he looked so much like Mary he could be her twin brother. They both turned when Mary come through the door she said she assumed we introduced each other and when we nodded then she took us for a tour of the new offices. She described the furniture and where the phones would go and went into a detailed description of the file room with stationary shelves, coffee tray and filing cabinets. I asked Mary when John would be back. She answered, "Who knows he's probably celebrating he's score from the Feline Follies". I asked too quickly, "What score".

She answered just as quick. "You ought to know you picked it up".

I looked confused and my mind when blank. We heard a tapping on the door jamb then the voice of the telephone man asking if he had the correct address. He said he had to go down to the main terminal in the building equipment room and heat up the lines and it should only take a half hour or so and left before anyone had a chance to ask any question. This suited Mary just fine she turned to me and said, "You wouldn't mind waiting would you? Allen and I haven't had anything to eat we'll just pop out and get something and be back in a jiffy". Of course, she didn't wait for an answer. I just nodded yes but they were already at the open door. I watched them walk to the elevator side by side in prefect cadence with Mary gesticulating with her finger to make a point. I was struck by the similarity of their body movements almost identical. I walked into what was my empty office stooped and felt the carpet then looked out the window on to Montgomery Street I was feeling quite full of himself when the phone man called from the main office. I gave him the layout of where the phones go and tried to stay out of the way. When the phone installation was finished the installer told me the phone numbers sequence and the intercom numbers and left. I didn't have time to think the new furniture arrived and I gave the movers the floor plan of which desks go where. I was standing with my arms crossed near the front door monitoring the furniture placement when Allen showed up without Mary. We were both dodging the movers so Allen told me Mary remembered an important appointment and asked him to let me know and if I would please wait for the storage company with John's filing cabinets. I told him sure and that I was free all day and it was no problem. When Allen left I got this eerie feeling I had talked to Mary in drag. As the furniture movers were finishing the storage people showed up. They started bringing in the cabinets when one of the storage movers told me accidently one of the cabinets got tweaked and the draw lock popped open and you need a key to relock it. I told the mover I didn't have a key so just place them in the filing room. I went over the delivery lists of the furniture and cabinets signed them and then I was totally alone. I closed the front door and took a quick look around the offices and was about to leave then decided to try and lock of the tweaked filing cabinet. I tried slamming it but I found I bent the first folder. I opened the draw to try and straighten it when curiosity got the best of me. It was labeled Addlemann I fanned through a few pages then stopped at a heading "Forensic Report Federal Detention Center Butner North Carolina". The report referred to a Michael "Mickey" Addlemann's psychiatric report. Reading the findings was confusing, but it mentioned murder and a penchant for violence. I suddenly felt I shouldn't be reading the file so I put the file back and closed the draw, but left it unlocked.

While Anne was making dinner she asked me why so glum you look like you lost your best friend. "Nothing's wrong it's just something Mary said today that's eating away at me and I don't know why".

"What she say"? "It's the way she said it; when I asked how long John would be in the East Bay she said she didn't know because John would be celebrating his Feline Follies score. When I asked what she meant by score; she said I should know I picked it up". I got quiet and waited for Anne's thoughts it didn't take long she said, "Whatever she was talking about it can't be money that manila envelope was too thin to have any amount of money in it so I would bet it's some kind of legal documents". I nodded an approval and then asked what was for dinner.

That evening John called me from the new office wanting to know what happened to the filing cabinet and who opened it? I explained it got tweaked by the movers. He wanted to know if Mary was there when the cabinets were delivered. I told him no and that I was the only one and I locked the office and left. John wanted to know if Mary took the office keys with her. I had no way of knowing, but told John I imagined she would. John wanted to know who went through the files.

I explained I tried to close the file draw and I bent one of the file folders I tried to straighten the folder out and just pushed it back in its place in the draw. John was quiet for a few moments like he was trying to weigh and balance what I just told him then asked what I was doing tomorrow. I told him I was free and asked what he had in mind. "We have property to look at tomorrow pick me up at ten use your truck with the ladders you may need them".

I picked John up at ten and he told me to go to Union Street and head for Pacific Heights. John was fumbling with a piece of note paper when I asked, "What's that". "It's the address of the property and I can't read Mary's chicken scratch". We stopped at a red light and I looked at the address and said, "I think I know the building it's on a corner of Union Street with three garages on the down slope of the side street. The garages are under the building". They parked in front of the building and John sat reading two pages of type written information on the building.

"This was written by the owner it says there are three flats one on each floor containing three bedrooms, two baths, full dining room and living room, commercial kitchen with a maid's bedroom and bath in the back and a garages under the building". John turned to me and asked, "What ya think"?

"How much"?

"Two hundred and twenty five thousand".

I looked skeptical and John quickly said, "I'm thinking of buying it for myself. I want you to give me your opinion on its physical condition and write up an appraisal that I can take to a bank. The owner's name is Budek he lives in the top flat and according to Mary he's a retired teacher and the place is too much up keep for him and his wife".

"Where did you get all that information"?

"Mary was in a cooking class with his wife the woman also told Mary they want to sell the place by them-selves to eliminate the broker's fee".

"That can be good or it can be bad depends on how much they know about Real Estate". I mused.

John looked at me grinning, "It's going to be good".

John hit the intercom button and a man's voice responded with a yes; John answered with his name and the door buzzed open. We started up the stairs and Mister Budek met us on the top landing then invited us into his flat. John introduced himself and told Budek I was his contractor and appraiser. We all shook hand and Mister Budek took us through a rehearsed tour of the Flat; mentioning all three flats were identical. He had a floor plan of the top flat all drawn with room measurements. John started talking price and who had the mortgage and obviously laying the ground work for negotiations so I asked Budek if I could walk around the building and check the roof. He said by all means; and in little over an hour we were on the way to John's apartment. We were sitting in my truck in front of John's apartment while John went over point by point what he want me to do; I asked myself if this was necessary or if John just wanted company. Finally I told John that when he gets the prices of any properties sold in the area to compare with Budek's it would give him a point to start his negotiations. John seemed satisfied and I headed home.

When I got home there was note from Anne saying she'll be a little late because she's going over the books with the accountant at her father's shop. The baby's at mom's and I'll pick her up on the way home it looks like left overs tonight. I went to the refrigerator grabbed some salami and cheese a cold beer and headed for the living room. I sat and was thinking of what Mary said about me picking up a score for John in Las Vegas it still bothered me, but I didn't know why. I suddenly was aware of the hum it was the wire cable under the street that pulled and controlled the cable cars going up and down Hide Street. I realized the noise was always there, but I only noticed it when it interrupted my thoughts. I heard Anne and the baby in the kitchen she must have driven through the alley while I was in the "o" zone.

She came into the living room with little Gina by one hand and a glass of wine in the other and maneuvered the baby to my waiting hands. I asked how was her day; she said, "Not bad mom wanted to come over for dinner, but I told her it was left overs then she offered to make some pasta dish".

"How did you get out of that"?

"I told her you were going to tear my clothes off as soon as I got home and ravage my body. She got embarrassed and didn't say another word and me and little Gina got out while the get'en was good".

I broke out in laughter then asked, "Did you really say that".

"Yeah I just didn't think I could take her questions that I knew she was dying to ask about my father's business".

"Where's your father"?

"He's at the Italian American Club with the boys".

Anne asked me about the property I looked at and if it was something we'd be interested in buying.

"It's not for us John is interested in buying it and besides it's' way out of our price range".

"How much"?

"Two hundred and fifty thousand".

"Where is it"?

"Pacific Heights".

"Well John certainly has expensive taste".

"I have to say it is a beautiful piece of property; it needs some work and its' over-priced, but I'll bet John will buy it. I'm supposed to do an appraisal for John to take to a bank and I need the comps for the area".

"And you want me to ask Larry for the comps"?

"Yeah".

"Jim I can't just ask Larry for comps he's a realtor that's his business he'll come up with comps when he buys or sells a house for us, not when the property isn't even listed".

"Why not, he has made a pretty of good amount money on us why not a favor".

"You have a point I'll ask him".

The next Monday when I got to the office Mary was not at her desk so I popped my head into John's office to say hello. John immediately asked for the appraisal for the Union Street building.

I said it wasn't totally organized yet, give me a half an hour and I'll be finished. John told me he was interested in the numbers and didn't care if it was organized or not. I stopped at John's desk and opened up my attaché case and fished through the contents then picked out a page and handed it to John. He quickly glanced at the page and said, "The price is too high you have to adjust it".

"What price are you talking about"? He pointed to a figure.

"That is his price it wouldn't be your offer look at the top of the page".

His eyes rolled up and a smile was grudgingly forming on his face.

"Let me get the appraisal organized and it will make more sense".

"Get it done as fast as you can we have a meeting with a banker this morning". I had it organized in twenty minutes and we went over the appraisal and when John was satisfied we were off to the Hanaford Savings and Loan. It was in walking distance and in fifteen minutes we were there. John told the receptionist we had an appointment with Mister Byrd, she told us to please take a seat and she would notify Mister Byrd you were here. Before we got comfortable a gentleman came to the reception area and introduced himself as Harry Byrd chief appraiser and Loan officer. He invited us to follow him to his office; on the way we passed a row of desks with young men either on the phone or with their noses in paper work. I was impressed I thought to myself that I never got this treatment when I was buying or selling a house. Harry Byrd had an office not a cubical which impressed me further. When we sat John introduced me as his contractor and appraiser which got a raised eye brow from Byrd he then bowed his head slightly towards me in what I took as professional courtesy.

He said he got a call from Phil Peresci at the Union Commercial Bank in Freemont I take it you've done a great deal of business with them he highly recommends you.

"That's nice to know, but that was a few years ago I've relocated back here in San Francisco. Since coming back I've tightened up the business to just me and Jim Kerry we work with a circle of independent brokers; it makes life a little less complicated".

"That sounds like good thinking; now how can I help you"?

"I'm negotiating to buy a building here in San Francisco and I've been told your S&L has the mortgage I've also been told it has a prepayment clause what I'm interested in knowing if I refinance through your S&L would you wave the prepayment"?

"I don't see why not if the mortgage is in good standing".

"I also would like to make out a loan application in my name and or my nominee".

"It's a bit unusual, but yes it can be done".

"To help things along Jim has done an appraisal; he then handed over the appraisal to Byrd and said he would take an application with him and they would keep in touch".

When we got back to the office Mary was at her desk and John seemed to ignore her he continued on into his office with me right behind. Mary was right behind me and put a series of phone messages on his desk and went back to her desk. John started to filter through the messages when I asked him about the prepayment penalty.

"This guy Budek thinks he has to pay a prepayment penalty on his loan when he sells; I'm not going to enlighten him and deduct the amount from the sales price and tell him I'm going absorb the cost. We've already discussed price and I told him when the appraisal was done we'll finalize the sales contract".

Mary was standing in the doorway until John said, "What"?

"One of those messages is from a man named Kalami he said he was referred to you by Dick Somers". John's expression changed into his brokers face and I knew if I asked him about this nominee thing I wouldn't get a straight answer so I went to my office and filed his copy of the Union Street appraisal. I pulled out my unfinished appraisal of the Tropicana and stared at it and had no idea where to start. I buzzed John on the intercom and told him I was at an impasse with the Tropicana appraisal and had no idea what to do. John didn't answer but in five minutes he entered my office with a file and said, "This is the appraisal done on the Feline Follies about three years ago just follow the format and plug in your numbers". When I opened it up the first thing I saw was Tom Valance's beautiful Picture layout of the casino and all its amenities.

Chapter 4

In the middle of the week I got a call from Harry Byrd asking me to get access to the building on Union Street for appraisal purposes. I made the arrangements to go through all three flats and when we were through I thanked the owner Mr. Budek and we left. Harry asked me if I had time for a cup of coffee. I said yes and we met on Union Square at Cafe Espresso. Harry told me he was impressed with my appraisal of the Union Street property and asked if I was interested in doing some appraisals for his S&L on a case by case basis as a contractor.

I was flabbergasted I couldn't answer I felt tongue tied. Harry realized he caught him by surprise then tried to relax me by telling me my experience in recognizing the need for repairs and my schedule of cost in the overall appraisal greatly added to the cost to value ratio. I seemed to be floundering so Harry asked, "What do think".

"I like the offer but I didn't understand a word". Harry grinned and said, "We'll get along great. The loan was approved this morning so you can drop by the title company any time today and sign the loan papers". I had a lost look on my face and asked, "What loan".

"You are the nominee that John was referring to for the Union Street property he opened escrow yesterday". I recovered and remarked, "How did you get the loan through so fast"?

"I sit on the loan committee and I'm the chef appraiser need I say more; but it is subject to a down payment of thirty five thousand dollars". I told him I would be in to sign the note sometime tomorrow afternoon then I made a bee line to the office. Mary was at her desk and handed me a phone message I took it without looking at it and went to John's office. He was on the phone and waved me in and pointed to a seat. John hung up the phone and asked, "How did it go with Harry Byrd"?

"Terrific the loan's a shoe in and it was approved this morning, but we're short thirty five thousand and your nominee doesn't have it". I was getting excited and upset and I thought John was enjoying it which made me angrier. John got up and walked to his office door and closed it then walked back to his desk and sat. "I've got the thirty five thousand so calm down we're going to the Bank in Fremont tomorrow to pick it up and then close the Union Street deal".

"So how did I become your nominee in this contract without being told"?

"Relax you and Anne are going to own a two hundred thousand dollar property that is in a positive cash flow; life couldn't be better".

I was numb the rest of the day I couldn't grasp what was going on. When I got home and told Anne she too was speechless; finally she said let's see what happens at the bank tomorrow.

I met John at his apartment in the morning and John drove to the bank in Fremont; on the way he filled me in on who we were going to meet and what to expect. "Philip Peresci is the president and will probably ignore you his vice president is EJ Boradine he'll ask you questions like how long you know me and then ignore you lastly there's the bank manager

Johnson he'll suggest a restaurant for lunch. Johnson should have information on a lease car for you and a modest unsecured line of credit". "Why would I need an unsecured loan account"?

"You don't have to use it but it's good to have; you never know when you might need it". We were expected at the bank so all three were waiting for us in Peresci's office. John introduced me and true to John's word the president ignored me the vice president asked how long I knew John and Johnson mentioned a new steak house that just opened in a nearby Mall. It was suggested that Johnson take care of my business and Johnson suggested they take an early lunch. I thought it was obvious they wanted me out of the room so they could talk business. They were just setting up for lunch when we arrived at the restaurant so Johnson stopped at the bar and had a drink while they setup a table. When we sat Johnson asked me if I minded eating a little early because the bosses wanted to go over the SBA loan John is proposing and they're always shy about discussing high finance in my presence; he let out a nerves laugh just as the waitress handed us the menu. Johnson ordered another drink and was asking questions that were too obvious not to realize he was pumping me for information; the one question that intrigued me was when he asked about a hotel on Sutter Street named the Cornucopia because I knew John had visited there a few time recently and alone. Before the bill arrived Johnson ordered another drink then disappeared into the men's room to avoid paying the bill it was obvious what John meant that he could be bought for a few drinks and a steak dinner. We returned to the bank and I followed Johnson to his corner on the main floor of the bank where he had a larger cubical then everyone else. He spent a minute or two thanking me for lunch then abruptly turning to the business of a lease car for me. He asked what kind of car did I have in mind. John told him to lease a prestigious car so I said a four door Mercedes sedan. Johnson didn't seem to be fazed he just jotted it down and picked up the phone and dialed a number; when someone answered he asked if they had any four door sedans. He cupped the transmitter and asked what color. I answered anything dark. I settled on a forest green and was told I could pick it up any time at the European Importer in Oakland. Johnson told me that a five thousand dollar unsecured line of credit was set up for him here starting immediately. Almost on cue EJ came out of the president's office and motioned for us to come to the office. Once inside it was John that had the floor he was standing near the president's desk with the president seated and EJ sitting in front of a coffee table with an open folder in front of him. He briskly told me EJ had some papers for me to sign this immediately alarmed me. I asked, "What papers".

EJ in his condescending tone launched into bank speak which made me even more alarmed. My face was telegraphing my panic so John stepped in with a quick explanation that it was the thirty five thousand to close Union Street deal and it was being funded as a second deed of trust against the property. Take a looked at it it's not simple interest with a balloon payment it's amortized over seven years. I was familiar with the difference between simple interest and amortization and I realized this was a very good loan but unusual.

I read it through twice more and made sure the check was made out to the title company. I overcame a slight reservation and signed it; I still had it in my hand when John handed me another document a Quit Claim Deed for me to sign. I balked I was familiar with a Quit Claim Deed and I said I would sign it when John took over both loans and of course, title to the property. EJ now in a pedantic tone said it was bank policy to have all the papers pertaining to the loan signed and in file here at the bank. I knew I was being bulldozed into signing these papers the second deed of trust was good business, but the Quit Claim Deed was too much. John realized this was going nowhere so he took the Quit Claim Deed back and said he would hold on to it until he was in a position to assume the property.

We drove for ten minutes in silence before we hit the freeway as soon as we got into the flow of traffic John in a voice of controlled anger said, "You sure made a jerk out of me at the bank".

"And you played me for a fool at the bank and I hope this incident was a miscalculation on your part caused by pressure from the bank. Where did you get the idea I would blindly sign a legal document giving up rights to the property but still be responsible for two hundred thousand dollars in loans"? The roll of teacher and student had reversed and I could feel John brisling with anger. Nothing else was said until we got to the Bay Bridge that's when John asked me if I was going to sign the papers at the title company and put the thirty five thousand into escrow.

"Why not I have everything to gain and nothing to lose, but be assured I'll sign that Quit Claim Deed as soon as you can take over the property and get me off the mortgages". It wasn't quite four o'clock when we got back to the office. John opened the door and stopped blocking most of the view of the office then a man's voice said, "Mister Mace I'm Agent Brophy and this is Agent Clark I hoping we may have a word"? John moved slightly and I could see the two men when John asked, "What about"?

"It's about Mickey Addleman". I could see the back of John's neck turn red that's when he invited the agents into his office. I continued to my office without a word. I dropped my attaché case on my desk and turned to see Mary in my doorway she told me Harry Byrd called and ask if you would call him he has a couple of appraisals for you. She had her arms folded and leaning against the door jamb when she asked, "Who is Mickey Addleman".

I replied, "Your guess is as good as mine".

I left the office and took the bus to John's apartment to get my truck and headed home. When I got home Anne had the baby fed and dinner was simmering in limbo on the stove. She was poking around the kitchen waiting for me to tell her about the visit to the bank in the East Bay. I went to the frig to get a beer when she asked, "How did it go".

"Well I can say interesting and informative and proceeded to tell Anne everything that went on since John drove him to the bank and the signing in the escrow office". She listened intently without interrupting until I finished. Her facial expression had not changed throughout my account of the day's events then casually asked, "Did John intend to move into the top flat and if so has a rent amount been established; after all we'll be collecting the rent and paying the bills and the top flat has to be at least $1,000.00 a month to put the building into a positive cash flow". I looked a little drained then said, "There's one more thing". Anne looked suspicious and asked, "What".

"When we got to the office this afternoon there were two F.B.I. Agents waiting to talk to John". "Do you know what they wanted"?

I thought for a second then said, "No when I left they were still in John's office". I thought about telling Anne about Addleman, then decided not to she had enough worrisome news for one day.

The following day I picked up my new car early and drove it around Oakland until the commute traffic cleared on the Bay Bridge then drove it to my assigned parking space under our office building. John had someone in his office so I went straight to my office and before I could sit the intercom buzzed. When I answered John told him to come into his office and there I was introduced to a man named Murray Beard who owned the Cornucopia Hotel on Sutter Street. John told me that Murray had an important meeting at our instigation at the Union Commercial Bank in Fremont; however he is without a car and it would be greatly appreciated if you would drive him there. I knew the request was an order so I said, "Murray if you're ready let's go". He smiled pleasantly and replied, "No time like the present". Murray appeared to be in his late fifties about five eight or nine well built, but a touch over weight with a few strands of hair on top of a bolding pate. On the drive down the conversation was limited to the weather at this time of year and the traffic this time of day. Murray was ushered into EJ's office and I went over to Johnson's cubical. Johnson saw me coming and bellowed, "Just in time for lunch". That remark made a few heads turn and he followed his remark with his patient nervous laugh. He waved me in and told me he was expecting me. "Really are you a soothe-sayer"? "I don't know what that is, but I know Mister Beard was coming here to sign the SBA loan papers and in all probability you would drive him. I realized Johnson knew pretty much what was going on at the bank so I said, "Let's go to lunch". His routine at the restaurant was the same one double Vodka tonic at the bar then another at the table before ordering lunch and one after lunch then escape to the men's room before the check came. While we were having lunch I started pumping Johnson about the goings on at the bank. He volunteered that the SBA loan was very unusual for the bank they normally won't do them because the government regulates the interest rate and it's a low yield plus the bank has to do all the paper work and brokerage commissions are forbidden; "So why are you and John involved "? "He's a good friend of John's and he is just helping him out".

"Well he must be a very good friend because he negotiated the bank to add one hundred thousand on to the two hundred and fifty thousand of the SBA loan". I grinned and replied, "What are friends for". I could tell Johnson could hold his liquor because he didn't slur one syllable, but his eyes got a little glassy so I decided to push the boundaries and asked Johnson what he thought of John. He didn't hesitate he said he was sure John had some unusual influence over Phil Peresci and it has something to do with the computer company.

"What computer company"? I asked.

"Phil and his family own the computer company that owns the property that the bank is on and we pay rent to them and I think John invested in the computer company because when he came back from Las Vegas I processed five, five thousand dollar bearer bonds into the company".

I was thunderstruck Mary's words hit me like a Mack Truck I had unwittingly accepted a payoff from Corsey or Corsenti or whatever his name was; that's why the mysterious envelope was so thin. I asked for the check using Murray Beard as an excuse saying he must be waiting to get back to San Francisco. When we got back to the bank Murray was waiting in the reception area and looking none too happy. I apologized and said I hoped he wasn't waiting too long, but Murray didn't answer. On the way back the conversation was minimal until I asked. "How did the meeting go"? Murray just said, "I just got a computer lessen and it was expensive".

I dropped Murray off at his Hotel and returned to the office. Mary said John was out and Harry Byrd called again. I called Harry and he told me he had two appraisals for me and one was a rush and if I could handle it. I told Harry I could pick them up in the morning if that was O.K. he agreed and I sat back in my chair and let my mind wander. Before long Mary appeared at my door and said John won't be back so could I give her a ride home? We got into the elevator to go to the garage for my car when I asked Mary if she knew Guy Corsey. "Oh yeah he was a second banana in Las Vegas for years I was even in a show with him; he would just tell a few jokes and introduce acts".

"How did he get to own a casino"? "He's just a front man he couldn't rub two nickels together there were lots of rumors who was behind him, but nobody actually knew".

"How did John get to knew him"? The question made Mary a little less talkative just then the elevator door opened and they were in the garage. On the way to her apartment she was obviously avoiding any more conversation about Corsey and filled in the void by telling me that John was with Dick Somers and a character named Max Kolblitz and she was sure I would meet him tomorrow.

I had to park my new car on the street because Anne had her car in their space in the back of the house so I came in the front door. Anne met me half way in the hall trailed by her mother and both wanted to see the new car. I said, "First get your car and take my parking spot out front it's only two spaces up the street then I'll park in the back of the house. I had to go around the block to get to the alley and drive into the back and there was Anne her mother and baby Gina waiting. Anne was admiring the car when her mother asked me why I got black. I told her it was forest green not black. "It looks black to me why didn't you get a nice grey that's an elegant color".

"Because I like forest green". Anne chimed in when she told her mother it was my choice and it's my car. "Well it still looks black to me". Anne sighed then said, "Let's go inside the fog is rolling in and it's getting cold". The kitchen was warm and reeked of delicious smells I saw a fresh loaf of Italian bread on the counter and was tempted to tear a piece off and dip it into whatever was in the stock pot, but I knew my mother in law was watching my every move.

Instead I asked, "What's in the pot". "Lamb ragout and don't touch it we're waiting for Carl he's bringing the fresh pasta from Baste Pasta he'll be here any minute and then we'll eat". Carl wasn't through the kitchen door when his wife told him I got a new green car, but it looks black. Then she began to explain why she thought a nice grey was a more elegant color. Carl looked at me with a, "What are you doing to do look"? I got the message and along with Carl let her babble on and just enjoyed dinner. Anne steered the conversation to the neighbors and local politics to get her mother off the subject of the new car and by the end of dinner the new car was forgotten. After Anne's parents left we sat in the living room and Anne was given a run down on the day's happenings. When I got to Johnson's tale of John processing Bearer Bonds through the computer company Anne became animated and asked, "What did he mean by processing bearer bonds? It sounds like laundering to me even the timing coincides with us picking up that envelope from that character Corsey".

"I'm afraid it hit me the same way; also Mary told me it was common knowledge that Corsey was a front for the real owners of the casino".

"Who are the real owners"?

"Someone or some group that wanted to be nameless or legally couldn't own a casino". I replied. Anne had a glass of wine and it seemed to be resting idly in her hand after my last comment she took a large swallow and said, "Jim I think the water is getting deep maybe you should rethink your relationship with Mister Mace".

I had a sleepless night and I was feeling edgy so when I got to the office and Mary told him that John wanted me in his office to meet a Max Kolblitz I felt a twinge of panic. I mustered up some self-confidence and walked into John's office and greeted them with, "Gentlemen". The man seated in front of John began to stand when I said, "Please don't stand I'm not Royalty". The man continued to stand and extended his hand in a greeting; while chuckling he said, "This is going to be a fun trip". John introduced Max Kolblitz from Simonson and Associates out of Cincinnati and explained that Max was here in California on business and Dick has a deal down in Hemet and Max has agreed to look at it while he's here. As Max was returning to his chair he kept smiling at me. I could tell his smile was natural and disarming, but brimmed with confidence. He was a tall lean man with unusually large hands and Nordic features his flaxen hair hid any grey so his age was hard to measure. John more or less nodded at Max as a gesture for an explanation so Max started to explain that his company specialized in warehousing new loans that have little or no history of repayment. Max could see he lost me so he broadened his explanation, "If a company or in this case a Real Estate developer has sold developed lots and assumed the loan themselves and want to convert them into cash we will buy them at a discount and service the loans while they mature to insure timely payment for a number of years and then resell them in a secondary market usually meaning insurance companies or private investors". I gave Max a glance then looked at John and said, "I can see this is going to be an education". Max gave out a belly laugh and said, "We'll get along fine". I had the feeling something was going on that I was not privy to, but was sure I was going to find out soon. I no sooner finished my thought when John told me he would like me to go with Max to Hemet and help with the documentation of the paper to be warehoused. Max obviously trying to lessen the surprise told me he was sure it'll only be a few days or no more than a week. I asked when all this was going to take place and Max replied he would like to leave tomorrow. My confidence had returned, but when I looked at John who was sitting back in this chair with a vengeful smile I had all I could do to control my inward anger. Max astutely read the icy atmosphere and told me he didn't have to leave tomorrow a few days wouldn't upset his schedule. I looked straight at Max and seemingly ignoring John told him it was no problem then asked where he was staying and what time did he want to get going.

I went into my office to finish an appraisal for Harry Byrd then called Anne to tell her that I was leaving tomorrow for Southern California and I would explain later and if she would start packing some things for about four or five days. Anne replied in a dutiful tone if I would like my silk under ware with the printed red ants or the cupid with hearts and arrows. I let out a laugh that startled everyone in both offices. By the time I got home Anne had all most everything packed and handed me a list and asked if I wanted to add anything to my suitcase now's the time; then asked, "What's going on". I told her I would like to explain this deal in Hemet, but I didn't understand it completely and I was sure it was part punishment from John for not knuckling under and signing the Quit Claim Deed at the bank. I continued, "I think there is another side to it if I drive this fellow to Hemet I'll represent John and he'll get a piece of the commission otherwise it would be an expensive punishment".

"So what are you getting out of it"?

"I hope experience this fellow Max sounds very knowledgeable and I would like to stay working for John as long as I can for the business contacts like Harry Byrd".

When I picked up Max at his hotel he was wearing a flowered Hawaiian shirt a Panama hat and waving a cigar in his hand to get my attention. He put his bags in the trunk and jumped into the front seat. I stared Max down until he asked, "What was the matter".

"I hope you're not going to light that cigar in the car"?

Max had a smirk on his face when he said, "No not really I'm acting like John to make you feel comfortable it's going to be a long ride". I looked at him oddly because I didn't know how to take him. A momentary silence then Max said, "That was an attempt at humor I've been told I'm quirky, whatever that means, I can't help it that's the way my mind operates before I know what I'm saying I've said it".

I began to relax and thought about what Max just said then I said, "John doesn't ware Hawaiian shirts". Max was grinning when he said, "I know so can I smoke his cigar"? I started choking through a laugh when I said, "Not in my car". I fully enjoyed the rest of the trip to Hemet listening to Max tell stories about his two ex-wives and of financial deals falling apart for ridiculous reasons and loans being written with all kinds of hidden or ambiguous clauses, but told in a cynical comedic way that was funny and entertaining. When we got to Hemet it was late afternoon and Max told me they were to call the developer named Habib Kalami and he would direct us to his place of business. It turned out to be a prefab modular building at the entrance to his development. It was a clean design with very attractive landscaping all around the building with a parking lot in back. Inside they were greeted as Mr. Kolblitz and Mr. Kerry by an attractive fortyish blond receptionist. Max said, "Please call me Max and this is my associate Jim Kerry and what may we call you"? She looked a little flustered and maybe embarrassed, but sang out Amanda. "Amanda"; he said it twice then told her it was a sensuous name and very English derived from the Latin meaning lovable. This time she was embarrassed when a door opened from an adjoining office and short man in a Hawaiian shirt said, "Hi I'm Harry Kalami". Max introduced himself and me as his associate, we all shook hands and went into Kalami's office. Kalami was grinning when he told Max they must have the same fashion designer. Max's reply was in the one up men ship tone, "you mean Madam Francesca of Targe'". Kalami's expression told you he was not going to pursue any further repartee. He told them he had motel rooms for them close by and when did we want to start. Max told him no time like the present and could we see the filing system of these mortgages you want to warehouse. He took us through another door in his office that accessed a long narrow room which had a second door to the hall and filing cabinets on the wall all along the parking lot side

of the building. In the center of the room there were seven or eight filing boxes on a long narrow table with several chairs. Max circled the table and settled in a chair in front of the first box. He took out six or seven folders and began reading; I stood at the end of the table and thumbed through the folders in the last box. Max asked Kalami what was the total amount of unpaid principal. It sounded rehearsed when he hesitated just slightly then said about one million six hundred thousand. Max made a grunting sound and to my relief Kalami got impatient and told us he would leave us to our work and left. I walked down to Max and asked if I could do anything. Max told me to open the second box and take out a few folders at a time and make sure they were dated and signed on the signature lines and by both parties if jointly owned if any of these things are missing put them in separate piles. I asked if that was all there was to it and Max said no but that's all for now. It was after eight o'clock when Kalami interrupted us to say he called the motel to make sure they didn't give away their rooms and invited us to dinner. Max stood and said we're done to no one in particular then left everything as is and we left with Harry Kalami. First stop the motel then on to the restaurant it was a typical steak house in rural area big steaks and full bar. Kalami took the opportunity with his captive audience to lay out his development.

"People come here for the weather because the winters are mild and it is a perfect place for retirees because it's close enough to L.A. but without the traffic and the price is right. He went on into his sales pitch, "A lot with water and septic system all for fifteen thousand add a manufacture home for as little as another fifteen thousand and move right in; where else in America can you get a deal like that"?

Chapter 5

Max and I survived dinner and met for breakfast in the coffee bar at the motel. It turned into a clinic on how to read prospective borrowers. "First take a page from that Chinese general who said, "Know your adversary like your second skin".

"What Chinese general? And before you answer that does Amanda really mean lovable in Latin"?

"To your second question yes; it was coined in some English Play in the seventeenth century. To your first question I don't know I'm shooting from the hip. Any way you get the drift any one hocking paper, by the way don't use that term in front of a client, who is selling or in this case warehousing a portion of their mortgages. They're looking to replace their cash investment not necessarily make a profit the discount rate we charge will make any real profit thin. Their profit should come when they either sell or collect the monthly loans as cash flow. The worst case would be if the borrower is in a position where he can't recoup his losses and is looking to pass on his losses to the lender which is us. That's why we got to check all the loan papers to make sure they were done legally especially from Mister Kalami who has a blemish on his credibility in this area. He had a development in Tahoe that had sloppy paper work; more than half the paper was unhockable. By the way that term is frowned upon in the financial world it kind of smacks of a pawnshop".

"It sounds like you did a through Dun and Bradstreet research on Mister Kalami right down to the Hawaiian shirt".

"You're very astute young man, but did you also notice I implied he bought his shirt from Target which bruised his ego; he wanted to correct me but didn't want to sound like a spendthrift by mentioning a high end expensive store".

"Or he's a class act and let the shirt speak or its self; one look and you could tell it was an expensive shirt". I replied.

"Point well taken, but I didn't use Dun and Bradstreet I got the information from a friendly competitor. Let's get to these loans there's more than I thought there would be and we may need some help".

"You're not going to ask Kalami are you".

"No I was thinking more like Amanda just a few hours in the evening; then I could reward her with dinner".

My expression went from sceptic to a frown.

When we got to the office we dove right in to the files. I thought we were making progress, but had no experience to make a comparison and when I asked Max what he thought of the progress he just grumble not bad. Amanda appeared in the doorway sporting a short skirt and very high heels exposing a beautiful pair of legs and announced she was taking lunch orders. She left after she took the sandwich order and Max followed her into the hall telling me he wanted to change his order. It took him a half an hour to change his order and return then told me Amanda will give them a hand tonight. As the afternoon rolled by I was beginning to question my scrutiny of my pile of files. I was on my third box and the rejected pile was twice as many as the legal pile. So I went back to the rejected pile and looked through them again, but with the same results they were averaging two for every legally signed loan file. I also noticed that the loans were new and the monthly payments were erratic. I told Max and Max told me that's why Kalami has to sell them to us we'll warehouse the mortgages in our portfolio for a couple of years to show a history of payments then we sell them to investors; just keep going and we'll look at them later. Amanda showed up at five o'clock with coffee so they took a break. Max dominated the conversation with questions about the development and if she liked her job; it was getting obvious Max was pumping Amanda for information on the loan procedures and this title company that handled the search and escrows. I thought Max was very clever the whole time he was pumping her he was fingering through the title documents and his voice was nonjudgmental just making conversation. When Max thought he was getting obvious he suggested they get to the loan files. That's when Amanda blurted out that Kalami was a partner in the title company that all the escrows went through. Max didn't seem surprised he just said, "Busy man". Seven thirty rolled around and Max told me he and Amanda were going to dinner and they would use her car I got the message and left. I drove back to the motel had a quick sandwich at the coffee bar and called Anne. I gave her an up to date on their progress and mentioned Kalami owning a piece of the title company. When I finished Anne told me to be careful it's not a good sign when the developer runs his escrows through his own title company and I'm not even sure it's legal; it leaves the door open for covering mistakes at the borrowers' expense or worse dodgy transactions.

I woke up in the morning to a message light on my phone it was from Max telling me not to wait for him at the motel he would meet me at Kalami's office. I got to the office before Max and was let in by a security guard I settled in at the work table in front of my two piles of folders. I immediately knew the piles were rearranged the legally signed folders were increased dramatically and the illegally signed folders were halved. I opened a folder I had rejected the day before and saw all the dates and signatures that were missing in place and to my eye they all looked like they were written by the same hand; even the ink was the same. I quickly looked through a few more to see the same thing. I calculated someone had doubled the legal folders with bogus dates and or signatures. I sat back and stared at the filing cabinets and let my mind race. I thought about the situation and concluded it probably wasn't Kalami he would have did it before they got here. I knew Max wouldn't leave Amanda here alone for the length of time it would take to alter all these files so Max was the culprit with obviously some help from Amanda. I decided to keep going over files with in the loan folders as I was instructed by Max until he got to the office. I was on the fifth box when Max showed up and he was with Kalami it was after ten o'clock. The phone which was ringing all morning was finally answered so I assumed Amanda was here also. Kalami was asking Max when he thought they would finish and Max replied probably tonight. When Kalami left Max jokingly asked me if I missed him. I was stunned by the events so far and was having trouble responding because of the feeling of being treated as an idiot so I stared ahead and said nothing. Max asked in a coy manner if anything was wrong which added to my anxiety and I really couldn't answer so I just pointed to the two piles I was working on the day before.

"I'll try to explain what's going on, all of the changes we made were really just simple omissions on the part of the sales person who made out these loan papers their ineptitude cost the developer a great deal of money we're simply correcting these mistakes no one is getting hurt and we're making it right". Before I had a chance to answer Amanda was at the door with an announcement that a Dick Somers was here to see Max. Dick came in through hall entrance and simultaneously Kalami came through the door from his office and everyone converged at the work table. Dick glade handed everyone and asked, "How's it going". I was sure it was a surprise to everyone that Dick showed up unexpectedly especially Kalami he looked a little flustered, but Max was unflappable he went into an account of the files being by far and large in good shape and he was confident they had more than a million dollars of loans acceptable to his company for purchase; of course, that's subject to the payment schedules being up to date for each loan, but there is plenty of room with all the lots involved, including our 25% discount and your 3% commission. Kalami seemed to be jolted by Max's statement and immediately told Dick that it was his understanding that his commission was based on the amount of the purchase; as the amount of the loans increase the commission decreases. Dick replied that is true, but the first five hundred thousand is at 3% the each hundred thousand above the first half a million is decreased by a quarter of a percent and the aggregate above a half a million not to exceed 2%. Kalami contradicted Dick and told him it was his understanding if the loans were more than five hundred thousand the commission was 2%. Dick was diplomatic but firm and told Kalami to read the contract again. Just at that point Amanda stuck her head in the door and told Kalami he had an important call and he went to his office to take the call. Dick continued his upbeat questions and then his voice change just slightly when he told Max he wanted to know exactly how much of Kalami's paper was hock-able? He checked his watch a couple of times then said he was on his way to Palms Springs and gave a card to both me and Max with his phone number and address telling us to stop by on their way to San Francisco and they could go over the deal; don't worry about a motel I have plenty of room and I love showing off Palm Springs. Dick said good bye as he knocked on Kalami's office door and went in; they both assumed to unruffled some of Kalami's feathers over the one percent difference in the commission. The rest of the day was a mirror of the day before with Max telling me he was having dinner with Amanda and in a joking manner said. "Don't wait up for me".

I finished going through the last of the files and folders and told Max I'd see him tomorrow then headed for the motel. On the way I stopped at a Deli to pick up a sandwich with chips and a six pack of beer. I went straight to my room and in almost one motion clicked on the TV and started dialing my home number on the phone. His home phone was still ringing when the pregame show came on for the LA Dodgers. Anne answered so I put the TV on mute and lay out on the bed when she said, "Your calling early anything wrong"?

"Well yeah, I have to hand it to you kid you were on the money; it's a little more than just dodgy someone is doctoring the loan documents and it has to be Max. It is not a matter of a few thousand dollars we're talking one and a quarter of a million dollars and I don't know how many of the documents have been tampered with".

"Did you sign off on any of the folders for the loan papers or sign anything at all"?

"No I didn't and no one asked me to, but Dick Somers showed up unexpectedly today and told us to meet him at his place in Palm Springs on our way back to San Francisco".

"I thought you told me out of all the people you've met through John he was the only straight shooter".

"Well I still think so but let's see what happens in Palm Springs I'll be on guard and be sure to cover my ass".

"Palm Springs sounds nice I wish I was with you and covering your ass would be the last thing I would be interested in doing".

"You're a dirty minded young woman". "Yeah isn't great".

I was laughing and told her he loved her then hung up just as the Dodgers were taking the field.

In the morning the message light was flashing on his phone it was from Max. He told me he had to finish the paper work last night because his boss called him from Cincinnati and the hour was late back east so he was in a foul mood. Something went wrong with some loan portfolio in LA and I have to get there ASAP please explain to Dick; I tried to call him but no answer I'll keep calling until I get him to give him an update. It was great working with you and I hope we can do it again; I left something at the motel desk for you and have a safe trip home. I looked at the time it was a little after seven so I dialed John's number at his apartment and he answered on the second ring. Before I could say a word, John in a very sarcastic tone, asked me if he lost their office number; then started to berate me for not calling and letting him know what was going on. I stopped him with a terse question, "Do you want to keep yelling or do you want to hear what happened"? There was silence on the other end of the phone. I took that as a yes so I gave John a blow by blow of the events since they got there; John tried to interrupt until I mentioned one and a quarter million dollars. There was silence on John's end again. I let the numbers sink in then John asked, "Is that the amount of the loans Kalami is trying to sell or is that the loan amounts Max is going to purchase". "That is the amount Max has O Ked for purchase". "I went on to tell John that Dick stopped in Hemet on his way to Palm Springs and asked Max and me to stop in Palm Springs on our way back to San Francisco to update him on the final numbers, however Max has left for LA on some emergency do you want me to stop in Palm Springs or do you want to handle it".

"Where are you now"?

"I'm still in Hemet".

"Stay there and I'll get back to you in a few minutes, give me your number". I went down to the coffee bar for a newspaper and a coffee to go when I returned in ten minutes the message light was flashing. It was John and he wanted to know, "Where the hell are you? I told you to stay right there call me immediately". I took a sip of his coffee and finished reading the headline story I had glanced at on the way back to my room. I picked up the phone and called John. He answered on the first ring. "I just talked to Dick I'll get a flight down there today you drive to Palm Springs and I'll let Dick know what time I'll arrive and you can pick me up at the airport". I packed up what little I had unpacked and went to pay the bill. I was told it was taken care of and was given a letter size envelope with my name JIM KERRY boldly written across the face of the envelope. I went to my car and sat for a minute or two deciding whether to open the envelope or not because I could tell by its' feel and shape it was money. I decided not to and headed for route 79 for what I thought would be a leisurely ride through Lambs Canyon Road to interstate 10 and a short ride to Palm Springs. It was anything but leisurely my curiosity became stress then stress became manic I thought if I opened the envelope I had accepted a bribe I decided not to open it until I got back to San Francisco. I couldn't help the feeling of being a one man conspiracy I knew it was some kind of fantasy intrigue but I was enjoying it.

When I got to Palm Springs I went to see Dick and was doing my best to deal with a guilty feeling. Dick invited me in like I was a long lost relative and introduced me to his wife Esperanza, a South American beauty, which age had not diminished, her face was framed by shoulder length black hair and laced with grey;

she was dressed in a tennis outfit and I had to admire her legs. She welcomed me to Palm Springs and then apologized and told me she was late for a tennis game and had to get going, but she'd see me later. Dick said, "Let me show you your room and when you get settled we can talk". Twenty minutes later I met Dick on the veranda overlooking the golf course. Dicks' condo was one of those up-scale units on the fairway in view of the green. There were three lounge chairs around a patio table facing the fairway with what looked like a pitcher of lemon aide. Dick offered me a cold drink and no surprise it was lemon aide. Dick didn't waste any time he got right to business. "I heard from Max and I'm afraid he was vague about the actual amount of sold lots that were left in Kalami's inventory. You guys were there all most a week you have to have gone through all the files and you would definitely know how many are left and if they are saleable".

"I can tell you there are two hundred and ten, give or take a few, that are left, but I couldn't tell you if Max could buy them all; we cherry picked the ones he wanted to buy and left the rest in there folders". I didn't sound convincing even to my-self and could tell Dick wasn't buying it.

"Did you find many missing dates or signatures you know things like that"?

"Yeah there were a few".

"Look Jimmy you're being evasive let me know what's going on I don't want us to get involved with something underhanded and then wind up in a law suit". The phone started ringing and it broke Dick's train of thought it also gave me time for second thoughts on how much to tell Dick.

"Yeah he's here you want to talk to him"? He handed the phone to me and said, "It's John". He told me what time he would be arriving at Palm Springs Airport then said, "Don't tell Dick anything that went on in Hemet I've already talked to Max just play dumb you should be good at that". "No problem I got a good teacher". As I was saying that I felt my face redden and my throat went dry. I handed the receiver back to Dick and made a grab for the lemon aide. Dick let the moment hang in the air, "How long have you known John"? I looked to be deep in thought but in truth I was feeling panic I didn't know how to keep the events in Hemet from Dick so I said nothing.

Dick seemed to stare out at the fairway then said, "Let me give you a little history three years ago I arranged an ill-advised loan to my company's biggest client it was very large and it went south quick. I was in a quandary and I had no idea how to get my client out of it. At the eleventh hour I got a call from John Mace who at the time I didn't know; he told me he knew of my position and had some one that could get me out of my bind. I jumped at it and he saved my professional life. I told him so and if I could ever help him out just let me know. It didn't take long he got me into a housing development in Union City with the Peresci family. I stuck my neck out for him because it was a little shaky, but I got them a three tier loan from Kissell Life insurance out of Chicago. The Loan stipulations stated the first tier was for survey and land improvement only, John volunteered to keep tabs on the money dispersal;

but as soon as the money was funded the Peresci family gave themselves substantial salaries and bonuses. As a consequence the rest of the project was constantly cash starved and subcontractors not paid on time and mechanic liens against the development started piling up. The only thing that stopped them from going bankrupt was the Real Estate Market went through the roof; you could sell a two car garage for one hundred thousand dollars. Then John got into trouble with the government and went to Lompoc, but I suspected he helped himself to some of the development money. It was only after John went to Lompoc that I found out from a contact at Kissell it was the Teamsters' Pension Fund that John used to get me off the hook; I have to admit I wasn't too choosey who it was at the time I just wanted out of the deal and I know I sound holier than thou and I'm still great full to John but I'm extremely careful when I'm dealing with him and in a roundabout way I'm telling you the same thing be careful with John".

I came out of my funk and in fact got very animated using my hands in a pleading gesture. "I really don't know what Max was doing but I felt uncomfortable he stayed at the office in the evenings with a woman who work for Kalami. He would leave a message for me in the morning that he would see me at the office and, of course, he and the receptionist would show up together at 9AM I thought it was pretty obvious what was going on. But I never signed anything or signed off on any documents".

"That may be but these kinds of law suits tend to paint everyone involved with the same tar brush". Dick replied.

We sat talking on the patio for another hour or two while Dick asked me some questions about New York and how I met Anne and some bordering on personal, but I didn't mind I admired Dick and felt he was sort of a Dutch uncle giving me a word to the wise. In a matter of fact tone Dick asked me if he ever heard of a guy name Cannelli. I said not the guy but my mother-in-law cooks those beans in a casserole. That started Dick laughing; funny you should say that because that's his nick name beans, "Freddy Beans". I thought for a moment and said, "No I don't think I have, why"?

"He was one of the people I dealt with when John got me out of the disastrous deal three years ago". I just shrugged and forgot about it.

At the bewitching hour I headed for the airport to pick up John. When I entered the terminal I looked at the arrivals and departures and saw that John's flight arrived early. I went straight to the smoking lounge and there was John puffing away on his cigar. His first words were, "You're late".

"Not really you're early".

"You've had little to do here so you could have come early and been here when I landed".

"Let's back up, you couldn't have been here very long your cigar was just lit and if this is the way this meeting is heading we're going to waste a lot of time and energy on," I said You said "instead of clearing the air on the Hemet deal". John just grunted something inaudible then wanted to know what I told Dick.

"About what"?

"Don't be a smart ass you know what I mean the files you and Max went through in Hemet".

"I told him that Max did all the profiling of the Loan folders I just did as I was told separating the files that were complete from the files that were not what else could I tell him that I was just the chauffeur".

John gave a quick sideways look at me and the look made it clear he liked neither the tone nor the word chauffeur remark. On the drive to Dicks' John told me they would drive back tonight to San Francisco after the meeting with Dick. I remarked it was an eight hour drive. "I don't mind driving and it would give me a chance to drive your new Mercedes". Esperanza answered the door and greeted them with a beautiful smile and told us Dick was in the back on the patio coaxing the charcoal grill to perform. There was Dick apron and all seasoning steaks, next to a tossed salad and two huge tomatoes just for John. He asked John how was his flight. When John answered fine Dick said great and pointed to the portable bar and said help your selves ice is in the frig under the bar. John picked a chair and sat then told me to get him a ginger ale. I said, "Hold on let me find it. Do you want anything in it"?

"Of course not I told you I'm driving tonight".

"No I mean ice".

"Yeah ice".

"Small glass or large"?

"Large glass".

"It doesn't look like there are any really large glasses, how about a medium size glass"? At this point John realized he was being put on so he exploded. "That's the second time today you're being an ass hole just pour me a fucken ginger ale". Dick half turned to face the sliding door and said, "Yes dear". Esperanza had a grin on her face when she said, "I'll leave you boys to your steaks I have a date with the girls for a little dinner and a little shopping".

"How nice just leave your charge cards at home". Dick said.

Her immediate response was "In your dreams". That even got a chuckle from John. Dick asked me how I liked my steak. I told him medium rare and ranch dressing on the salad if you have it? I looked over to John as if waiting for his order; it prompted him to tell me that Dick knows how I like my steak grilled.

"Yeah, he likes the meat cooked to death with beef steak tomatoes sliced a quarter inch thick and no rabbit food or potatoes". John finally began laughing and replied, "You got that right all except the tomatoes they should be five eighth of an inch thick".

They were half way through their steaks when Dick asked John, "What was so important that you had to fly down here on such short notice; Jim was leaving here tomorrow and would be in your office the next day".

"Max called me from LA and said it was a done deal, but no specifics when I pressed him he said he hadn't finished putting together the package and his company told him to get to LA immediately to meet with their lawyers because one of the loan portfolios was in default and heading for chapter eleven. He said he didn't expect to be in LA long and he would stop in San Francisco on this way back to Cincinnati with all the particulars. He then turned to me and asked, "Can you tell us where the Hemet deal stands". I realized John never answered Dick's question, but it did confirm his decision not to tell them everything that went on with Max and the mysterious signatures. On his way to Palm Springs he had given this a lot of thought on what and how he would tell both Dick and John what went on in Hemet and came to a conclusion what they don't know could not hurt them in a court of law. He told the same story that Max told him to segregate the files into two piles those that were complete and those that were not then Max cherry picked the loans he wanted. He heard Max and Kalami discussing one million and two hundred and fifty thousand dollars; Kalami seemed ecstatic so I assumed that was the figure Max was going to recommend his company buy".

I thought John bought the story but Dick still looked skeptical. After dinner I put my bags in my car while Dick and John admired the Mercedes and Dick especially liked the color Green. Dick's taste in car color made me respect him all the more in the financial world and patio barbeque chef-dom. We left Dick's and John was driving and heading for the freeway when I said you're heading for I-15 and Las Vegas.

Chapter 6

I was trying to figure out what was going on then asked John, "Why didn't you mention Las Vegas before; because I already called Anne to tell her I would be getting in very early in the morning and not to worry".

"You can call her back from Las Vegas we'll be there in a couple of hours".

"That's not answering my question why all this secrecy and misdirection"?

"I don't like the whole world knowing our business".

"I don't know what you're talking about Dick is your partner and if you mean he can't keep a secret you're wrong".

"Well Dr. Brothers I didn't know you can analyze a person so thoroughly knowing them for such a short time".

"John you're getting into I said you said argument and you know it leads nowhere if you're pissed off at me or if it is something else tell me".

"No you're all right I'm frustrated with this guy Max he's really avoiding me and Dick which always means something is wrong. I was hoping you could tell us what". I stared out the side window at the scenery and John gave me a quick glance then said, "I don't care if he forged signatures and dates to tell you the truth I expected that from him what I'm concerned about is that he made a deal with Kalami to buy only half or less of the good loans for now and come back in the near future and buy the rest to cut us out of our commission on the second purchase; I calculate that at around twenty thousand dollars now that's getting into serious money". They were nearing Las Vegas when I decided to confide in John. "I kept a written record of twelve files that Max picked that both the dates and signatures were missing or incomplete along with their names and addresses of the people on the loans. I hope that will help you as a hedge against what you think Max might be up to".

"I knew I hired you for a good reason you're starting to understand the game plan".

"Do you think I should call Dick and give him a heads up"?

"Nah Dick doesn't know how to deal with people like Max it would be the last thing he would expect in a deal like this; although he researched Kalami pretty good and told me we would have to watch him his last development was a little shady". They pulled into the Tropicana and registered. I got to my room and called Anne; she answered on the second ring and before I could tell her where I was she asked me if I was still in Palm Springs. I told her we were in Las Vegas at the Tropicana because John has a meeting with Kusterson, but we are leaving tomorrow for home. "Well that may be but Mary call me and told me the FBI was at the office right after John left and she thought he knew they were coming because he told her he was going to LA on business; she said she knows he has no business in LA and she said it feels like a replay of the last time John got in trouble. There's this case over in Oakland it's been in the papers the last day or two about a guy named Cannelli accused of extortion and money laundering and Mary thinks it's the same guy John was involved with the last time". I had a numbing feeling when I recalled Dick asking me if I knew a guy named Cannelli, "Freddy Beans Cannelli". I recouped my thoughts then told Anne not to over think this because John was going to the meet this guy Max Kolblitz in LA but at the last minute decided to see me in Palm Springs because he couldn't locate Max in LA. We had a meeting with Dick and then John called Kusterson and was told they had some minor details to work out we were so close to Las Vegas it would be silly not to drive there and take care of business". That even sounded feasible to me and Anne's voice lost its' panic then she said she missed me. We exchanged a few I love yuzu's and how little Gina was doing and her mother and father then before I signed off I told Anne not to bother Mary where John is now it might confuse the issue. Anne's voice got dead serious when she said, "You mean the FBI". "You know you could tell her he's in Palm Springs with me and I'm sure when John finishes here he'll contact the FBI and find out what they want". By now it was after eight o'clock PM and I thought the meeting John had was very short because I saw him in the Casino at the craps table yelling for some drunken woman to make her point. I went to the bar opposite the craps table and ordered a gin and tonic then watched John's antics for a good half an hour before John noticed me at the bar. He picked up his chips and met me at the bar and ordered a ginger ale. No one said anything for full minute then I broke the silence with a question, "Did Kusterson change the meeting time until tomorrow"? "No there is no meeting and I think you know that; what do you hear from home"? "Well Mary is in a panic because right after you left the FBI came looking for you". "Yeah well that was the reason I told her I was going to LA otherwise she would have told the Feds where I was and I need a little time to get organized before I talk to them".

"Is the craps table part of the organization or is Nero playing the fiddle while Rome burns"?

"What the fuck are you talking about, what organization and what has Nero got to do with all this"?

"John how long are we going to be here"?

"Just a few days at most I'm seeing a lawyer tomorrow I got to be careful with the feds every time someone I knew in the past gets in trouble they start squeezing me so I need help to keep them in line". I decided not to bring up Cannelli's name and see where all this goes. John went back to the craps table I finished my drink and headed back to my room to make a few phone calls. My first call went to Tom Valance, but he wasn't home Nancy told me he was at a meeting at the Jolly Friars and asked if she wanted Tom to call me when he got home. I told her it wasn't necessary anyway I was out of town and I'd call him when he got back.

Second call went to Dick in Palm Springs, but I got his answering service who told me that he and his wife left this evening for San Francisco. I spent a restless night in my room thinking. John called me in the morning to meet him in the buffet for breakfast when I got there John was at a table near the entrance and waved me over. There was a family of six in front of me sorting out their buffet price with the cashier. John yelled at the cashier that I was in his party and she waved me through the line. Before I could sit John told him to get a plate and they went through the buffet line and picked what they wanted and returned to their table. "I thought you didn't like buffet's lines and would rather be served your food"?

"Ordinarily that true, but I don't like waiters standing just close enough to ease drop; you don't have them at a buffet and it's a little noisy".

"So John what's up"?

"Things have changed a bit I'll be here a little longer than I expected, so here's what's up. There is no need for you to stay here so take a flight back to SF today because I'll need the car and when you get home don't go to the office for a few days. I'm sure Mary has been calling Anne to find out where we are and it would be impossible to avoid her so tell her as far as you know I'm still in Palm Springs. There's another problem the Union Commercial Bank in Fremont the one we financed that SBA loan for Murray Beard has been audited by the banking commission and didn't pass muster".

"John why would the failure of the Bank in Fremont have anything to do with us outside of the Lines of Credit we have there and I never pulled down a dime of it; the SBA loan was between Mister Beard and the Bank we were never involved".

"Phil Peresci's family owns a computer company that owns that shopping center that the bank is in; it looks like the bank was paying an exorbitant rent and now the IRS is looking into both the bank and the computer company because too many of the banking customers have made payments to the computer company for serves that were not rendered".

"What the hell are you talking about"?

"They were using the computer company as a conduit to cover transactions that were border line or out and out illegal".

"You mean laundering money".

"Call it anything you want, but this is what I want to talk to you about if the feds talk to you get dumb say you can't recall any specifics of any deals".

"I can't because I don't know any specifics you did all the deals remember I was just a chauffeur".

"That's great just like that tell'em you were just a guy who ran errands.

One other thing don't use any of your charge cards from the Fremont Bank use your American Express".

I ignored him and used the Fremont bank card and I was on a flight heading for SF by noon Anne told me she'd pick me up when I arrived at the Oakland Airport. She was right at the arrival exit waiting when I left the terminal; I threw my bag in the back seat then jumped into the front and we were off. "Why did you come into Oakland and not San Francisco"?

"I took the first flight out of Las Vegas that was going to the bay area and it happened to be going to Oakland".

"Wow it sounds like someone was chasing you".

"No not really I didn't feel like hanging around Las Vegas and took the first flight I could get".

"Where's John"?

"Bad question you got two more".

"Oh boy; it was that kind of a business trip". She tried to smile while she was saying it but I was too serious she knew then things were worst then first imagined. I changed the subject to Little Gina and her mother and father and by that time we were over the Bay Bridge and on to the Embarcadero and five minutes from home. When we pulled into the back of the house and parked Anne asked, "Where was my car"? I looked unconcerned when I said John had it. Anne gave him a look of anxiety. I asked, "What's the matter". "My mother, she watched little Gina while I picked you up at the airport; are you ready for all the questions about your car"? As soon as I walked into the kitchen I bellowed out, "I left the car with my Boss in Las Vegas he's involved in business deal that doesn't affect me so I flew home and he'll follow in the car when he's done".

"Stop yelling you'll wake the baby". That gave Anne an opening. "Come on Mom it's getting late and I'll drive you home". When Anne returned she joined me in the living room we sat in silence for a few moments when Anne asked, "What else happened that upset you so much"?

"Max left an envelope for me it's obviously money; I didn't open it and I don't know what to do with it. If I open it I'm complicit in their scam but I don't know where he is or if it was actually him that left the envelope".

"Anne was thoughtful and said let's put it in our safety deposit box at the bank for now and you can give me all the details later".

The morning was foggy and cold made to order to just stay in bed, but my mind would not cooperate. When I got to kitchen there was note on the frig telling me I was on his own today Anne had work to do at her father's business and Gina was at the babysitters. I was half way through my coffee when the phone rang. It was Tom Valance apologizing for not returning his call sooner; he said he just got lost in work and forgot about me. "So what's new"?

"Tom I'd like to talk to you about John some things have come up that is making me nervous. I'm not going to put you on the spot, but I do need some advice do you have any time or are you against giving advice".

"Jim I'll be in my studio for a few days and if you don't mind talking in between photo takes come on over any time".

"Give me an hour".

"Good then I'll see you in an hour".

"Tom's studio was in the Ice House Complex on Townsend right at the I 80 and the 101 split no more than a half an hour so I had time to finish my coffee and to organize my thoughts.

Nancy greeted me from her receptionist desk which was an antique dining table. The phone rang and she put one finger straight up to let me know she would be one minute. I started perusing the photographs on the walls and I stopped dead in my tracks on one; it was Mary and her gay friend all decked out in a tuxedo and black tie and she in an evening gown striking a dancing pose. Two more with Mary in a Marlena Dietrich pose on a piano and in top hat and tails with gorgeous bare legs controlling your eyes. The last one was a shot of her in a chores line. Nancy hung up the phone and came over to where I was viewing the photos and with a Cheshire smile asked, "Any one you know"?

"These are great shots of Mary".

"They're not Mary; well she's in one of them but that's her friend Allen or as he was known in the theater by his theatrical name Luana Dune". He was the star attraction at Bimbos, and advertised on a large poster "Woman Impersonator Extraordinaire". He and Mary were attracted to each other because of their extraordinary likeness; Mary actually taught him to dance".

"I think you're going to tell me they're in reverse rolls in the dance picture".

"As you can see she is a very attractive woman, but has a masculine side she can exploit and in the right lighting can pass for a man".

"Are you hinting Mary is a cross dresser"?

"I'm not hinting like I said she has a masculine side that she likes to exploit". I was staring at the dance picture when Tom and a man and a woman followed him out of his studio. Tom introduced them to me as the chef Ellen Marx and her producer Peter Molden; he told me they're doing a food lay out for her book and now they're taking a lunch break.

He asked me if I was hungry; I said no then Tom told me he generally doesn't eat lunch, but he said Nancy does. She looked up a bit surprised and said she could take a hint and left with the Chef and her producer.

"After you called I thought about your situation and I believe it'd be better to give you John's history as I know it rather than advice; then you can make up your own mind".

I gave him an affirmative nod so he continued.

"I met John through my younger brother who went to Saint John's College with him; they were in some classes together and hit it off they even played intermural basketball together. When they graduated my brother was hired by a stock brokerage house and John went into insurance, but they stayed in touch. This was a year or two after the War around 1948 it was a year or two after that John made the headlines. He worked for a guy named Itkin and he was found stuffed into the trunk of his car with a bullet in his head. Itkin had an insurance agency on Long Island and he primarily dealt in key man insurance insuring heads of corporations who took out big loans; to insure the lender's protection if the key man dies. John was sort of second banana he wrote other insurance but primarily the agency's specialty was writing Key Man insurance. One of the key man they insured owned a factory and a line of clothes in the Garment Center in Manhattan; evidently his business was failing and he missed some payments, but before the lender could foreclose on the loan and try and salvage whatever they could from the business the key man was found dead from a fall down an elevator shaft; apparently the door malfunctioned. The lender was the Teamster Pension Fund and Itkin had insured the owner of the factory through New England Trust and Assurances Co. They held up the insurance settlement subject to a full investigation that's when it started to fall apart. Itkin had a guy working for him named Mickey Addlemann. John told my brother he was a real dummy, but would do whatever Itkin told him. The police liked Mickey for the murder of the factory owner and indicted him. Now it comes out that there was a substantial payment made in cash by the factory owner to Itkin as a conduit to someone in the Teamsters for the loan. Now that Itkin is dead it's a moot point, but no one knows what happened to the cash. John was sort of the last man standing and he had access to the company accounts so he's a natural to continue working with the Teamsters Pension Fund under his own company. He is not only writing key man insurance but he is brokering their loan packages for a healthy commission. This is when he hits the papers Addlemann pleads guilty to man slaughter and accuses John of being the actual mastermind behind the key man insurance scheme and bag man for the Teamsters; he knows there was hidden cash accumulated over time by Itkin and Mace knew where it was; if there is any cash missing he got it. My brother told me that's when things got hot for John. He started going to Cuba he was spending one and sometime two weekends a month in Havana. No one thought too much about it because John loved to gamble, but there was no checking carryon luggage and there was a consensus amongst his friends that John over time took the cash to Cuba. Then Castro came out of the hills and in a flash he was in Havana; he headed for the American Express Office, the Bank of Havana and any other institution with Yankee dollars. While everyone on the mainland was scrambling to get to Havana to get their hidden cash John was already there. Everyone that got their cash out was trying to get back to Miami, but not John he got on a boat going to British Honduras. He stayed there for a few months and with all the press Castro and his revolution were getting John was forgotten and when the heat died down he returned by way of Las Vegas".

"I'll bet this guy Addlemann still thinks John has the missing cash". I said.

"He's not the only one so does Mary the IRS and I'll bet a few Teamsters".

That remark from Tom got to me I started laughing.

"Tom did you know Addlemann was released from prison and is searching for John ".

"Where did you hear that"?

"Direct from the mouth of the FBI".

"I have a pet theory". Tom replied.

"What is it"?

"John didn't keep all the cash; I think I know him well enough that he gave the cash to the Teamster it was supposed to go to and took the rest, a substantial portion of the cash, to Cuba".

"Do you think Addlemann can squeeze any cash out of John"?

"I think he will try to get some money from John, but as stupid as he is he must know John would be protected by someone in the Teamsters".

I asked, "Does Cannelli fit that bill".

"Perfectly, Cannelli owes him; John took the blow back for the Feline Follies Loan and got Cannelli off the hook, he got eighteen months in Lompoc for his trouble but Cannelli has problems of his own, so the News Papers say, it would be bad timing for John with all the exposure Cannelli is getting right now".

"Blow back on what. I was led to believe he got caught by the IRS".

"May be that was part of it, but the feds got him for conspiracy to defraud".

"Defraud who"?

"The government".

Chapter 7

I left Tom's studio and felt compelled to go to the office to check it out and return a call from Harry Byrd. The door was locked so I unlocked it and when I entered I closed it and without thinking I relocked it. I was heading for my office when I heard Mary ask, "Who's there". I answered then told her I didn't expect anyone was here because the door was locked and continued to walk into John's office. Mary was sitting behind his desk going through some of John's papers. She looked exasperated then said, "They took everything".

"Who took everything"? "The feds you just missed them they had a warrant for John's files so they took all the filing cabinets and anything in his desk". I quickly glanced toward my office I thought of the file on the Union Street property with the loan papers from the Bank in Fremont it made my skin go cold. Mary saw me glance then got from behind John's desk and then told me the warrant only covered John's files so they never went into your office. I felt my circulation coming back as I rubbed my hands together and started thinking of what to do next. I was going over my options when Mary volunteered that the mysterious Mickey Addlemann showed up looking for John when the feds were here they started questioning him and he couldn't get out of here fast enough. "What did the feds do"? "Nothing one of them wrote something in a personal note book, but they didn't stop him". Then out of the blue she said she was leaving John and was staying at Allen's place temporally until she decides what she is going to do. I said I was sorry to hear that, but she raised her hand with an acknowledging expression and said, "It has been coming for a long time. I've been trying to get John to commit to some compensation for all the years I've put up with his moving around the country plus his prison time when half my weekly salary paid for his cigars while in Lompoc. I dutifully made our conjugal visits to Lompoc every week and I have to admit there were times I was not only tired of the trip but put off by his new found appetites".

I got a little embarrassed that she was telling me more then I really should know, but I was feeling sympathetic until she started pumping me for information on the Hemet deal. Her demeanor changed completely her questions were not only persistent, but beginning to question me personally about covering for John and helping him conceal his assets from her. Just then the phone rang and we both looked at each other with the same should we answer it expression. On the third ring Mary answered it with the familiar office greeting and then said yes good morning would you hold please then put the line on hold and said, "It's Harry Byrd for you". Harry wanted to know if I had finished the two appraisals he sent him a few days ago. I didn't know what he was talking about so I told him I was out of town and just got back and if he could give me an hour or so to get organized I'd get back to him with some timing on the appraisals. That satisfied Harry so he rang off. I handed the phone back to Mary and as she hung it up I asked her about the appraisals from Hanaford S&L. She said she put them on my desk they came the day you left. I went to my desk thumbed through the appraisals for their addresses and got a mental picture of their neighborhoods then pulled out a list of properties recently sold in those areas and made some notes then took a few punch lists from my appraisal file and put them all into my attaché case. I started to leave then stopped and seemed to reflect on something for a minute then picked up the phone and dialed Dick Somers number. The receptionist put him through and Dick answered with an unconventional greeting, "What's up neighbor"?

I whipped out a snappy retort "Sputnik comrade". I could have bit my tongue after I said it I felt it sounded wise ass and kind of disrespectful to someone like Dick Somers. I was surprised when Dick stayed in the game with, "Ah comrade Kerrylinsky what brings you all the way from Moscow to this decadent city center of capitalism"?

"Robles, Filthy Lucre, Yankee Dinero any currency to support my Dacha on the Red Sea". There was a momentary break then Dick said, "Ah Jimmy you light my day with your wit; is there something I can do for you or is it a social call"?

"It's a business call and I'm going to tell some tails out of school and I'm afraid it's going to upset the apple cart".

"This sounds serious you better come up here for a cup of coffee". I took the elevator to the sixth floor and read the lettering on the double doors that read Scranton and Associates Richard Somers Managing partner. I opened the door and the receptionist told him Mr. Somers was waiting for me in the conference room. She showed me to the conference room opened the door for me and discreetly disappeared. Dick was seated at the conference table with a stack of construction prints and building drawing going through them one at a time and looking confused. "Jimmy sit down you're just in time I need a hand matching these drawings and prints".

"What is all this"?

"This is the new hotel here in San Francisco; the construction prints I get, it's the details of the corresponding drawings that are confusing".

"I would think the square footage would be the matrix you would use and the details would be factored in". I replied.

"You would think so but the developer is applying for a takeout loan to get rid of the construction loan but the last three floors of the hotel are unfinished; however I have a lender willing to give him a mortgage, subject to a tentative clearance by the building department if the inspector will sign off the first ten floors for occupancy, but they want me to justify his higher dollar per square foot of the project in their loan package that states the cost of the upscale details".

"Do you believe him or do you think he's just hedging his construction cost as an abundance of caution". I asked?

Dick looked thoughtful then said, "That's something to think about, but I have a favor to ask".

"Shoot". "I'm to meet with the building inspector and the construction superintendent to get some answers could you go with me and hold my hand; you know so to speak".

"When and where and I'll be there".

"That's great it is a load off my mind and I'll get back to you with the day and time".

"You better contact me on my home phone I'm not sure how long I'll be with John". "Understood; enough of my problem you said you wanted to talk to me".

"Can I ask you if you heard from Max Kolblitz"?

"No I haven't yet why do you ask".

"John thinks he is playing footsy with Kalami to dilute the amount of the commission he would have to pay to you and John. To do that he would recommend his company buy a smaller loan package then return later after you both are out of the picture and buy the remaining loans".

Dick said, "What do you think"?

"I think John is right and let me tell you why; I helped Max separate the loan papers that were missing signatures or dates or both and he would volunteer to stay with Kalami's receptionist after work hours. The next morning he would leave a message telling me he had a lift to Kalami's office. I would get there early and security would let me in then Kalami would get there around nine, but Max and the receptionist wouldn't show until ten. I naturally thought Max and the receptionist were playing house and that was the reason they stayed late. The second day was replay of the first and I was early, but I was curious why some of the loan files that I found had no signatures or dates were place on the good pile of files. I thought may be Max and his lady friend got sloppy because they were distracted the night before with pleasures of the flesh so I went through the good pile and found a number of my rejects perfectly signed and dated even the ink matched. This went on for another day and we were just about through all the files when I heard Max tell Kalami he cleared one and a quarter million dollars for purchase. It now occurred to me that the evening trysts between Max and the receptionist were more to keep me out of the way while they doctored the loan papers. The next morning the message light was flashing on my phone, this was the third morning in a row, so I knew it was Max and he told me he had to get to LA immediately and had finished the paperwork last night and that I was on my own. I called John and told him the amount I heard Max tell Kalami and the rest you know except when I went to pay the motel bill I was told it was already paid and there was an envelope for me with my name in broad letters across the front".

Dick stopped me and in a deliberate tone said, "Don't tell me there was money in it, right".

"I think so but I didn't open it and I didn't tell John about the envelope; I told him I wrote down the names and addresses of ten people who have loans with Kalami that someone altered their paper work".

Dick was nodding his head in agreement then said, "I have to say John has a sixth sense when it comes to spotting untrustworthy people, but Max made me nervous the day I met you both in Hemet he only half answered my questions and Kalami was dodging me so I called his boss Karl Simenson in Cincinnati. Karl and I were classmates at Purdue; of course, Max didn't know that if he did he wouldn't have been so careless. I was told Max called his office and said he only had enough time to clear two hundred and fifty thousand dollars in mortgages, but there was probably another million that was buyable at a 30 % discount and on his next trip to the Coast he could verify that".

"You sly fox you were a head of this the whole time can I ask what you're going to do with Mr. Kolblitz".

"That would depend on Mr. Kolblitz; I didn't mention his antics to Karl I made it more or less a social call however it won't be a social call with Max and I have my cross hairs on Kalami".

I looked at my watch then asked if I could use Dick's phone explaining I was trying to get someone so I could do an appraisal on their property. Dick was there when I made the call and when I finished Dick asked a question in a statement form, "You're doing appraisals for the Hanaford S&L". "Yes on sort of a piece meal bases when Harry Byrd is too busy he calls me".

"Would you mind telling me what kind of arrangement you have with John"?

"Not at all it's a draw against commissions I get a thousand a month and after I meet the office costs I share in the commissions I bring in".

"What your bogey"?

I said, "Twenty five thousand".

I finished the walk through for his appraisals and was home before nine. Anne was waiting for me in the kitchen while doing the crossword puzzle from the evening News Paper. She asked if I was hungry and I said no and that I had grabbed something on the way home. Our eyes lock and she said, "So what are you going to do cowboy".

"I've got to get away from John; I've kidded myself that everything borderline illegal or actually illegal I've seen him do could be explained away as bad timing or coincidence. When I went to the office Mary told me the FBI came in with a warrant and marched off with all his recorders. When she told me my heart stopped I thought of the loan papers in my desk from the Union Commercial Bank in Fremont, but it wasn't until she told me their warrant only covered John's records that I started to breath normally.

"Why would the loan from the bank in Fremont cause you panic"?

"Before I left Las Vegas John told me the bank was closed by the Banking Commission and the IRS is involved this has all got to tie into why the FBI wants to talk to John and believe me John is rattled; he made an effort to coach me on what to say to the FBI; I told him I didn't know anything so it didn't matter what they asked me. It wasn't until I got to the office and Mary told me about the FBI taking all the records that the second mortgage the bank put on Union Street would raise a red flag".

"I don't see a problem it's a second mortgage they're as conventional as any other bank loan". Anne replied.

"On the surface, but suppose they start asking the bank why they are making second mortgage fifty miles away in San Francisco and not in Fremont or the East Bay and then our name is brought into this mess and that I work for John".

"I wouldn't worry it is a perfectly legal loan maybe a little unconventional a personal loan made into a second mortgage but legal and legally they can do business two hundred miles from their main office".

"That's the red flag I'm talking about it's a little unconventional".

"Maybe we should get some legal advice"? Anne said.

"I've given that some thought, but maybe we should wait until all this mess starts to play out and we can see where we actual stand; getting an attorney involved might be another red flag".

The next day I was working at home finishing up the two appraisals for the Hanaford S&L when the phone rang just before noon. It was Dick Somers he told me they were to meet the building inspector and the construction superintendent tomorrow at ten o'clock at the hotel under construction. I told him I would be there. I was about to hang up when Dick asked me if I heard from John. I told him no. He told me John called him last night about this Hemet deal and mentioned he'd be back in San Francisco sometime today. I thanked him for the heads up and got back to my appraisals. I finished the appraisals and dropped them off at the S&L and out of curiosity stopped at the office. As I approached the office I could hear John and Mary arguing from the Hall way. I opened the door gingerly and Mary was sitting at her desk and John was in the doorway to his office yelling at her and it was about money. Mary was being out shouted by John so she looked up at me and said, "I think I have had enough". She stood gathered some of her things and left without another word. John told her good riddance. She looked back and if looks could kill John would be splatted all over the wall. I stood in limbo while John muttered something about ungrateful women then seemed to recognize me. He brightened a bit and said good you're here come on into my office we have to talk. John was talking while he was walking to his desk and I paid no attention and as soon as John took a breath I told him I was leaving. I couldn't imagine why John looked surprised, but he did and his face started turning red and he exploded. "Another rat abandoning ship; let me tell you I'm coming out of this smelling like a rose and don't think you're fooling me you're taking advantage of my position. I know you're angling to keep the Union Street property, but I still have a trick or two you don't know about. While we're on the subject what is this pussy footing around with Dick you think by leaving my company you can screw me out of my fifty % of that $130,000.00 commission from the Hotel on Pine Street". I just told him I had one or two things to get from my desk and I left, but not before John followed me into my office and told me not to take anything that was not mine personally. I was surprised I felt so even keeled after the one sided confrontation with John. Before I got to the elevator I thought of the meeting at the Hotel with Dick I realized there were complication now and decided to go see Dick. I took the elevator up to the sixth floor and asked the receptionist if Dick wasn't busy I would like a minute of his time. Although she appeared to be in her late thirties she had a very matronly smile and replied, "I think he's available let me buzz him. She said he's in, first door passed the conference room". Dick offered me a seat and as soon as I was seated I told Dick what John said about me trying to leave his company to get a piece of his fifty % commission of the Pine St. Hotel deal. Under the circumstances it might not be a good idea for me to go to the meeting tomorrow. Dick was quiet until he was sure I had finished. "John has nothing to do with this broker contract, all of the loan sources were located by me or my company; I'm even surprised he knows so much about the loan, but I'm sure it is all over Montgomery Street by now". I looked confused.

"The owners of the hotel were shopping for a bridge loan of $13,000,000.00 for a month or two to pay off the construction loan that's coming due; then have it rolled over into a mortgage. So it wasn't a secret so somebody told somebody and now everyone knows that my company located the mortgage money, but believe me John had nothing to do with it. If you still feel obligated to John I certainly understand, however I would appreciate it if you could make the meeting". I said, "I'll be there".

It was raining heavily the next morning and when I got to the hotel I parked with all the other construction trucks hoping I'd blend in and not get a ticket. I found the freight elevator and told the operator I was the loan appraiser and to take me to the tenth floor. I looked at my watch and realized I was fifteen minutes early so I started to nose around and ran into a plumber. I said hello and started into some small talk and eventually asked him what was left for him to do on the tenth floor. He told me not much he's going to install the fixtures this week, the electricians have just the trim to do; then they can lay the carpet and the painter has some touch up to do and we're done. I asked him if he knew if it has all been inspected. He said he hasn't seen the inspectors sign off sheet, but he's been all over these three top floors the last few days so I suppose so. I heard the elevator gong and voices from the end of the hall. I thanked the plumber for his help and stepped out into the hall to see three men heading at me and one of them was Dick. Dick was smiling when he introduced me as an associate and for reasons I couldn't understand I felt important then I followed the three listening to their conversation. They stopped at one of the rooms and stood in a circle discussing the progress of the top three floors when the building inspector told me I looked familiar and asked if I was a contractor. I said no, but you inspected some houses I own. The building inspector cocked his head a half degree sideways and asked in a good natured way if my houses passed his inspection then started smiling. I smiled back and cocked my head in a similar manner and replied with flying colors. Dick almost sounded like he interrupted when he said that I was working on the loan package with him. There was a momentary lull and I followed that up with a quick synopsis of the loan requirements and I was told there's no more than two to three weeks away from finishing, but the loan commitment may not be available in that time so with the top three floors all roughed in and only two to three weeks to go it would be extremely helpful if you could give a final inspection clearance subject to the finished three floors. Just then as luck would have it the electrical contractor and his foreman got off the elevator and as he passed he nodded to the building inspector and with- in a few seconds of passing told his foreman he wanted him to get his men on the final trim tomorrow. The building inspector said they should walk through the three floors but he doesn't see a problem; with that Dick had his loan package secure. An hour later me and Dick stood out in front of the new hotel and Dick was uncharacteristically giddy he said, "If I were a drinking man I'd suggest an early liquid lunch at Lefty's".

John invited Tom, Nancy, Anne and me to Jack's Restaurant on Sacramento St. and everyone wondered if Mary was coming. Mary was there and things were tense from the get go. John had reserved a privet room upstairs this in hind sight was done on purpose. The conversation started on the menu then a little political gossip with Mayor Alioto's personal life being kicked around by Mary who at this point was referring to John as a third person. When the food arrived it took center stage and the conversation changed to the sounds of food appreciation. All the while there was this surface tension and finally Mary broke it with a statement presented as a question, "Did you know John is buying those flats on Union Street in someone else's name; he told me the reason was the IRS is still after him and they'll confiscate the property, but I know it's because he wants to divorce me and keep it hidden from the settlement along with all the money he has buried". Then she accused John of being in cahoots with Cannelli and the Bank in Fremont in bribery and money laundering and predicted he was going back to Lompoc. John was stoic through Mary's tirade, but when she tried to push food off the table onto his lap he stopped her by grabbing her wrist and squeezing it until she began to cry. She took her purse and left in tears. As typical of John he mumbled, "Hysterical woman I gave her twenty grand what'd she want from me"; then went on to explain how the Feds will take him in for questioning every time someone he knew in the old days was being accused of something. His rhetoric was getting old and everyone was tired so we all thanked John for dinner and went their separate ways.

Chapter 8

Two things happened at the end of the week that surprised me; one I was hoping for and the other was unexpected. Dick sent me a check for $1500.00 and a thank you note for my help in the Peresci water crises and the help in expediting the Hotel on Pine St. loan and expressing his hope for future collaboration; that was the surprise I was hoping for, but more than I thought I deserved. John sent me a case of French Cognac, I had once said I liked, with a note apologizing for his bad temper and his reasoning why it should be all forgotten and return to normal. I called John and thanked him for the cognac then said they should talk and what time would it be convenient. He told me this evening after six would be fine. I thought this was a good omen because it would be a perfect time to tell John I was definitely quitting and leaving or otherwise it was a distinct possible I would go hand and hand with John to jail. I knew John had something important to discuss and the cognac was to loosen me up. I had previously told him of my intention to quit and I wanted to make sure I got my three thousand dollars owed me; but I was curious why John wanted to meet at his office after hours.

I got to the Montgomery St. office at 6:30 PM and parked in my assigned spot in the subterranean garage. When I got to the elevator there were movers loading furniture and had set the elevator's over-ride switch to buy pass the main floor. I asked if I could hitch a ride so they made space for me and as I was squeezed in one of the movers told me I just missed the show. I asked what show. One of the men looked to the heavens and said a Madonna; the other told me some broad had on white boots and a skirt up to her ass when we whistled she put on a show walking from the fire exit to the garage exit. They stopped at the second floor for me to get off and as I was getting off I questioned the one mover; didn't the Madonna have a car. The two men looked at each other and just shrugged. In comparison to the 9 to 5 traffic in the building there were few people wondering the halls so except for the movers I saw no one else. When I got to the office it was unlocked so I walked in and called out John's name. I got no response so I called his name again then entered his office and stopped in my tracks. John was seated and slumped over his desk face down with one hand on the desk blotter and his left arm dangling somewhere behind the desk. I immediately thought he had a heart attack but when I went to help him I saw blood all over his white shirt collar and his blue suit jacket had a dark stain down the back. My disbelief and confusion momentarily paralyzed me; is all I did was stare at my Boss's head it was laying on his right cheek on the desk and I could see a neat little hole behind his left ear with blackish blue discoloration. I got hold of my-self and realized I shouldn't touch anything so I went to my old office next to my Boss's and called the police. After I gave the police the location, my name and telephone number of the office I opened the door to the hall and waited for them. I was about to call my wife Anne, but then decided against it I would wait until I was calmer and could talk without this hyper emotion I was feeling. The first ones to show were the uniform police and building security. One of the patrolmen asked the security officer to wait at the entrance to the office to keep out inquisitive people then went into John's office when he returned he conferred with his partner for a minute or two and his partner called homicide. One of the policemen asked me some obvious questions, what was the name of the deceased, what was my relationship to the decease, what time I discovered the body and all the while he jotted down my responses in a small personal note pad. In a little more than an hour two detectives from homicide and the Lab team arrived and a detective named Oscar Norman asked me the same questions as the patrolman did and jotted down his answers in an identical little note pad. Norman was an inch taller than me and a bit rangy with dark hair and eyes and his eyes were penetrating; he never took them off of me while continually asking questions and writing in his note book. He looked to be in his early thirties, but with a strangely mature demeanor. I had a meaningless though that all the San Francisco police were issued those little note pads and taught short hand. The second detective named Medwin was a bit shorter and at least fifteen years his senior. He had flaxen hair and hazel eyes and decidedly more muscular both wore dark suits with loosened ties and opened collars. He accompanied the forensic team into John's office when he returned he had more questions, but I kept getting distracted by the camera flashes from John's office and the gravity of death was sinking in deeper so I couldn't concentrate and often asked detective Medwin to repeat the question. Detective Medwin seemed to take my haziness in stride then told me they could continue this at a later date and suggested I go home and rest, but before you go the lab Guys want to make a quick test on your hands.

Anne was speechless while I told her the whole gruesome story. Even after I finished she was mute. I waited a moment or two when I realized she was in some sort of shock. I got up went to the pantry and broke out a bottle of the Remy Martin Cognac that John had sent me; I poured two stiff drinks and returned to the kitchen table. Anne was looking at me but not seeing me her eyes were far away; I put a glass in front of her and her eyes dropped to the cognac. She seemed to hesitate for a second then took a sip and made a sourer face then with-in a moment or two she smiled and told me that when it hit bottom it gave her a nice warm feeling. I asked her if she was feeling better and she said yes fine, she stiffened her posture and then told me is all she could think of was if I had been just a little bit earlier I might be dead along with John. I had two confusing thoughts one was what Anne had just said about me being lucky because I wasn't a little bit early to the meeting and here they were drinking French Brandy that John had sent him as an incentive to meet him that night. The irony turned my body cold I downed the brandy in one gulp then sat and looked at a speechless Anne. We both mopped around the house for most of the evening and into the night then about ten o'clock the phone rang. We were still sitting at the kitchen table Anne looked at me and I told her she was the closest to the phone. She took a deep breath and turned still sitting in her chair and reached for the phone receiver and took it off the wall phone then turned back to face me. She said hello as she was turning back to the kitchen table;

then said, "Yes Tom it's true" she had a fixed stare of someone listening intently then said yes a few more times and whipped the long extension cord toward me and handed the phone to me.

"I called to see how you are because I just got off the phone with Oscar Norman the detective that is handling the investigation of John's murder; he said you were pretty shaken up so they sent you home".

"Yeah I was but I'm fine now. What was this guy Norman calling you for"?

"Oscar is a friend of mine we both belong to the Jolly Friars and he knew John was a friend of mine so he called me to tell me the news but also to ask about you and John".

"What did he want to know"?

"If you got along were you feuding over money or women the usual questions it really was routine. They are thinking it could have been a professional who killed John because of his shady back ground and the latest connections to the Cannelli case and the defunct bank in Fremont; except he was shot twice from the back and they're trying to figure out how John would let someone get behind him when he was sitting at his desk that gave them the idea he must have known whoever it was".

"I didn't see a second wound and the wound I saw was not in his back it was behind his ear".

"Well yeah, but he was shot first in the back of the neck through his spinal cord which paralyzed him and the wound behind his ear was the shot that killed him. According to Oscar they think the first could have been intentional so he would be conscious and know he was going to die; this to them didn't look like a pro-hit the pro would be in and out as fast as he could he wouldn't be interested in punishing anyone".

"Unless he or they were paid extra to do exactly that". I replied.

"That's interesting you say that because they're looking for Mary and her friend Allen they found a check from Allen made out to John for over nine thousand dollars on his desk and it's dated the day John was murdered. They tried John's apartment with no dice so I told him they broke up and as far as I know she is staying here in San Francisco with her friend Allen who owns a women's boutique shop somewhere near the Sir Francis Drake Hotel".

"Why didn't you tell him he was that woman impersonator from Bimbo's Luana Dune"?

"I didn't think of it and I'm sure as soon as Mary finds out about John's murder she'll call the police".

The next morning Anne told me she didn't feel like mopping around the house today so she was going the work. She packed up the baby for the baby sitter then told me there was coffee on the stove and biscotti's in the bread box and left me to my thoughts. Around nine o'clock the phone rang and it was Dick Somers; he wanted to know how I was taking all this and asked if he could do anything. The question struck me as useless and couldn't imagine what Dick could possibly do, but immediately got my mind back on tract and answered no I told him I was fine. "I got a call then a visit last night from the two detectives investigating John's murder they wanted to know about any business dealing I had with John; they asked a lot of question about a guy named Mickey Addlemann. I'm telling you this because a guy by that name was here at my office that morning asking my receptionist about you and if she knew where you lived". I told Dick is all I knew was that this guy Addlemann worked with John back in New York and I've been told he just got out of prison and was looking for help from John; but I have no idea why he would want to talk to me. Dick again told me if I needed anything don't hesitate to call. I thanked him and hung up.

I thought it was obvious Addlemann was after the money and figured I either knew where it was or at least suspected where it was.

I no sooner had I put down the phone when it rang again I picked it up and it was Detective Medwin. He asked me if I could come down to the police station at City Hall to answer a few more questions to help in the murder investigation. When I got to City Hall I was directed to the homicide division then to the cubical of detective Peter Medwin I was surprised to see Agents Brophy and Clark of the FBI. Everyone voiced a friendly greeting and Medwin suggested they move their meeting to a more comfortable room. When we entered this room I got nervous it was obviously an interrogation room two way mirror and all. Brophy and Clark followed us in and Medwin said Oscar would be here in a minute. Detective Medwin and Agent Brophy sat opposite me and Agent Clark slowly circling the room but lingered behind me. Medwin started off by tell me that the reason Agent Brophy and Clark are here because this is a joint investigation between the Police Department of San Francisco and the FBI.

There are some of the opinion that Mr. Mace's murder may have far reaching ramifications such as money laundering and bank fraud and we were hoping you could help us understand what if anything Mr. Mace had to do with the Union Commercial Bank in Fremont. The door opened and Oscar Norman came in and gave the Agents a surprising glance he smiled and pulled up a chair and sat to the left of me. My nerves morphed into aggravation I said to myself this is just like the movies good cop and bad cop and decided I better get a lawyer. Medwin pressed on asking me if I could tell them how I got an unsecured loan from the Bank in Fremont and a credit line with no previous dealing with the Bank. I stopped him and asked, "What has that got to do with the murder of John Mace". That's when agent Brophy jumped in with the statement, "May be more than you think we believe they could be related and we're asking for your help in connecting the two". I knew this was bullshit they were looking to create a suspect or worse and thought I better say no more and leave. Before anyone could say another word I announced I was leaving and stood to leave when Agent Brophy said, "If you have done nothing wrong why are you acting like you did; getting a lawyer and refusing to answer any of our questions does not bode well in the eyes of the law".

I couldn't help giving Brophy a dirty look and left.

After I left there was some discussion amongst the Agents and Medwin, about me and how best to handle me, but Oscar Norman was notably quiet until the Agents left. Medwin asked Oscar, in a coy way, if anything was wrong. Oscar's reply was terse, "What the hell was the

FBI doing here"? "What are you talking about we're in a joint investigation why wouldn't they be here"?

"Because you know very well they have their own agenda and they never include us unless it benefits them. We're investigating a murder, Mace's shenanigans are a peripheral matter, but to the Feds it's really the money laundering they're interested in and the murder is a peripheral matter. They only share what they want to share that's what they call cooperation. Keep in mind the Agency has been after Mace and a number of dirty Teamsters for twenty years they only nicked him for eighteen month at Lompoc it would be a huge feather in their cap if they can nail down the people Mace was involved with. Getting back to Kerry the Lab found no paraffin or gun powder residue on his hands. The movers established his arrival time and of the time of the black and white's arrival. Mace's phone call to Mister Somers at five thirty establishes he was alive at five thirty. That leaves him approximately an hour and a half to shoot Mace; get rid of the gun and clean any residue off himself and call the police. You interviewed him and told me at the time he was really shook up so much so you sent him home. His back ground is clean as a whistle. He'd worked for this guy Mace for less than a year and the information we got was that he was going there that evening to quit the job so where's the motive. The Feds would love to have a big conspiracy and murder with a pro hit over money laundering and bank fraud; to them Kerry looks like the perfect dupe and with pressure he would crack. Let's get back to our investigation and let the Feds do theirs if we can help fine, but we can't let then derail our investigation so they can build some case at the expense of some dupe. Let's keep in mind the facts as we know them first the security of the building was not designed to tract people it was designed to prevent someone coming in afterhours and stealing office furniture so there are many ways in and out of the building without being detected. The movers even saw a sexy woman come down the fire exit into the garage and opened the gate electronically and walked out minus a car, which seems suspicious and the idea Mace would let someone he didn't know get behind him with only a couple of feet clearance to the window while he was sitting at his desk still bothers me. His wife has an alibi she was in San Diego that day with an aging Aunt, Her friend Allen paid off his note to Mace earlier in the day, so it appears he had no motive, but the following morning he cancelled the check could be he knew Mace was dead before anyone? We were told it appeared nothing was missing except we couldn't find Mace's electronic key card for the garage gate. To me the way he was shot smacks of a well-planned murder of vengeance by someone who was familiar with Mace and the building routine not a paid torpedo".

"Great theory, but you just eliminated all our suspects". Medwin said.

"Did any one check this character Addlemann's alibi"?

"Yeah he said he was at the theater, "Beach Blanket" he had the ticket stub with the time and date they even stamp your hand at half time so you can get back in the theater and he had the blotch of the ink on his hand".

Oscar was thinking out loud when he said, "How many people keep their theater tickets and don't bother to wash off the ink stain; I don't know it could be common it's just a thought".

"You know there is a neighbor of Mace's that called police about a guy hanging around his apartment the uniforms responded and the guy was sitting in his car evidently told them a convincing story so they left".

"How do you know this"?

"It was in the daily patrol reports it struck me because it was Mace's address".

"Let's hope the responding officer wrote down the guy's license number".

Chapter 9

I left City Hall Police Station furious. I thought of all kinds of things I could have said or done instead of just getting up and leaving, but by the time I got to my truck the gravity of my situation was taking hold. My thoughts ran to what Brophy said not only about the loan and credit line from the Fremont Bank, but the Las Vegas trip and my connection to Guy Corsey and what I thought were IOU's were more likely those bonds Johnson told me about, that John took to the bank. I sat in my truck trying to focus; I turned the ignition key and immediately thought of Murray Beard and realized I drove him to the bank to sign the SBA loan; I was now sure John was involved in something illegal and I drove Murray to the bank so everyone would think I had something to do with the loan especially Murray. I didn't remember driving home I realized it when I pulled into our parking space in the back of the house. I sat in the kitchen doing nothing and getting more paranoid I looked at the clock and it was near four so I called Anne at her father's business. When she answered she asked me what kind of a day I had. I replied it's hard to explain what time are you coming home. She could tell by the tone of my voice it must have been stressful so she suggested we ask the baby sitter if she would take Gina tonight and we could go get something to eat and talk things out.

We walked down to Ghirardelli Square to the Oventi Forno on the second floor and watched people below milling around the street musician. I was locked into listening to a violinist so Anne brought me back from the music below by asking me what I thought we should do. "From what you told me the police and FBI are obviously zeroing in on you and I agree we should get a lawyer".

"I know but I don't know what kind of a lawyer to call"? I said.

"Well a good defense attorney or maybe a criminal attorney not a run of the mill lawyer". Anne said.

We were finishing our coffee and watching the people below in the court yard when she said, "Why not call Tom he knows everybody here in San Francisco he must know a good lawyer".

When she said that a light bulb went off in his head and I replied, "You hit the nail on the head I thought of someone who definitely could point us in the right direction".

I waited until mid-morning of the following day to call Dick Somers. When the receptionist answered with usual company business greeting and a "How may I direct your call" that always sounded mechanical and insincere. I had a knee jerk reaction to be a smart ass and make a joke about how she could direct the call, but servility prevailed and I told her who I was and asked if Dick was available. Her voice became a live saying, "Oh Jim how have you been I recognized you voice its very New York you can't miss your accent".

"My accent, I don't have an accent it's you and all these foreigners from LA that live here San Francisco; I'm making provisions to have some of the boys from home to come out here and give elocution lessons in the King's English". That set her off in her matronly giggle then said, "Wait I'll let Dick know you're on the phone". I had a mouth full of coffee when Dick came on the line so I gulped it down, but it went the wrong way and it put me in a fit of coughing. Dick asked if I was all right in a sincerely concerned way. When I answered my voice was rough and halting and Dick asked again if I was all right and said it sounds like you're choking on something. "It's the dryness in my throat from the police and FBI interrogation".

"I thought one of them would be grilling you soon because yesterday both of them questioned me about the Bank in Fremont and your relationship with the Bank and John. To ease the dryness in your throat I told them I had no dealings with the Bank in Fremont so I couldn't help them and we were both in Hemet down near LA on a business deal and on the way back you told me you were resigning from John's company as soon as you got back to San Francisco".

"I can't thank you enough for all your support and I actually called for a favor could you recommend an attorney that could help me in my situation".

"My corporation has a law firm that can handle just about any situation that comes up in our business; let me make a few calls and I'll get back to you". While I was waiting I figured I'd call Harry Byrd to see if he had any appraisals he needed done. I was angered at first when Harry Byrd told me. "Due to the publicity of the fraudulent bank failure and your connection with it; it wouldn't be prudent of me to have you associated with our S&L; however if and when this matter is resolved discretely and in your favor we would be happy to reconsider employing you on a contract bases". I said something like "Really" and I hung up. I sat for a half hour or so with the feeling of abandonment then oddly I remembered what John said the last time he saw me about rats leaving a sinking ship and with that the phone rang and it was Dick. When I answered the phone Dick told him he thought he had a solution and could I meet him at his office sometime after three o'clock. I said, "Absolutely".

At three o'clock I opened the door to Scranton and Associates and was greeted by the smiling face of Dick's receptionist the name plate on her desk read Beate Olsen and told me Dick was waiting so go right in. The door to Dick's office was opened so he heard me enter the receptionist area and told me to come in before I was ten feet from the threshold of his office. Dick had an open file on his desk with his hand on the cover when I entered he closed it and said take a seat. I said, "How did you know I was in the hall are you clairvoyant or does your receptionist have a button she pushes to signal an intruder". "Neither, I could hear your clodhoppers crushing my carpet twenty feet away". "Clodhoppers I'll have you know these are cordovan loafers from Spain".

"If they told you that maybe you should get your money back".

"No problem I bought them off the back of truck next to Pier twelve from a guy who guaranteed my money back if I wasn't satisfied".

Dick was grinning when he said, "I think you better find his guy and try and get your money back".

"I know where he is I'll just have to wait a while he's doing eighteen months for breaking and entering".

Still grinning Dick said, "You just have to get the last word don't you"?

"Well yeah, my social worker told me it's a product of my environment".

That put Dick into rolling laughter then said, "Jimmy if nothing else you lighten my day. And I hope I'm going to lighten your day. We have on retainer the law firm that handles all our needs their name is Sloan and Pacemann they're over on Pine Street opposite the Stock Exchange. I talked to Myra Pacemann and she has time tomorrow between twelve noon and one fifteen. Now here is my plan, I have already sent you a check for services rendered I have a few papers for you to sign that are already back dated and you will be officially an employee of Scranton and Associates that will take care of most of any legal fees; in the paper work you'll see the usual employee package, you know, healthcare plan, 401K plan and other assorted benefits. It is only two pages so if you could read through them and if you approve sign them then all your legal fees should be covered. This could be temporary or I could certainly use you to do my leg work and if that appeals to you we could work out a similar financial arrangement like you had with John".

This took me completely by surprise; I came here with my hat in my hand looking for sound advice and given expensive legal representation free and a Job offer that some brokers on the street would kill for. I scanned the employee paper work then signed them and told Dick whatever he thought was a reasonable salary was fine with him.

I was so excited I drove right passed my street; I had to go around the block. I told myself to calm down or I'll have an accident. When I got into the house there was a note from Anne to put on the water for pasta, this I did in a large pot with a low flame then grabbed some salami and cheese with a can of beer and headed for the living room. Within an hour Anne was home with bags of fresh vegetables. I was adjusting the heat under the pot of water and asked where did she get all the vegetables?

"Dad he was out in South San Francisco and stopped at the Produce Market and pick up tons of veggies so I was thinking Panni with veggies in garlic and oil".

"I'm in; give me the cutting board and I'll start on the vegetables".

I watched Anne as we both were preparing dinner and it became obvious her silence was meant to stimulate conversation and it worked. I told her I saw Dick Somers today and he made an appointment at his company's Law Firm; I'll see an attorney tomorrow. She thought for a moment then said, "That sounds expensive".

"I haven't told you the best part Dick's Company is paying all of the cost or a major part of it".

"He's really a nice man, but why would he do that"?

"Because it's part of the employment package".

"I still don't get it is he fudging some company rules that might come back to bite him, in the you know where, or is he absorbing the cost him-self"?

"Neither; he hired me".

"He hired you to do what"?

"The best explanation is he needs a gofer and I'm available".

"Are you putting me on"?

I quickly decided I better stop playing with her and tell the whole chain of events. When I did her eyes weld up and she threw her arms around me then said, "You're one hell of an Irishman, but the Italian business sense you received through osmosis will always win the day".

She tried to pull away from my grasp when I said, "Are we in the mood for some of the Italian osmosis".

"I have to pick up Gina after dinner, but I am told she is very tired and she's in for an early night so let's hurry up and eat".

It rained all night and it didn't clear until ten thirty the air was crisp and clear I had the time so I decided to take the cable car it was literally at my front door. I took the Hyde Street car up Russian hill to the Fairmont hotel had a light lunch and then took the California Cable Car down to Montgomery Street and walked the rest of the way to Pine. As Dick had said the office of the Law Firm was across the street from the Pacific Coast Stock Exchange. I looked up at the four story building that was surrounded by buildings twice its size and thought to myself it must have survived the 06 big quake. It looked out of place amongst the taller newer buildings, but it did have commercial charm. The entrance was in a small hall set back five or six feet from the street with a single glass door with bold face lettering "Law Firm of Sloan and Pacemann". A quick look at the directory told me they occupied the whole building and I was going to the third floor. I got off the elevator and was greeted by a young woman seated behind a roll top desk in the middle of the room; the walls were retro-fitted with steel beams in a decorative baroque motif extending strait up to the ceiling of the fourth floor with a very wide spiral stair case connecting the two floors with offices off the fourth floor balcony; it gave you the effect of an atrium. I told the young lady my name and that I had an appointment with Myra Pacemann. Without taking her eyes off of me she pick up the phone and hit a button and still looking at me said, "Mister James Kerry to see you". She acknowledged an answer and then asked me to take a seat Ms. Pacemann will be right with you. Within a convenient two or three minutes a women called my name from the top of the spiral stair case. I looked up and she waved a hand and said come on up and I did just that. She ushered me into the first office and it had an eight foot sliding glass door looking directly into a roof garden. She offered me a seat then skirted around the corner of her desk and sat then said, "I'm glad you're a little early I just ordered a sandwich for lunch if you're hungry I can made to two"?

"No thank you, I had lunch".

"So what can I do for you"?

I started with John's murder then everything leading up to it and everything that happened after including the envelope from Max. Myra had a legal pad in front of her and was writing as fast as I was talking; the only time she stopped me was to ask the names of the detectives and the FBI agents. When I finished she seemed to be rereading what she wrote. To me she looked to be in her fifties, well-groomed with black hair turning grey, but natural not touched up. She was attractive in a hard sort of a way and starting to lose the weight battle. By the time I finished telling my tale of woe her lunch had arrived. She asked me if I would mind continuing their meeting out in the garden while she had her lunch. I told her not at all. The garden was well done with a paving tile floor a few potted small trees and a small hedge row along the parapets and accented with a few flowers. The adjacent buildings towered over the garden from contiguous walls from all three sides. The front of the building was open and the street noises were muted; sort of a white noise back ground. We sat and she left her sandwich and coffee untouched then asked about the Bank Fraud and when did I find out about it; the another question was about this character Guy Corsey and when did I realize I didn't pick up IOU's but actually bearer bonds and last but not least she wanted me to explain why I thought there was something illegal about the SBA loan. While I was answering her questions she was writing it all down on her legal pad; when I finished she started unwrapping her sandwich and asked again if I would like half as she was remarking that the sandwiches are too big she only can finish a half. I declined then she began asking me more about me without writing anything on her legal pad. When we concluded our meeting she told me she'd get back to me in a week or so with some information and her opinion on my legal status and if I was culpable in any of these deals. She cautioned me in the mean-time don't talk to the FBI or any other Police at least not until I get a handle on this situation.

I was half way to my father in law's business so I decided to go see Anne. When I got to his shop I parked in the alley in back of his warehouse. I entered through the back door and made my way to the office where Anne was on the phone. She kept staring at the phone and subconsciously slightly moving her head from side to side. She waved at me and then in a burst of controlled anger said, "I did not say that; what I said was Gina's Baby School will not allow anyone to pick up a child that is not one of the child's parents anyone else I have to call and identify anyone else picking up Gina. There was a short heated exchange when Anne raised her voice to say, "No, NO, NO, You are a grandparent not a parent you have to call me first before you go over to the Baby School and further more I don't want you to go over to that School on a whim and disrupt their routine". The next exchange was calmer and then Anne hung up. Anne looked at me and said, "That women does not understand the word no or not and she'll press a syllogistic argument until she wears you down".

"Syllogistic where did you get that word"?

"I read it in a psychology book when I was trying to understand and deal with my mother, but I gave up I now use brute logic; I read that in the psychology book too".

I had to turn away and make believe I heard something outside so Anne wouldn't see the smiling smirk on his face. It didn't work; she said half seriously, "If you think it's funny I could go and stay with my mother for a week or two and when I come back I'll be as squirrelly as she is"."

"Is that part of the Italian osmosis you kept telling me about".

"It maybe; you'll get a full dose of it tonight dad's going to the Italian Men's Club tonight and mom's at the house right now cooking dinner".

"It's a little early, but do you want me to pick up Gina"? I asked.

"No let me do that I'm sure the school has some questions about my mother that I better smooth it over or we'll be looking for another baby school. I better ask you now and not in front of my mother so how did the meeting with the lawyer go".

"I thought very well, I'll give you a whole break down when we have time".

"On your way home stop at Macaluso's and pick up some bread make it two loaves to keep my mother quiet".

"What kind"?

"One better be Tuscan the other doesn't matter; Oh and by the way you better have a good story why you don't have that forest green black Mercedes any more my mother hasn't stopped asking about it for a week".

As soon as I walked into the kitchen I was met by the inquisitor.

She wanted to know where my black car was. I immediately knew I made the mistake of correcting her by reminding her it's not black but forest green. This started her out on a long worn out tirade about the car's cockamamie color and she didn't know why I didn't get a nice color grey. I made my second mistake by telling her the truth that I quit the job and I gave the car back. This opened up a floodgate of nonsensical and temperamentally driven questions that by their shear nature were rhetorical and by design can upset and infuriate the receiver. I realized my mistake and before she could finish berating me I asked what smelled so good. That got the response I wanted; she went on for ten minutes on the sauce preparation and the difficulty of making the manicotti without decent ricotta cheese then with an approving nod said, "You got the Tuscan bread good if you want you can take a piece of bread and taste my Marinara sauce it's the best". I was not only playing along but was dying to dig into the sauce. I was making all kinds of yummy sounds, to the delight of my mother in law, when the phone rang. It was Tom Valance he wanted to know if I had any time tonight for a little get together at the Jolly Friars Club. I hesitated to answer, but Tom sounded different almost mysterious so I asked what time and said I'd be there. After dinner while her mother was entertaining Gina in the living room I had a chance to tell Anne all that went on at the lawyer's office and a graphic description of the unique building especially the roof garden; and that Tom called and asked me to meet him tonight at the Jolly Friar's Club he was unusually insistent and the impression I got was because Tom couldn't talk on the phone.

I wasn't a member of the Club so when I arrived I didn't know what to expect. I immediately recognized several well-known business men and a would-be politician they all nodded a polite hello and then I saw Tom. He was talking with a clergyman and when I approached Tom introduced him as Father Gorman; he asked me if he was a prospective member I smiled and said I'm here to reconnoiter. The priest nodded in recognition then said, "Me thinks we have a military man amongst us Tom".

"No I just did my two year obligation and got out".

"I too did a stint in the military during the Korean Conflict".

"Carrying a gun or wearing a chasuble"?

Father Gorman looked confused then smiled broadly and said to Tom, "Sign him up Tom he has wit we need some more of that here". He told me it was nice to have met me then excused himself leaving Tom and me alone. When priest was out of ear shot I asked Tom, "What did this club do"?

"We raise money for the Catholic Seminaries". I made an approval sound then asked Tom what was on his mind and that he sounded mysterious on the phone. "My brother in law called me the other night to tell me he thinks your phone is being tapped".

"By who"?

"He's not sure; he is a test desk man for the phone company and he works in the Central Office that handles your telephone exchange. In his daily routine of testing circuits he observed an unusual capacity reading on the circuit assigned to your number when he reported it he was told to ignore it. When he was on his break he asked the wiremen, who work on the cables in the volt of the Central Office, what's going on with the number of your circuit and they said they were told the same thing to ignore it, but one wireman suspected a Fed tap".

"Can they do that"?

"The point is they're doing it and if I were you I'd tell my lawyer to see if it is legal or not".

"But I didn't hear any clicking or drop in volume and why wouldn't it be the S.F.P.D. why did the wireman think it was the Feds".

"I'm told you wouldn't notice any difference they're very sophisticated and have people that do nothing but surveillance and I'm told the S.F.P.D. would not use the telephone central office to tap you phone".

I thanked Tom and left for home on the way I stopped and bought a bottle of Anne's favorite wine I was going to try to fortify her for all the upsetting news. When I got home it was quite my mother in law was gone and the baby was asleep. Anne was sitting at the kitchen table listening to music on the radio and reading the evening paper. I put the bottle of Prosecco on the table with a grin from ear to ear and said, "A slice of cheese cake would go very nicely what do you think"?

"I think you're on the right track, but don't chill the wine any more than it is I don't like it refrigerator cold". I got the cheese cake and served a piece to Anne and proceeded to open the wine. Anne looked up at me and with her wildly grin said, "What did you do wrong".

"Why is it when I do a little something special you accuse me of forgetting something important like the time I celebrated our anniversary on the wrong date because if you turn a 6 upside down it could be a 9 it could happen to anyone".

"O.K. let's get real what happened at the club"?

"Our phone is being tapped".

"Tapped by whom"?

"The finger is being pointed at the FBI"

"Who's pointing a finger at the FBI"?

"Tom has a brother in law who works for the phone company and his job is to test the phone lines he came across a problem with a particular line and was told to forget it and leave it alone. That made him curious so he checked further and discovered it was our line and it was being tapped by a government agency need I say more".

Anne took a long pull on Prosecco then sat back and said, "You better tell your lawyer as soon as possible".

Chapter 10

Oscar and Medwin were sitting in their car waiting outside a cheap hotel in the Tender Loin for Addlemann. Oscar asked Medwin, "How did you find Addlemann".

"The young officer got his license plate and it was a rental car and he left the hotel number as a call back".

"Boy they're training these young guys real good nothing sloppy did you give him an att'd a boy".

"Yeah and I let his lieutenant know". Medwin told Oscar he came across something interesting about that woman impersonator Allen a.k.a. Luana Dune. Oscar asked, "What was it". "He grew up in Philadelphia so I got his prints off of his DUI record and sent them with a request for any convictions. He was a convicted gang member way back and a Local Judge gave him an alternative of two years in jail or join the Army; he did two years in the Army as a medic. It kind of struck me he certainly was introduced to firearms and being a medic he would get training in the human anatomy so he would know where a neck shot would paralyze someone".

"Can we get a hold of anyone in Philly to find out what he was convicted of"?

"I'm working on that now". Oscar's voice dropped to a serious note; "Here comes someone give me that mug shot that's him".

"I could have told you that I interviewed him". Medwin replied.

"Yeah, yeah don't be a wise ass let's talk to him"."

Addlemann slowed his walk to a stop when he recognized Medwin. Medwin greeted him with an insincere friendly hello and introduced Oscar as his partner then invited him to join them for some coffee.

"Do I have choice"?

"Not really besides we've been waiting for you for hours and we're dying for a cup of coffee; come on we can go to that new coffee house from Seattle, the coffees are great".

They settled in at the coffee house with three coffee grandees and Oscar took the lead trying the friendly approach by calling him Mickey this prompted a frown from Addlemann. Pressing on, Oscar told him they were interested in knowing more about Mace and could he fill in some blanks.

"I'll tell you what I told the Feds Mace was the real master mind behind that garment business fiasco. Itkin was just a go between Mace was the guy who put that deal together. He and his buddy Merrick formulated the loan for the Teamsters to get the key man insurance to protect the loan and made off with all the loot scot free". He swung his head in the direction of Medwin and in a condescending tone asked, "Hay Medwin would you get me one of those carrot cakes". Medwin glanced at Oscar then Addlemann and in a tired voice said, "Yeah don't go-way I'll be right back". Oscar asked him why he came to San Francisco. "To find Mace and ask him for help".

"I take it you meant money so what did he say"?

"He gave me a quick grand with a promise of more".

"How much more"?

"I don't know he got wacked before he could make good his promise".

"Why would he give you money in the first place"?

"Because I kept my mouth shut; I'm going to tell you the short version of what happened in New York twenty years ago. Itkin was getting heat from this guy Anastasia so he told me to go see this guy that owned a garment company because he was late on his interest payments. This is the second time I went to see this guy so he knew what I was going to say; he was next to the elevator and when I got close he put something into the door seam and the elevator doors opened. At first I didn't realize the elevator wasn't there, but when he grabbed me and tried to throw me down the shaft I twisted away and he fell down the shaft. The New York D.A. had me on a murder for hire and I was heading for the chair when by luck I was assigned a free lawyer who was real sharp. He dug up an eye witness, one of the women who worked there, to corroborate my story and they found the tool he used to open the elevator door that only had his finger prints on it. I pleaded out to manslaughter but the judge didn't like my previous record so he gave me the max twenty years, but thinking back I was lucky if I opened my mouth I could be in the cemetery at Sing Sing".

Medwin looked bored when he said, "We were hanging on every word but what has that got to do with Mace's murder"?

"Maybe nothing, but I'm not a murderer I've leaned on people but I never killed anybody and that includes Mace besides he was going to give me money". Oscar jumped in with a question, "Who is Anastasia".

"He was the head of the crime family in New York he was involved because he lent money to the owner of the garment business and was tired of late payments and contacted Itkin to get this guy a loan from the Teamsters Retirement Fund so he could be paid off".

"So who killed Itkin"?

"No one knows, but my money's on the Crime Family and Gambino he had Anastasia wacked to take over the Family and maybe they thought Itkin knew too much of the family's business".

They finished their coffee and they offered Addlemann a ride back to his hotel. "Never mind I'd rather walk". He said.

They were sitting in the car when Oscar asked Medwin, "What do you think".

"He certainly sounds convincing, but I'm not taking him off the top of my list of suspects".

The next day I was with Dick Somers in his office when I called my lawyer Myra Pacemann. I told her I was at Dick's office and that I found out my phone was being tapped and more than likely by the FBI. Then my bank called this morning informing me the Feds had a warrant to search my safety deposit box and all my accounts. She said she had to be in court this afternoon and could I meet her at her office tonight at six o'clock and as a precaution both you and your wife be careful and limit your conversations on the phone and most important do not talk to the Feds without me present; I agreed and hung up. We were sitting in the spare office that I assumed was going to be mine that is if this knew turn of events doesn't cause Dick or his company to distance themselves from me. Dick spoke first, "Your handling of this is right; go at them don't wait until they get some insignificant transaction and pick up a few others and come up with a circumstantial case".

"I know you're right and I'm sure Myra feels the same and I sure would like to know how they're going to make a federal case out of anything I did".

"Find out from Myra if I can send you out of town for week I need you back at Hemet. I got a call from Simenson and Associates they're sending out there accountant to go over the loans to be warehoused and now Kalami wants all million and a quarter presented in one package. I'd like you to go over all the original paper work with the accountant and keep an eye on Kalami".

"Where is Max"?

"I don't know and they didn't tell me but he wasn't mentioned in the conversation which means he won't be there so you're the only one who knows what went on".

"Dick that leaves me in a possible untenable position; if I ignore the document tampering that I'm sure Max did to increase the loan portfolio that would make me complicit. If the FBI found out that would be another nail in my coffin".

Alright Jimmy here's where we are at; there is a possible commission of more than thirty thousand dollars that will more then cover your salary and office overhead for the year. The rest you make this year you will get a healthy commission now if I were you I would meet with the accountant from Simenson and tell him Max did all the loan profiling and you just compiled the paper work, which by the way is technical true. Let the accountant do his job he's a professional and if there is anything wrong let him handle it and above all don't try to cover for Max let everything fall at the accountant's discretion".

I didn't get home until eight o'clock. Anne had dinner in orbit and I sat down at the kitchen table and told her to bring it on I was starving. She asked if I wanted anything to drink and I said just ice water. She served me a plate of meaty pork ribs braised in her mother's marinara sauce with a half of a loaf of bread; I swooned, "I love you". As was her custom when I was late for dinner she sat opposite me with a small plate of salad and a glass of wine more or less to keep me company. She waited until I was well into my dinner then asked me; how did it go at the lawyer's. "No surprises she cautioned us again not to talk long on the phone and be aware of what you are saying and if we could get our financial statements in the same time frame I worked for John".

"That's no problem I have them in our tax file".

"Dick asked me to go back to Hemet to meet with an accountant from Simonson and Associates to explain to the guy what I know about Max's loan portfolio. It should only take a couple of days I'm flying down to Palm Springs and I know there is scheduled flight at nine AM to Oakland on Saturday".

"The rental agent called me to day to let us know that by the time you get back the new tenants will have moved into the Union Street flat; however what are we going to do about the Union Street property? Do we own it or does it belong to Mary".

"Good question, of course, legally we do, but John had an unsigned quit claim deed and I wouldn't put it passed him to forge my signature we'll talk about that when I get back".

I took the first flight in the morning out of Oakland International on PSA bound for Palm Springs. I opened the folder Dick had given me in it was a copy of the contract with Kalami and the name of the accountant from Simenson and Associates. There was also a note telling me that the accountant was already there and had called with a few questions so he was informed you were on your way and could answer any questions when you arrived. I rented a car at the Airport and got to Hemet and Kalami's office by early afternoon. Kalami wasn't there but Amanda his receptionist greeted me with a friendly hello and ushered me into the file room where the accountant was going over a pile of loan papers. When he looked up I said, "You must be Neil Lyons; I'm Jim Kerry". They greeted each other in a business-like manner and got right to work. Almost all Neil's question had to do with the payment history of the loans he had separated from the pack and his main concerns were if the payments were currant and on time. I went to the delinquent loan file pulled it out along with a list of chronic late payers. He spread out the lists and they started cross referencing the delinquent loans from his list and checking the late payers at the same time. All was going very smoothly and the time passed quickly and before we realized it Amanda was at the door telling us it was five o'clock and she was leaving and the security guard was alerted you'll be working this evening. We stayed at it another hour or so then decided to get something to eat and pick it up in the morning. We realized we were staying at the same motel and thought the café in the motel was a good choice for dinner. I got settled in then met Neil in the café. Neil was all business he talked about the loan portfolio all through dinner and surprised me by discussing Kalami's financial health; he went into some detail of his company's books judging a few things a little shaky but overall it's in pretty good shape when we buy these loans he'll be in very good financial shape. This left the door open for me to ask, "Are all the loans in the portfolio going to be bought as the original package of one million two hundred and fifty thousand dollars".

"I can't see why not, I'll certainly recommend it as a matter of fact I can see about forty to fifty thousand more that could be bought". When we wound up the evening I went to my room to call Anne to tell her I'm going to try to get out of here tomorrow and I should get back to Oakland that evening. I then called Dick to tell him the one and a quarter million was going through as one package, but he didn't answer so I left the message with his answering service. I was lying in the motel bed surfing the TV for a ball game when a thought hit me Neil never questioned the legitimacy of any dates or signatures just the payment history.

As I hoped we were done by noon then I said my goodbyes and was heading home. I was somewhat relieved but also mystified that I saw neither hide nor hair of Kalami while his loan package was being scrutinized. When I arrived in Oakland it was Dick that met me not Anne. He quickly explained he called and told Anne it would be easier for him to pick me up with such a short notice to get a babysitter. As we drove away from the airport Dick wanted to know the whole story step by step and how Kalami was reacting to the scrutinizing of his loan package and did he mention the commission. After ten minutes of driving and me talking; Dick told me to save it we'll stop at the Buena Vista Cafe down from your house where I can concentrate on what you're saying. We stopped at the Café went to the back room where it was quieter and I gave Dick a blow by blow of the events in Hemet and when I told him of Kalami's absence it raised Dick's eye brow and he said something like, "Interesting". Dick sat back and took a pull on his drink then said, "I'll call Simenson tomorrow in Cincinnati to confirm the sale and open escrow in a title company in Palm Springs to avoid Kalami using his escrow company. Jimmy we'll both sleep better tonight so drink up and let's go".

When I got home Anne was in bed and half a sleep so I told her I'd catch her up on the events in the morning. In the morning true to my word I filled her in on all the twists and turns of the Hemet deal and she was laughing and asking questions in joke form then said, "This is like a soap opera".

"It might sound like it but they're paying a price; the money makes it real".

I waited until Monday to call my lawyer to tell her I was back in town. She told me she notified the two FBI agents Brophy and Clarke that she was now representing me and there will be no more conversations with my client unless she was present. Then she explained Brophy called the following day and asked to schedule a meeting at the Federal building; I explained you were out of town and as soon as you got back we would contact them for an appointment. Let's do it a.s.a.p. and see what's on their mind. I agreed so she called them to set up a meeting. I met Myra in front of the Federal building then entered and navigated security and eventually to Brophy's cubical. His partner Clarke was sitting on the edge of Brophy's desk with a file folder in his hand. Myra introduced her-self and they in turn did the same; then suggested we go to an interview room for convenience sake. As we were leaving the cubical Brophy asked me, "How was Hemet"?

Without missing a beat I answered, "Hot". I knew this was going to be just like the last time they were not really interested in information gathering but rather intimidation and guilt by association by thinly vailed accusations. My attorney and I sat next to one and other at the table across from Agent Brophy with Agent Clarke wandering about the room looking bored and uninterested. When everyone was seated Clarke stopped long enough to place the file he was carrying in front of Brophy then continued wandering. I thought this looked like a replay of the last time I was here. Brophy opened the file and seemed to be looking for something then abruptly looked up at me and asked, "Are you familiar with Small Business Administration loans"? Myra put her hand up and stopped me from answering then asked Brophy, "In what context".

"I'm asking a simple question is Mr. Kerry familiar with SBA loans".

"Mr. Kerry didn't come here to be quizzed on his general knowledge please be more specific with your questions so he can help you in your investigation". Clarke spoke for the first time, "Are you aware that commissions are regulated by percentage that anyone can charge for helping a client obtain a SBA loan"?

"I've heard that".

"Are you also aware that your client Mr. Beard, owner of the Cornucopia Hotel in San Francisco, secured a SBA loan from the Union Commercial Bank of Fremont"?

"I was told that, yes".

"Were you also told that he paid a thirty five thousand dollar payment to the computer company owned by the same people that own the bank in question"?

"NO I was not".

"We have it on sworn testimony that you drove Mr. Beard to the bank to deliver the bribe and discussed it with one of the bank employees".

I looked at Myra and she nodded a go ahead gesture so I said, "Half of your statement is correct I drove Mr. Beard to the bank after Mr. Mace asked me to because Mr. Beard had no way of getting there, but to the employee you're referring to he was quizzing me on what was going on with the Beard loan more or less to qualify him to spread the in-house gossip". Now Brophy weighed in, "I find it quite a coincidence that we find a thousand dollars in an envelope in your safety deposit box at your bank".

"If you check the dates that my wife last went to our safety deposit box you'll see it coincides with me returning from Las Vegas and that was part of my winnings".

"If that be the case why didn't the casino have you declare it with the IRS"?

"Because I won the money in increments too small to declare".

Clarke was now sitting when he said, "Speaking of Las Vegas what is your relationship with a man named Guytano Corsenti aka Guy Corsey the alleged owner of the Feline Follies Casino".

Myra cut Clarke short by asking, "What he meant by alleged".

"I think it is common knowledge he's a front man for someone who can't get a gaming license".

"Well I think you ought to go to the Nevada Gaming Commission and inform them of that fact; if of course you have proof if not I strongly suggest you confined your accusation to the facts". Myra said.

Clarke stared at Myra momentarily then continued, "Mr. Corsenti gave Mr. Kerry twenty five thousand dollars in bearer bonds for Mr. Mace who in turn used them at the Union Commercial Bank to create a credit line for his business. We would like Mr. Kerry to verify this".

I looked at Myra who nodded a go ahead then I said, "I was told by Mr. Mace that Mr. Corsenti held IOU's of his and he wanted me to pick them up because he was in an important meeting at the Tropicana all day so being a good employee I did so and that is the extent of my relationship with Mr. Corsenti".

"What was Mr. Mace's relationship with Mr. Corsenti"?

"I don't know I just assumed he lost money at his casino and was paying him back".

"Were you aware that Mr. Mace negotiated a loan from the Teamsters Pension fund for Mr. Corsenti to finance the Feline Follies Casino and Mr. Mace was indicted and convicted of bribery, money laundering and defrauding the government"?

I was genuinely surprised my eyes focused on the wall behind Agent Clarke then replied, "No I was not aware of that".

Myra stepped in at this point and told the Agents she thought Mr. Kerry has been very cooperative, but she also thought her client had answered enough question for today and they were leaving.

Before they left Agent Brophy asked, "What happened to your black Mercedes"? I didn't answer him we just left. When they were outside Myra asked me what was that all about. Just a warning shot he's letting me know my phone is being tapped; the question about Hemet and the black Mercedes he got from my mother in law she doesn't know the phone is tapped.

I headed for my new office just two floors up from my old office at 300 Montgomery Street. I stopped at the news stand in the lobby and was perusing the head-lines when I felt some body behind him. I casually turned not wanting to seem to be spooked and there was a man standing too close behind me to be comfortable. The man apologized for interrupting my thoughts then said, "My name is Addlemann I was a friend of John Mace and we worked together back in New York many years ago I wander if I can speak to you in privet it's important".

I glanced around the lobby as if we shouldn't be seen together then asked, "What about".

"Please it is confidential it will only take the time to drink a cup of coffee there's a place on the corner we can talk in privet".

I agreed on impulse so we found a table in the corner and ordered coffee. Addlemann got right to it and asked if I knew anything about him. I started to nod yes then said, "I know of your stint in prison and the story of what happened twenty years ago, but what do I have to do with you and John".

"John owes me I kept my mouth shut and saved his ass. When I got out he was going to take care of me, you know money wise, than he got wacked. He buried a ton of money and between the two of us we can find out where it is".

"What makes you think I know anything about his buried money"?

"Because Mace always had a go to guy; back in New York he had this guy Merrick and when the money disappeared so did Merrick".

"Then why don't you go find Merrick"?

"I don't know what he looks like or where he is John kept him up state in Troy New York in a different insurance business".

"Even if I wanted to help you I wouldn't know where to begin and I have my own problems the police think I killed John and the FBI wants to arrest me on money laundering charges so I'm sorry I'm a dead end".

I left Addlemann in the coffee shop and was back in the lobby of Montgomery Street building heading for the elevator when I realized Dick was in front of me. When Dick saw me he raised an eye brow in surprise then asked me how did the meeting go? I answered O.K. with a sardonic grin. We didn't say much until we got off of the elevator and into Dick's office then I filled Dick in on what was said at the meeting with the FBI. Dick listened quietly until I had finished then told me he thought it best to let Myra handle it; then he turned to the business in Hemet. "I heard from Cincinnati their accountant had nice things to say about you and even better they're going ahead with the warehousing loan with Kalami for the full amount; I opened escrow in Palm Springs so we should be seeing our commission in a week or two and congratulations on a job well done".

"Out of curiosity do you know what happened to Max"?

"No I don't; however I imagine he has a lot of explaining to do".

"Yeah he probably does, but he is cleaver and very persuasive he might come up with the right answers and get off the hook".

"He's a little too clever for my money". Dick replied.

Chapter 11

Oscar and Medwin were sitting in their car waiting for someone to show at Allen's apartment. It was early evening and they thought it would be the best time to catch someone home; so far they were drawing a blank. Oscar asked Medwin if Allen could shed any light on where Mace's wife was. "No I caught him at a bad time he was flitting around his shop talking to two women about colors and fabrics and when I asked him he said very dramatically she had her own key and he guessed she was over twenty one. I was tempted to kick him in the ass and watch him fly around the room".

"Now, now you have to be a little more sensitive and understanding he is only living his dream". Yeah, yeah speak of the devil here he comes. They both got out of the car that's when Allen saw them and with a discussed look said, "I'm going to get a lawyer and sue you for harassment and I'm going to get a restraining order to keep you away from my business".

"Calm down we're trying to find Mace's wife if you think our questions are harassment maybe we should treat you as material witness and take you down town for questioning".

"Alright I don't know exactly where she is, my boyfriend Jean and Mary didn't get along so she left. She said she was going back down to San Diego and then mentioned a friend she wanted to see in Las Vegas". Oscar asked if they could continue the conversation in his apartment. "No I don't want you in my apartment".

"Well people will get nosey if we continue talking here in the street so get in the back seat of our car and we can finish the conversation". He glanced at both of them and reluctantly got in. Medwin knew it was obvious he was disliked by Allen so he let Oscar ask the questions while he stared out the front windshield. "Where exactly did she say she was going in San Diego"?

"She didn't say but the last time she was there she stayed with a grand aunt so I guess that's where she is".

"Did she give you an address or phone number you could contact her down there".

"No she didn't and I don't know where to contact her in Las Vegas either".

"That's surprising you're her best friend you would think she would let you know how to keep in touch with her".

"Yeah; well she's kind of flighty I'm sure eventually I'll hear from her".

"Something else came up in the investigation that maybe you could help us out with; it's on recorded that you were given an choice of jail time or a hitch in the army by a Philadelphia Judge for gang related crimes could you explain what they were"?

Oscar thought he freaked out he started screaming and yelling obscenities and accusing them of illegally obtaining his juvenile records that were sealed and he's going to have them thrown off the force".

It was clear to Medwin they got him rattled and felt his juvenile record would be an important piece in the investigation and worth pursuing. Oscar was trying his best to calm Allen down is all he accomplished was to stop him from shouting, but he continued to threaten and curse the two detectives even after he got out of the car. When they pulled away from the curb he was shaking his fist and you didn't have to read lips to know what he was saying. As they were heading for Mission Street Medwin said, "What happened to his demure personality I believe we just triggered his more violent side".

Oscar replied, "Could be let's see what happens next".

The following day Oscar's lieutenant came over to his desk and told him Medwin would be tied up in court the rest of the week on that Sanchez homicide. Then asked, "How's the Mace investigation going.

"Not bad we're narrowing down the suspect list".

"I see from your notes it's quite a list".

"Yes it is and I have a question for you".

"What is it"?

"I want to check out a suspect's time of her alibi she claims she spent in San Diego with her Aunt. I have some vacation days coming so I'll take a few and go check out her alibi. I'm hoping you could OK a travel voucher for four days".

"We're really thin in coverage so let me think about it; Oh by the way have you updated the murder book the last time I looked it was pretty thin". After the lieutenant left Oscar opened the murder book and began re-accustom himself with the forensic report from the FBI. He read the report twice on the 22 caliber slugs recovered from Mace's body. The slug that entered his head behind the ear disintegrated into fragments, but the slug that they removed from his spine was intact and showed no discernable rifling marks. He sat at his desk thinking about any reason the slug wouldn't have any defining rifling marks at all and couldn't think of any except if it was a smooth bore so he put a note on a sticky tab on that sentence and closed the book. Two days later Medwin showed up in the squad room and told Oscar that Sanchez copped a plea to manslaughter so they were back in action. Oscar got Medwin up to speed on the Mace case and the odd forensic report on the slug that severed Mace's spine and asked for his thoughts on how that can happen. Medwin was also at a lost, other than the use of a smooth bore, so they went on to the suspect list and Oscar told him he asked for time to go down to San Diego to personally check out Mace's wife alibi. "We better update the murder book I couldn't find the name of the officer that you talked to at the San Diego PD that checked out Mace's wife's alibi it must be still in our notes".

"His name is Morales he's in some sort of detective pool they fill in where needed you can contact him through Central Booking".

"Come to think about it Pete maybe we could call Forensics and ask one of their experts about the absences of rifling marks on the slug"?

Medwin shrugged why not.

Oscar got the O.K. from the Lieutenant and left for the day to pick up his wife and get a head start for San Diego; he wanted to get out of the city before the commute traffic started if not it would be as long drive; he'd worry about the travel voucher when they got back.

Oscar wasn't gone ten minutes when the Lieutenant came out looking for him and asked Medwin if Oscar already left.

Medwin just nodded yes and the Lieutenant told him he wanted the two of them to check out a call he just got from the DA's office in Oakland; they got a guy being held by the Major Crime Squad who says he knows who the hit man was on the Mace murder; here's a number to call and the ADA is a Latisha Morgan she's handling the case. Why don't you go and have a look see and when Oscar gets back you can fill him in. Medwin called the ADA over in Oakland she answered on the second ring with a formal, "This is ADA Latisha Morgan". Medwin replied just as formal, "This is Detective Peter Medwin of the San Francisco Police Department I understand you are holding a suspect on an unspecified charge that has volunteered information on the John Mace murder here in San Francisco".

"That would be correct, but right after I called your Lieutenant I got a call from the Federal District Attorney's office informing me the FBI is working in conjunction with the SFPD on the Mace murder case and no one is to interview our suspect until an Agent named Clark has a chance to interview the man".

"Well do you have any idea when we can interview your suspect"?

"I'm afraid not it seems Agent Clark is in Las Vegas and won't be back until this coming Friday".

"That's three days away; boy that will slow things down. Can you tell me anything about who he says was the hired gun"?

"You know I'm not to discuss the case until Agent Clark gets here, but there was a name mentioned "Hugo Bettencourt".

"Was his location mentioned, you know where he might be"?

"No, but it was mentioned he was a Mexican National".

"Was there anything else mentioned about Senior Bettencourt like a Rap sheet or priors".

"I believe I heard nothing of note".

"I would like to thank you for your help and if you can remember anything else that was "mentioned"; I'd appreciate a call".

"I will do that Detective Medwin and have a nice day".

Medwin was still holding the receiver to his ear when she hung up; he pulled the phone away from his ear and looked at it questioningly then hung up.

Then two days later Medwin was crossing his office to start his workday when his phone rang. He quickened his step and got it on the fourth ring; it was Oscar. Oscar gave him a bad time accusing him of being late because he could see him running across the office to answer his phone. Medwin's reply was a sarcastic, "Yeah, yeah what'd you find out"?

"The old Aunt, by the way her name is Mable Mac Leash, how's that for an old fashioned name. She confirms Mrs. Mace was in San Diego on the day in question, but not after three o'clock. She said they had lunch and then Mace's wife spent over an hour in her Aunt's garage; she doesn't have a car and she uses it for family storage".

"Did she know what Mace's wife was looking for"?

"No, but the old lady went to the garage after she left to put things back in order and said she had rummaged through her father's military memorabilia and left photos and his medals all jumbled up just stuffed back into their box. I asked the Aunt if anything was missing, but she said she couldn't tell because she hadn't been in that box in many years. But listen to this, there was a photo of her father sporting a target pistol with a notation "Champion 25 yard target competition of the 377 fighter group 1947". I asked the Aunt if Mace's wife took the pistol, but she said she couldn't remember if there was one in the box".

"Was it a 22"?

"From the photo Yeah; there was also a bill of sale made out to a Cornelius Mac Leash for a Ruger competition rim-fire pistol along with a serial number and an advertisement photo and it looks like the one in the snap shot. Mrs. Mac Leash agreed I could take the box of photos and the bill of sale so I gave her receipt and I'll bring them back with me.

I don't want to put a damper on all your good work; and I'm serious but, something came up just as you left. The lieutenant gave me the number of an ADA over in Oakland that claimed they had a prisoner who claimed he knew who the hit man was in the Mace murder. When I called her she told me the Federal District Attorney called right after she talked to our Lieutenant informing her that no one was to interview the prisoner until the bureau interviewed him and you'll never guess who the Agents are".

"Wait, wait don't tell me I'll take a wild guess Brophy and Clark".

"Yes, but they're in Las Vegas until Friday and she gave me the name of the hit man he's a Mexican National by the name of Hugo Bettencourt. While you're there why don't you check with detective Morales down there in San Diego and see if they have anything on this guy. Who knows we may find something to connect this guy to the Mace murder; it beats waiting for Brophy and Clark to share their information on the Mace case".

Anne and I were getting into a heated discussion on the Union Street property; I wanted to keep it and Anne wanted to deed it over to Mary Mace, John's wife. The more the discussion went on the more I felt my argument was sounding flimsy even though I didn't think she could qualify for the mortgage; I found himself agreeing with Anne's long time premise if you do something sleazy it comes back to haunt you. I said I didn't know where she was or how to contact her. Anne said Tom told Nancy she was in Las Vegas and she worked with Guy Corsey so call him and see if he knows where she is. I had to think about calling Corsey or Corsenti whatever name he went by because of the investigation and it wouldn't look kosher calling him in the middle of the investigation. I was in my office late in the afternoon and was deciding whether to call Guy Corsey. I decided to do it and was put through to Corsey in just a minute or two. Corsey's voice was almost accusing when he told me he was trying to get a hold of me in San Francisco, but the phone was disconnected. He continued on without giving me a chance to ask about Mary. "Listen, John gave me a key to a privet mail box here in Las Vegas when he went to Lompoc. He would get letters every so often and I would mail them to him at Lompoc. I would have done this as a favor, but he insisted on greasing my palm the funny thing about it the letters weren't for him they were for some guy named Merrick. There was a letter in the box after I heard about John's murder so I put it in my desk waiting to see if anyone would claim it; seeing as though you're the last man standing I thought you would like to have it"?

It took me a minute to take in all that was just said and the name Merrick hit a familiar note his name was just mentioned by Addlemann; now the question who is Merrick?

"Mr. Corsey I'm sure at this point you have been interviewed by the FBI so you know what's going on here. My phone is being tapped so be careful what you say to me on my home phone; the other thing is I'm trying to find John's wife Mary I was told she has moved to Las Vegas; do you have any idea how I can contact her"?

"No I haven't; are you interested in the letter to Merrick"?

"I might be what's in it"?

"I don't know it's sealed".

"Knock it off; I'm not buying anything in the dark you tell me what it's about and how much".

"Who said anything about money"?

"OK let's stop playing games you could have contacted me at any time I'm in the San Francisco telephone book. As soon as you found out John was murdered you opened the letter and it's obvious you don't know what to do with it. You've been trying to figure out who you could sell it to when I called and now you're shooting from the hip; tell me how much".

"My book keeper was going over my books the other day and found one of your IOU's for five hundred dollars, of course, if you're strapped you could pay it in two payments and then I'll send you your IOU".

"Tell me when and where the IOU came from and more about it".

"It has the name and address of the sender and a reference to money".

I thought for a moment then said, "It sounds like something John was into and it really doesn't concern me so I'll pass especially with this investigation going on, but it might be worth fifty bucks if you could get me in touch with Mary".

"I'll tell you what, I'll give the letters to you for three hundred and throw in Mary's address".

"Make it two fifty and it's a deal".

"They're yours, "When are you going to pick up these IOU's"?

"I'll call you and let you know and remember what I told you about the phones yours included".

Anne called me at my office and asked me to pick up some bread on my way home tonight Mom's making dinner so make sure one of the loaves is Tuscan. Then said, "I may be a little late I'm buried this week in invoices".

Before we hung up I told her about the crazy conversation I had with Corsey.

"Are you going to Las Vegas"?

"Yeah you better catch up on your invoices and find someone to baby sit for a few days".

"Sounds like you're inviting me".

"Only if you bring that sleek black dress the one that's so tight you can't wear underwear".

"You have quite an imagination for your information I always wear a bra and panties but maybe the lack of slip constitutes not wearing anything".

"Why do you have to be so technical you're ruining my mental image"?

"I think we should retire that black dress I may have a few new mental images for you". After I hung up I was enjoying the mental images my wife had just prompted when it occurred to me I should call my lawyer and tell her of this conversation with Guy Corsey and if it was a good idea to follow up on it and go to Las Vegas. When I called her I was told she would be unavailable for the next four days so I said I would call back. I decided to go because primarily I was going to see Mary and tell her about transferring the deed of trust for Union Street flats to her.

I asked Dick if I could take a few days off to track down John's wife Mary. I'm told she is in Las Vegas and explained the situation with the San Francisco property.

"I have an idea you might like; I got a call from the escrow company in Palm Springs they have cut a check for the Kalami deal and I told them I'll pick it up in person. I'll pick up the check and Esperanza and I could meet you and Anne in Las Vegas to celebrate the closing, of course, the company will pick up the tab. We generally stay at Caesar's so we'll book you two there".

"That sounds great just let me know when".

That night I came home with a bottle of Perseco I could tell by the whiff from the kitchen that my mother in law was at the stove. I stood outside for a moment or two and a thought occurred to me I could channel information that I wanted the FBI to hear by using my mother in law unknowingly as a FBI informant. I stopped at Macaloso's for the bread and a few cannolis's, but with all that had happened when I got home I forgot them in the car. As soon as I entered she asked me, "Where was the bread". I told her yesterday was my bread day Anne's picking it up today. "You should pick up the bread every night she's a hard working girl and has a lot to do".

"Well that's true but Anne likes Gina to get use to going to the bakery she wants it to be part of her San Francisco neighborhood besides they always give Gina a sweet and that kills two bird with one stone".

"Yeah well she can do that any time you should pick up the bread it's on your way home". I bit my lip when I realized the logic I was dealing with, than I had to laugh to himself because I knew I was milking this too long and went out to the car and got the bread and cannoli's and when I returned my mother-law's comment said it all. "See I told you it wouldn't take long Macao's' only minutes away". I could let the FBI deal with my mother in law's logic after all they'll be listening to her conversations on our phone while we're gone.

When we got to Caesar's there was a message from Dick telling us he and Esperanza would be delayed a day and he would explain later. That actually gave us a day to take care of our own business so I called Corsey and made a date to meet at his Casino that evening. Anne wanted to go with me and told me she would play a few slots while I finished my business with Corsey and they could go to dinner afterwards. As we entered the Casino Anne sat at the first twenty five cent machine and I continued on to Corsey's office where I was ushered straight in to a smiling Corsey. As soon as I entered I thought I should have arranged to meet him some place other than his office the smile on his face gave me an uneasy feeling. I glanced around quickly to see if they were alone and then asked in a no nonsense tone, "Where is my IOU's".

"I have them right here".

I took an envelope out of my pocket and handed it to Corsey saying, "Here's my check now where's my IOU".

Corsey's smile disappeared when he said, "Check, what's with a check I expected cash"?

I was now smiling as I took the Merrick's letter then said, "I want a record that I paid off my IOU". Corsey frowned and said something about playing games then started to open the envelope and stopped and said, "I couldn't find Mace's wife, but you can ask her old roommate Mara Pace she's working out in Sumerlin at the Star Burst as the wardrobe lady for their knew production; if anyone knows where John's wife is she would". Then he got a good look at the check and bellowed, "Wait a minute this is made out to the Casino".

"Well yeah, I could probably turn the check into cash if you could get a number or place I can contact Mary Mace".

"Kerry you're a punk, a typical New York punk".

"Well thank you I take that as a compliment we're staying at Caesar's give me a call when you get the information". I left Corsey's office and motioned to Anne as I was heading for the Casino exit. She caught up with me and we left arm and arm. Outside she said, "What did you have in mind for the rest of the evening"?

"I don't know do you have any suggestions".

"As a matter of fact I do; you could take me to early dinner and I would like to discuss this whole chain of events and we can take a look at this two hundred and fifty dollar letter".

"Sold, I'll take you to my privet dining room at the Stage Door Deli".

We got to the end of one of those community tables and I opened the letter addressed to John Merrick. I was scrutinizing the contents when Anne impatiently asked me what was in it. I handed her the letter then said, "Not much something about an annuity payment and this guy Merrick has to file his quarterly taxes". Anne asked me if I ever heard of this lawyer De Long or this Essex Trust and Assurance Co. "No I haven't, but if anyone would know it would be Dick he deals with insurance companies for many of his loan commitments".

In the morning I was in our room reading the newspaper and drinking coffee when the phone rang. It was Corsey he said he had Mary's phone number and address and to meet him down stairs in the coffee bar; bring the cash and I'll give you back the check. Anne was still snuggled up under the covers so I told her I was meeting Corsey downstairs and I'd be back in an hour. Corsey was seated at a booth near the entrance drumming his fingers on the table to a military beat and looking annoyed. I slid into the booth and said, "Good morning sunshine". "Yeah, good morning to you here's the info you wanted now give me my two fifty".

"Just a few preliminary questions and I'll go to the cashier in the casino and get you your money, but first I hope you have my check with you and second the original envelope that the letter to Merrick came in was replaced by one of your own; I'd like that original envelope".

"Well mister smart ass that will cost you another two fifty, and I just happened to have that envelope with me".

"Mister Corsey I was hoping we could work this out in an amicable way, but I see dealing with you is like walking in mud; so let's just stop. I have no intention of paying you more money than we originally agreed on so keep the envelope and Mary's address. You see I have already talked to Mary's friend Mara and she put me in contact with her and the letter head on the letter to Merrick had the name and address of the lawyer Merrick was dealing with so I don't need that information, but I was thinking with this FBI investigation of John's business dealings and both of us in their sights we could be of some value to each other". Corsey's attitude changed completely when he said, "Your right I'm acting like a jerk we could definitely help one and other. How much do the Fed's know about what I was doing for John when he was in Lompoc"?

"It's not what they know it's what they suspect. You just having evidence of communicating with John while he was in Lompoc will get them to start digging into your business not only with John but the Casino and all your associates; they may even uncover a silent partner or two that at this point is strictly confidential and the Nevada Gaming Commission might take exception too. If I were you I would start covering my tracks by getting rid of anything that could connect you with John while he was in Lompoc".

"There's not much just the key to the P.O. box and the Letter you have".

"What about the envelope I picked up for John when we were here for the Tropicana deal"?

"Well yeah, but I just held on to them for safe keeping until John was sure it was safe".

"What was in the envelope"?

"I don't know I was just holding on to them for John".

"Did you open the envelope to see what was inside"?

"No".

"Then why did you refer to the envelope as them and not just the envelope"?

"What are you the FBI; I told you I was just holding on to the envelope until John thought it was safe".

"You keep saying safe what was in the envelope that would be incriminating"? Corsey's eyes were now darting around the coffee bar showing a hint of panic. "Look Kerry I did a favor for John that's all".

"Listen Guy I'm trying to help; we both had our hands on that envelope and if there is nothing incriminating in it then if the Feds question me I can tell them about the envelope".

Corsey suddenly got animated when he responded with, "No, no don't do that there was bonds in there and I don't know if they were clean".

"How many and what were there amounts".

"Five bonds at five thousand a piece".

When I got back to my room Anne was dressed and with the news that Dick and Esperanza are waiting for them at the café downstairs they drove in from Palm Springs this morning. "You mentioned Corsey before you left what was that all about"?

"We had a meeting of the minds and I found out the address of that lawyer and Mary's phone number".

"How much did it cost us"?

"Nothing I'll tell you about it later, but John must have been desperate to use this guy as a go between and confident while he was in Lompoc; he leaks out information under the slightest pressure. He tried to hold me up for another two fifty for the lawyers address, but I told him I didn't need it because it was on the letter head and of course, he couldn't remember if it was or wasn't".

"Yo my hero, you're so smart".

"I know". But then it occurred to me Corsey kept the key to Merrick's P. O. Box.

I called the number for Mary Mace, but got an answering machine so I left my number at Caesar's and a short message explaining why I needed to talk to her. Then we met Dick and his wife Esperanza at the café down stairs and plotted our soirée into Las Vegas night life. Esperanza took the first step by informing them she had four tickets to see the Helen Ready Show that evening. I didn't hear back from Mary and we left the next morning so the Union Street property was still in limbo.

Chapter 12

Back in San Francisco I used the company account to run a Dun and Bradstreet on this law Firm of De Long & De Long in Salt Lake City. Then called my lawyer Myra Pacemann for an appointment; I was asked to wait a minute then Myra got on the line almost interrupting the receptionist and said she heard I was in Las Vegas. I told her I had come across a piece of information inadvertently that was related to the FBI investigation. She asked if they could meet at her office sometime after six o'clock today. I told her I'd be there a little after six. I was organizing my day when Dick buzzed me and asked me to come to his office. I left everything as is on my desk and went to Dick's office. Dick was on the phone and pointed to a chair waving a greeting all the while raising an eye brow at the phone as if it was actually talking to him. When he hung up he let out a sigh then asked me if I had ever heard of a man named Jonathan Welsh. I told him no. "Well this fellow was asking if we represent any lenders that finance startup businesses in Las Vegas and he wasn't bashful at all about mentioning John's company U.S. Brokerage; also for good measure your name was mentioned". I was struck by a cold feeling; I immediately thought of Guy Corsey and somehow he was involved. Now should I tell all to Dick and possibly get him involved in the FBI investigation or stone wall all knowledge and keep Dick and his company out of it. I choose to plead innocents and denied knowing this man Welsh after all I actually didn't know this man.

Dick went on telling me he had a shopping center project down the Peninsular he wanted me to look at, but I wasn't listening. I was getting an eerie feeling it was like a controlled panic because a thought entered my mind that maybe somehow John Mace's past was now becoming my legacy. I took the paper work for the shopping center back to my office, but hardly looked at it. At around a quarter to six I left the office and headed for my meeting with Myra. The receptionist knew I knew the way so she just said she's expecting you and I hopped up the stairs and into the open door of her office. She had her back to me looking out the sliding glass door to the roof garden. I said, "Good evening Myra". Without turning she said, "I miss this garden, I've been in court all week, its solitude helps me think. So what information did you inadvertently come across in Las Vegas"? I told her about the P.O. Box under the name of John Merrick and the letter from the law firm of De Long & Delong; I didn't want to mention Corsey so I just told her that was where John Mace received the bonds from an annuity. She asked, "What kind of bonds and what annuity "?

"The bearer bonds Mace used for his line of credit at the Union Commercial Bank of Fremont".

"Is that the ones the FBI has been questioning you about"?

"Yes".

"Do you have that letter from De Long & De Long with you"?

"Yeah I do".

"Let me see it".

She read the letter then asked where I got this letter and did I have access the P. O. Box of Mister Merrick?

"The letter was left at the desk for me at Caesar's with a short note explaining it came from a P. O. Box belonging to this guy Merrick".

"Was it in its original envelope"?

"No it was in an envelope from Caesars".

"Do you have the note that came with the letter"?

"No I threw it away".

She gave him the fish eye in a prolonged stare then said, "We better get something straight you never lie to your lawyer and don't hold critical information from the police, because if you do I will no longer represent you; I'm I clear"?

I had a wise ass grin on my face when I replied too quickly, "Perfectly".

"She continued her stare then said, "It has been said confession is good for the soul".

"Yeah but it plays hell with your personal life". I replied.

"Is that some sort of admission".

"No it's just me getting in the last word".

"Well I'm going to spoil your last word; this Merrick is making this case very complicated I strongly suggest you bring all this new information to the FBI and let them sort it out".

I got quiet then asked, "Every detail".

"Yes even what you conveniently left out of the account you gave me".

At this point I didn't hesitate I told her how I was contacted by Guy Corsey and that he was John's bag man while he was in Prison and this guy Merrick was paying John off or was John's partner in whatever shady business they were in.

The last statement brought a smile to her face when she said, "You can take a kid out of Gotham but you can't take the Gotham out of a kid".

I looked questioningly at her and said, "What does that mean"?

"It means there is more that you're holding back".

"The rest has nothing to do with this case its part of John's personal life".

"Why don't you let the authorities figure that out"?

I left the lawyer's office and headed home. It started raining pretty heavy and the people were driving too aggressively so by the time I got home I felt all rung out. I gave Anne what amounted to an air kiss then went to the frig for a beer and sat at the kitchen table. Anne was playing with Little Gina in her high chair and looked over at me and I was far away. "We have left overs tonight and I was waiting for you to get home so you could choose your poison. There is beef stew from Monday night or we have a few veal cutlets from last night". I suddenly perked up and asked, "Is there any mozzarella cheese". She hummed a yes then said, "I could put them under the broiler add a little tomato sauce and slip them into an open piece of Italian bread".

"Woman you're a saint".

"I didn't think you noticed"?

"How could I not your mother reminds me every chance she gets".

"Stop picking on my mother she adores you and your black car". I almost chuckled, but Anne's sense of humor brought me out of my funk. I gave out a sigh and told her our lawyer strongly recommend that I tell the FBI everything that I found out in Las Vegas. I don't know who this Merrick guy is so I'm not concerned about him, but I told Corsey I'd keep him out of it. I feel like I'm on a rock or a hard place.

"You told me Corsey still has the key to Merrick's P. O. Box so if I were you I'd cover myself; remember how shifty he can be I think he is well adapted at self-preservation". I was mulling this over when Anne told me Mary Mace called from Las Vegas. I replied, "And"."

"And when I explained the situation of the Union Street property she wanted to know if we could just sell the property and give her the money; she said she was afraid to come back to San Francisco".

"Did she say why"?

"Get this; she told me that Allen had borrowed some of her clothes the day John was killed and among them was her large shoulder travel bag. Sometime later when she went to use it she found three small bullets in the bottom of the bag. Now she wants to stay clear of San Francisco and Allen". I rocked my head then said, "I knew this was not going to be easy. Do you think she's telling the truth"?

"NO, she certainly seems to come up with these revelations when she has time to think about her position in the investigation, but who knows".

The next day I called my lawyer and told her she was right and if she could set up a meeting with Agents Brophy and Clark to tell them what went on in Las Vegas. Later that day she called me back, "They told me they were in a sensitive stage of the investigation so they would have to get back to us in due time. It seems on the scale of importance you got put on the back burner".

"Well that could be good or bad, but something just came up that we should talk about; could we meet at your office this evening at the usual time"?

"Sure; bring Chinese".

I called home to tell Anne I had a meeting this evening and wouldn't make dinner; she said fine but don't make plans for Friday night we're going to the Valance's for dinner.

I was forty minutes late so when I rang the inter com expecting the receptionist to answer I was taken back when Myra answered and asked if I forgot the Chinese. "No mam, mushi shrimp with duck sauce". The door release buzzer was still buzzing when I got on the elevator and Myra was waiting for me when he got off the elevator then led me to the main conference room. The table was set for two with napkins, plates, silverware and pitcher of ice water. Myra dove right in with her own ivory chop sticks; then with a gratuitous wave of her hand and a matching statement; tell me all about it. I started off with my first impression of Mary when I first met her. Myra stopped me and said just get to the quick I'm starving. I felt a little hurt, but I knew that was Myra's way of telling me at this time of day she was doing me a favor seeing me. I told her of Mary's reaction to the news of her gift of the Union Street property and the story of the three bullets she found in her bag after Allen had borrowed it the day Mace was shot. Myra told me the Union Street property was a privet matter between you, your wife and Mrs. Mace; the bag with the three bullets is an altogether different matter it's a matter for the police or in this case the FBI. I strongly suggest you alert them to this matter when they get around to having time to interview you. Myra's sarcasm about the FBI helped ease the apprehension about being interviewed by them.

Brophy and Clark were leaving the Oakland City Hall of Justice after their meeting with the Assistant District Attorney Latisha Morgan and the unnamed snitch when Brophy asked Clark what was his take on the snitch's story. "Well we've been through this before he's a three time loser and he probably would say or do anything to avoid life in prison however his story is more than plausible. The ADA had a substantial sheet on this guy Bettencourt and that's just here in California we'll contact the Mexican authorities and see what they have on him, but it won't be easy finding him ". Brophy went quiet and Clark asked him, "What's the matter"?

"Every time we brought up Cannelli's name he went deft and dumb. That makes me believe he's shifting the facts around you know he never once said Cannelli and this guy Bettencourt in the same sentence".

"I'm with you on that, but once we get Bettencourt and he faces the charge of murder for hire his only alternative is to finger Cannelli and take life in prison".

When Oscar got back from San Diego Medwin called Agents Brophy and Clark and asked about the interview of the prisoner over in Oakland who claims to know who the hit man was on the Mace case. Oscar was livid when they got a lot of maybes and they're not sure type of answers. Then when he asked the name of the snitch and the hit man he was told it was too early in the investigation to divulge any information, but they will keep them abreast of the event as they unfold. Oscar asked Medwin if he thought that the Oakland ADA let the FBI know she told you the name of the hit man. "No I would be willing to bet she didn't".

"Good we can follow up on this guy Bettencourt on our own. I'll call Morales in San Diego and see if he can dig something up on this Hugo Bettencourt while we look through our records".

Their records showed Bettencourt was arrested on buying arms illegally here in California for transport to Mexico. The charge was later dropped and he was deported back to Mexico; that was November 1969. He was arrested again in 1971 illegally entering the country for the purpose of laundering money; he again was deported and nothing after that, but both times the Feds were involved and both times he was arrested in Oakland you don't think it's possible he was a FBI informant. Anything is possible. Morales called back with surprising information on Bettencourt. He told Oscar Bettencourt had a mistress in San Diego who he visited occasionally there, but mostly she meets him in Puerto Vallarta. It was Morales's understanding that he had a Villa up in the hills, but no one seems to know exactly where. He told Oscar his mistress had a very nosey neighbor who would give Morales a blow by blow account of everything his mistress did including the make and model of her new BMW. The neighbor reported an unusual change in his mistress she came back from Mexico and hunkered down in her apartment for the last week and when the neighbor next saw her she seemed distraught and had obviously been crying. My conclusion was he either broke off their relationship or something happened to Bettencourt. I'll follow this up; I have someone in the area of Puerto Vallarta who will try and find out where his Villa is and check his usual haunts. He told Oscar he would call him if he gets any more information. He ended his conversation by giving Oscar his opinion of Bettencourt he told him he couldn't see him as a hit man because he never got his hands dirty all of his illegal activities he kept at arm's length, but who knows he could be your man.

In less than an hour Brophy called and told Medwin they found out the hit man's name was Herman Bettencourt and they believe he's in Tijuana and they are talking to the Federales and when they locate him they'll contact us. When Medwin told Oscar he went silent for a full minute; then with a sarcastic question asked, "Who do you think has accurate information the ADA Morgan and Morales or Brophy and Clark"?

Chapter 13

Friday evening the baby sitter was late which saved me from further petulance from Anne since I was also late, but not as late as the baby sitter. I emerged from the bedroom in casual clothes just in time to hear Anne giving last minute instructions to the young teenager who looked bored. I knew Anne was not totally comfortable with the neighbor's daughter so I figured it would be an early evening. We arrived in plenty of time everyone was still working on their second cocktail and we were hardly noticed until Tom started to introduce us to Tom's brother Jason and his wife Helen who were visiting from New York. There were three other couples which Anne and I had met before so everyone began to mingle except for Tom's brother. He coaxed me away from the group while starting a conversation about John Mace that's when I remembered Tom told me his brother went to school with John. He said he was sorry to hear about John's murder and if there was anything I want to know about his back ground that could help in the investigation just ask. "Yes there is; I understand you went to school with John". "That's right Saint John's College in Brooklyn".

"I'm curious if you knew if John had a friend named Merrick"?

"Absolutely, Merrick and John were class mates of mine and they were thicker than thieves no pun intended. I lost track of Merrick right after graduation, but John I would see socially from time to time. When he got involved in that murder and extortion business

I saw a lot less of him. It was by his own design he got wrapped up in his insurance business and he seemed to be in Cuba more than New York".

"Really Cuba what was the attraction there"?

"Gambling it was the gambling capital of the Caribbean John loved the excitement and someone mentioned to me a while back that Merrick would often go with him. I heard they were both in Havana when Castro roared into town".

"Was there any connection business wise between John and Merrick"?

"Probably like I said they were very close they grew up together in an orphanage in Brooklyn on 12th Avenue, but I can't remember its name. They even resemble each other both had red hair and about the same size they were often taken for brothers. They were always covering each other's back; especially John, Merrick had a congenital heart problem in fact the doctors made him quit playing intermural basketball in college. I remember Merrick getting annoyed at John for mothering him and John getting embarrassed when he realized what he was doing".

"I understand John left Havana for Belize do you know if Merrick was with him"?

"No I don't, but if Merrick was with him in Havana I would bet he went with him to Belize". After dinner Anne made our excuses and we left early to satisfy Anne's anxiety over the teenage baby sitter. On our way home she asked me, "What was the secret conversation you had with Tom's brother about". "It was interesting he went to school with John and this fellow Merrick I'll give you the whole story when we send the baby sitter home".

The lieutenant called Medwin and Oscar into his office he offered them a seat then with a slight hesitation said, "We're handing over our part of the Mace investigation to the Feds; It seems they have connected Mace's murder to their investigation to the bank fraud down in Fremont and they have just indicted the President and vice President of the bank on money laundering and conspiracy to defraud the government. It is my guess they're going to offer them a deal to implicate this guy Cannelli and if they can hang this murder rap on him he might give them bigger and more important fish. So bring the murder book up to date and get it over the Federal Building". The first one to reply was Medwin, "We'll need a few days to get the book organized". Then Oscar chimed in with, "We can't give them our sources so we might need a few more days to cover the sequence of events so they can't figure out who they are".

"That's fine just contact someone over in the Federal Building and tell them you'll send over the murder book as soon as you bring it up to date. In the mean time I want you both to help Morrison he is on his own out in the Mission; he needs leg work done on that triple murder and drug mess, in fact he needs all the help we can give him".

They both stood and left the office and headed for their desk's Oscar was mumbling obscenities under his breath which triggered a sardonic smile on Medwin face. When they got to their desks Medwin said, "I don't know why your upset we both knew this was coming; so as soon as they changed Bettencourt's name and the most improbable location of Tijuana the hand writing was on the wall".

"Don't be so smug when you're right; so do you want to help Morrison or bring up the murder book to date". Medwin hesitated a beat then said, "You got a fixation about this Mace Murder so why don't you bring up the murder book to date and I'll help Morrison out in the Mission until his partner is back".

Oscar nodded his approval then reached for the keys to the filing cabinet all the while mumbling new obscenities about the Feds especially Brophy and Clark. He went to the filing cabinet and retrieved the murder book then sat at his desk and began going over the book page by page. He came across a few questions that were never answered one was the juvenile record of Allen, Luana Dune of Bimbo's fame. The request for his records from Philadelphia was denied because of age the records were sealed but there was a contact person and her direct number. He was annoyed with himself for not following up on this information because he had the feeling it was important. Then he saw a note from the Lieutenant that he didn't know was in the book it referred to Mace's profile from the FBI. He went back to the filing cabinet and found it under FBI profiles he had to laugh to himself because where else would it be. He took it back to his desk and started going through it and was fascinated by the profile and the following sorted history of Mace's adult life including his brush with Castro and his escape to Belize then his circuitous route through Mexico and eventually to Las Vegas. A name was mentioned briefly, Merrick; he knew he heard the name before, but couldn't remember where. It went on to Mace's connection to some Teamsters and organized crime figures and his eventual prison term for conspiracy to defraud the government. The file ended with James Kerry then Mace's murder. He sat back and thought about what he had just read then started to read it all over again. The second time he read it he realized what bothered him. He went back to the Lieutenant's office gave a perfunctory knock and entered. The Lieutenant looked up and asked, "What's the matter". He explained he was reading the FBI profile and the history of John Mace and there's something in the report that is unusual especially for the Bureau. The Lieutenant wanted to know what it was.

Norman fished out a page of the report and as he was handing it over to the Lieutenant he said, "This is the sequence in the report where Mace leaves Cuba but there is no mention of a guy named Merrick and when they get to Belize Merrick is the only name mentioned he is never again mentioned all through Mexico and Mace is the only one reported entering the States". The Lieutenant mused, "Interesting was this guy Merrick in Cuba with Mace"?

"On the previous page they state because he accompanied Mace on all his other trips to Havana they surmise he was there".

"How did Mace get from Havana to Belize"?

"A Dutch Tramp Steamer called the Curacao she circles the Caribbean on an organized schedule she was in Havana on her schedule when the Revolution started and left at its height and arrived in British Honduras on schedule all this was reported concise and accurate as usual in the FBI reports except the mention of Merrick landing in British Honduras minus Mace. By the way it was renamed Belize in 1973".

"Oscar this is all fascinating but it really doesn't concern us leave it to the Bureau to figure it out just update the murder book and send it over to the Federal Building". Oscar collected the pages of the report from the Lieutenant and headed back to his desk. He looked at the clock and tabulated the time in Philadelphia at 3:30 PM so he called the contact number and asked for officer Spann. She was at her station so they exchanged greetings and the usual questions about the weather and what was his take on the war protests; that said he got right to the question if she was familiar with the request they sent to Philadelphia about the records of one Allen Monk. She replied she was, but as you know his records are sealed however I was involved with this case at the beginning and I can give you an idea in a general sense why he was singled out from all the other gang members and given the alternative he accepted. Oscar said her general sense of why he accepted the alterative to prison would be appreciated. She told him it was a weapons charge with a stiff penalty. It was rumored he went into the business of making zip guns for sale, if you're not familiar with the term it refers to homemade guns and his were quite sophisticated and professional looking. Oscar thanked her and hung up. He was thinking out loud when he said, "That's why there were no identifying marks on the slugs he used a steel tube barrel with no rifling".

"Who used a steel tube barrel"? He turned to see who said that and there was Medwin, he was almost on top of him.

"Sit down we have to talk I just came across some interesting information on the Mace murder".

"I thought we were punting that case over to the Feds"?

"Well yeah, but these things could help them out".

"Since when did you become the FBI's little helper".

"Shut up and sit down".

"Make it fast I have to meet Morrison in the Mission".

"It seems your friend Allen had a thriving business as a young man in Philly making Zip guns; that would explain why there were no rifling marks on the slugs that killed Mace".

Medwin answered in a low condescending tone, "And there wouldn't be if Hugo used a smooth bore barrel that he could change after every time he used it. It would be easy especially if a revolver was used all the spent shell casings would be trapped in the cylinder leaving no evidence. This could further strengthen the FBI's case that it was a professional killing".

"You're a kill joy go meet Morrison".

"I'll let you know when Morrison's partner will be back right now I gotta go". Oscar was sitting looking into space when the phone rang. He lazily picked it up on the third ring and it was Morales from San Diego. Without preamble he said, "Do you read Spanish"? A little confused Oscar answered, "No". "Well I'm sending you a copy of a newspaper from Puerto Vallarta it's an account of a car accident on the date of your Mister Mace's murder and the unfortunate victim was Hugo

Bettencourt. The article goes on to say he was an important business man in the area and author of many charities and a full page of extemporaneous horse shit. I'm sending you a copy of the paper by registered mail and a conformation from my department of evidence transfer and signed by me. Oscar this is one less bad guy the world has to worry about I hope this helps in your investigation; if you need anything else just call me and I hope you haven't forgotten our fishing date we better schedule it soon the Marlin are biting off the coast down in Baja". Oscar thanked him and said he'd keep in touch then hung up. He sat for a full minute staring into space trying to get a handle on what Morales just told him.

I had just got back from a morning at the Planning Department down the Peninsular checking out the proposed shopping center off 101. I saw a phone message from my attorney M. Pacemann. I called and was put right through to Myra. She said, "Wonders of wonders we heard from Brophy and Clark and get this, they want to meet here at my office".

I asked, "Is that unusual"?

"Highly, they typically prefer there interrogation room using the intimidating factor in their favor".

"Well what do you think it means".

"I don't know we'll play it by ear and see what is really on their mind. Do you know if they still have a tap on your home phone"?

"I don't know but I can try to find out".

"Do that and also ask you wife if your mother in law knows anything about your Las Vegas trips that she might have talked about on the phone".

"When do they want to meet"?

"That's one reason I called you when would it be convenient"?

"Just set it up and I'll be there".

"One more thing I talked with S J De Long the Attorney representing this fellow Merrick; S J is the only one in the firm that has met Merrick and that was almost twenty years ago. I was told they are a law firm that specializes in financial management and they handle his annuity payments from New England Trust and Assurance Company for his quarterly tax returns. The interesting part is he gave them his power of attorney to send his taxes into the IRS for a period of 18 months because he would be out of the country and to put his annuity payments into a trust account. Then told them he was cancelling his P.O. Box in Las Vegas and would notify them of his new P.O. Box when he returned. They sent him notice that his quarterly payment had already been sent, but it appears he was already gone. They're still waiting for his new P. O. Box address. I don't know if you want to give the feds all this information I would just give them the law firm's name and let them talk to the attorney". I thought for a moment then said, "What are your thoughts on this because I'm totally confused".

"To be candid I have a suspicion Mister Mace and Mister Merrick is the same person".

I said, "No that can't be they were best of friends they grew up together in an orphanage in New York they went to the same college and had the same friends I was told they were closer than brothers".

"All that might be true but this overlap of their business and the mysterious non presence of Mister Merrick leads me to that conclusion".

I went quiet then said, "Call me when you set the meeting". I hung up and called Tom Valance. Nancy answered and told me Tom would be in the rest of the day and probably into the evening. At this point I didn't even want to use the office phone for fear it too was tapped so I left my office and headed for Tom's studio. When I got there Nancy told me Tom was in the dark room and he'd be out in a minute or two. While I was waiting I scrutinized the pictures on the wall of Allen and Mary in reversed rolls I marveled at their likeness and still had trouble distinguishing one from the other when Allen was in drag. Nancy chirped up and said you're still having trouble telling them apart. I turned toward her as I was nodding yes and she told me Mary is getting a little wider in the hips as she ages; except from a distance that's the only real way to tell them apart. Tom said hello from the door way to his studio and that broke my fixation with the wall. I helloed back and we went into the studio. Tom wanted to know what was up and I got right to the point. "I'm here to ask for a favor".

Tom said, "Shoot".

"Could you find out if my phone is still being tapped"?

"I'll try, give me a day or two and I'll call you at your office if I say I got tickets to the Giant's game they still have the tap on if I say I don't; of course, it means they don't but I don't know about your office phone that's why the entire spy talk".

"I just got off the phone with my attorney and she told me an interesting theory she has it that John and

Merrick are the same person; does that make sense to you"? Tom looked at me until it became a stare then said, "No, it's not possible my brother went to school with both of them".

I looked dejected and said, "Mysteries, you get a handle on one and another pops up".

"I've got another mystery for you Mary called me wanting to know how to get in touch with Micky Addelmann". Tom said.

"What did you tell her"?

"I told her the last I heard he was staying in some flea bag in the Tender Loin".

"Did she say why she wanted to talk to him"?

"No".

By the time I got home I was convinced Myra was wrong about John and Merrick, but I ran it passed Anne to see if it made any sense to her. She thought it was intriguing and wanted to hear once more the sequence of events from the time John left Cuba and when and how John arrived in Las Vegas. I went through the sequence once more, as I knew it, and looked uncertainly at her because I was expecting her to agree with me and Tom. "I've been thinking about this whole situation, she said, I mean John and his relationship with Mary and this fellow Allen and if it had anything to do with John's murder".

"What do you mean"?

"It is possible they had a three way relationship that went sour and the outcome was they murdered John".

"What do you mean a three way relationship"?

"I mean sexual the French have a word for it, ménage a trios".

"No that can't be right I can't see John in a situation like that".

"Well Allen owed John a lot of money and Mary felt she was financially being taken advantage of and if John felt they were using their intimacy as leverage against him it could start fireworks".

I frowned then said, "I don't buy it".

"What's to buy? I said it's just a possibility". Anne replied. "So back in the early fifties John and his friend Merrick were going to Cuba on a regular basis and both possibly were chased by the revolution and went through Mexico by way of Belize and winding up in Las Vegas; it is bizarre and it's something of an adventure novel. However no one knows for sure if Merrick was with John in Cuba, but somehow he disappears before John gets to Las Vegas; sounds like a name change to switch identities".

"Then what happened to Merrick"?

"Your guess is as good as mine".

When I got to Myra's office she was in her roof garden with Brophy and Clark. The sliding glass door was closed so with no sound all their actions looked animated. Somehow I felt like a voyeur so I tapped on the glass to get their attention. It was Brophy who saw me first and I could read his lips saying its Kerry as he was pointing at the glass. I slid the glass door open and couldn't resist a wise ass remark asking if this was a horticultural class or just getting some fresh air. Brophy laughed, Clark frowned and Myra said, "Somehow I expected that". Back in her office they settled in around Myra's desk in an arranged seating with Myra behind her desk framed by an oversized picture by Georgia O'Keefe, of what else, flowers. Myra got things going by saying, "Well gentlemen could you tell us what's on your mind"? "Brophy jumped right in; we would like to ask Mr. Kerry what is his relationship with a man named Guytano Corsenti, a.k.a., Guy Corsey the licensed owner of the Feline Follies Casino in Las Vegas".

"Do you want me to start from the beginning or where we left off; where I picked up John's IOU's"?

"Start where Corsey calls you about the P.O. Box for this man Merrick".

Myra noticed Clark gave Brophy a dirty look but he ignored it and kept staring at me waiting for an answer.

"Right, well a while back I called Corsey and told him I was trying to find Mary Mace's phone number. He was more interested in selling me a letter addressed to this man Merrick that he was keeping for John. I told him I wasn't particularly interested in this Mister Merrick but if he could locate Mary Mace and her phone number it might be worth something".

Now Clark lost his frown and interrupted me by asking, "Why were you so interested in the whereabouts of Mrs. Mace".

"Let me finish so I don't lose my train of thought and I'll get back to that".

Everyone seemed to be satisfied with that so I continued. "Corsey then said he could find out where Mary is in Las Vegas and throw in the letter for two hundred and fifty dollars. I told him if and when he could get me Mary's phone number we could talk business. At the same time my boss invited my wife and me for a Holliday in Las Vegas for a job well done in Hemet so naturally I told Corsey I'd be in Las Vegas at Caesar's. We met in the coffee shop at Caesar's we exchanged envelopes and he went nuts because I gave him a check and he expected cash. I told him I needed a record of this transaction and the check was made out to the Feline Follies Casino so he could easily claim it was a payment for a gambling debt. That explanation didn't calm him down he called me a putts and then said something about it's not the IRS he is worried about, but a partner or two that would want to know where it shows in their records. We discussed it further and decided to just wash everything clean and forget about the two hundred and fifty dollars it wasn't worth the trouble".

"So you didn't pay him the two fifty". Brophy said.

"No I didn't".

At this point Clark jumped in with a question about what if anything was in Merrick's P .O .Box.

"Corsey had a key for the P. O. Box and a letter from an attorney up in Salt Lake City telling Merrick his taxes were paid for the quarter but the date was a few years old".

"Who was the attorney"?

"De Long & De Long their letter head said financial planners".

"Did you contact them"?

"No".

"Did Corsey contact them"?

"I don't know ask Corsey".

"Did Corsey introduce you to a man named Jonathan Welsh"?

"No, wait someone by that name called my office".

"What did he want"?

"I don't know I didn't speak to him my boss did; it was an inquiry about loans for small businesses in Las Vegas".

"What was so important that you were willing to pay Corsey for Mrs. Mace's phone number"?

"Both my wife and I wanted to know if Mary had been contacted by anyone from John's probate"?

"You mean if she knew about the flats on Union Street"?

Myra stopped the questioning by asking Clark what he meant.

"During our investigation of the bank fraud and money laundering it was disclosed that Mr. Mace arranged for the loans to buy the property on Union Street and put it into Mr. Kerry's name to hide the asset from Mrs. Mace; all to revert back to him by way of a quit claim deed from Mr. Kerry after Mace got a divorce from his wife. Upon further investigation it was disclosed Mr. Kerry refused to sign the quit claim deed and frustrated his boss by going to work as a contract appraiser for the same Savings and Loan that Mr. Mace had secured the Mortgage in Mr. Kerry's name for the Union Street Property making it legally his and his wife's property. He then looked over at me and said, "I'd say you turned the tables on your boss and it couldn't have made him happy. However it might have been all for nothing because the IRS is putting a hold on all Mister Mace's real property and they would certainly look at this as a thinly vailed attempt to hide this from them".

Myra put her hand up to stop Clark then in a less professional tone asked, "If this was a fact finding meeting or an interrogation. After all it was my understanding that Mrs. Mace was the one who knew the owners of the Union Street property and told Mr. Mace they wanted to sell it so I hardly think that Mrs. Mace didn't know her husband was involved in the ownership of the building".

There was a moment or two of regrouping by the Agents then Brophy said you're right we went too far afield we're really interested in this man Merrick; could you tell us anything at all you know about him".

"Not much; just his name and he was a long-time friend of Mister Mace. I suggest you call this Law firm De Long & De Long and they could give you more information than I can". I replied.

That seemed to satisfy them then I was surprised when Clark asked Myra about some plants on her roof garden. He even used the Latin name and it was obvious he was interested in horticulture. Myra and Clark got into a brief gardening conversation while Brophy and I looked at each other totally disinterested. They wind up the meeting and the Agents left. After Myra followed them out to the staircase and returned she said to me sit down let's talk. I don't know if you noticed but they had the beginning of a sun tan and you don't get that in San Francisco this time of year. I'm sure they got it in Las Vegas. Brophy let slip that they interviewed Corsey when he mentioned Merrick and his P. O. Box which means they were checking his story against yours. That's a good indicator that you're falling off their list of suspects, of course, that's if your two stories are similar.

Chapter 14

I was walking across the lobby of 300 Montgomery heading for the elevator when I was abruptly stopped by Guy Corsey. In my surprise I said, "What are you doing here"?

"What the hell time do you start work I've been waiting for you for an hour".

"I asked you what are doing here".

"Some things have come up that we have to talk about".

"Why didn't you call and let me know you were coming"?

"I don't trust the phones I think the Feds have every body's phone tapped. There is a little café around the corner we can talk there".

"To set you straight I've been at a meeting across the street for two hours so don't think I've got bankers hours. Come with me my car is under the building in the garage we can talk there". We took the elevator to the garage and sat in my car. I asked Corsey what was so important that they had to meet in this cloak and dagger fashion; the question opened up a flood gate of disjointed and hyperventilated sentences until I told him to stop and to get himself under control. Corsey got quiet then as he looked around the darkened garage and then he said, "I've got a friend who is not happy that I am involved in an FBI investigation and to make matters worse your friend Mary Mace is constantly in my face about the Merrick P. O. Box and is threatening to tell my friend that me and John had an arrangement while he was in Lompoc".

"Tell your friend it's none of his business about the FBI investigation and let Mary know Merrick closed the P. O. Box".

"When I say friend I mean a business partner and if he's not happy I'm out of the Casino or worse and somehow Mary is convinced I know the new one so I need your help".

"How can I help I don't know this guy Merrick or his new P. O. Box. Why don't you just tell Mary you don't know the new P. O. Box for Merrick"?

"She won't believe me".

"Then why would you think your partner would believe her if she told him you sent John this guy Merrick's mail while he was in Lompoc".

"It's complicated".

"You better start telling me everything if you expect me to help you".

"Yeah, yeah ok about twelve years ago Mary and me were in the same show my future partner was in town looking for new business ventures and we were introduce by a mutual friend. He saw Mary back stage in between acts and asked to be introduced. They hit it off and she was his squeeze for almost a year, but he had a wife and family back in New Jersey and when push comes to shove he eased out of this predicament gracefully and they stayed friends. That is when John got in the picture he picked up where my future partner left off; by the way John was the mutual friend that introduced me to my future partner, that's what I mean about it getting complicated. To complicate matters more she remembered seeing a similar letter while she was visiting John in Lompoc. When you came to pick up the Bonds she figured out that John was using Merrick's identity to collect his Bearer Bonds". Corsey's last statement hit me like a lightning bolt Myra and Anne's theories were right John had two identities. I managed not to show any reaction to this eye-opener then said, "So she is holding a hammer over your head threatening to tell your partner about John and you"?

"You got it Einstein".

"Listen you jerk, if you keep shooting sarcastic remarks at me you'll get Jack-shit".

"Hey relax you know the New York banter it's all a knee jerk reaction they call it "come back". He immediately thought of Myra's comment about the kid from Gotham. "It's obvious you're in a bind, but I have no idea how I can help".

"You were his go to guy he had to have said something about a Post Office Box or a key he kept in an unusual place or a place he seemed to visit regularly".

"No look, I was a go-fer not a go-to, when he needed someone to drive his clients around I was the guy; that's why he got me a Mercedes so it looked good. You knew John he was all Glitz and Glamor to disguise the smoke and mirrors I was nothing more than part of his smoke and mirrors. I was never part of his inner circle and never part of his Shenanigans and believe me I was never his confident, if anything I was just the opposite he rarely took me into his confidence unless it benefited him".

Corsey grunted in disbelief then said, "You know there are some bad people that believe John buried a ton of money and now that John is dead they're looking at you because you're the last one standing". There was a long pause and Corsey saw it got the effect he wanted, my demeanor changed I was vulnerable.

"If we can find John's P. O. Box and maybe the key I can smooth out these people and we can get a piece of the stash if not they might start getting nasty". I tried to recoup, but my response was weak I told Corsey I was sorry but I couldn't help because I had no idea if John had a stash or if he did where it was. I then asked if I could drop Corsey off anywhere. He said no and got out of the car and left. I sat in the dark garage thinking; my thoughts were on Corsey's threat I knew it was bogus, but it still unnerved me. I suddenly remembered my Boss was waiting for me to fill him in on the meeting this morning so I locked my car and headed up to my office. The day went slow by the time I left the office my mind was muddled with all kinds of possibilities so by the time I got home I was a mess. I no sooner walked into the house when Anne said, "Bad day huh".

I mumbled yeah then said, "You can't imagine".

"Try me, I had a set-to with my mother she is convinced we are ruining our daughter's life by sending her to a child care school. Her fix is for me to quit work and she could help me raise Gina properly".

I was non responsive; that alerted Anne knowing me something bad must have happened so she waited until I seemed to be a bit more approachable and asked if she could get me anything.

"Sure do we have any coffee"? "It's on the stove give me a minute and I'll heat it up".

I belatedly muttered, "What did your mother say about Gina"?

"Never mind it's not important, what happened today"?

"I got a visit from our friend Guy Corsey; it looks like you and Myra were right, evidently John had two identities and was using Merrick's to hide money. To quote Corsey "To complicate the matter Mary also knows and is harassing him to find out where John's present P. O. Box is or she is threatening to tell his partner in the Casino that the FBI is investigation his connection with John when he was in Lompoc. All this, according to Corsey will get him moved out of the Casino business or worse".

"Do you believe him or do you think he's exaggerating the whole thing especially about the bad people zeroing in on you"?

"I have to admit when he first told me I started looking over my shoulder but not so much now, I'm going to call Myra and ask her what she thinks".

Myra's answer was call Brophy and Clark. They did and this time the Agents wanted the meeting to be at the Federal Building. The officious tone alerted Myra, but she said nothing to me. When we got there we were met with friendly smiles from both Agents then ushered into a small conference room that subbed as a library or vice versa. They all sat at an oblong table and when Myra realized they were being manipulated into prearranged chairs, she balked. She moved me next to Brophy who was seated at the head of the table and across from Clark; this gave her a view of everyone at the same time.

Clark frowned at the chair rearrangement and Brophy gave her his theatrical smile then said, "If we are all comfortable now, could Mr. Kerry tell us what is this new development in the case"? I started off with the encounter with Guy Corsey and the revelation that John Mace and this fellow Merrick were the same person at least John was using Merrick's name to collect Bearer Bonds from a P. O. Box in Las Vegas and Corsey was being threatened by John Mace's wife Mary. She told him if he didn't give her the new P. O. Box number she would tell his partner that he was in cahoots with John and that the FBI is investigating him which could jeopardize their Casino License. He ended with a threat telling me there're bad people involved in this and they're looking at me as John's confident. I got the message it was his partner who was the quote "bad people".

All the time Myra was watching Clark and Brophy they had the perfect neutral facial look a tried and true way to keep a suspect talking. She decided to step in and stop their momentum before I said something that would come back to haunt me. She asked them both in a general way what did they think of my situation and could they protect him from what Corsey calls "bad people". Clark nonchalantly glanced over at Brophy then at Myra and said, "They would be willing to extend their investigation to Las Vegas to look into Mr. Kerry's allegations of threats and intimidation, but we need some help in doing this". Myra knew what was coming and went ahead and asked, "What would that be?"

"If Mr. Kerry would work with us to get Mister Corsey to incriminate himself in any fashion it would definitely help us and we would be there to protect him". "When you say there, do you mean Las Vegas or here in San Francisco"?

"Both, of course".

"So you're planning to have Mister Kerry travel to and from San Francisco and Las Vegas to do your bidding as an informant"?

"He is not an informant he's part of the team we all help out one and other". Myra was starting to have fun with this sham of an interview she thought she'd keep it rolling thinking I would see what they are really after. Now she couldn't stop she wanted to see how transparent this interview was so she said, "Then I take it, since Mister Kerry is now part of the team, he will be under immunity for any charges from before and after this particular investigation"?

"Well we expect Mister Kerry to comply with our overall investigation and in affect clear himself of any cloud of suspicion".

I was livid and said, "What cloud of suspicion; do you think I had anything to do with Mace's murder or money laundering"?

Brophy interrupted Clark and said "Not at all, as a point of fact, we have someone who was told by the hit man that he murdered Mace and we can verify that but, of course, this is an ongoing investigation so we can't divulge names or places".

"If that's the case why hasn't there been an arrest"? Myra asked.

"LET me say it again; it is an ongoing investigation and to divulge any names or places could compromise our investigation".

"So what you're saying is your "someone" is a jail house snitch and his testimony is shaky at best". I was antsy I was moving around in my seat like a school kid with the answer but nobody would call on him. I finally interrupted by saying, "This so called interview is going nowhere so let's stop playing games. When we contacted the Agency we thought we could help out with your investigation by giving you the information that John Mace had a second persona and the source of the Bearer Bonds. It's pretty clear now is all you're interested in is using me as an informant and, of course, that would leave me vulnerable to Corsey and his "bad people". That's contrary to what I had in mind and it's obvious the Agency is either unable or unwilling to protect me and my family so there will be no more voluntary meetings ". I looked over at Myra, who was grinning from ear to ear, and said let's go".

We were on the street looking for a cab when Myra said, "You handled that well did you know I was bluffing about immunity or did you know it was only the Federal District Attorney that had that power".

"No I just wanted to leave".

I walked from Myra's office to my car at the garage under 300 Montgomery Street. I thought it would give me time to think, but it didn't. Driving home my car was on automatic I hardly remembered driving the route I finally realized where I was as I was turning into Bergen Alley and home.

The fog had rolled in so everything was wet and cold. When I got out of my car I was hit with the aroma of something beefy like stew. The smell perked me up; I hopped up the stairs through the pantry and into the kitchen and the aroma disappeared. To my disappointment I realized the smell was from next door. The baby sitter was feeding Gina and looked up at me and told me Anne was in the bedroom changing. I couldn't think of any place we were going this evening that's when Anne came into the Kitchen and told me she made reservations at Scoma's for tonight at 8 o'clock. I did it at the spur of the moment I think we both need a break. I was all for it I took ten minutes to wash up and we were off to Soma's. It was only six or seven blocks to the pier where the restaurant was and we were early so I alerted the night crew where we were going and we took our time. The fog was spotty, but you could see the strobe light coming from Alcatraz flashing intermittently through the fog with a perfect view of Alcatraz. This was the atmosphere for a glass of wine and a hardy crab Ciappino dinner. We quickened our step when we got to the pier and hustled up the few steps and into the restaurant. We were a bit early so we went to the bar and low and behold there were the Valances. Nancy and Anne immediately picked up from where they ended their last conversation. The girls stopped talking when they heard me mention the Feds. I was telling Tom what the Feds said about my situation with Corsey all the while Nancy was glancing at Anne who was nodding in agreement on every word of mine. In the middle of their conversation the hostess told me and Anne our table was ready. Tom perked up and asked the hostess to combine the reservations and make it a table for four. She said no problem and we were off to the dining room. We sat and ordered more drinks that's when Tom changed the subject and began telling them about a new client and how he was looking at his composition and the first shoot in hopes of impressing his client and maybe get some commercial work out of it. The rest of the dinner went the way of good friends and good conversation go and ended with coffee and dessert; Tom and Nancy had their car so they offered to give me and Anne a lift home. The girls got in the back and I sat next to Tom. When we started off the girls got right back into their last conversation and Tom, in a somewhat subdued voice told me to call him at his studio and we'll discuss Giant tickets and dates as cover; I'll give you the dates then you should come to my studio I think it is important. I smiled to myself and wandered what all this cloak and dagger stuff was about. I called the following day and went through the Giant ticket ruse and Tom told him he would like to wait until next week when the Cardinals were in town and he could get seats behind home plate. I agreed, but I was in the dark on what exactly Tom had in mind. I was tempted to call Tom during the week but realized Tom was being careful that one of their phones might be tapped. Tom called the following week and told me to come and pick up my tickets on Wednesday right after lunch and dutifully I trudged over to Tom's studio on Wednesday after lunch and to my surprise Detective Oscar Norman was sitting behind Nancy's desk.

Before I could say a word the detective told me Tom had asked him to talk to me about this guy Corsey and his threats. I was so surprised I couldn't respond. I heard someone clear their throat and I half turned to see Tom standing in the door way to his studio. In response is all I could say was "Tom"! Tom replied hesitantly, "Jim

I was so upset by your situation and the seemingly nonresponse by the Feds I talked to Oscar about it and he wanted to talk to you, I hope you understand". While Tom was talking Oscar sat expressionless still behind the receptionist desk and when Tom had finished he asked him to leave and explained he would feel better talking to me one on one. Tom said, "Why don't you two go into my studio and I'll stay here at the receptionist desk and monitor my phone calls because Nancy won't be in today". I looked at Oscar and shrugged in a questioning way and Oscar said let's go. We maneuvered around a camera tripod and found two director chairs in front of a large screen with a photo of the Pyramid Building. Oscar rearranged the chairs to face each other and we both sat. Oscar wasted no time he got right down to facts. "If you haven't surmised already the Bureau and to be more accurate Agents Brophy and Clark have had Mister Corsey under surveillance from the time Mace was murdered. They have a short list of murder suspects but their main investigation is into the Mob's involvement in the money laundering, bribery and anything else that they can uncover. Hence they convinced themselves that Mace's murder was ordered by someone in the Mob and they're searching for a hired killer. They knew about the Bearer Bonds but they couldn't make the connection with this guy Merrick until you told them about the P. O. Box and the attorney handling the Merrick Annuity. They have a history of Mace and Merrick until the Cuban Revolution; they have Mace leaving Havana, ostensibly with a lot of cash, for Belize, but no Merrick and Merrick landing in Belize but no Mace. They believe that is where Mace bought an annuity in Merrick's name from an English Company called Essex Trust and Assurance Company which wholly owns its subsidiary the New England Trust and Assurance Company which Mace dealt with in New York. That's the history as we know it in the Department, but we have been taken off the murder case and turned everything we had over to the Bureau because, as they tell it, it dovetails into their Mob investigation which, of course, is confidential". I was attentive through Oscar's explanation and when he finished I asked, "You don't sound convinced that the Mob was involved in John Mace's murder and how does your explanation of the Feds lack of interest in protecting me and my family help me".

"First of all I would bet your phone is still being tapped and the Bureau has a team watching you and your family. Whatever you think of the FBI they are not stupid; they're organized and have very bright and dedicated people working there, but they can be full of themselves and that gives them a negative attitude while working with others. As far as the Mace murder case, you're right, I don't think it was a hired killer; I think it was someone familiar to Mace just from the murder scene its- self and the manner in which he was killed".

I interrupted him, "I don't know if the Feds told you about their murder suspect. They told me it was a hired killer and they know who he is and are in the process of tracking him down". Oscar was rocking his head no, "The name they got is Hugo Bettencourt from a jail house snitch; he's a Mexican National and was in Mexico the night Mace was murdered, it was verified because he was killed in a motor vehicle accident in Puerto Vallarta on the same night Mace was murdered. Your guess is as good as mind why they keep this fellow Bettencourt on their suspect list when they must know he was killed in an auto accident".

"Do you have a suspect in mind or are you at a standstill because you are off the case"?

"Yeah I do, the irony is you gave me the first clue".

"I did, how did I do that"?

"At the murder scene you told me the moving men were drooling over a woman who came out of the stairwell and left without a car but opened the gate with an electronic key. We searched Mace's office, car and his apartment and couldn't find his key. Then the murder scene its self; the position of the body it was obvious someone got behind him. I doubt very much if he would let a stranger or someone he didn't trust get behind him so his wife or her friend Allen in drag or both are a good bet".

I said, "That could make sense, but to get back to Corsey you obviously think he is a windbag and harmless; however a man named Jonathan Welsh called my office asking if we made small business loans in Las Vegas. My boss got the call and let the man down easy by telling him we had no plans to broker any loans in that part of the country; then told me he didn't think it was a good idea to get involved in Las Vegas. At one point I mentioned it to both Agents and they got very interested but when I told them I ever met this Mister Welsh they reluctantly dropped the subject. I think they either know or believe this Mister Welsh is Corsey's partner and the "Bad People" he kept mentioning in his threats. My attorney thinks that is who the Feds are really after and they want to use me as bait and dangle me out there in Las Vegas".

"How would they use you to do that"?

"Use me the same way John Mace brokered loans through the Teamster Pension Fund to startup new casino's or buy up existing ones. Essentially I would be a bag man for whoever is running the Pension Fund by delivering cash from the bad people to the controller for a favorable loan from the Pension Fund". Oscar was staring at me and it made me uncomfortable finally Oscar said, "I believe, through no fault of your own, you are in a lot deeper than I thought". I winced and asked, "What do you mean deeper than you thought"?

"I think you have inherited the mystique of Mister Mace's legacy of corruption by simply being at the wrong place at the wrong time. The safest advice I can give you is to not cut off the FBI cooperate with them short of being their pawn; I'm sure they'll watch out for you and your family".

I left Tom's Studio just as it started to rain, I ducked into a doorway and watched the rain when out of nowhere I realized Oscar was trying to tell me he thought the killer of John was Allen or Mary or both. The rain let up so I joined the throngs of people scurrying for their offices or cars. My thoughts went back to John's murder and I couldn't believe Mary had anything to do with it, but Allen he certainly had a motive and the beautiful woman escaping through the parking garage would be something he could easily do.

When Oscar got back to his office Medwin told him there was a message to call Morales in San Diego. Oscar had a peculiar feeling while he was dialing Morales and it continued when Morales answered because without so much as a hello he said, "Bettencourt may not be dead".

"Could you tell me why you think he may not be dead"?

"There is now a report that the body in the car crash was not Hugo Bettencourt and the official government responds was "no comment" which usually means the report is true".

He thanked him and said, "I'll keep in touch"; and then hung up.

Medwin was curious and asked, "What was that all about".

"He thinks Bettencourt is still alive".

"You're not still chasing that Mace murder case are you"?

"NO, I don't think so".

Chapter 15

When I got back to the office it was before three and ran into Dick as he was leaving. He said he had an appointment and had to run but he told me to let him know tomorrow what is going on with the shopping center down the Peninsular. That prompted me to head straight to my office and pull out the file on the shopping center. This was the first time I actually looked through the particulars of the loan request. The loan request had an addendums A and B they were alternate business plans written by the son of the owner of the property. This was the young man who showed me the existing mini-shopping center and the adjoining property that was once a drive-in theater; it was now being used as over flow parking lot, but it was not really necessary the existing parking was more than adequate. Addendum A was a detailed proposal to build a new complex on the sight of the old drive in theater with a twenty thousand square foot Pacific Coast Super Market chain store a movie complex of three different theaters and to refurbish the existing twenty two stores along with repaved parking lots and upgrading the lighting. Addendum B was the same buildings on the old drive-in theater property, but the existing twenty two stores would be razed and replaced with new buildings with removable interior walls for better flexibility. Both Addendums had detailed plans and square footage cost for buildings and parking lots. I sat back and thought why would they need a broker to procure a loan; with this comprehensive loan package they should be able to go to a local bank and get this approved and funded. I checked again and it stated the land was owned by the family and the original mortgage was in the final years of the principal being paid off. I decide to call the son of the owner David Mills; he was the author of the loan package. I got him on the first try; it was he who took me through the property so the conversation was friendly and almost like longtime associates discussing business. I complimented David on his professional loan package. David replied that it was good to hear his time in Stanford's business school was not wasted. This was the natural time in the possible negotiations to ask the burning question, "I see in one of your addendums there is a letter of intent by a national grocery store chain to lease a portion of the new complex and of course that would be a perfect anchor for the deal. Why don't you just go to a local lender and eliminate a broker who will charge you an additional fee"? He was obviously ready for the question his answer was smooth and deliberate, "Our Company is a limited liability company we have acquired debt from the maintenance and repair of the existing building and parking lot repair and are unable to service the debt with the vacancy factor at 40 % hence we filed for chapter 11. This is the main reason local lenders have shied away from the loan, however there is a Real Estate and investment company that specialize in shopping centers that have offered to remedy the debt and build the new shopping center for a fifty one percent participation. I'm sure you understand our position we don't want to give up control by selling away fifty one percent; however we would certainly entertain any offer of participation of anything less of fifty percent". On impulse I made another appointment with David Mills for the following afternoon. I gave Dick the package the next morning with an explanation that this was a golden opportunity or a complete sham that's why I was going to look at it again.

We met at a pet store in the small shopping center David gave me the high sign while he was talking to the owner of the pet store. I decided to look around while they were talking. They were discussing DMSO some sort of salve for the joints of horses; the proprietor was telling David to be sure his father uses gloves and washed his hands before and after applying the DMSO because it was known to take something's with the DMSO through the skin and into the blood stream by the process of osmosis. For some reason I thought this was fascinating, so when David was through buying the salve and other articles all related to horses I asked him if the family owned horses. It came as no surprise when David told me his father bred race horses but now with the Bay Meadows race track closing the cost of transporting horses all around California, being what they are; we're down to just two. That explanation made it apparent why the shopping center was neglected their family horse farm had drained its cash flow and that would be the reason investors wanted fifty one percent control of the center. We walked the property extensively with me making notes and David pointing out what the new center would look like at that point I told him I was satisfied, but cautioned David it would be a tough sell. We left it at that and David headed for his car. I stood and watched him drive away than on a whim I went back to the pet store. The proprietor was at the window watching David leave as I entered his store. He turned his head still smiling and asked me if there was anything he could help me with. "Yes; where is your dog treats"? "They're one isle over come on I'll show you". They past two women at the checkout and the owner told them he'd be right with them and continued on to show me where the dog treats were. I fiddled with his selection waiting for the owner to finish with the two ladies than just grabbed one and headed for the checkout. I put the dog treats on the counter and was told they'd be one dollar eighty seven cents.

"I'm curious do you have many big animal veterinarians as customers"? "You mean horse stables"?

"Yeah more like racing stable".

"Yeah there are a few owners and trainers that deal with me".

"I'm a little surprised because from the outside your store looks like any other small animal pet store".

"Yeah well we cut our floor space down to about a third of what it was when we gave up the store space next door but we kept the horse product business because we do most of it by phone".

"I noticed in the paper work you're on a month to month this is a good location why not sign a lease"?

"We tried that but the owners deduct their horse purchases from the rent and the accounting got messy so we decided to go month to month". I started to leave then thanked the owner for his help and pocketed my change when the owner replied, "Not at all, I want to thank you for paying for the information and handed me his dog treats". It took a moment for me to catch the humor; it had me laughing all the way to my car.

When I entered my office I put the dog treats on the receptionist desk and said, "Here's some treats for your dog".

She replied, "I don't have a dog".

"Well then give them to your cat".

"I don't have a cat why don't you give them to one of your neighbor's dogs".

"My neighbor's dogs eat people". In mock surprise she said she hoped he was joking. "Don't worry my mother-in-law's shear presents keeps the hounds at bay". As I was passing Dick's office I glanced in the open door just as Dick was looking up from some papers on his desk; he signaled with his hand and said come in. He pushed his chair back from his desk and stretched while he was rubbing his eyes with the knuckles of both hands. While still rubbing his eyes said, "What are we doing with that shopping center package"? "It's such a beautiful piece of property, well located and great potential, but the owners have run it into the ground; because they were using it to finance their horse farm which is sucking them dry".

"Do we want to go any further with the deal; for instance find a money partner for a percentage in ownership"? Dick asked.

"I don't think it will work they want controlling interest and under the circumstances we would have to disclose their financial history and I can't imagine anyone going for that".

"Why don't you put it into the inactive files and we'll keep it for reference".

"Will do, I have already mentally done that".

I continued on to my office and pick up my messages that were on pink memo paper that were placed next to my phone; for no apparent reason I wondered who picked out that color. I sat behind my desk and began thumbing through them and discarded the first two because I had already answered them the third one was from Mary Mace. Her area code was 702 so I knew she was still in Las Vegas; so I dialed her number and got the answering service for the office of Adrian Goslar Laboratories. I said I was returning a call from a Mary Mace and wanted to know if I had the right number. I was told I did and I could leave a message and that she picks up her messages twice daily. By this time it was getting late so I packed it in at the office and headed home. When I pulled into the back of the house I could smell something mouthwatering coming from the open widow of our kitchen; it dawned on me Anne took the day off from work and as she would like to do; spends all day in the kitchen. The scene in the kitchen was positively domestic. Baby Jean was fed and quietly playing in her playpen away from the stove near the hall; Anne was at the stove and the table was set with our best plate ware with an open bottle of wine breathing hopefully to enhance its flavor. Anne glanced sideways at me then said, "You're right on time". I left my attaché case at the door and sashayed over to the stove kissed her playfully and ran my hand from her waist to her derriere. She just snickered then said, "Watch it the baby's looking at us".

"She'll never breath a word to anyone she has joined a family that is the last word in discretion".

"What got you all wind up? Sit down and have a glass of wine, dinner is going to be another half hour or so". After I settle in I told Anne I got a phone message to call Mary Mace; her area code was 702 so she's still in Las Vegas but the interesting thing was when I called her back I got the answering service of a Laboratory. They took my message and told me she checks her messages twice a day; now she must be working for a laboratory with a doctor's name".

"What kind of laboratory"?

"I don't know, I didn't think to ask. I have her number you could call her back from your father's business just to be on the safe side".

"You know Tom keeps in contact with Mary and Nancy told me Allen is very sick, it maybe AIDS and his partner, at the boutique, is having trouble running it by himself and Mary is talking about coming back to San Francisco to help them out".

I said, "Tom once told me she was very charitable and always trying to help out the underdog".

"Well I'm sure there is something to that but Nancy believes she is also devious and uses other people's misfortunes to cover her own secret agenda and from what I've seen of Mary I agree".

O. K. enough said, "Dinner must be ready by now I'm starving".

"If you pour me a glass of wine I'll start serving it".

"You didn't tell me what it is".

"Osso Buco with creamy polenta".

"You just made my day".

When we finished dinner I was helping Anne with the dishes when the phone rang; it was Tom. In a bright and airy way of talking he said he was down at the Cannery at Mecco's and in an argument with our friends that share the box at Candle Stick for the Giant games about who gets the front seats. I need you down here they're ganging up on me. I realized what Tom was doing and told him to keep them at bay until I could get there in about twenty minutes. I hung up and told Anne that was Tom and he wants to tell me something he can't tell me on the phone. "I'm going down to Mecco's to see what is so important that Tom can't tell me on the phone". Anne told me go ahead she would keep the dinner in orbit until I got back. As soon as I got to front of my house I could see the fog rolling in on the bay from my vantage point on Hide Street. I continued down the street to the Cannery and on the Mecco's. Tom was at a table with his friend Oscar Norman; somehow I was not surprised. The place was busy so I just dragged a chair from an adjoining table and sat. Tom looked very serious and Oscar had on his policeman smile, it prompted me to ask, "What's up". Tom just said, "I'd rather Oscar tells you". I went along with it by using a hand gesture for Oscar to speak.

"After Corsey threatened you we called the Las Vegas police for a run down on this Guy Corsey. They gave us back ground information and almost all of it was common knowledge and of course, you know the rest. However there are some knew developments; Mister Corsey was found at the bottom of the elevator shaft at his hotel Casino. It appears the elevator door on the fourth floor mysteriously opened with the elevator still on the first floor resulting in him falling to his death. Anyway that was the official report we got from the Las

Vegas Police Department. Then it struck me your friend Addlemann was involved in a similar death back in New York where a man was killed by falling down an elevator shaft. We had all the flights to Las Vegas scanned from here looking for familiar names including yours. We checked all the flights prior to Corsey's accident but no Addlemann then guess what, Mickey Addlemann rented a car from here and drove to Las Vegas two days before Corsey's accident; coincidence right"? The noise at the bar was loud enough to distract me from answering the question that needed no answer. Oscar continued, "Now what makes these events so interesting is we were told Corsey had Key man insurance from New England Assurance Company, which pays off the loan on the Casino or in this case reassigns the loan obligation to a third party that guaranteed the original loan with no penalty, only if the cause of death is accidental. The third party is a reasonably successful Real Estate broker in Las Vegas named Raymond Morgan. Does any of this ring a bell"? I didn't have to think too hard Raymond Morgan was the Real Estate broker John had sent me and Anne to for the Real Estate comparable on Casino's in Las Vegas. Oscar waited for me to respond and I was slow in doing so, but eventually told Oscar I met him through John Mace and the circumstances. Oscar just nodded and continued, "The day after Corsey's death Addlemann was found dead in his hotel room in Jean Nevada about twenty miles from Las Vegas. The cause of death was from cocaine laced with arsenic. In his effects there was a business card of yours with Corsey's address and phone number on the back and the word dangerous.

I've been told that the address and phone number's hand writing didn't match the comment dangerous so it would follow Addlemann wrote the word dangerous. Pretty soon you'll get a call from the Las Vegas Police and they'll ask you about the business card in Addlemann's effects and ask for an interview. If you hear from the Bureau and they ask for an interview they think they have a match on your hand writing; we sent them our murder book on John Mace and in it was your hand written account of finding his body. If you don't hear from the Bureau it's not a match". I didn't say anything I just sat transfixed; staring into space. A very bubbly waitress seemed to come from behind Tom and asked if she could get anyone a refill. Tom and Oscar shook their heads no, but I came out of my trance and told her vodka on the rocks. Tom and Oscar were waiting for all this to sink in and played with their drinks until the waitress returned with my vodka then Tom made an obvious comment, "You can be sure the FBI is aware of the Las Vegas police report and in short order will be interviewing you so you might want to contact your lawyer". I finished my drink, thanked Tom and Oscar and left.

On my way to my office in the morning I began to regret not telling Anne what really went on at Mecco's the night before and decided to fill her in on the conversation I had with Tom and Oscar when I got home that evening. When I got to the office the receptionist was on the phone so I gave her the high sign and took my messages out of my in-box and headed for my office. Dick was on the phone and waved as I passed his open door. I sat at my desk picked up my phone and dialed my lawyer's number. I was told she was in court and wasn't due back until after five o'clock. I asked if she would call me as soon as she got in it was very important. I was trying to keep my mind on my work, but I couldn't decide if I should tell Dick just yet which was helping to confuse the issue even more. I looked at my clock and realized time was passing and I hadn't done a thing. At that point the intercom buzzed and I was told my wife was on the line. I pushed the flashing button and said, "What's new kid". "I just got off the phone with Mary; she told me Guy Corsey fell down an elevator shaft at his Hotel, but she doesn't think it was an accident".

"Did she say how or why she came to that conclusion"?

"No, but she is worried for her own safety; she knows the people he was involved with and they know she was involved with him trying to locate John's P. O. Box and that brought the FBI too close to their business".

"So what does she want"?

"Well according to her Allen has AIDS and she is coming here to help his partner take care of Allen and also help run their boutique business".

"So what do you think is she coming here to just get out of Las Vegas or is she truly Florence Nightingale"?

"Jim there was a cruel edge to your voice maybe she has another motive but the willingness to nurse an AIDS patient is proof in its self she has a good heart". "You're right I'm in an ugly mood; I had some unpleasant news last night it's put me in this mood I'll tell you about it tonight when I get home".

The day moved along and at five thirty Myra my lawyer called back and I told her over the phone that I heard Guy Corsey was dead and Addlemann was found dead in a hotel room in Jean Nevada from poison and they found my business card on Addlemann incriminating me. She was quiet for a few moments then asked me where I got this information. I told her I had a friend on the Las Vegas police department and the FBI was getting involved so I might be getting a call from Brophy and Clark. "I've got court tomorrow at nine can you get to my office by seven AM"? Without hesitation I said, "For sure I'll see you then".

When I got home that evening I told Anne about the conversation I had with Tom and Oscar Norman the evening before from its start to finish. She was quiet and tense all the while I was talking when I finished she said, "The card must be from John's business you just got your business cards from Scranton and Associates so do you remember giving Addlemann your business card or even Corsey for that matter"?

"Yeah I thought about that and the only thing that makes sense is when Addlemann was in our office looking for John he could have taken one of my cards; they were displayed on Mary's desk".

At six thirty the next morning I was at the Pine Street Luncheonette across the street from the Pacific Coast Stock Exchange buying coffee and cheese Danish. I left the café and walked down three doors to Myra's office and intercepted her as she was opening the outer door. She had a smirk on her face when she said, "What'd you got there"? I replied in an exaggerated Brooklyn accent, "Corfee and". They walked to the inner door to the elevator and I could hear the lock snap shut on the outer door. Myra inserted her key into the key pad of the elevator for the top floor bypassing the reception area on the third floor. We went from the elevator strait to her office. The drapes on the sliding glass doors were open and let in plenty of light but Myra automatically switched on the lights. Myra produced some paper towels and spread them on her desk while I deposited the coffee and Danish. No words were exchanged we both grabbed a pastry and coffee and sat and said nothing until half of our coffee and Danish were gone; then Myra said, "What's with this business card"? I took another slug of coffee then began to give her a blow by blow of the events that I was told about Corsey's suspicious accident and Addlemann's murder from arsenic poison. "I'm dragged in because Addlemann had one of my business cards on him with Corsey's name and address and the word Dangerous written on the back of the card. Anne and I talked about this last night and we think the best explanation of how Addlemann got my business card is when he came to see John my business cards were displayed on the receptionist desk and he took one".

"What is the connection between Corsey's accident and Addlemann's murder outside of your business card"?

"Addlemann rented a car here in San Francisco and drove to Las Vegas two days before Corsey fell down the elevator shaft. Addlemann spent twenty years in prison back East for man slaughter when the man he was fighting with fell down an open elevator shaft; then one day later he is found dead in his hotel room from cocaine laced with arsenic. The clincher was he was seen on the night after Corsey's accident on the elevator heading to his room with a good looking woman. The police don't believe in coincident".

"So far what you told me about the case against you is a stretch it's circumstantial, what else do they have"?

"I've been told the FBI is involved and they're matching my hand writing against my statement on John's murder and if I hear from them then they think they have a match and if I don't then they don't".

"Where are you getting all this information and don't tell me some police officer in Las Vegas it's all too comprehensive".

"I know I sound like some newspaper hack but I can't divulge my source".

She looked over her reading glasses and said "please"!

"I know it's corny but I couldn't resist saying that but seriously I can't tell you".

"Well I suspect it's your friend Detective Norman here in San Francisco so I won't bring it up again".

We finished with the idea that we would wait and see if and when the FBI would come calling then I left for my office.

Chapter 16

I got to the office before everyone so I let myself in and put on the coffee. Before I got comfortable at my desk I heard the front door open and a voice call out is anybody here? I knew it was the receptionist Mrs. Olsen. So I went to my office doorway and told her I was the early bird. To my surprise she was arranging her desk and chair as if all was normal. I thought she would be upset or frightened to find the door unlocked and the lights on until she said, "I figured it was you I could smell coffee perking and that's not in Dick's job description".

I smiled then asked if she wouldn't mind telling him the origins of her first name. She cocked her head in a questioning manner and asked why. Because Beate is unusual and obviously European but I wondered if you were named for a place or it was an actual name. Her eyes brightened to a radiant blue when she told me Beate was a Scandinavian derivative of Beatrix and in this country Beatrice.

"So it's not a nick name you were given that name at birth".

"Tell me why you are so interested in my name".

"No real reason, but names especially unusual ones trigger my curiosity I have an uncle we called Sepp and I thought it was a nick name for years until I saw his full name on his daughter's wedding invitation".

"Would you like to know where the German name Sepp was derived from"?

"Yes I would"."

"It's from the Latin Josephus, but I can't imagine how they got Sepp from Joseph".

"Where did you learn all that"?

"We were all taught Latin in School and a lot of names were translated into German and Swedish".

"Where did you go to school"?

"In Sweden".

"You don't have an accent; you must have come here when you were young".

"NO, not too young I was twenty".

"I know people that have come to this country even younger than that and they have a tell-tale word or sentence that will let you know they were born in another country".

She just smiled and said, "My husband was an English teacher and taught elocution and so my accent was corrected over a seven year period and according to you very successfully".

"I didn't realize you were married".

She was no longer smiling when she said, "I'm not any longer I am divorced; I have a son who is a career student majoring in illegal plant chemistry and Olsen is my maiden name. I think that covers my personal life up to this point is there anything else you would like to know".

I was taken back by her sudden change in tone and didn't know how to respond so I just said, "The coffee is ready would like a cup"? She nodded yes and when I returned she apologized for snapping at me, but said no more. I took my coffee to my office and began to dig into some papers in my in box as Beate appeared in the doorway. I began to apologize for being so nosey when she dismissed the apology with a wave of her hand and told me not to apologize and if I could try to ignore an old woman's hyper-sensitivity. I shrugged instead of answering so there was a moment of silence until she said, "Mister Peresci called from the Blackstone Corporation for an appointment with Dick I'm sure it's about resurrecting that loan package on the Union City Development. I haven't told Dick yet so I would appreciate it if you played dumb when he tells you". "Not to worry I've had plenty of practice at it". My remark brought a smile to her face and melted her concerned demeanor. She than continued, "I made a call to the Union City Planning Department about those water meter permits and they told me they issued all two hundred and twelve permits to the Hill Crest Housing development that's the advertising name of Mister Peresci's development". I didn't seem to respond so she asked if I can recall the Blackstone Development Corporation. My response was not very enthusiastic so she counted with, "I take it then you've meet Mister Peresci". "Yes I have".

"How much do you know about Mister Peresci"?

"Not much I meet him or I should say I had a run in with him over the same project when he tried to bulldoze Dick and me to broker his development without water meter permits. He told John I was personally sinking his project; John more or less took his side and told me to get with the program. I suspected John knew about the missing permits before we even talked to Peresci".

"How much do you know about Johnny Peresci and his family"?

"Pretty much what I've read in the papers about his cousin and the failed bank". "Did Dick mention he brokered a development a few years ago in the same area"?

"Yes as a matter of fact I was with John and Dick when that came up and Dick said it was sheer luck they didn't go under and it was only the tremendous housing demand that saved them".

"I'm sure that's true but there were tell-tales right from the beginning that put a cloud over the project. First of all, their father pulled out of the project right as it got started and he was the experienced builder and land developer. The loan was made in three installments the first one was for the first fifty houses and the second stage of seventy five houses was funded when fifty percent of the first stage was sold and a percentage of the second stage was to be sold to get the third stage funded; I'm sure you get the picture. Along with the building loans there was a "Seed money loan" of one hundred and fifty thousand dollars to pay off the engineering and surveying companies which filed their mechanic's liens. As the Development progressed it was uncovered by the lender's accountant that some of the contracts of sale on the first stage of housing that were sold were fraudulent. They just made up factious buyers and phony contract of sale to cover the short fall in sales on the first stage. But the worst thing to be uncovered was the one hundred and fifty thousand dollars disappeared and the engineering and surveying companies were never paid. Dick went berserk because John Mace volunteered to be the watch dog on the project and told Dick he was as shocked as

Dick was but was told Johnny Peresci's father would replace the money. It was later revealed that the title and land company that dispersed the money was also part of the family business. Later the Union Commercial Bank filed a lien on the property for the exact amount of $150,000 now the whole family was involved in the project. I know Dick suspected John had his hand in the missing seed money". Just then the phone started ringing, rather than run back to her desk to answer it Beate took two steps to my desk and picked up my phone then began to give the standard greeting then stopped and put the call on hold and said it's for you it's Dick. He told me to stay at the office until he got back he wanted to go over the Blackstone package.

Forty minutes later Anne called telling me she just got off the phone with Mary and she'll be delayed a week or two because her Aunt died and she'll be in San Diego to settle her Aunt's Estate. Anne didn't know if the timing was good or bad for me because she knew Mary wanted me to get her financing on the Union Street flats. I was looking through the housing development on my desk so I was a little slow in answering but then told her it didn't matter Dick wants me to go over Johnny Peresci's old package on his housing development. She asked me if that's the same Johnny Peresci that was a friend of John's. I replied a flat yes. She asked me if I could stop at the bakery on my way home and pick up two loaves of bread just make sure one is Tuscan Mom's doing the cooking tonight. I replied sure then hung up and started going over the housing development with an increasing negative attitude. I heard Dick in the outer office talking to Beate so I was sure I'd be getting a call on the intercom. I didn't have to wait long as soon as Dick got into his office the intercom buzzed and lit up. He told me to get the old file on the Blackstone Land Development Corporation and bring it to his office. I sort of chuckled to myself and gathered up the file on my desk and was heading for Dick's office when I thought better of it. I didn't want to march right in with the file so I fiddled around at my desk for a few minutes then went to Dick's office. When I entered I sat down in a chair on a slight angle to the right of Dick's desk; I saw he had just gotten a haircut a little closer than usual and it showed a very prominent scar just above the hair line over his ear. I hadn't noticed it before and Dick caught me staring so he told me it was a memento from an old girlfriend and then asked if I had the file. I stopped gapping at the scar and handed over the file. Dick told me he thought it was odd he didn't see me pass his office to get to the records room which means you already had it on your desk which means Beate told you Johnny Peresci called to resurrect his loan package. I didn't know what to say I fidgeted in my chair like a ten year old caught telling a lie. My embarrassment was showing in my ears they began to glow red. Dick was enjoying this little game that had me twisting and turning in my chair when Beate appeared at his office doorway. Dick looked up and said, "What". Beate in her Mrs. Olsen's voice said, "If you're done embarrassing Mr. Kerry Mr. Peresci is on the line and I'm sure it is in reference to his earlier call". "Let him wait I'm having fun".

"I'll tell him you're in conference and too busy to talk right now and he'll have to call back".

"Alright, alright which line is he on". "The only one blinking".

He turned to me and told me he was fuzzy on the particulars of the package and if he had a chance to read it. I just rocked my head yes. He starred at me with a smile on his face and took on the tone of a Dutch uncle when he said, "You're lucky Beate really likes you. Dick picked up the phone punched the blinking button and in his most proper tone said, "Mr. Peresci how are you"; as he was smiling at me.

It was a little after six when I came through the pantry and into our kitchen with a loaf of bread under each arm. My mother- in-law glanced from one arm to the other then said, "You gotta be different you can't hold both loaves under one arm"?

"Well I start off with both loaves under one arm when I got out of the car, but then I decided to show you that I'm ambidextrous".

"Now you're telling me you got only one arm".

"Never mind what's for dinner"?

"Rollitini".

"What's that"?

"It's like Lasagna only different".

"Oh good that explains it so what's the chicken liver container for".

"Chicken livers".

"I'm sorry I knew that was a stupid question, but where did you put the chicken livers"?

"In the Rollitini".

"Of course, how do you put up with me; where's Anne and the baby"?

"In the front room, out of the way". I smiled my salesman's smile to let my mother in law know I got the message. As I was heading there my mother in law complained the bread was squashed in the middle from your stupid way of carrying them. Before I even thought of responding a voice from the front room came the melodic tones of my wife, "Keep your remarks to yourself and when are you going to stop fussing with dinner we're all getting hungry". I heard some unintelligible mumbling and then a shrill voice from the kitchen, "When it's ready, that's when". I stepped into the living room where Anne had the baby corralled on a mat playing with the box one of her toys came in. Anne looked a little frazzled; she had a glass of wine in her hand and both hands were draped over the arms of the chair. I grinned and said, "Busy day huh".

"She's been in that mood since I got home with the baby and it's starting to wear thin".

"As soon as we get something into our stomach's we'll all feel better and by the way what's with this chicken livers and what is Rollitini"?

"Oh that's what my mother calls Cannelloni so let's go with it to avoid an argument and the liver makes the sauce and the filling rich with flavors you can't identify but you know they're different it's my mother's specialty. Put the liver out of your mind and you'll fall in love with it.

Were you right did Dick want you to streamline the old package of Peresci's"?

"Yeah he did he already had a lender back East interested so he wants me to bring it up to date".

"That means you're going to go through the same Punch and Judy act like the first project".

"Not necessarily; Dick is going to use a land and title company here in San Francisco to control the distribution of the payments".

Just then a voice from the kitchen informed them dinner was ready.

Anne ignored the call and asked me if Peresci would go along with that. I told her Peresci had no choice Dick told him he's calling the shots and if he felt it too confining he should shop the loan package on the street; meaning the financial street. Anne frowned and I realized she was familiar with the expression then I added, of course, you know all that. They both looked up to the doorway where her mother was standing in her uniform of an apron with the words Basta Pasta on it with a flowered babushka covering her hair and tied at the back of her neck. She was shaking a big spoon, like a weapon, in our direction going on about being harassed about getting dinner ready and here we are talking and not answering her call from the kitchen. Anne made a face and told me to put the baby's high-chair next to the kitchen table then picked up the baby and we headed for our liver Rollitini.

In the morning Johnny Peresci was at the office bright and early with a gentleman who resembles Johnny; he was a few inches shorter then Johnny but the same coloring with dark hair and eyes and his name was Alex Albo. After all the introductions Johnny told them he was his construction coordinator for the new project. They all sat at a around conference table with everyone, more or less, facing each other. Mister

Albo reached into his attaché case and pulled out the new construction package and put it on the table toward Dick. Dick read the cover letter then pushed the package over to me. Dick was beginning to ask Mr. Albo if the package was similar to the old package when he noticed Johnny watching me thumbing through the package; when I abruptly asked Johnny if the land was still free and clear. Johnny was slumped in his chair and frowning; he suddenly leaned forward with a crocodile smile and said yes. When Dick finished the question he was watching Mr. Albo who delayed answering; because he was watching the simmering chemistry between me and Johnny Peresci. He focused back on Dick and told him there were few minor changes but essentially it's the same. They were discussing the interest rates and the brokerage points while I was looking through the package when again I abruptly asked Johnny if the surveyor's stakes were still secured in the ground or would they have to be resurveyed. Johnny asked me why I asked that.

"Because I didn't see any numbers for surveying in the package".

"That's because it was already done on the original survey which was already paid for".

I rocked my head in recognition then asked, "Was the loan for $150,000.00 lien on the property to the Union Commercial Bank being paid off or retired; I ask that because I don't see that in the financial page or does it show up somewhere else". At this point Mr. Albo stepped in and told them to his knowledge that loan has been paid off. He then looked over at Johnny with a stern expression to shut up and he got the message. The meeting ended with Mr. Albo explaining he wanted their lawyer to look over the brokerage contract and they would get back to us in a day or two. They exchanged business cards and I mused Mr. Albo's card read Alexander "Albo" Albononi and an address in Oakland. When they were gone I asked Dick if he thought it was odd that Johnny introduced Mr. Albononi as Mr. Albo. Dick replied knowing Johnny's lack of business decorum, "No I'm not surprised".

"Or maybe it was done with a purpose I think Johnny likes to intimate and maybe we're supposed to be intimated". I replied.

"Intimated how he's a straight forward business man; his business card reads financial advisor".

I was quiet for a beat or two then asked if Dick knew anyone over in Oakland who could run a check on Mr. Ablononi. "He said he probably could but why are you so suspicious". "It's because of Johnny, I know some of his attitude is because of our mutual dislike for each other, but his smugness hiding behind Mr. Albononi's apparent reputation makes me feel uneasy about this deal".

"Well I guess it can't hurt I'll make a few calls; his address is at the industrial park at the Oakland Airport".

I sat and made no move to leave so Dick asked if there was anything else on his mind?

"Yes actually there is; while I was doing appraisals for Harry Byrd at the Hanaford S&L I came across property owners trying to refinance their income properties. I found it odd that many lenders didn't seem interested in going the extra step in helping the owners in packaging their property for a loan consideration if they were eight units or less. Consequently many requests languished in a loan committee or died on the vine waiting for an approval. Harry had a system of cherry picking his own appraisals for loan approval and pushing them through on his appraisal in one loan committee meeting. In about a month and a half I saw eight or ten properties fall into this category of being put on the shelf; although I only saw the paper work and an actual inspection might put thumbs down on any loan, but their rental income verses expenses made them a good bet to refinance. If there could be a deal worked out with a lender or two to give these types of loans a serious consideration we could package these loans for the owners and the lenders for a point or two. I believe this could work out to be serious money for what I consider a fast turnaround; figuring a loan like Johnny Peresci's might take a few months to close, with the possibility we might not be able to find a lender willing to go with it; where as these small loans are easier to place and we would be ahead in the numbers game if one or two didn't close the percentage would be that the majority would". Dick listened then said, "The problem I see with that is when you show some S&L or bank how lucrative it can be they eventually cut you out for your portion of the refinance and do it all them-selves".

"That's true unless we make it either not worth their while with a modest brokerage fee or provide a secondary lender and package these loans for sale by using our license as a mortgage banker".

"You mean get paid points on both ends of the loan".

"Exactly".

"Let me think about it".

The better part of the following week passed when Dick told me he was going to Pittsburg to his annual school alumni bash and while he was there he'd see if he could sell Johnny Peresci's housing development project to the usual lenders. I also heard from Oakland and I was told this fellow Albononi has only been there about a year and he's from Pittsburg so I'll check him out while I'm there.

Chapter 17

I got the call I was hoping I wouldn't get; a message from my attorney Myra Pacemann. Brophy and Clark from the Bureau wanted to talk to me and they strongly suggested the sooner the better however she suggested we ignore their pushiness and make it at our convenience.

The meeting was arranged at the federal building and Myra wanted to meet me before-hand because they were going to take a deposition she explained there will be a court stenographer to transcribe the proceedings, but not to worry because she'll be there to represent me. We met briefly and she went over the procedure before we entered the building. We were admitted and directed to Brophy's cubical where we were introduced to detective M. L. Slough from the Las Vegas Metropolitan police; he was tall and on the thin side with grey hair and light eyes framed in gold eye glasses that were more pronounced by his tanned face. We were taken to the same small library that we had our last meeting ostensible to give the feeling of an interview rather that an interrogation and the court stenographer was already there sitting in the corner behind her steno machine. Detective Slough began by thanking both me and my attorney for agreeing to meet on such short notice. Before he asked a question he seemed the preface it with an explanation of why he was even asking the question. I glanced at Myra who was smiling in a general way which I realized was her way of telling me to be careful this guy was slick. He explained he was also here on behalf of the sheriff's department from Jean Nevada where Mr. Addlemann, the suspect in the murder of Guytano Corsenti a.k.a. Guy Corsey, was found dead believed to have been poisoned. He started off by asking me for some identification. He apologized telling me it was procedural and he didn't doubt who I was. I took out my driver's license and handed it to the Detective who seemed to look at it a little to long for Myra so she asked him if he was studying it. He smiled and said he just got new glasses and he's still getting use to them. At this point he slid a photo out of his paper work and asked me if he recognized the business card? My reply was, "Of course, it's one of mine". Then he turned it over and the other side had writing on it and asked if I recognized the writing? Myra stopped me from answering and then addressed all three detectives, "This is like some procedural entrapment Mr. Kerry's hand writing is in the murder book given to the Bureau by the San Francisco police department. It was a hand written account of his movements before, during and after he discovered Mr. Mace's body. Surly it was enough to compare the writing on the back of that business card". This is when Brophy jumped in by stating, "The handwriting is still in question, but more important where did Addlemann get Mr. Kerry's business card"? Myra frowned then replied, "Business cards are given out all the time and often from person to person without the owner's knowledge".

"That may well be, but we're trying to establish the relationship between Mr. Addlemann and Mr. Kerry".

"What relationship; you could see in the photo's in the murder book that the S.F.P.D. sent you that the business cards were on display on the receptionist desk anyone could have taken one and as a point of fact Mr. Addlemann came to Mace's office when you two were there impounding his records". Brophy and Clark went stone faced. Myra let it hang in the air for a moment or two then said, "Neither one of you read the murder book did you or more accurately you read the parts you thought to be pertinent, but you didn't go over it thoroughly. It's my understanding that, that is part of detecting one goes over all the facts thoroughly and it is also my understanding that is why there is a murder book. This is apparently a fishing expedition where there is no water. My client has repeatedly tried to help and you have persistently tried to coerce him into cooperating with nefarious types for your own benefit with no thought of protecting him. As for the hand writing on the card it's not even close to Mr. Kerry's and I'm willing to bet you've been already told that buy an expert. Mr. Kerry and I are leaving. Detective Slough suddenly came alive by putting his hands in the air imploring both me and Myra to please be patient he would like to ask a few questions and try and establish a time frame just for his own investigation. I looked at Myra who gave him a reluctant nodded so we sat down. He apologized again and then asked me when I first met Guy Corsey; interrupting himself he turned to the stenographer and said; for practical purposes we'll refer to Mr. Corsenti by his stage name Guy Corsey. He turned back to me and motioned me to continue. I told him while in Las Vegas on business Mr. Mace asked me to run a few errands for him because he would be at a meeting all day and one of them was to deliver an envelope to Mr. Corsey and he would in turn give me an envelope and later I was told they were IOU's belonging to Mr. Mace.

"Did you have an occasion to meet him again"?

"Yes he approached me in the lobby of the building where I work in San Francisco about a month later".

"Could you tell us the nature of that conversation"?

"Sure, he talked me into an impromptu meeting at a local coffee shop to enlist my help in locating a large sum of money that Mr. Mace had stashed somewhere. I told him I didn't know what he was talking about and left him in the coffee shop".

"What was his response"?

"I really don't know I just told him I didn't know anything about it and left".

"I understand he told you later he had access to a P. O. Box that Mace had under an alias".

"Yes that's true".

"How did he contact you"?

"He didn't I called him to find out Mary Mace's phone number and that's when he offered me the letter to a man named Merrick that was in the P. O. Box for two hundred and fifty dollars".

"Why would you call him about Mary Mace's phone number"?

"He knew her well they were in a show together in Las Vegas and he introduced her to John Mace so I thought he would know how to get in touch with her".

"What was so important that you had to get in touch with her"?

"I wanted to know if she knew how to get in touch with the probate attorney here in San Francisco to settle some property issues; so I told him I'd be in Las Vegas and I could look him up".

"Did he give you that information"?

"Well yes, I met him at his Casino and offered him a check for that amount and in return he gave me IOU's in my name for that amount and along with Mary's phone number. He told me he didn't take checks only cash I told him I didn't do business in cash. He went through a minute or two of profanity then more or less tossed Mary's phone number at me and left".

"Did you threaten him in any way"?

"No but I'm sure it occurred to him the money wasn't worth it if his partners found out he was shaking someone down for two hundred and fifty dollars".

"Did he ever mention any of his partners"?

"No".

"Did he mention a man named Rolondo Visconti"?

"No".

"How about Ray Meise"?

"No".

"You mentioned a Jonathan Welsh that called your office did Corsey ever mention his name"?

"No why".

"They're all the same person and we believe the major partner in the Feline Follies Casino. So you had no intention to pay him for the letter and the phone number".

"You could say that".

Detective Slough was jotting down notes on a small pad then looked up at me and with a vague smile said, "I think that's all and then turned to Brophy and Clark and asked if they had any more questions".

Clark piped up and asked if I knew of any connection with Corsey and Cannelli or if Corsey ever mentioned Cannelli. I told them no so the interview ended. Before leaving Myra said to the stenographer she wanted a copy of the transcription and then handed her a business card.

The interview had only taken a little more than an hour so I was back at my office before noon. Beate gave me a few messages and she pointed out one was from Dick; it was from Pittsburg telling me to call before two o'clock Pacific Coast time it was important. I glanced at the clock in a knee-jerk reaction but I knew it was only eleven fifteen so I continued on to my office. I took a brief look at my messages then picked up the phone and called the Pittsburg number. Dick answered on the second or third ring and asked me, "How did the interview go". I was upbeat and answered, "Very good and I'll fill you in when you get back".

"That's good to hear, I also have good news we have a lender interested in the Blackstone development in Union City and a group that was interested in the mini-shopping center development down the Peninsular; until I explained the complications in the percentage of ownership the owners were willing to give up".

"Well we knew it would be a tough sell". I said.

"Wait, wait there is more; I chuckled at Dick mimicking of those T. V. commercials then he continued telling me he talked to an investment group that is very interested in his idea in financing small income units than after warehousing them selling them off to secondary lenders in a package here in Pittsburg. The usury law in California can be overcome by getting a lead bank or S&L to take a portion of each loan they're not governed by the usury law of a ten percent yield, that's what made them interested, but be mindful they're interested in the idea we'll have to do the leg work to make it happened. This has been the most successful business trip I can ever recall and I should be back by Tuesday of next week. If you have to get me call this number and Beate has my Hotel number, but only in an emergency I'm hooking up with the boys for some fun and games see you in a few days".

I started to thumb through my messages again when a name struck me, Larry Armorson. I recognized his name I recalled he was one of the loan officers in the Hanaford S & L. I thought this may be something to do with the contract job of appraisals. I wasn't sure I wanted to get involved with the Hanaford S & L, but it couldn't hurt giving him a call. I called and to my surprise the receptionist answered Cordy Savings and Loan. I asked for Mr. Armorson and I was told he wasn't in so I left a message that I was returning his call and this lead to a game of phone tag. On the second day we finely connected and to my surprise Mr. Armorson wanted to know if I knew of any multi-unit building looking for refinancing. I was speechless, but I recouped quickly and told him I didn't at present however our brokerage company was just now seriously considering that field of finance; I ended by telling him I would keep in touch. On a hunch I moseyed out to Beate's desk and asked if she knew anything about Cordy S & L. Of course, she was a wealth of information; she knew when they started, generally its size and that it was a small family business with two offices, one here in San Francisco out in the Mission and the other down in Belmont on the Peninsular. She told me she could drop by their Office here in San Francisco and pick up a brochure. I told her not to go out of her way and she told me she lived in the Mission and their office was on her way home. She had an all knowing smile when she said, "I can see you're interested in knowing more".

"Yes please".

"The S & L was started by the father his name is John and a few investors. He was a hard driving local Realtor who saw the advantages of not only listing properties, but buying or financing them. He told some people later that he got into refinancing properties as an off shoot of the Real Estate business and for idem by idem the most lucrative. Of course, as the story goes the son had big ideas and wanted to expand and started and office down in Belmont where he lives and has an insurance broker's office. I'm not sure if that is working out, but evidently the old man has hired Mr. Armorson to take control". Armed with this information I retreated to my office and when I finished my phone calls and left for home.

Oscar got to this office in the homicide division late and there was a message on his desk from Morales in San Diego. He fumbled with the note as he looked at the picture on his desk of him and Morales on a dock in Baja with a huge Marlin hanging between the two them. He started to relive the moment then caught himself and dialed his number. When Morales answered he immediately started needling Oscar telling him the captain of the fishing boat wanted to hire him to cut bait on the next trip to insure Morales would land another Marlin. Oscar had to counter with his side of the event by telling Morales that while he was cutting bait no one knew whose pole actually landed the marlin and it was widely speculated you switched the poles to your seat. Oscar could hear Morales roar with laughter. "Now that we settled that what's up"?

"Something came up and I don't know if you're still interested, but the old lady that lives next door to Hugo Bettencourt's girl friend called and told me she has been getting mail from Mexico and after the last letter she packed all her things and left".

"It's probably too much to ask, but did the old lady see where the post marks were from". "No, but the movers were from Mexico and she asked them where they were heading and they told her Cheturnal that's all the way down to the Yucatan Peninsula. The location struck me immediately because it's on the border with Belize; if he went any further he'd be in Central America". "I'll pass that on to the Bureau, but he may be out of their reach". "I have another note of interest that elderly lady Mable Mac Leach, the one involved in the Mace murder, was found dead by her caregiver. It was reported by the caregiver that there was a strong smell of garlic in her bed she died of an apparent heart attack and her bladder emptied her urine when she died. I've been told arsenic has that effect to make urine smell like garlic but so far nothing has come of it".

"You mean nobody is looking in to it"?

"I talked to the uniform who first responded and he said the caregiver claimed someone was in the house and went through the old lady's desk, and he did report the desk looked like someone had gone threw it but the rest of the house looked normal. Because of her age and her medical history they discounted the caregiver's claim and ruled her death from natural causes. The caregiver also claims there was a will and she was mentioned in it, but she didn't know if an attorney made out the will, but she knew the old lady had stationary with Last Will & Testament printed on top of the paper. But there was none found and according to the caregiver she and a now deceased neighbor were the witness to the will's signing. The only thing missing according to the caregiver was a Hummel a figurine of a boy under an umbrella she also claimed she was willed the Hummel. Oscar didn't respond right away he asked Morales, "When did the old lady die"?

"Three weeks to a month ago".

"How creditable is the caregiver"?

"Kind of iffy she changed her story a few times so they thought she was working the story to benefit herself". He decided to give it more thought later and told Morales he would keep in touch and before he could hang up Morales told him the figurine was valued at $500.00.

Oscar was staring into space when Medwin asked him, "If that was Morales with more fish stories".

"No as a matter of fact he told me Mrs. Mac Leach, Mary Mace's aunt died about a month ago and there is some question that she may have been poisoned with arsenic. That is an uncanny coincidence that our friend Mickey Addlemann also died of arsenic poison a few miles from Las Vegas where Mary Mace in now living". In a low conspiratorial voice Medwin said, "Why can't you give up on the Mace murder that's now the Bureau's problem and if the Lieutenant finds out you're spending time on the case your ass is grass".

"I know, I know, I just can't seem to let it go. It just doesn't look like a professional hit to me." He thought for a minute then told Medwin he had to make one more call and it was to Morales and asked him, "Aside from what the caregiver said did the old lady have a will and who benefited". His reply was, "No not as far as we know; she died intestate".

Chapter 18

On the way home the fog was thick and mesmerizing. I maneuvered around the cable car at the Columbus and Powell crossing. I wasn't sure if I was upset with the cursing and the yelling from the cable car questioning my driving abilities or my stupid decision to beat the cable car through the intersection. I drove on trying to look as dignified as possible. When I got home Anne was sitting in the front room drinking coffee and reading the evening paper. I gave her a peck on the cheek and asked where the baby was. "She's at my mothers and she'll be there overnight I had to agree to the one night because my mother feels I'm treating her like a foreigner, that's her words; and dad said he misses her too. So what do you want to do for dinner? I could whip up something if you don't feel like going out or we could go someplace in the neighborhood". "That sounds like a plan how about the Buena Vista Cafe? Is all we have to do is walk down the street and tonight they have bangers; I feel like sausages and a beer how about you"? The back room was full so they sat at a community table. The people sharing the table were tourists and of course, they were telling me and Anne what a beautiful city we lived in, but is the summers this cold all the time? In a dead pan I seriously told them this isn't bad in August we wear our woolies. The older man which I took for the father of the small group leaned back and folded his arms with an expression of being put upon while the younger twentyish girl swallowed the yarn hook, line and sinker. She asked, "What are woolies". I never cracked my dead pan expression when I told the girl, "Special long handle underwear to the ward off the frost". At this point the older man was visibly annoyed with me he must have felt I was making a fool out of the young girl probably is daughter so he paid their check and they left. Anne said she thought it was time to go they paid their check and on the walk home she asked me, "What was that all about".

"I don't know I had a stupid incident with the cable car coming home and I probably took it out on the young girl, but think of it this way there are too many people here already we don't want any more people moving here do we"?

"Were you told we wore woolies here in August when you moved here"? "O. K. I'm two for two today let's just go home". As soon as they walked into the house they both looked at the answering machine the red light was flashing and they both had the feeling it couldn't be good. Anne looked at me and said, "I hope that isn't my mother". It wasn't it was Mary Mace and the message was she was packing up and moving back to San Francisco, but it will probably take her about a week and she'll call when she gets there. Her last sentence was about getting her a mortgage on Union Street. I was looking into space when I said, "That makes it an even three for three".

When Dick returned from Pittsburg I filled him in on the call from Larry Armorson. I remarked how coincidental that he should be looking for income units to finance when we were looking for a lead S & L to invest in the same type properties. Dick mused for a moment or two on what I said then told me not to lose focus on the Development down in Union City; "We've got a signed brokerage contract for three percent of a three stage loan with an extra ½% to service the loan so concentrate on that for now".

"Our friend Albo; I was told he was somehow involved in a Teamster scandal when the dust cleared he was exonerated then shortly after left for California so I guess no indictment no foul".

"Can you tell me how you got this Reliance Industries in Pittsburg Pa. to accept a loan proposal when they told you they knew this guy Albononi has a sleazy reputation"?

"I put them into good loans in the past and that carried the day".

"I heard he went back to Pittsburg to try and sell the Blackstone development; what happened"?

"He tried to sell the Blackstone Development to the same investment Company that financed their last housing development and needless to say they gave him some lip service, but they never seriously considered it".

"Don't the investment companies talk to each other about near disasters like the Blackstone Development from payment manipulation"?

"There are some, but there is a certain amount of competition and one firm may not tell another for fear of seeming incompetent. You have to remember they have investors looking for a return on their investment so they have to get that money working it can't just sit idle".

"I have to ask you why you brought that shopping center refinance and improvement loan with you I wouldn't think that was saleable with all the family contingencies".

"I couldn't resist taking the package it was so well written and I wanted to do a little fishing and see if anyone took the bait".

"And did anyone"?

"You'd be surprised among the three or four interested parties was an old friend who is very interested so much so he's coming out to see the shopping center and talk to the owners about rethinking the percentage of ownership".

"That's going to be really tough they're set in their ways, at least the old man is and they have turned every offer down that didn't give them controlling interest".

"We'll see this old friend is very persuasive".

"Is this one of your old school mates"?

"Yes; Peter Travillian an upper classmate and we served a year or so together in the army".

"Was that in the Eighth Air Force"?

"Young man we were in the 96th Bomber Group. To be more precise the XVI Bomber Group and he was skipper on "The Fan Dance" that was the name of our Seventeen; I flew eighteen missions with him and he got us back every time. His folks were from Wells England close to where we were stationed so we called him the "Third Earl of Nothington". His family's English lineage went back to 1066; they accompanied King Billy across the Canal. After all we were in a foreign country and he spoke the language". This remark tickled me, but gave me an insight into the closeness of their comradery and friendship.

"When do you expect Mr. Travillian"?

"Soon he said he'd call ahead and I'd like to see the property in question so I don't look like a complete moron when I take him to see it".

"When do you want to see it"?

"A. S. A. P.".

"Let me call down to the owners and tell them to meet us. One more thing I'd like to talk to this fellow Larry Armorson at the Cordy S & L about being a lead for our loans".

"I'd hold off on that for while I want a firmer commitment from the investors back East".

"Do you think the proposed idea is a little shaky"?

"No not at all it's a solid idea it's been done before and successfully. I want to make it clear what we and they should expect in the amount of profit it would yield". I returned to my office and as soon as I sat Baite was on my intercom to tell me while I was in conference call with Dick I got a call from Mary Mace and she left a number for me to call her. I wrote down the number and realized it was local. I toyed with the idea of ducking her call and claiming ignorance if she called back then I realized how stupid that sounds so I picked up the phone and dialed her number. A man's voice answered announcing a boutique something which I didn't get. I asked for Mary Mace and he said she was with a customer could she call me back? I said sure and gave him my name and told him she has my number. I went about my business when I realized it was near 6 o'clock and Mary had not call back. I was again toying with the idea to forget all about the return call and play dumb, but I knew this would not go away. I picked up the phone and called the boutique where Mary called from. The same male voice answered with the same greeting and I asked if Mary was there. The man apologized for Mary telling me the place has been a mad house and that she was just finishing up with a customer and he'd shake her loose right now and get her to the phone. Mary came on in a matter of a minute or two apologizing and saying the same thing about it being a mad house. She seemed to pause to catch her breath then said, "Could we meet some where this evening I have papers I'd like to give you. They're from my Aunt Mable's Estate she died without a will and I'm her only living relative so when all things are settled I'll inherit enough money to buy the Union Street property out right".

"Well Mary that simplifies the problem so there is no rush why don't you just hold on to the papers for the present and let me find out if there is a prepayment penalty if the loan is paid off early or what arrangements can be made with the lender. Can I get you at this number anytime or is this strictly a business number"?

"This is their business number I'm staying with Jean and Allen at their Twin Peaks apartment; then she gave me their home number. I'm helping Jean out right now; he's overwhelmed with the business and with Allen being so sick. I stay with Allen a couple of nights a week to give Jean a break so you can generally get me there in the evening".

"I'll get back to you as soon as I get more information". I said.

As soon as I had a chance I called the Hanaford S&L and got a young man that was in charge of existing loans. I told him who I was and the property address and the situation with the Quit Calm then I asked him if my client could pay off the bulk of her mortgage and if there was a minimum amount that could be left as a mortgage that could avoid a prepayment penalty. He asked if I would hold on he would be back in a minute and when he returned he asked for my phone number and said he'd get back to me. I thought this was strange because they generally have a policy that covers that and I thought we could start negotiating from that point. At that moment I had a thought that maybe Mister Byrd was somehow involved in any decisions in the disposition of that mortgage because he was involved in the original loan and that would fall into that old adage "Cover your ass". I knew this could be a bargaining chip for Mary.

When I called to make an appointment for Dick to see the shopping center down the Peninsular I thought their reply was a little slow or maybe a touch of resistance in making an appointment. Eventually we agreed on a time and day, but I felt some sort of reluctance so I thought I'd better do a little reconnoitering to see if my feelings were correct. I called the owner of the pet shop in the old section of the shopping center and after I reminded him of who I was asked if he had any dog treats left. I got the reaction I was hoping for he chuckled then said, "We have just received a new shipment however the price has gone up". I smiled to myself because I knew the game was on. "Well that shouldn't surprise me the last treats I bought from you were definitely underpriced".

"I'm glad you realized that; you know some people don't and complain about them being overpriced".

"It just shows you can't please everyone".

"That's true, but I knew a discerning man like you would appreciate that".

"Well thank you. I thought I would call and see if anything was new and if you're still supplying horse farms with that joint remedy DMSO".

"Yes I still have my dedicated following but there has been a flurry of activity lately with those original buyers and their contractor discussing their plans with Mr. Mills; at some point it would be nice if they decided what they really wanted to do so I know where I stand".

"It sounds like they're still vacillating on that sticking point of percentage of owner ship".

"Well yeah but it also sounds like they're weakening on exactly that point".

"It sound like you'll be getting a new owner at least a controlling owner and who knows if that would be good or bad".

"That my friend is my burning question".

"Well I'll be down Wednesday with a client so save me a big bag of dog treats".

"I'm loading up the biggest bag I have right now".

"Good man I'll see you Wednesday".

I buzzed Dick on the intercom and told him we had a meeting with the shopping center owners this Wednesday and that it sounds like they're weakening on the percentage of the controlling interest.

"Who told you that?"

"I have my sauces". Dick laughed and said, "We'll take your truck it will put a different wrinkle on our meeting with this young fellow David Mills".

Wednesday showed up in a slight drizzle and the road was slick so I drove down to the shopping center in the slow lane which annoyed Dick. He said more than once, "Can't you get a little more speed out of this bus"? It annoyed him more when I slowly increased our speed only to return to below the speed limit. He gave up complaining when we got to the shopping center, but he couldn't resist a frustrating comment "Finally". David Mills was waiting for us sitting in his car in front of the pet shop. I introduced Dick and David went right into his sales pitch so I let them be and went into the pet store to talk to the owner. As soon as I entered he was waiting for me with a smile on his face and enormous bag of dog treats. That set me off into a laugh just short of hysterics. This man had a sense of humor. Little did he know I had put a fifty dollar bill in an envelope as an incentive for more information if needed as it turned out he refused the envelope and gave me a bill for three dollars and thirty five cents for the bag of dog treats I gave him a five dollar bill and he gave me change. I took the bag out to the truck and got a quizzical glance from both Dick and David Mills. I gave them a gesture of surprise and returned to the pet shop. Dick and David wandered off on a tour of the property and I and the pet shop owner were discussing his rollercoaster ride of his business. We got on to his business with DMSO and his clientele mostly horse trainers. In the conversation he mentioned he also had some doctors and their patients as customers. I asked why doctors I would think they could go directly to the manufacturer. "Well they could but I buy enough DMSO to get a good discount and I pass on a certain amount of the discount to the customer that insures customer loyalty. I also guarantee 25 % concentration in the gel form which many other suppliers sell 10 % concentration in the gel form which obviously dilutes the product".

"Well what exactly does DMSO do?" I asked.

"It's a supplement that eases joint inflammation in big animals and that includes people".

"Why isn't it advertised more?"

"Well it has its detractors the main objection is that people should be under a doctor's care because it has the properties to be absorb through the skin and into the blood stream so anything that is on the skin or anything foreign in the gel can be absorbed into the blood stream".

"Then why isn't it being regulated"?

"Because it's a supplement and therefore not regulated by the FDA".

"So it's not considered medicine and anyone can buy it".

"That is correct".

Chapter 19

I said good bye to the store owner when I saw Dick wandering in the old outdoor theater parking lot so I moseyed over and not seeing David thought it was time to leave. Dick was more than ready and said let's go. We no sooner got into the truck when Dick said, "You were right about the lack of enthusiasm on their part to discuss terms and conditions I felt this young man was just going through the motions. I'm having second thoughts about bringing Peter out here for this deal I think they already have a buyer and that would put any negotiating in their favor". I decided to take 280 the scenic route back to San Francisco. Dick was quiet just taking in the scenery then broke his silence by remarking he forgot how pretty this freeway was and he generally takes 101 and has his eyes on the road so scenery is secondary he thought he should take this freeway more often it mellows his mood. His mood changed as soon as we got to the city limits. He asked me how the Blackstone Development was progressing. I told him I haven't had a chance to get down there, but I'll have time this week. He told me to check with the Escrow Company to make sure the loan is mapped out in the same distribution instructions as the construction draws and as in the loan package we don't want the same thing that happened in their last construction loan.

As soon as we got to the office Baite told Dick he just missed Peter Travillian, he called no more than a minute ago; Dick nodded and headed to his office.

I glanced at my messages and saw a call from Larry Armorson and then just to round out my day a call from Johnny Peresci.

I called Larry Armorson first and he had two small appraisals, which I accepted and then I called Johnny Peresci and in his first words the fight was on. He wanted to know what the hell was going on; the Escrow officer told him he couldn't get his second construction draw until he sold half of the first stage of the first stage. I told him that's what is in the contract he signed he has to prove his company has sold 50 % of the first stage before you can get the second draw on the first stage. I could hear him breathing heavy then in a hissing string of obscenities told me he was sure I was behind all this and he was calling Dick to straighten me out. Before he hung up I tried to tell him I thought it might be a good Idea to call Mr. Albononi to clarify the loan commitment you and your company signed, but he hung up on me before I could finish. I got Dick on the intercom to tell him to expect a call from Johnny Peresci and the same pattern of robbing Peter to pay Paul on the construction draws has started already. I asked Dick if he thought I should call his financial advisor Mr. Albononi to clear up Johnny's misconception and confusion or try and deal with Johnny directly. Dick told me to call Mr. Albononi and let him straight out Johnny I'm assuming they speak the same language. Dick told me not to hang up and told me he just got off the phone with Peter and he's coming out to San Francisco any way on business and is interested in your idea that I told him about in Pittsburg. So sharpen up your paper work on your idea because he'll be here soon. While I was talking to Dick I fingered through my rol-a-dex to A. Albononi's number and when Dick finished talking I left the intercom by punching a button to an outside line and dialed his number.

I got an answering machine on the second ring, I started to leave a message for Mr. Albononi when he cut in with a friendly good morning and what can I help you with, it was obvious he was monitoring his calls and it made me wonder why. I got right into the conversation I had with Johnny and thought it would be a good idea if he talked to Johnny and explained the terms and conditions of the contract. I told him if he could clear up this misconception Johnny has it will make it a lot smoother dealing with the Escrow Officer on subsequent construction draws. "Please call me Alex and yes Johnny called me not more than a few minutes ago and I did bring him up to speed on the terms and conditions of the contract and I must say you sound like a lawyer".

"Well it could be because I'm spending a lot of time with my lawyer, but in reality I'm using all those big words so people think I know what I'm talking about". There was a hesitation then "Albo" began to laugh. He continued by saying he was meaning to talk to me about refinancing a piece of property in Berkeley. "It's my understanding that you do appraisals for S &L's and I was wandering if you could steer me to one you might recommend. Of course, nothing is for nothing and I expect to compensate you possibly by having you give us an appraisal on this property". My response was sure and asked for the particulars and the address and then for a contact person to see the property. He told me he would meet me there at my convenience. We set a date for the next day and I hung up. I got back on the intercom with Dick to tell him that Mr. Albo is taking care of Johnny's misunderstanding of the contract he signed and wanted me to do an appraisal on a piece of property over in Berkeley tomorrow; also I told him I had two other appraisals from Cordy S & L so I'll be out of the office all day. In mock surprise he said don't tell me tell Baite she runs the office. I did just that and then made an appointment with Larry Armorson in the afternoon. We met out at Larry's office in the Mission. I picked up the information on their two appraisals and asked him if he was interested in refinancing a property in Berkeley. He told me if I thought it made sense bring it in and we'll look at it. His confidence in me trigged a half-baked proposal that I hadn't yet formulated for his S & L to be a lead lender in California for an out of state investment group. He was obviously surprised and it took a moment or two for it to sink in; then he asked me to elaborate further. I told him it was still in the planning stages but generally what I had in mind was for your S & L to take the lead on a series of real property refinances at say 10 % of the loan and the investment group put up 90 % and your company service the loan for small percentage of the payments, say an eighth of one percent. He looked to be contemplating the proposal then said, "I like a quarter of a percent better and started to laugh. It certainly is an interesting idea I take it the purpose of our participation is to get around the California usury law of 10 % and increase their yield". I said, "Exactly". He said he would have to take it up with the owner Mr. Cordy and get back to me.

I went to the Berkeley address early to get a lay of the land before I met with Mr. Albononi. I thought I had the wrong address it was a series of three two story building each contained eight apartments and a laundry room with beautifully well maintained landscaped. I drove around the back to a black top off the back street there were twenty four garages and twenty four storage lockers. This was not what I had expected. I thought the property would be four or six units. I blamed myself for not asking how many units. I left my truck on the street and took my Polaroid Camera and was on a path heading toward the units when I saw Mr. Albononi and a woman heading my way. We met half way and he introduced me to a Mrs. Wright and told me she and her husband were the managers of the complex. Mrs. Wright had a fact sheet of the property's age and all of the upgrades and Mr. Albononi had an income and expense sheet and a profit and loss statement for three years. With that Mrs. Wright excused herself and went about her business and by now we were calling each other Alex and Jim. He told me they had an apartment for me to see and all the units were identical and if that was alright. So we took a look at the unit. It was a one bedroom six hundred square foot unit with a fifteen by eight balcony. The bottom units had patios they were all modern and up to date with new appliances in the kitchen and tiled bathroom. I spent about forty five minutes checking the outside of the buildings and their laundry rooms which had coin operated commercial washers and dryers. When I was finished with my walk through I looked over the income and expense statement and the existing mortgage and had to ask

249

him why he wanted an independent appraisal from me because the property speaks for its self. You could easily refinance this property from someone local and net three hundred and fifty thousand dollars or more with just the lender's appraisal; you really don't need my appraisal. He thanked me for my honesty but said he didn't want a curbside appraisal from some Savings and Loan only interested in making a loan based on income. I like to know what the property is worth in square footage cost and income compared to similar properties these are the things necessary to know if and when you sell. I told him I'd have the appraisal ready by the end of the week; I'll be down the East Bay Monday I could drop it off at your office Monday afternoon if that is O. K. He agreed and I looked up several Real Estate Brokers for sale comparisons and was back in my office a little after lunch.

The office door was locked so I assumed Baite had taken a late lunch. I unlocked the door and went straight to my office and started on the appraisal. It didn't take long before I could see something didn't add up. I was going over the fact sheet that Mrs. Wright had given me and the cost of rehabbing the three building was short of the actual work reported done. The first thing that caught my eye was the window replacement; they claim the cost of purchasing and replacing the windows at about half the actual cost for duel-pane windows. The units are fully electric but the laundry appliances are gas yet there is no cost for gas installation although there are gas hook ups. There is no cost for new roofing yet it is obvious it's just a few years old on all three buildings which would be a major cost. The discrepancies were glaring.

I heard the door to the office being unlocked then Dick's voice telling someone that everyone must be still at lunch. I called from my office saying I was holding down the fort. Dick appeared in my doorway and asked if I locked the front door because I was afraid of being taken advantage of by one of these man hungry secretaries roaming the hallways. I told him that was not the case it was the fear of someone slipping into the office as I was so diligently at work and I wouldn't hear them steal the millions we got stashed here. Someone behind Dick started to laugh and a gentleman stepped forward and Dick introduced me to Peter Travillian. I got up from behind my desk and offered my hand he shook it and his eyes scanned everything on my desk in an instant. Then in a statement form asked, "Your property appraisal". I nodded yes and then Dick said you don't look too enthused. I made a face and Dick immediately asked what was wrong and if there wasn't any room for refinancing Albononi's units. I replied on the contrary there is too much and the few units turned out to be twenty four units. I hemmed and hawed then Dick told me to speak up we're all friends here no secrets. The condition of the building does not jell with the reported cost of the rehab. I'd roughly say about one hundred and fifty to two hundred thousand dollars unreported. Dick raised an eye brow and said really.

I watched Peter Travillian cock his head a little like he had a question, but he said nothing. When I came around my desk and offered him my seat to more comfortably read the appraisal and we brushed shoulders. I realized how solidly build he was; he was my height but ten or fifteen pounds heavier with no pot belly. He had the regal English nose that was only prominent on his profile, but full faced it fit perfectly into his features along with his green hazel eyes and thinning grey hair he was the picture of our American English Aristocracy. He thanked me and as he was sitting he said you know I know Mr. Albononi and his reputation back in Pittsburg. I just looked at Dick with an approving smirk and he returned my approving smirk. Peter asked me where I get my construction material figures from. I explained I was a general contractor and of course, it was my business to know. He then said, "I'm sure you're right and I'm sure he intends to keep your appraisal in-house and not for publication. The only thing a lender would be interested in is the income and expense statement and he has plenty of positive cash flow". Dick took a quick look at the appraisal and asked me, "Why do you think Albononi would give you that rehab statement". I told him I didn't have a clue. Peter was thumbing through the income and expense statement and smiling at us as he said, "It's obvious he's washing money, but why is he being so obvious about it unless for some reason he wants you to know. Just one more question did he give you the fact sheet with the improvements or was it the manager"?

"It was the manager". Peter's reply was short and vague he said, "Interesting". I looked at Dick and asked him what I should do". He answered almost immediately, "Give him the appraisal and charge him like we're behind in our rent here, but keep a copy photos and all." Dick decided to leave me to my work then Peter asked if I was going to hand deliver the appraisals to Cordy S & L today. When I said yes he asked if he could come along. I naturally said yes and just give me a half hour and we'll be on our way.

Chapter 20

This was my first real look at the office of the Cordy S & L. Not too surprising it was a store front on the oldest part of Mission St. but the front was nicely rebuild into a modern edifice. It stood out from the rest of the street and I'm sure it was intentional. When we entered we were greeted by a good looking Latino young lady receptionist. Her beautiful deep brown eyes almost make you forget why you came in. Her business attire was professional, but with a flare; she was wearing a beige suit with a bolero jacket and a pink man tailored shirt. Her jet black hair was combed back into an extreme pony tail making her eyes even more riveting. Inside was also redone in a modern motif and the colors had your eyes follow one from the other until they landed you on their Logo; which was a group of black gull like silhouette figures in flight starting large and then all graduating smaller to give you the impression they were leaving or may be coming.

Peter casually said, "Very impressive some one knew what they were doing". The receptionist's name plate read Teresa "Terry" Munoz so I addressed her by her nick-name Terry and told her who I was and that Mr. Armorson was expecting me. She smiled then picked up the phone and called him on the intercom then asked us to take a seat and he would be here directly. I sat but Peter was looking at the poster size replicas of modern masters on the far wall when a gentleman appeared from a hall to our right he was obviously Larry Armorson. He glanced at both of us and I could see the light go off in his eyes when he recognized me. With a big smile he said, "Mr. Kerry" I remember you from Hanaford and extended his hand to me then looked toward Peter so I introduced Peter Travillian. They shook hands and he saw that Peter was looking at the painting reproduction that took up half the wall and asked Peter if he was a fan of modern art. His reply was slow and vague as he said, "I'm not sure if you'd call me a fan, but this of "Guernica" it's one of Picasso's most fascinating works it's his anti-war painting of the bombing of the city of Guernica by the Condor Legion of the Luftwaffe".

"Well you seemed to recognize that particular Picasso do you agree with him?" "Not necessarily but I do believe in payback". I thought I'd better change the subject before it went to some place other than business so I mentioned Peter was from out of state and interested in the subject of the California Usury Law. That alerted Larry that the subject should be discussed privately so he ushered us into his office. His office was much of the same as the receptionist area with a chrome and glass desk and credenza, but the walls and ceiling were painted more neutral colors. He pointed with an open hand to two chairs of similar glass and chrome and we sat. He had to maneuver his six foot 4inches frame into his chair from behind his desk it was only then did I notice he favored one of his legs. He was a large man and I was sure negotiating the space behind his desk made his moving around very uncomfortable. He reminded me of a friend of my father's a big Swede with flaxen hair turning grey and fleshy skin on his face making his blue eyes appear small and recessed behind his cheeks and under a thick set of greying eye brows. I apologized for not telling him that Mr. Travillian would be with me but it was the spur of the moment decision. He just nodded with body language that said no problem. I turned to Peter in effect to give him the floor. He began by telling Larry, "I got into San Francisco late last night on other business, but there was a glitch in my timing so I showed up at Jim's office this morning to see his boss Dick Somers and of course, upset their schedule. Then Jim told me he was bringing his appraisals to you this afternoon so I hitched a ride. I hope this isn't inconvenient, but I would like to discuss the possibility of funding loans through a financial institution here in California."

"Of course, you're referring to getting around the usury law here in California". Larry said.

"Yes that would be my intention".

"When Jim called me last week about this I talked to the owner of the S & L Mr. Cordy to see what his feeling was about the subject and he's interested in more particulars in the structure like how much percentage of each loan would he have to come up with to participate and what kind of profit his S & L would realize."

"This is all negotiable". Peter replied.

Larry looked slightly perplexed then said, "Would you mind waiting a minute or two I've got to make a phone call"?

Peter said not at all and Larry left to go to an adjoining office. We could see the button on his desk phone light up for an outside line. It stayed lit for no more than a minute then Larry returned and told us he just talked to Mr. Cordy and he's very much interested in meeting you and if you wouldn't mind waiting his office is only a few minutes walking distance from here. Peter looked at me and I shrugged why not so we traded some small talk until Mister Cordy arrived. For some reason I was not surprised by Mr. Cordy's appearance neither physically nor his aggressive presence. He entered with a certain swagger and even while being introduced he began controlling the meeting. His looks are what my wife would call handsome. His facial features were small his nose, cheeks and chin all seemed to be in perfect balance, but when he talked his expression seemed contrived or learned not natural. When he entered he had on a grey fedora which dated him, but I suspected it was intentional. He removed it with what would be called 1930 panache a bit theatrical but effective. He by passed the chair and sat on the edge of Larry's desk facing Peter and myself as we sat strategically oblique to Larry giving him a perfect view of Peter and me. When he leaned against the desk he was in a sitting position because of his height. He was probably five foot eight, but his shoes looked to have lifts in them; his hair looked too good for his age it was probably tinted professionally with just enough grey around the ears to give it the proper age look. That aside he was in excellent physical condition bordering on the athletic. He looked to be in his late fifty's or early sixty's, however I was told he was actually in his mid-seventy's. He kicked off the meeting by asking Peter where he called home and when Peter told him Pittsburg Pennsylvania then he had an amusing story about a time he was in Pittsburg. We all chuckled and then he got right to the business at hand asking Peter, "I'm told you're looking for a business partner here in California to deal with Usury Law".

"Your information is correct". Peter replied.

"I have to ask you how much do you know about the Law here in California".

"Not enough that's why I'm here to be enlightened".

"I'm just the man to enlighten you". It was said with tongue in cheek so no offense was taken. In fact it started a good natured banter between Peter and Mr. Cordy smoothing the Segway into the pros, cons and pitfalls of dealing with the usury law.

"The first and most important thing to know is that the Lender found willfully in violation of the usury law is deemed to be loan sharking, a felony punishable by jail time up to five years. The financial cost of a usurious loan could be forfeiture to the borrower of all interest on the loan and not just the usurious part but triple the amount of interest paid to the lender by the borrower". Cordy eased up by unfolded his arms then put his hands on the desk to reposition his body to a more comfortable stance. It was obvious to me this whole scenario was practiced beforehand and by now I knew Peter was thinking the same thing, but it was done well so we were going to neither suffer through it or sit back and enjoy it. We choose the latter. By the time Mr. Cordy finished he got through the laws not applying to the California banks or saving and Loans associations on loans secured by real property. I could tell Peter was thinking the same thing it was well done and not over windy. Peter thank him and got down to brass tacks when he said, "We were thinking along the lines of as 90% participation on our part with your company servicing the loan at negotiable rate with a buy back of the 10 % at a specific time interval, that's also negotiable. All loans are subject to Mr. Kerry's appraisal. That's the outline of the proposition it is really just the bare bones and any input on your part would be welcomed". Almost before Peter had finished Cordy added a provision he would like to see a money injection into his Savings and Loan in the form of a certificate of deposit from Peter's company as a good will gesture.

Peter said, "That's also negotiable". He unzipped a small leather bound file size folder he'd been carrying and took out some papers. He inspected them until he was satisfied then handed them over to Mr. Cordy telling him this is our proposal and pretty much what I told you so you could let your lawyer look them over and get back to us. That seemed to take the wind out of Mr. Cordy this was obviously unexpected and took away all his momentum. With that Peter stood extended his hand to both Larry and Mr. Cordy then gave them his business card and said, "We hope to hear from you soon I'll be here until Friday of next week and,of course, you can contact me through Mr. Kerry's office after that I'll be back in Pittsburg". We left them with a slightly confused look and headed for Peters hotel. I dropped Peter off at the Ramada Inn at fisherman wharf not two blocks from my house so I just continued on home.

It was Friday morning and when I got to the office I had all intentions of finishing up the appraisal for Mr. Albononi so I could deliver it Monday. Peter was in Dick's office with the door opened talking business; when I passed I heard my name so I stopped and retreated back to Dick's office. I was invited to sit and then Peter asked if I had any time today to accompany him to the lawyers office. Of course, I said yes and he replied good let's go I just got off the phone with her and she is free. He hustled me out the door and into the elevator before I could ask what lawyer and where is her office. That's when he mentioned Myra then told me he had asked her to write up an offer to buy Cordy S & L, of course, the offer would be subject to a look at the books. I was dumb founded I didn't know how to respond. When we got off the elevator he told me he would like to stretch his legs and if I wouldn't mind walking to Myra's office. I mumbled something like sure and we were off on a trek similar to a forced march with Peter in the lead. Peter seemed to know where he was going and in record time were climbing the stairs to Myra office. As soon as we entered the law offices of Slone and Pacemann I noticed everyone seemed more reserved and to my surprise most of all Myra I wondered if it was Peter's presence. Myra had met us at the doorway to her office where Peter took her hand then said, "It's so nice to see you again". She thanked him and suggested we sit out on the roof garden. The garden table was set with coffee cups and linen napkins; a thermos of coffee was almost camouflaged under as vase of flowers. I thought this was a first and confirmed my impression that Mr. Travillian was being treated especial. Peter and I sat and Myra followed us out with a folder and the lawyer's ever present legal pad then put the file in front of Peter. As he was reading the papers from the folder Myra had sort of a frozen smile on her face and was glancing back and forth from Peter to me without changing her expression. I smiled back and raised an eye brow to let her know I was also in the dark as to what Peter's plans were, but she never changed her expression. The weather was cool and the wind pick up and the napkins started to luff. I put my hand on mine and Peter's blew into his lap. Myra made a move and I thought for a minute she was coming around the table to grab Peter's napkin and save the day. This was all new to me I never saw Myra this rattled and it was obvious to me Mr. Travillian was much more than what Dick had portrayed him to be. He palmed his napkin and never stopped reading the file then said, "It looks good let's go with this as a beginning offer, but what I would like is to incorporate the name Cordy and the logo in the deal. I like the name Cordy because we can write it out like an acronym and add the proviso Mr. Cordy can-not use the name Cordy in any business or advertising any business or promotion of any entity". Myra was writing on her legal pad as Peter was talking and when he finished she look up and said, "That can be done is there anything else"?

"No that's pretty much for now, but I would like to take you out to dinner before I leave. Dick and I are going the Palm Springs over the week end and as you know I've compressed my time here and have to get back to Pittsburg before next Friday; I know I'll have thought of other things and of course I want your input".

"Just name a time and place".

"Wednesday and you name the place".

"I don't know it would have to be someplace quite so we can talk and be heard". Peter looked over at me and asked if I had a place in mind and I replied, "Jacks on Sacramento Street they have small dining rooms up stares".

"That sounds perfect, Jim would you make reservation and bring your wife, Esperanza told me she's beautiful and bright I'd like to meet her". I was slow in responding because I was caught off guard I had assumed he wanted to discuss business with Myra in privet, but I said sure how about 8 o'clock. Everyone agreed and Peter reached for the coffee thermos and poured everyone a cup then sat back and started on a critique of plants and flowers on the roof garden. As I was sipping my coffee I realized Myra had been watching me when Peter was talking plants and flowers she had a grin on her face that was unreadable. We left after coffee and on the way back to my office Peter handed the file folder to me then said go over this and anything you don't understand or are not familiar just tell me and I'll explain. I like you to be prepared for these negotiations because you're going to be part and parcel of it.

When we got back to the office Dick was waiting for Peter to head out to the airport for their flight to Palms Springs. I went into my office and broke out the appraisal for Mr. Albononi. It was four o'clock on a Friday afternoon and I was making progress on the appraisal when I looked up to see Baite leaning on the door jamb to my office. She didn't try to mince words just said, "I've heard you're going into the saving and loan business". This was the second time to day I was taken off guard and my response was weak and not very convincing when I coyly said, "What do you mean"? Her smile went to a frown, "I heard Dick and Peter discussing the deal and I see you wound up with the folder".

"Well yeah, Peter gave me the file to read over to familiar myself with the deal; it's no big thing". Her frown went back to a smile then she said, "What do you know about Peter Travillian"? I thought it was a peculiar question so I said, "Just what I've been told by Dick and the limited conversation I've had with him; why"?

"I can give some back ground on Mr. Travillian that might help you with dealing with that S&L proposal are you interested"?

"Fire away".

"You will probably come across the name of a company named P&O Enterprises; I know it's a holding company, and it stands for Pennsylvania and Ohio Enterprises, but you would have to do research to find out what the holding company holds, but Mr. Travillian is the P&O Enterprises. In the course of answering Dick's correspondence I've sent letters from Dick to P&O Enterprises either approving or disapproving a deal or transactions always referred to by an account number and occasionally a proxy vote to Peter Travillian. Two of the accounts in the holding company are Reliance industries and Scranton & Associates.

In the course of these letters the one name that is often mentioned is Ohio Valley Oil and Gas Association they, of course, support the exploration of Gas and Oil in the Ohio Valley and Mr. Travillian is financial supporter of the Association".

"Is P&O Enterprises into Oil and Gas"?

"Draw your own conclusions".

She then said she was meeting some friends and would I mind covering the phones because she would like to leave a few minutes early. My response was not at all and I went back to my appraisal of the Albononi's property. I was hard pressed to concentrate on finishing the appraisal but I did and headed for home.

Chapter 21

I lost track of time and it was all most 7 o'clock by the time I got home. When I walked into the kitchen Anne was sitting at the table reading the paper and sipping a glass of wine with the baby in her high chair playing with her Cheerios. The lack of cooking smells and pristine condition of the kitchen gave me the first clue we were going out to dinner and Anne gave me the second clue when she told me we were going out to dinner. It being Friday a good guess would be Scoma's and that was the first thing Anne said, "We have reservation at Scoma's at 8 with Tom and Nancy so you got time for a glass of wine are you in"? I just pointed to my empty glass and she poured a perfect two ounces in a ten ounce glass I played with the swirl and then the aroma and drank it. I emptied my glass and begged for more and Anne poured me a man size glass and at that moment the front door bell rang. She put her hand up for me to stay put and told me it was the baby sitter. I barely finished my wine when Anne finished with instruction to the baby sitter and we were on our way. It was only a ten minute walk down Hide Street to Beach Street then angle through Jefferson to the pier and Scomas. We were right on time and Tom and Nancy were at the bar waiting for us. We alerted the hostess and were escorted to our table with Tom and Nancy trailing with cocktail in hand. Dinner was the usual best with a wrinkle Tom ordered two dozen Oysters Rockefeller with a glass of the French liqueur Pernod. He carefully spooned a drop or two onto the oysters and voila. It was an experience, but not so much for the girls they said they could live without the liqueur; me and Tom were sucking on the shells. The conversation at dinner filled everyone in on their respective family's highs and lows then invariably got around to Mary Mace. Tom said he ran into Mary down town and she looked beautiful as ever; we talked for a few minutes and she said Allen was improving and Jean is holding down their business quite well. Nancy had a frown on her face and Tom looked at her and said, "What's the matter"?

"That's not what Jean told me he said Mary still has that attitude when she feels like doing something she'll do it if not she won't so that's a problem at the boutique and Allen seems to be getting weaker the only thing she does for him that seems to help is the salve she gives him for his arthritis". The talk got back to local politics and when that was exhausted everyone decided to call it a night. As they were leaving I asked Nancy what salve was Jean talking about. She said she wasn't sure he just said it penetrated the skin and brought warmth and relief to Allen's arthritic joints. When we got home Anne paid off the baby sitter and I went to the front room and collapsed in an arm chair. In due time Anne followed me in sat opposite me then asked what's wrong. I closed my eyes like I was concentrating then told her I am being educated and I seem to be a little slow and it's embarrassing.

"Can you be a little more specific"?

"I've been lead around by the nose by Dick and now Peter Travillian to show me how their business is structured and it took Dick's secretary to explain it to me".

"OK, try it again; I didn't get it the first time what business and what structure".

"Peter Travillian owns all these companies that are financing the projects we broker and Dick is a partner or major stock holder".

"Well that makes life a bit easier for you doesn't it; I mean you're almost like a banker you already got the money if the deal is good you fund the money".

"True, but I'm not sure I want to be a banker or control a saving and loan mainly because I know nothing about running these types of businesses; it's called getting in over our head".

"I think you might be over thinking the whole situation people like Dick and Mr. Travillian do not jeopardize their investments by putting their employees in impossible situations, stop and think a minute, you told me Larry Armorson is in complete control of Cordy S & L you don't think for a minute they'd replace him with you; do you"?

"No, but things are moving too fast it's making me nervous".

"Stop over thinking your position it's the same as when you first moved here you gave it a try, did your best and it worked out; I remember you telling me you had nothing to lose if it didn't work out you would go back to square one. Essentially this is the same thing".

"I hate it when you're right".

"Good now that you know I'm right we'll go over the file tomorrow together". Then Anne reached over and touched my arm and said, "It's time for beddy- bye we can discuss this under the covers".

"Could I be the naughty chauffer and you could be Ava Gardner the barefoot Contessa"?

"You could be any body you want I can always fake it".

Anne's wise cracks always had the effect of putting a hose on my fantasies this was no exception.

Monday morning the office was quiet. I was in twenty minutes before Baite and I had no idea where Dick and Peter were so I went ahead with my plan for the day. First I called Johnny Peresci at the construction site and left word I'd be there around nine thirty then I called Mr. Albononi's answering service to tell him I'd drop off the appraisal around noon. I ran into Baite as I was leaving and told her I left a note on her desk of my whereabouts today so I could hit the Bay Bridge at eight thirty. I was going in the opposite direction of the commute traffic so the trip was uneventful. I got to the Hillcrest housing development about ten after nine so I started walking around looking at the construction at all stages. I thought it was going well the road and sidewalks were all in and the model houses were finished with green lawns and flowers. By the time I looked at my watch it was ten to ten and no Johnny. On the way to my truck I was passing Johnny's superintendent talking to the building inspector about back flow valves for the individual water meters to each house that was completed. Evidently the superintendent argued all the plans were approved without back flow valves and obviously the inspector disagreed and was claiming it's now a requirement of the City and it's up to the developer to know this and comply. I caught the gist of this on the way to my truck and decided to make a few notes. While

I was writing I felt someone at my driver's window and I looked up to see Johnny motioning me to roll down the widow. I did just that and Johnny started on a tirade about me sneaking around the job site looking for minor faults so I could delay the construction draws just to get back at him because of jealousy. I opened my door and he retreated into what he would call a fighting stance. I slammed my door and walked passed him and headed over to where the building inspector and the superintendent were discussing the back flow valves. As I approached, the building inspector's back was to me and Johnny's superintendent faced me with a questioning look. I introduce myself and apologized to both men and told them I was here today to notify the plumbing contractor of the new requirement of the back flow valve because it's so new I wasn't sure he was notified; and also we ordered fifty valves and were told they were overwhelmed by orders because of the new requirement that they could only deliver thirty and twenty are on back order. The building inspector said he understood the problem, but he personally sent out memos to all developers and contractors and followed up with phone calls to insure everyone knew about this new requirement I talked to Mr. Peresci over a month ago and my only concern is no one here seems to know anything about it. The superintendent looked over to where Johnny was standing and we both could see he was nowhere to be seen. The building inspector said he would sign off on everything but the valves and as soon as you can install them I'll give you a final. The confab broke up and after the inspector left I told the superintendent no one as ordered any back flow valves so tell the plumbing contractor to do it now before it really becomes a back order problem. I was getting into my truck when the superintendent approached my driver's window. I dropped the window and he told me his name was Joe Peavy and he asked me for my business card then thanked me and said they would have to change the line of communication here and would I mind if he kept in contact with me on some of these types of issue. I told him not at all and don't hesitate to call me because it appears I'll be monitoring the progress here for the construction lender through the Title Company until it's finished. When I left I was smiling all the way to Mr. Albononi's office I relished the thought of Johnny twisting in the wind.

This was the first time I'd been to his office and the first time I'd been at the Oakland Airport Commercial Complex and I was impressed so I drove around to see how it was laid out. His office was in a series of two story buildings all of the same size with some all one company and others broken up into smaller offices. His office was in the very first building and the very first entrance with his name and company prominently displayed. I parked right in front and entered to a smiling face of a young lady who seemed to be ready for any one coming through the door. I told her that I was dropping off an appraisal of a property I'd appraised for Mr. Albononi and I'd like to discuss it with him. She asked me to wait while she told Mr. Albononi I was here. I sat and was fiddling with the pages of a magazine when Mr. Albo appeared in a half opened door way and asked me to come in. As soon as I entered he introduced me to an Oriental Gentleman named Doctor Chester Yee we shook hands and found seats then sat. Mr. Albononi told me Doctor Yee was in the market for finance for a Residential Care facility for the elderly here in Oakland I mentioned that you had lenders that were interested in loans of this nature. I was totally taken back I was unprepared and had no idea who would finance a project like that so I fake it. I asked Dr. Yee if he had any experience in operating a Residential Care Facility. That turned out to be the right question; he began telling me he has been a doctor of geriatrics for ten years and the rest of his qualification that sounded more like a resume. I nodded through most of it trying to look intelligent enough that I actually understood what he was telling me. He mentioned an old abandon school here in Oakland and plans to convert it into a Care Facility for the Chinese Community. He emphasized the need for this facility to care for the elderly in the Chinese Community and the government is willing to participate but what is needed is a primary lender. I had a thought so I asked Dr. Yee if he planned to raise the existing building or remodel the structure to earth quake standards. He told me the architect has preliminary plans for both to get an idea of cost because the building is somewhat historical it dates back to nineteen thirty six public works program of the NEW DEAL with its sculptural Sandstone paneled façade everyone is for the remodel for the art work alone, but of course, the cost will dictate one or the other. I was struck by the eloquence of his presentation, but I thought with all that preparation he should have little trouble getting finance locally so I told him I would look into it and if he would give me his card I would get back to him.

After the doctor left I laid out the appraisal for Mr. Albo. He hardly looked through it he just looked at the property value and the bill then buzzed the young lady out front and asked her to come in. He opened up his check book and gave a check to her then told her to print out the check in the name and amount that was on my bill. While we were waiting for the young lady to print the check I brought up my problem with Johnny Peresci. I recapped his latest antics and then told Mr. Albo I was now monitoring the construction stages for the lender through the title company and it's now important he start to cooperate; if not the lender will not hesitate to pull the plug. "I can't help feeling, regardless what he thinks of me, he seems to be in some kind of self-destruct mode. It's obvious he is not in any real communication with his contractors or even his superintendent so you have to talk to him and try and bring him around to reality".

"I'll answer your concerns in a minute, let me ask you is it Reliance Industries that is worried about Mr. Peresci or are you being over-zealous because if Mr. Travillian actually looked at the progress and sales of Johnny's development he wouldn't be quite as critical as you. As for Johnny I've already talked to his partner and he assures me he will put in more controls".

"I wasn't aware that Johnny had a partner involved in this project; at least it wasn't disclosed on the loan documents". Mr. Albo immediately answered, "Well he's a silent partner".

"That's good to know Johnny has a silent partner I'll tell Peter Wednesday when I take him out to see the development".

"Travillian is here in San Francisco"?

"Yes he is; I am sorry I thought I told you".

"NO you didn't mention it and there is no need to be sarcastic".

Just then the young lady returned with the check so I waited until she left then I apologized telling him I was sorry if I sounded sarcastic it is the frustration dealing with Johnny that clips my speech and it sounds sarcastic. My explanation seemed to mollify him and he went on to Dr. Yee's care facility and wanted to know if Reliance Industries or any other company of Peter Travillian would be interested in either funding or participating in the venture. I told him I could ask him and see what he says. He nodded an OK and with nothing more to discuss I left.

I was back in my office by 1:30 and at my desk when I could hear Dick and Peter enter the main office and Dick ask Baite if anything was new. I couldn't hear her reply, but I could tell by Dick's reaction she handed him his messages. Peter appeared in my doorway at the same time as he tapped on the door jamb lightly with one knuckle like he wanted to wake me slowly. I was tempted to be a wise ass and yawn, but I caught myself and just smiled and then asked, "How was Palm Springs". He said, "Hot".

"Too hot for golf"? I asked.

"Not for Dick, but I don't play golf I enjoyed the dry dessert weather as opposed to the humid weather back home". I counted with everyone needs change. He made an affirmative nod of his head and then asked if I had a chance to read through the file on the S & L acquisition. I pushed my chair back from my desk and moved my hands in an imploring gesture then said, "I read the file from stem to stern twice, but the legalese had me snowed I couldn't understand a word".

"Don't be discouraged that's why we use lawyers; to begin with the legalese confuses the other side so we can establish a better position than the other guy. So they get their lawyer to decipher the legalese and then we let the lawyers fight it out. We know we have an edge because Myra is an excellent negotiator and if you have a willing seller and a willing buyer the best negotiator wins". I nodded my head like it all made sense, but I knew Peter was placating me to help me through my confusion and insecurity. He let me mull that over for a second or two then asked, "How is the Blackstone Corporation or to be more precise the Hillcrest Housing development getting along".

"Well the construction phase looks solid. The streets are in and the model homes look very good. The first phase is all most complete there is only six houses left to finish however Johnny is still an obstacle; I went on to explain his antics and then mentioned to him about a mystery partner that Mr. Albononi told me about when I delivered his appraisal".

"Mr. Peresci is full of surprises do you have any idea who that partner could be"?

"Not a 100% sure, but when the hillcrest Development stared there was a Teamster strike throughout the East Bay however Johnny had little or no trouble with delivery of building materials especially concrete plus there was no picket line at his job site and the East Bay Union Representative for the Teamsters is Freddy Cannelli".

Peter's eyes lit up, "That name is familiar I believe Dick told me he was involved with your previous employer in some sort of corruption case; I'm I correct"?

"Yes you are and I know the FBI has been trying to nail him for years so I'm thinking they must be watching him pretty closely".

"That makes sense I think you know Mr. Albononi had a run in with the Feds in my home town of Pittsburg".

"Yes I heard that, but Mr. Albononi introduced me to a Doctor Chester Yee who has a Geriatrics practice in the Chinese Community in Oakland and I gave Peter the doctor's plan for residential care facility with apartments for the ambulatory all the way to those in dementia. I didn't see any plans but he told me he already has local and Federal government participation. Do you know of any one that does these kinds of loans". Peter looked amused then smiled and said, "Intimately, we have participated in two of these facilities one in Pittsburg and one in Cincinnati and both are solid investments when you have the right partner. Would you contact the doctor and get all the information on his project and some back ground on the good doctor; especially from the Oakland Chinese Community".

Chapter 22

Dinner at Jacks went well Peter increased the reservation to six guests Anne and my-self plus Dick and Esperanza and, of course, Myra and Peter. We all fit perfectly with room to spare in a privet dining room above the restaurant. Drinks were ordered and then menus were passed out. There was little if any business discussed, but it was obvious to me Peter and Myra had thrashed out all the kinks in the S & L contract before coming to dinner. Peter and Dick told some funny stories about their tour of duty in England during the war then Myra added a story about Dick and Peter getting taken by an old lady on a lumber yard loan; it seems she inherited the lumber yard upon her husband's death. They gave her 70 % loan to its evaluation on the land and the lumber inventory being stored there. She took the money and never made a payment and the lumber was missing along with the old lady. They were setting up the papers for a tax-loss when they were approached by the county assessor's office and offered twice what they paid for it; the county needed the land to finish a proposed road project. Myra ended with a quip, "Crime doesn't pay, but it's even better to be lucky". We all laughed, but Dick and Peter fell apart laughing to the point Dick had tears in his eyes. We all ordered dinner and another drink and needless to say things were swimming along and it struck me it seemed to me this was like we did this every week. Especially when I listen to and watched Myra she wore two hats one for business and one for pleasure and she seemed comfortable in both. However as the evening progressed it occurred to me the position of everyone looked contrived with Peter at the head of the table with Anne to his right and Myra to his left and Dick at the other end with me on his right and Esperanza on his left so the conversations were different at each end. Dick was talking about South America and Esperanza's home town in Argentina with Esperanza half giggling and laughing saying Dick was exaggerating and that it wasn't as beautiful as all that but it was simpatico and the whole atmosphere was easy to slip into. I had my other ear on the other end of the table and I couldn't help but notice Peter was talking to Anne in his soft interrogation mode that sounded like normal conversation. I thought back to the two hat theory and my thought was Peter wore only one hat, but he could tilt it in any direction.

Flushed with an in house social success Peter arranged a meeting with the principals of the Cordy S & L. at their office. This was all by his design it was 9 o' clock Friday morning and he had a midnight red eye flight back to Pittsburg so when he made an offer to buy the S & L the negotiations were compressed into a few hours at least with him present. He began by saying for those who haven't met my attorney this is Myra Pacemann of Sloan & Pacemann and my associate James Kerry then he refer to us as his negotiators and apologized for his short stay, but he had to attend an important unscheduled meeting first thing Saturday morning back home. I liked his choice of words "back home", but I could see the cagy Mr. Cordy was not taken in with the back home ploy. He replied, "We could do this another time when you have time to be here for the negotiations after all the offer is a surprise". This was hardly true because he had his son Bryan junior, a partner named Munoz and Larry Armorson with profit and loss statements a half inch thick all with pen in hand and an elbow on a legal pad. The dance began when Mr. Cordy introduced his side of the table then started reading through the proposal and was making small grunting sounds that were made to sound negative then occasionally stopping to look up at our side of the table and run his eyes passed us in an accusing manner. My eyes dropped down to Myra's legal pad and I was fascinated by her doodling's. At times when nothing of importance was being discussed she was drawing wolf heads facing one another. After an hour of going nowhere with the talks suddenly Mr. Cordy asked Peter why his stenograph was drawing dogs on her legal pad. Peter glanced at her pad like he was suddenly aware of her doodling then said, "I take it you mean my attorney; she's relaxing her mind because there's nothing of substance agreed on as of yet". That seemed to bring things to a crawl so it was mutually agreed to let Mr. Cordy have time to read through the contract thoroughly and convene at a later date at Mr. Cordy's convenience. Mr. Cordy told Peter he wanted to deal directly with him and Peter replied he would certainly look forward to negotiating the contract, but when that was not possible my negotiating team of Counselor Pacemann and my associate Mr. Kerry would be here in my stead. This didn't sit well with Mr. Cordy, but bit his lip and the meeting ended.

We met back at Myra's office and it was almost 1 o'clock; there were tea sandwiches and finger food and, of course, tea. The weather was a little raw so it was set up in the conference room with a full bar. When we entered the conference room Peter went straight to the bar with the familiarity of an out of work brother-in-law. He was making himself a drink when Clifton Sloan the other partner of the law firm joined him. He looked the part with steel grey side burns blending into black manicured hair with facial features that could only be described as Plantagenet. They were joking in a way that friends do not just business acquaintances. I felt a hand on my arm and I was surprised when it was Myra she just said, "We'll talk when Peter leaves". The buffet lunching was joined by six or seven associates of the firm and there was a lot of smoozing this went on for well over an hour then it started breaking up. Peter told me he was walking back to our office to meet Dick before he left for Pittsburg than shook my hand and told me it was a pleasure meeting and working with me. He looked over at Myra and said, "She has all the information you'll need to negotiate with Mr. Cordy and good luck". The weather was still raw so we settled in at Myra's office. She opened up the Cordy File and after shuffling a few papers around she asked me what I thought of the meeting this morning with Mr. Cordy and company. I raised an eye brow and shrugged then told her I couldn't quite get the gist of what was going on, but it looked like a penis measuring contest between Peter and Mr. Cordy. Myra dropped her head and blurted out a belly laugh then moved both hands along the edge of her desk like she was brushing off dust then looked up and said she appreciated me sanitizing that expression, but that's what it was.

When Peter and I first discussed the deal he told me about his first meeting with Mr. Cordy and what he expected from him when he made an offer to buy the S & L. He expected all that sparring between them and the only thing that Mr. Cordy respects is the power position that controls whatever he is involved with so Peter told me he was coming out swinging and not expect anything of substance from the first meeting. Peter said Cordy was the Alpha Dog in his pack and it was important not to cause him to lose face in front of his people so he would try to be subtle when he put him in his place. Mr. Cordy did the job for him when he called me Peter's stenograph his people at the meeting knew it was a cheap shot. It became obvious to them that he blinked first and shot himself in the foot that was what Peter was waiting for. He then graciously let him off the hook and that gave him the wiggle room to appear to be in control of the outcome of the meeting, but it weakened his position on all the subsequent meetings. That's, of course, if he is really interested in selling the S & L; the first meeting established that one way or the other and saved a lot of time. She gave me time to absorb all that, than we went over the contract knowing it was all to be negotiated to its final form.

When I got home I had a lot to discuss with Anne she was my sounding board because she wrote many contracts for a Real Estate lawyer. She thought the whole concept was perfectly routine to have an independent audit and then the negotiations but the rest was brilliant get all the minutiae and posturing out of the way and get to the transaction.

The first half of the next week was slow so I was catching up on my general office work then on Wednesday I got a call from Doctor Yee asking if I made any progress on financing his project. I told him I may have and if he could send me his loan package request along with the building plans. He said he would bring them over in person so we made a date for the following day Friday. As soon as I hung up Baite buzzed me telling me there was a gentleman named Peavy calling from the Hillcrest Housing Development. It took me a minute to recognize the name then I remembered Johnny's superintendent. I punched the flashing button and said hello he started to apologize for calling, but that he should if the same type of problems came up and they have and it's going to hold up the final inspection. I moaned for affect and in my best martyr's whine asked, "What did Johnny do now".

"It's not what he did it's what he is not doing he insisted that he be the one to order those back flow valves and he hasn't. Then he called for final inspection and when the building inspector came he told the inspector that they were on back order and the supplier told him they wouldn't be available for another month so if he could give him the final he would have the valves install when they were immediately available. The problem is it was a lie and the inspector knew it because he is in contact with the plumbing supplier because of all the problems with the other contractors getting the same valves. Now our credibility is shot with the inspector and he's pissed and he's taking it out on our subcontractors by not giving them an inch of slack. This type of sleight of hand gets around quickly and paints everyone here with the same brush which means I could lose some of my subs and replacing them can really slow a job down". I let him talk for a bit longer and I was trying to more or less pacify him and then I finally told him. "I'll take care of it". I called the Title Company and asked the Escrow Officer if the final payments have been made on the first stage of the Hillcrest Development construction loan. He told me no and he was waiting for my clearance; however he has a request on his desk from Mr. Peresci with a picture of a construction permit all checked off and signed by the inspector. You're absolutely right don't cut a check until you hear from me in writing. Next I called Mr. Albononi and told him of Johnny's egregious act and could he tell me why I shouldn't turn it over to our lawyer. He pleaded with me not to do anything until he got back to me and he was sure they could get it all straighten out. I told him he would have to have some resolution by Monday if not I have no choice but to give it to our lawyer. I personally called the plumbing supplier and asked if they could ship fifty back flow valves to the Hillcrest Development job site and I would give them an escrow number from the title company for billing. I was asked to hold on while they connected me to the book keeper. I waited for over a minute when a lady answered asking me to give her a telephone number of the escrow company to verify the escrow number and if I would please give her my name. I gave her that information and my number and asked if she would call me back and let me know if and when the valves would be sent; she agreed and called me back in fifteen minutes with the information. I know sooner hung up the phone when Baite told me the escrow officer was on the line and wanted to talk to me. I punched the blinking button on my phone a little too hard and the phone slid across the desk and sent my pencil cup to the floor. I calmed myself down and tried to sound normal and asked if he got a call from the plumbing supplier he said yeah and she told me they were behind in their account and until they settle the account they were on COD. I thanked him and told him I'd be in touch. I felt like a one armed paper hanger I rearranged my phone to a more normal position on my desk and called Mr. Albo with the scintillating news that the Hillcrest Housing Development is now on COD from the Plumbing supplier. This smells like he is behind in all his accounts plus I have to look into his payments to his subcontractors and if their mechanic liens are not cured he's going to have a hell of a time closing those mortgages on the first stage of the development. Mr. Albononi didn't interrupt through my tirade when I was finished he calmly told me all of these problems will be addressed on Monday Johnny's partner has been notified and is moving to remedy the short falls. We ended our conversation, but I wasn't convinced so I waited until Dick got to the office and when I thought he was settled at his desk I buzzed him on the intercom and asked if he had some time to discuss the Hillcrest Development. With his Dutch uncle sigh he told me sure come in. We sat in his office and I gave him the whole story from stem to stern and in his unperturbed manner told me Monday will be a crucial time for Mr. Peresci, but we'll find out who this silent partner is; further more we have the upper hand if we took receivership of the project we would make the profit and Johnny and his partner would not only not make a profit but would lose their original investment so we're in good shape. Try not to obsess about Johnny Peresci it sounds like he's trying to cover his mistakes so let his partner worry about him and his antics. Why don't you take a half a day off tomorrow and take Anne out to lunch and put this out of your mind until Monday. I told him I would love too, but Doctor Yee is coming in with his loan package with all building and renovation plans for his residential care facility and I asked if he would like to sit in on the meeting. He just smiled and said no this is your baby.

Doctor Yee was a bit early Friday and my desk was a mess so we took over the conference room which actually was a third office but Dick never hired anyone so now it was our conference room let's just say it is cozy. It did have a very efficient work table with draws for markers and pencils with a portion that could be elevated from 0 to a 45 degree angle this was ideal for reviewing plans and making revisions. I was fumbling through the paper work and actually getting a good sense of what was going on with the financial structure that the Doctor laid out and how all this was going to be paid back with profit to spare. I got caught up in the renovation plans and realized I was suggesting changes. We finished up near noon and I promised the Doctor I would get on this by next week and hopefully have some answers then we ended it there. I thought of what Dick said about going to lunch with Anne so I called her at her Father's business and she was definitely available so I told her I'd swing by in twenty minutes and be outside.

I took my truck over to Howard Street went a block or two past my father-in-law's location and swung around to be on the side of the street that Anne would be on. I saw her a good city block in front of me but so did a burly, leather clad, helmetless, bearded motorcyclist with a Hells Angels logo on his back. He moved passed me then cut in front of me as soon as he saw Anne lift her skirt with one hand and signal with her thumb in a going my way gesture. I thought it was comical because she was looking at me when she made the gesture, but then realized she had attracted someone other than me. He pulled up next to her at the curb and I could only imagine what she said to him, but he glanced back as I pulled in behind him then gave me a sneer and pulled away. When Anne jumped in and I asked, "What did you say to him"? She said she told him if he didn't get moving the guy behind you will kick your butt. "You didn't say that did you"? She chuckled then said, "No I just told him I don't sit side-saddle I'd tell you what else he said in response, but I don't want to soil your delicate ears". "You're so protective of my sensibilities, where do you want to go for lunch"? We sat in my truck at the curb and I asked if she had a preference and her answer surprised me she said she didn't care as long as she could get a vodka gimlet. I pulled away from the curb slowly then asked, "What up"?

"My father is selling his business".

"Make that two vodka gimlets I'll join you". I said.

We wind up at Fiore de Italia near her father's men's club. In between the salad and pasta she bemoaned the fact that without his business to occupy his time and as a safe haven from my mother's prying question about everything from his business to why his family ignores her; he'll be a sitting duck. At this point I could be tempted to interject some pearls of wisdom, but timidity and good sense took over and my only words were, "Who knows maybe things will work out". My remark was a wimpy cop out but it calmed her down or maybe it was the vodka at any rate she enjoyed the rest of her lunch and we decided to take the rest of the day off.

Monday came around too quick for me; Dick was on me about the Hillcrest Development so I dropped everything and headed down the East Bay to the job site. I got there before 10 o'clock in time to watch the fur fly. As I pulled in I could hear Mr. Albononi dressing down Johnny in the construction trailer and it was loud enough for half the construction site to hear. I decided to wait in my truck until things quieted down and saw the construction superintendent heading my way. I rolled down my widow and he told me the back flow valves came in this morning then thanked me explaining their installation held up his bonus. I told him I was confident things would get resolved today and incidents like this would not happen again. He smiled and motioned toward the trailer then said it sounds like it. It quieted down but I could still hear a one sided conversation going on and it was Mr. Albononi's voice I recognized and not a word from Johnny. This went on for another twenty minutes so I pulled out my personal file on the project and started to reread my comments to fix some of the problems I had Johnny Peresci's name underlined twice that the double line represented my solution to fix the problems; remove him from the project. The door to the trailer opened and Mr. Albononi motioned to me not to leave. I got out of my truck and he cupped my arm just above the elbow and steered me away from the trailer toward the building site. In an even voice that was obviously controlling his anger told me he was sure the problems of the past were resolved and thing will return to a smooth operation with no more hitches. I told him I had to be honest and I didn't think so and I was sure he knew or suspected what I knew that Johnny is skimming money from the construction draws because he is not paying his suppliers and worse than that he's stalling on payments to his subcontractors and in one case I know of their bonuses. I don't think he can dig himself out of the hole he dug for himself so I'm recommending you have his partner replace him. Mr. Albo was rocking his head no and said he thought it was harsh and he was sure he had learned his lesson. I told him he may think that but I'm going to take control of the final construction draw. I'll straighten out the mess he's made and bring all accounts up to date. Which should leave him with a clean-slate and the sale of the fifty houses in the first phase would be the company's profit and the sale of fifty houses would be substantial. Mr. Albononi was quiet for a moment or two then said he didn't think Johnny's partner would go along with that.

I was trying to avoid this kind of situation, but I decided to play hard ball, I counted with a bold threat reminding him to read the contract and that any misappropriation of money would force the development into the receivership of the lender, in this case Reliance Industries and they would sell the houses to recover their losses. His demeanor turned dark he glanced at me then away to something on the horizon then said, "I'll take this up with your boss". I told him it was his prerogative and started back to my truck.

As soon as I walked in the door Baite pointed to Dick's office and told me he wanted to talk to me and I didn't have to think too hard what it was about. Dick heard me coming and said, "Come in Robespierre but leave the guillotine outside". I didn't know what he meant so I said, "What"?

"Never mind I was trying to be funny; I'm sure you've figured out Mr. Albononi called as soon as you left to cry foul and he thought you over stepped your authority by demanding Mr. Peresci be removed from the Hillcrest Development and furthermore the contract doesn't stipulate any such codicil and he went on bla-bla-bla. I stopped him at some point to explain the Hillcrest Development was your account and responsible for its success and if you saw fit to recommend Johnny's removal from running the project and it was not complied with then we would be forced to stop all payments then appeal to the courts for relief in the form of receivership and no matter how it all turns out you people will lose because time would be on our side. I also explained that it has come to our attention that Mr. Peresci has a silent partner and of course, has nothing to do with the contract that Mr. Peresci and the Hillcrest Development signed so Mr. Peresci will appoint someone to take his place and officially resign as managing partner of the corporation. So where do we go from here"?

"What did Albononi say to that"?

"He asked me if I could get you to reconsider and I told him I wouldn't then he said something about getting back to me and hung up".

"OK moving right along I've talked to the superintendent, a fellow by the name of Joe Peavy, he told me the valves had arrived that morning so they'll be installed shortly also he's compiling a list of subcontractor who have not been paid. Next I'm going to get a list of suppliers who have filed mechanic liens and contact them to find out if they have been paid or not then I'll have the Title Company pay them off from the escrow account of the last construction draw. There is one thing that the escrow officer mentioned to me a while back that I more or less paid little attention too, but now seems to be important. At the time the amounts were small, but now I'm told they have grown to a serious amount. It's a supplier that did not file a mechanic's lien but was being paid COD upon each delivery but now the superintendent doesn't remember any deliveries".

"Find out who this mystery supplier is and what kind of construction material they were delivering and who signed for them"?

"I'll have to get the copies of the inventories from the girl at Hillcrest Development for an address and phone number".

"Good, do that and let's see where this is going and in the mean time I better call Peter and let him know what's happening I can't help feeling stupid for getting him into this mess especially because they did this same thing on the last housing development".

Chapter 23

I was at my desk penciling in a list of things to check to see if they were paid by Hillcrest when Baite buzzed me and told me Anne was on the line. I picked up the phone and asked a little apprehensively, "How's it going".

"As well as you would expect my father is apologizing to me for dropping that bomb shell on me, but what's making me crazy is he wants me to explain the sale of his business to my mother. I said to him, what's there to explain, just tell her you want to retire. The poor guy is paralyzed with guilt because he knows if he is around her all day there will be fireworks. I was sitting here thinking about the situation when Mary Mace called to tell me the probate of her aunts will is taking longer than she expected and wanted to make sure we hadn't changed our minds about turning the property on Union Street over to her so I had to reassure her nothing hadn't changed and soon as she is ready we will transfer the Flats over to her". I called Anne back to tell her Mary called and wanted to know if we changed our minds and wanted to keep the Flats.

"Out of curiosity did she mention how Allen was doing"?

"No I didn't think to ask her, why did you hear something".

"No not really it was just something Nancy said the last time we had dinner together".

Jim asked. "What'd she say"?

"It was probably nothing but it was about Mary using a penetrating salve on Allen's joints to help sooth his arthritis I just didn't think it fit her personality".

"What do you mean"?

"Well you know a Las Vegas dancer also being a caring competent nurse didn't seem to fit and also Jean told Nancy Mary promised to help him out financially when her Aunt's will was settled".

"Hold on, I thought you were there when Nancy mentioned Mary's father sent her to lab technician school for training in pharmacology I would guess that's where she was taught about arthritis and how to help sooth it". That explained her working for the Doctor in Las Vegas in his lab but also triggered latent feelings going back a few months to a chain of events that now made sense but they disturbed me so I put them out of my mind. I must have drifted off because Anne startled me by asking me if I was all right. I replied I was and then asked what's for dinner.

"That was my next bit of news Mom is at the house making dinner and if I would pick up two loaves of bread at Macaluso's and may be some cannoli for dessert, it's Mom favorite and she doesn't know about Dad selling the business yet".

"So you're planning to tell her before or after dessert"?

"Actually I was going to ask you to tell her".

"ME! What are you nuts; right after my first sentence she'd hit me with a frying pan". Anne snickered while saying, "I got ya".

As soon as my heart started to beat normally I said, "Don't ever do that to me again unless you want to be a widow". I knew this was going to be a close family thing so I planned to make an excuse before dessert and head back to my office at least that was my gutless plan. To my pleasant surprise Mr. Montalvo, Anne's father, arrived without fanfare like it was a Sunday afternoon. Anne had a grin on her face all through dinner that led me to believe I was not in the loop as to what was going on. After dessert Mr. Montalvo excused himself and announced that he and Anne's Mom were going down to Ghirardelli Square for coffee and to start planning their retirement. After they left Anne told me her father unbeknown to her call her mother and told her he just got an offer for his business that was so good he couldn't refuse and he would explain the whole thing after dinner tonight. When they left their faces were lit up like teenagers on their first date. Anne looked at me with those big beautiful brown eyes and said, "Looks like the first round went well so let's hope the next few go as well". I got the message.

Myra had scheduled a meeting with me on the Cordy S & L acquisition so I put everything else aside and we spent the afternoon and into the evening in the conference room at her office. It was great because she encouraged me to ask about anything that I didn't understand and there was plenty. One of the questions I had and the answer she gave me was revealing of how Peter's mind worked. I wanted to know why Peter was so insistent on keeping the name Cordy in the sale of the S & L because to me it was a small thing and not worth making it a big deal.

"Probably two things one the obvious one the transition would be very easy and cheap all the stationary was in place along with the logo and the crisp new officer on Mission Street and a minor thing that can be a major legal problem if not done right is the conveyance of all the existing loans. Second It would exclude Mr. Cordy from using his name on his other businesses including his Real Estate business which I have an educated guess Peter is going to make an offer to buy with the leverage knowing Mr. Cordy no longer can use his name and I'm sure he is predicating this on Mr. Cordy's willingness to retire".

"So essentially he is buying the saving and Loan with the Real Estate business thrown in".

"Exactly".

We finished up and it was after 6 o'clock I gave Anne a tinkle telling her I'll be late and then started walking back to the office. It was a typical San Francisco office rush hour everyone crisscrossing the streets dodging cars horns blasting everyone trying to get to their destination before whatever bewitching hour was driving them. I turned the corner onto Montgomery Street and was surprised by the flashing red and blue lights of a police car in front of 300 Montgomery. My pace slowed but I dispelled any thoughts of what happened a few months ago. When I entered our security guard waved to me and then turned to a policeman next to him and that prompted the policeman to head in my direction. He stopped me and asked if I was James Kerry I said I was and asked me to wait that Detective Norman wanted to speak to me. The officer left to get the detective and I walked slowly over to Nick the security guard and asked what's up. He said David the garage attendant was shot and I think he's dead. It took the patrolman ten or fifteen minutes to find Detective Norman while he was doing that I asked Nick what he knew about the shooting and he told me he didn't know anything he just heard David was in my truck when he was shot everything else is speculation. My mind went sideways for a minute or two I couldn't even visualize the Garage Attendant then everything cleared and I had a picture in my mind of David the Attendant and the conversation we had that morning when he told me if I wasn't back by five o'clock today he would have to move my truck around because they were painting the parking lines tonight. Then I was brought back to the moment when I heard my name and realized Oscar Norman was asking me a question. I told him I was distracted and if he could repeat the question. He said, of course, "I understand you met the parking attendant this morning could you tell me what it was about"?

"Sure he told me if I wasn't back before five o'clock he would have to move my truck around because they were doing some work in the garage this evening".

"Did you know him well enough to know if he seemed nervous or may be apprehensive"?

"Not really, but he was always up beat with a good sense of humor and this morning I didn't notice any change".

"Did he ever mention any problems with anyone, you know like a confrontation with anyone in the building".

"No not at him, but you always had people being grumpy about something usually the gas shortage; he would generally fend these situations off with some home grown San Francisco humor. I have to ask you does it look like a robbery".

"Well at this stage it's hard to tell it appears the perpetrator tried to shot it out with a patrol car near the Ferry Building and lost".

"You got him already"?

"Yeah, it was a great piece of police work all around a meter maid heard gun shots and spotted him running out of the garage entrance then followed him and using her radio gave the police his progress street by street they caught up with him on Drum Street and he tried to shot it out with them". I told Oscar I wanted to go up to my office and make a few phone calls and he told me go ahead and of course, we'll have to impound your truck so if you need a lift I'll have a black and white run you home.

"Why do you have to impound my truck"?

"I can't give you all the specifics but the Attendant was either sitting in or getting into your truck when he was shot so it's obviously part of the crime scene". I called Anne from the office and filled her in on the shooting and my truck was going to be impounded so I'll be a little late getting home. Baite had already left and Dick wasn't in that afternoon and what I thought I was going to do when I got back from Myra's office went out the window the murder of David Farrell began to consume me; why would anyone want to kill such a nice guy. Good to his word Detective Norman had a patrolman drive me home and he turned out to be the same officer who first responded to John Mace's murder. He obviously recognized me and I him and his conversation with me gave me the impression I was involved in this murder with more than just my truck. I gave Anne a blow by blow of what I was told of the murder and it made for a somber evening. I couldn't stop thinking of what the patrolman said, "Don't worry Detective Norman told us to watch your back".

The next morning I decided to walk from my house to Columbus and catch the bus at Union Street which dropped me off just about in front of 300 Montgomery. I walked through the lobby and nodded at Nick the security guard; he nodded back and I got on the elevator then it dawned on me they didn't have a security guard during the day just an elevator supervisor to monitor the people capacity for weight load.

Baite beat me in but Dick was waiting for both of us sitting in one of the reception chairs. It was a strange sight to me with Dick talking to Baite sitting in the reception area. Everyone said good morning and Dick asked me how was I feeling and if everything was OK. I told them I was fine and then they wanted to know if I knew what happened in the building garage last night. You may have heard the garage attendant was shot and killed in the garage maybe a little after five while he was parking my truck. They caught up with the guy near the Ferry Building and he was killed in a shootout with the police. The only other casualty was my truck I think it has bullet holes because they impounded it last night. I was kept away from the scene and the Detective had a patrolman drive me home that's about all I know. Baite had a few questions and so did Dick, but I didn't know the answers so we started our workday with little enthusiasm. Dick asked me to get the files on the Hillcrest Housing Development and the

Residential Home project and bring them to his office. We sat at his conference table and spread out the plans for the Residential Care Facility and I put the Hillcrest file to one side. As Dick was looking over the plans he was asking question if I knew where they stood with the Oakland planning commission and if they ran this passed the building department. I told him there were letters of approval for both and construction permits were issued for the plans in front of you for a totally new facility however they also have got approval to rebuild the existing building with an additional building because of its historical value. Cost will have a great deal to do with which they ultimately choose. Dick looked impressed then said, "I like this project and it is something Peter would be interested in; we already have two elderly care homes in our portfolio and if run well are a great asset". My slight head turn to the "We" in Dick's statement about elderly care homes alerted him to my obvious surprised reaction. He smiled with the smile of I should tell you more and he did. In short chopped sentences he told me he and Peter were in many enterprises some partnerships others stock in Peter's companies, but Reliance Industries is not one. I made some facial expression of acknowledgement and he pointed to the Hillcrest file and asked, "What's happening with that project". I told him I heard from Mr. Albononi and he reported that Johnny is done and he's been replaced by Joe Peavy the General Superintendent. I told him I thought that was a smart and logical move he is competent and easy to work with. I haven't heard from the girl out at the Hillcrest construction site about the address and phone number on those mystery invoices I may have to drive out there and see what's what. Dick left me at the conference table and went and sat behind his desk I remained standing and turned to face him when he said, "I'm past being curious about the silent partner of Johnny's we better find out who this guy is".

"How do we do that"?

"I'm not sure, but try looking in the construction company's check book register see if you see any person or company that Johnny made out checks to fairly regularly and you might try and get Mr. Albononi to tell us who he is really representing Johnny or the mystery partner".

I left Dick and went to my office and called the Hillcrest construction company. The girl who handled the books answered and after we greeted each other I asked her if she found those mystery invoices. She apologized and told me mostly all the invoices and for that matter parts of the check register are nowhere to be found she told me Johnny was here into the night the day he was leaving and it appears that's when everything disappeared. I should have been more surprised, but I wasn't it fit Johnny's mindset under pressure cut and run, but maybe in this case grab and run. I buzzed Dick on the intercom and told him things look a lot more serious the girl at the construction site just told me Johnny stayed late last night and most of the records, invoices, and the check register are missing. "Call Albo right now tell him either he find and produce these missing documents with the check register and schedule a meeting with this silent partner or we are going to the authorities and charge Johnny with fraud and embezzlement and anything else the authorities can think of. This, of course, will prompt the calling due of the remaining loan and our Lender will appeal to the court for relief which would mean your Silent partner will lose his investment". I asked Dick to start again at where he said our Lender will appeal because I was writing down exactly what Dick said so I could repeat it verbatim. I called Mr. Albononi and told him verbatim what Dick said he was quiet for a moment or two then asked if anyone knew where Johnny was I responded by telling him we were hoping he could tell us. He then asked me if I could meet him out at the construction site today. I told him the police impounded my truck last night because the garage attendant in our office building was shot and killed in my truck and it's part of the crime scene now so I'll be without wheels for a couple of days. He paused again then asked where I was when the attendant was shot. I told him I was an hour late getting back from a meeting with our attorney so the police just asked me a few questions and I had to leave my truck so a patrolman drove me home. He then asked where the attendant was when he was shot. I told him in the building garage parking my truck. He asked if they have any idea who shot the attendant and I told him he was shot and killed in a shootout with the police. Do they have any information on the identity of the killer? I told him not yet but I was sure it wouldn't be long before they match his figure prints and identify him. He went on to ask me all kinds of questions about the police who were handling the investigation and was any other law enforcement agencies involved in the investigation other than the San Francisco Police. I told him what I knew which wasn't much, but I had the feeling his questions were more than just idle curiosity. Just as I was hanging up I saw Dick in my door way he had his hands in his pockets and started for one of the chairs in front of my desk. He took his hands out of his pockets and repositioned the chair to give him more leg room then said, "I heard half of the conversation so fill me in on the rest". I told him what he hadn't heard and the peculiar questions Albo had about the investigation. He told me Myra called while I was on the phone with Albo she heard about the murder and wanted to know if you were OK. I told her outside of being truck less you were fine which brings me to why I came to your office. We have a deal with a local Ford dealer on leasing cars Baite has all the information on where and how so talk to her and see if you can get a car you like a.s.a.p. I think you should retire that truck because it probably will have gruesome memories even if you repair and clean it up. I walked out to Baite's desk to more or less stretch my legs and to get the information on leasing a car and the person to call at the dealership. I was standing at her desk when the phone rang she picked it up and gave the usual business greeting then said, "Please wait one minute while I see if he is available". She looked up at me and told me it was Detective Norman and he wished to speak to you. I just pointed at my office and told her I'd take it in there. I thought he was calling to tell me they were releasing my truck so I popped behind my desk sat and answered my phone. He asked in a mechanical sounding way how was I feeling then asked if I had time to come down the headquarters tomorrow morning for a briefing on Mr. Farrell's murder. I told him sure and asked what time and he said any time before 10 o'clock. I told him I'd be there and hung up. I didn't think too much about the phone call from Oscar because I had the car leasing on my mind; so I called the person in charge of car leasing and made a commitment for a four door sedan that I could pick up any time tomorrow and she had a choice of three colors.

Chapter 24

I could literally walk to the Vallejo Street Station from my house and I knew the way through the formalities when I entered Head Quarters building so I headed to the second floor to the Homicide Division. I saw Oscar sitting at his desk that was spotted in the corner of this small field of desks and most of them humming with activity with privet offices ringing the field. There was someone sitting with Oscar with his back to me and when I got close enough I realized it was Agent Brophy from the FBI. He turned half way in his chair and gave me a big hello. I answered in kind and we all shook hands and I was offered a seat. I sat, but I had the feeling this was more than just a briefing. Oscar excused himself and said he wanted to tell the Lieutenant I was here. That definitely put me on guard not so much calling the Lieutenant, but that Agent Brophy was here and I couldn't understand why he would be here. I was soon to find out. Brophy tried to make small talk while Oscar was gone and surprisingly he was congenial and told me he was flying solo because his partner Clark was on vacation with his family in Disneyland for the week and his tone was natural and chummy; it did help to calm some of my apprehensions. In due course the Lieutenant came out of his office and headed for us with Oscar in the lead. He introduced me to his superior, Lieutenant Harrison then we formally shook hands. He pulled over an extra chair from another vacant desk and the Lieutenant started the proceedings with a brief explanation that it appears David Farrell was not the intended victim. In a bout of surprise I looked around the desk and everyone was looking at me it was a chilling moment and I got the message. The lieutenant motioned to Oscar and he directed his conversation directly at me and me alone like no one else was there. He started with why they suspected the wrong man was murdered because he was in the wrong place at the wrong time and it sounded feasible to me. He said at first it looked like a murder of revenge or passion mostly because the victim was shot four times by someone not very familiar with guns. The first shot went through the edge of the door while it was slightly open the second went through the window shattering it and the third and fourth rounds went into the victim's body killing him. He reminded me about the fine police work put in motion by a very alert and smart Meter Maid, he said by the way the papers got her name wrong her name is Nora Tomas not Norma Thomson. When the Officer on the scene searched the suspect they found his car keys, wallet, a half empty pack of cigarettes and a half of a round trip ticket on the Alameda Ferry to Oakland. His wallet had a driver's license identifying him as Nathan Bule with an address in Sacramento. We called the Oakland Police and asked them to check and see if they could match this guy's name and address to his car in the Marina. It didn't take twenty minutes to locate his car because he parked it in a restricted zone and they already had ticketed it. They opened the trunk and found torn money rappers used by banks to stack money into specific amounts and the rappers had the identification numbers of the Union Commercial Bank formally of Fremont. As you know that bank was closed by the feds for money laundering so we called the Bureau and that's why Agent Brophy is here. That seemed to be the segue for Brophy to take over the story or briefing or whatever we were in now I was really confused at this point I was getting the drift where they were going, but I couldn't understand how I was involved.

Brophy told me they went back to the crime scene and they found that the door to the Main Power and Telephone room that fed the building was unlocked it was directly across from where David Ferrell, who was now in his street clothes, parked your truck. When they checked it he said they found twelve cigarette butts on the floor by the threshold all the same brand as this guy Bule had on him this suggests a murder in waiting not a crime of opportunity and further inspection they found a crumpled note paper in the trash can with the address 300 Montgomery, the color of your truck and its license number with a notation between 4:30 and 5:30. The note paper is at our lab for figure print analysis and we hope to get results shortly.

It was like a revelation all at once the briefing became a testament to a murder for hire and I was the intended victim.

For almost a full minute I vacillated back and forth from anger and fright to a feeling of desperation. They let me go through my silent emotions then Brophy in a very even voice asked if I knew of anyone who wanted me dead. I looked up and zeroed in on him then rocking my head back and forth I almost said no one when I suddenly could visualize Johnny Peresci threatening me with that sardonic smile in my office and the job site confrontation. My expression must have registered with Brophy because he said who is it? I told him I'd rather not say until I give it more thought. He made some nasal sound that I took for understanding my plight, but then told me about the finger prints. He said there were no prints on the gun except for this guy Bule, but the shell casings had the prints of a guy named Ponzine who works for a concrete company owned by Freddy "Beans" Cannelli. Ponzine and Bule at one time shared a cell in Folsom Prison. Nino Ponzine has been out for two years, but Bule just got out three months ago it's an easy stretch to prove they have been in contact with each other and the prints on the shell casings will bring Ponzine into this as a conspirator if not the one who ordered the paid for the hit. It would be a slam-dunk if his prints are on those money rappers from the bank. He asked if any of the names of these people rang a bell. I told him yeah Cannelli, because he was in the papers, but I never met him. Then he asked me if I could think of any one that might be connected to these guys from the East Bay Alex Albononi immediately came to mind. I finally realized I better tell them about Johnny Peresci and the problem at the construction site in Union City mainly because I thought he was capable of murder and also stupid enough to hire those morons that left this trail probably right to him. Both Oscar and Brophy took notes of my whole story of the missing mystery invoices and parts of the check register and forcing Johnny Peresci to resign as managing partner and appointing someone to take his place and now Johnny has disappeared. Oscar was a little more reserved about my revelation, but Brophy smelled blood he jumped right on the phone and was calling someone over in Oakland, but they weren't there so he left a message for them to call him a.s.a.p. While he was doing that Oscar asked me if I knew of any of Johnny's hang outs. I told him I wouldn't know because our only contact was business. There was more questions than Brophy's pager went off it was a number from Oakland. He pointed to Oscar's phone and asked do you mind if I use your phone. Oscar just moved his phone closer to Brophy so he could dial. He reread his pager then dialed the number and when they answered he just said great and hung up. With a big smile he blurted out they found a key hidden it the car's upholstery; it's a locker key so they're checking the bus terminal, train station and the airport. Without thinking I asked why he would take the money out of the rappers if he was going to stash it in a locker. All three quickly glanced at one another, with the who's going to tell him look, then the Lieutenant told me he probably wanted to count it and that old adage about there is no honor among thieves still holds true. That news got Brophy on the move he excused himself and said he had to get over to Oakland and left. The Lieutenant made his excuses and headed for his office that left just Oscar; he asked me if I had any questions I told him no so we ended it there. I left the Police Station then walked down to Columbus and on the spur of the moment decided to walk down Columbus to my office it was a pleasant walk and all downhill and I really had to do some thinking. When I got to the office it was after lunch and Baite asked me when I was going to pick up the lease car she said they have all the papers made out is all you have to do is sign them and drive it away. I apologized and said I couldn't imagine how it slipped my mind I'll get moving as soon as I check my messages. As I was heading for my office she told me Joe Peavy called twice. I sat at my desk filtering through the messages and I put Joe's aside to call him first then I saw a call from a Bryan Cordy junior. I was uneasy about a call from the son of the owner of the S & L because I was sure it was without his father's approval. Before I called Joe Peavy I called Myra and let her know about this call from Bryan Cordy junior; she told me to return his call because he was either selling his father down the river to better his position when the business was sold or his father is behind this to find out the starting price we're willing to offer. Either way we'll find out more than they do. I hung up and called Joe Peavy he told me he was going through the Trailer Office with Joan the office Girl-Friday/manager trying to piece thing together and they found three blank invoices from the mystery company and a cancelled check from the Oakland State Bank made out to Sunloc Building Materials the same name as the mystery invoices and signed by John Peresci. I explained my truck was down and I'm in the process of leasing a car so it was more than likely I wouldn't be able to get out there until tomorrow so guard them with your life and I'll see you then. I buzzed Dick and asked if he had a few minutes and I was off to his office. I told him what Peavy just told me and he seemed elated he said this is the leverage we can use to have Mr. Albononi reveal Johnny's partner it could make everyone's life a lot easier. I told him about the call from Bryan Cordy junior and asked him if he could give me some idea of how to handle the situation; he said the best thing to do when you really don't know what is on this fellows mind is to let him do all the talking and say nothing more the "I'll see what I can do" or anything to that effect in that way you'll get an idea what this fellow is really after. Before I left the office to pick up my lease car I called Bryan Cordy junior telling him I was returning his call and we agreed to meet at my office around 5 o'clock. Of course, Baite was right the salesman was waiting for me with all the papers and I signed them then we went to the lot to pick out the color car. Wouldn't you know there was a forest green, a blue and a dark gray? I was really tempted by the forest green, but for the sake of, "Peace in our time", I picked the gray. The salesman got the information he needed from the car and I was off to the parking garage under 300 Montgomery I passed the crime scene still taped off and parked in my old space. I got to the office around 4:30 and first thing Baite said, "Do you like your new car"? I told her fine it was a nice solid car and handles well. Then she asked what color. I told her gray and she called me a wimp for caving into my mother-in-law.

"What makes you say that'?

"Anne called right after I talked to the salesman and he told me the colors available then Anne told me about your mother in law's aversion to green or black so we bet what color you would pick. I told Anne definitely green she just laughed and told me gray and I owe her lunch at Momma's". I told her to enjoy her lunch. On my way to my office Baite told me Anne wanted me to call her at home when I got a chance and there were no other messages. I settled into my chair and began preparing for Mr. Cordy and I noticed Dick's privet phone line was lit and at that moment I heard Bryan Cordy in the outer office. Baite was getting ready to leave so I went to the doorway of my office and told him to come right in. You couldn't help noticing the resemblance to his father, but not as athletic looking and less out going. His hair was strawberry blond as his father's once was but his hair line was receding much too fast for his age. He sat and I offered him coffee or tea and he looked at me strange like it was a joke so I couldn't resist I went into my routine, "I used to go with an airline Stu and it rubbed off". He thought that was strange too so I dropped it and asked the safe question, "How can I help you". He hemmed and hawed then finally got to why he wanted the meeting in sort of a roundabout way. "I have an insurance brokerage and Real Estate business down the peninsular along with a few investments one of which is a commercial sausage company that is going very well and expanding; my father has a piece of them all. One of the stipulations he made when he invested in them was that the Cordy name would be prominent and as the S & L is also named Cordy their name is linked inseparably."

"Let me stop you there when you say prominent you mean he wanted his name on the businesses".

He nodded then said, "Yes".

"I'm sorry please continue".

"Well the preliminary offer to buy the Cordy Savings & Loan stipulates that the name goes with the sale of the S & L and all businesses owned or promoting, advertising or otherwise selling any product under that name cease".

"I believe you're right so what's your point"?

"I would like to discuss removing that proviso and that the final offer say that".

"Say what"?

"Spell out that the original name Cordy of our businesses be exempt from that proviso. Of course, we would compensate you for removing that proviso".

I automatically glanced at Dick's privet line on the phone and it was still lit so I stalled by looking at something on the wall and pondered if I should bring Dick into this surprising offer. I thought not and decided to tell him later rather than have him blindsided by this offer. The silence was getting embarrassing so I said the first thing that came to my mind, "I'll see what I can do". That seemed to mollify Bryan as a smile of satisfaction crossed his face then he asked how long did I think it would take to get back to him.

"Well Mr. Travillian has the final decision, but I'll see what I can do".

That seemed to satisfy him and out of the blue asked if he could have that cup of coffee. I told him no problem and I went to the file room and there was a problem Baite had cleaned up the coffee station so there was no coffee. I didn't know where half the stuff was to make the coffee so I limped back to my office with the word we were out of coffee. He took the news stoically and after a brief hesitation said he should be on his way to beat the traffic commute down the Peninsular. He thanked me and left.

I waited until the light on Dick's privet line went out then went to his office. I told him of Cordy junior's proposal that would eliminate the name proviso and he was offering compensation. Dick looked incredulous he said, "That means the old man wants to let the name go with the sale of the S & L and the Son wants to keep it; at least for the businesses he controls. Well at least we know the old man will sell the name along with his business". Dick asked me if I made any verbal commitments and I told him no and he said that's good that means the old man must have financed this Son's business ventures and has control of the son's businesses otherwise he wouldn't be here making this kind of an offer. That's a good and bad situation I don't know if you would want to eliminate that proviso for junior because it will weaken the final offer. I'll call Peter and let him know about the Son's offer. By the way I just got off the phone with Peter he told me to tell you not to go any further with the Residential Care Facility over in Oakland he wants to handle it so he's coming out here to meet with Dr. Yee. Peter wants me to find him a condominium somewhere close to the office so when he's in town he can walk to the office, but the main thing we talked about is increasing the office space. He wants to have his own office as a center for his San Francisco and Bay Area projects and for that we need room for expansion so I was looking around and the management here told me the office space next door will be available in a month or so. I'd like you to look into that and may be do a lay out then if it looks feasible we'll have plans drawn up. I asked him if he could give me an idea how big a space we would need. He told me, "Two large offices facing Montgomery with windows and two other offices and a storeroom for office material and files and a mid-size conference room and a larger reception area; any questions ask Baite she can help you with it. Before you go I thought of something after you mentioned that mystery building supply company Sun-something I think that company was involved in the first project Johnny and his family were involved with. See if you can check with John Mace's files he kept them meticulously I'm sure he kept track of all payments".

"I wouldn't know where to start the FBI took all those files last year". "Start with the FBI they were asking for your help see if they'll extend theirs". I did just that and left a message on their answering service at the Bureau for either Brophy or Clark to call me. I buttoned up the office and left.

By the time I got home it was after seven and I noticed my father-in-law's car right in front of our house for an instant I got the notion this would be a frequent sight. After all his new found freedom from the business would give my mother-in-law new found freedom of movement with her personal chauffer. I swung around into the ally and parked in the back when I entered the kitchen the first words out of my mother-in-law's mouth was let's see your new car. I just pointed to the back and went to the frig for a beer. Anne and her father were sitting at the kitchen table elbow deep in paperwork. He looked up and said inventory what a pain in the ass, but it has to be accurate for the sale. I just put my hand up in a I understand gesture. Five minutes later my Mother-in-law came back and wanted to know why I got a dark color gray; you should have gotten the light gray so it doesn't show the dirt. I told her my choices were either the black or forest green. She remarked it's not much of a choice and the forest green would hide the dirt better.

I saw that no one else was paying any attention to my Mother-in-law that's when I realized it was the secret to family harmony so I commented, of course, you're right and kept nodding as she babbled on. I have to say her cooking was worth the aggravation.

I was a little late getting into the office the next morning and Baite was on the phone so she just held up my messages as I passed. I speared them on the run and waved to Dick as I was passing his office on my way to mine. I put my brief case next to my desk and slid into my chair. There were two messages one from Bryan Cordy and the other from Agent Clark of the FBI. Clark left his direct number which I thought put me one notch higher on his list, but I wasn't sure what list. I called him first and he answered on the second ring with a flat sounding "Clark". In contrast I gave him my Sunday greeting and asked, "How was your trip to Disneyland". The tone of his voice changed and got more excited or for him titillated as he told me how much his kids enjoyed the whole experience and found himself enjoying all the excitement of the rides just as much as the kids; it's a hell of a place I highly recommend it. He ended this flurry of emotion with his usual flat sounding greeting or maybe it was a question, "How can I help you"?

His tone made me cautious so I decided to be as vague as possible so as not to let him know I was fishing for something in particular in any of Mace's files. I told him I had an idea that there was something in one of Mace's files that pertains to one of my projects and it was right on the edge of my mind but I couldn't remember so I wanted a quick look into his files to see if it triggers anything. He asked if I could be more specific so he knew which files I was talking about. I was right he was trying to find out which file I was looking for and, of course, I would never get to see it until he reread it, screened it and sanitized anything he didn't want me to see then maybe he'd show it to me if I promised something in return. He finally agreed after the more he asked the vaguer I got so he told me it would take at least a week to locate the files and he would call me when they were located. I thanked him then hung up.

I looked at the message from Bryan Cordy and was trying to decide if he was going to be a pest about this name change proposed in the preliminary proposal and if so how to handle it. Should I give him the same chorus of "I'll see what I can do" or actually try to help him. I decide to call him and find out what he wants. He picked up this phone on the second ring so I was two for two; he told me the Accountants were here and they looked serious and they're moving along with a purpose so could you please get me an answer about the name change? I explained there would be no decision until Peter Travillian came to San Francisco which would be in the next week or so. At any rate there would be no final offer until he's here so you'll have to wait until then. That seemed to satisfy him and after a few apologies for pestering me I ended with a now familiar I'll see what I can do. I popped into Dick's office and told him about Bryan Cordy's concerns and how we left it then to Agent Clark's response to my request for a peak into John Mace's files and the vagueness of that request so he would need me to figure the specific file of interest after all there must have been two hundred of them. Dick just nodded his head in agreement then told me he agreed and also he remembers some of them an inch or two thick that would keep Agent Clark in reading material for his career at the Bureau; that was very clever being vague let's see how critical he thinks the information you're interested in is? While we were talking Baite buzzed Dick to tell him Joe Peavy wanted to talk to me and it was important. Dick handed the phone to me and said it's Joe Peavy and it's important. When I answered he sounded half excited and half annoyed when he told me Mr. Albononi was at the trailer late yesterday and went through the office and Joan tells me the majority of the phone records are gone it is obvious he took them. I asked Joe if he still had the mystery invoices and the cancelled check he told me he did and I told him I would be out there this afternoon and please wait for me if I'm a little late. After I hung up I told Dick what Joe just told me and I thought it might be a good idea to get the police involved because it's apparent something underhanded is going on. Dick looked to be thinking ahead of me when he said let's hold on I think the Bureau is going to get involved sooner or later so let's give them a chance to sell a few of those houses. I went to my office and got the file for the Blackstone Corporation and the Hillcrest housing Development then headed for my car in the parking garage. When I got off the elevator I naturally looked to the spot where the garage attendant was murdered. The crime scene tapes and my truck were gone, but I could still visualize them and it gave me a chill; I wondered how long I would get these uneasy feelings when I go into the garage. I put that idea into the back of my mind and drove to the construction site in the East Bay.

Just about all the workmen were gone with the exception of a few plumbers probably finishing off the back flow valves. The Development looked beautiful with all the lawns and walkways snaking through the project framing the stucco houses with red tiled rooves into a picture of the American country dream. I drove over to the trailer and parked between two sedans and saw Joe's truck and a familiar car that must be Joan's Johnny's girl-Friday. When I entered Joe was standing talking to a gentleman I thought I recognized but I knew I never met and Alex Albononi sitting in one of the reception chairs with his shirt collar opened and slouching in a somewhat bored looking attitude with Joan Girl-Friday behind her desk. All conversation had stopped when I entered and Joe said he wanted to introduce me to Mr. Peresci, Johnny's father. If the expression "The spitting image" applied it was here Johnny was the walking replica of his father except for the greying hair and a softening of his features; age was treating Mr. Peresci very well. He was dressed in a perfectly tailored suit probably European with a silk tie and soft Italian leather shoes. I was the only other one with a tie on and my off the rack sports coat and chino slacks looked tacky next to Don Peresci. We shook hands and exchanged brief pleasantries I then acknowledged Alex with a nod and smiled at Joan then told her it was nice to finally meet her after talking on the phone so often. She smiled back and mouthed thank you. Joe more or less announced that this was the biggest room so why not have our talk here. This sounded reasonable so Mr. Peresci took the other reception's chair Joan pushed her chair back from her desk to a more relaxed position and Joe and I got folding chairs from the utility room. Before Joe could get into a comfortable position and start this impromptu meeting Alex jumped in with a forceful request that was more like a demand that all material pertaining to the Hillcrest Housing Development be organized into a file and handed over to Mr. Peresci. I couldn't let this go by he was obviously trying to control this meeting and if he got his hands on it no one would ever see this file again. Joe was speechless but I was ready for him so I could hardly disguise my sarcasm when I asked him if he hadn't already done that last night when you searched the office. He got highly indignant and said he was merely trying to find some phone numbers that he was sure were here. Mr. Peresci in a controlled business like voice said, "Let's get to the real issues Johnny has disappeared and God knows where and left this development in a mess; the Hillcrest Development is owned by the Blackstone Corporation which our family owns so if the lender Reliance Industries has no objections we'll sell the remaining houses and make good all debt incurred by Hillcrest Development". It was a sober statement and I didn't know quite how to respond so I fell back to my favorite response, "I'll see what I can do, but by contract the title company handles all the escrows on the sale of the houses and their instructions from the lender is to reimburse all principle and interest to Reliance Industries and the balance is your profit. I'm sure our lawyers will want to talk to you personally".

"Well that's only reasonable, but I'm interested in the chain of construction draws and how were they structured I understand the first stage is completed and sold, but the title company is holding up the final payment can you tell me why"?

I had the feeling Mr. Peresci was being coy or at least partially in the dark as to the sham that went on when Johnny was here. I explained how and when the draws were available, but then told him of the antics of Johnny forging the building inspector name to the final inspection and lying to the same inspector about the availability of the back flow valves from the plumbing supply company that the inspector contacted to distribute the valves to expedite there installation. Now the final inspection is held up until every bit of construction is one hundred percent finished and of course, those back flow valves are still being installed. In the interim it was revealed none of the sub-contractors had been paid so they were paid from the proceeds of Hillcrest's final draw by the escrow officer. Now it has come to our attention that contracts of sale of at least nineteen houses in the first phase were signed buy fictitious buyers making the second phase of the development void. The silence was palpable nobody's eyes were looking in the same direction when Mr. Peresci turned in Joan's direction and said, "Miss Kitmer is in charge of all final sales and I'll ask her to explain the present situation".

"Thank you Mr. Peresci. I've been working for the Blackstone Corporation for seven years in that time I've handled the Real Estate sales for the Company including the last housing development. In practice we try to sell as many houses on the drawing board as we can; that's to say before they're built. In the last two projects Johnny has handled all those sales and when the first house is completed, we make it our model house and the sales are turned over to me and my three sales people who by the way work on commission only. There was actually twenty one sold on the drawing board as you say to fictitious buyers we sold two of them and they're ready for escrow along with the other twenty nine that have been sold with approved mortgages, but that leaves nineteen still bogus. We have plenty of interest every weekend there will be somewhere around thirty people going through the models every day which by the way are sold with the furniture as an incentive to wait for the rest to be sold before they take occupancy. I knew what was going on, but I thought it was all a promotional gimmick you know like, "Gettem while they're hot" or "Don't miss out". Johnny did the same thing in the last development and it work fine".

"Thanks for being so candid, but it's more than just a promotional stunt it changes the dynamics of the deal it's not only illegal to ignore the wording of the contract, but it puts the lender at risk of being in a second position encase of a default".

Everyone seemed to be letting all this sink in when Joe broke the silence with the news that the building inspector has agreed to issue final inspections on each house as the back flow valves are installed instead of all houses being done this means Joan can start the paper work for the escrow company to close these mortgage loans. That news certainly lightened up every one's mood. Alex Albononi left after Joe's news about the final inspection with what sounded like a lame excuse about being late for an appointment. Mr. Peresci asked

Joe to come into Johnny's office to give him an update on the entire development which left Joan and I alone in the reception area. I was fascinated by a design on her blouse it was tiny multi-colored flowers in a vine like configuration circling her collar. Her blouse was white cotton sort of man-tailored, but with sort of puffed sleeves and dark blue slacks. We both tried some small talk I followed her facial expressions as she was talking I was guessing she was in her late forties well groom and trim along with her voice she was a perfect sales presentation package but when it got stale then Joan said, "All this intrigue started with that guy Mace". She said it so unexpected I didn't respond so she must have thought she had to explain what she just said. "When the other development started about three or four years ago Johnny was going through a divorce. His wife got the house, family automobiles and what was in the savings account so Johnny was trying to hide cash and he was using the construction draws from the development, but it was Mace who showed him how to do it. I didn't catch on for quite a while because I was at the other end selling them not in the construction. I still don't know how they did it but somehow Johnny was siphoning off money from the construction draws and charging it to expenses. It was when the project almost went belly up then I realized something was definitely wrong but as luck would have it the market went nuts and the demand and the prices sky rocketed it saved the project and Johnny. Johnny came out smelling like a rose he settled the divorce and the only thing he wound up with was his wife's property in South Lake Tahoe. The property in Tahoe was both a blessing and curse because Johnny liked to gamble and I know he spent too much time at the Lake".

"Do you know how John Mace got involved in Johnny's skimming money from the construction draws"?

"Not really, but Mace had financial connections and I now suppose they used the now defunct Union Commercial Bank here in Fremont; his cousin's bank as a filter for the money".

"I heard Johnny wrote all the checks, but did you ever hear of a building material supplier named SunLoc that he did business with"?

"No and yes, that was a company that Mace dealt with in the first housing development a few years ago, but I've seen neither hide nor hair of them since". I gave her my business card and asked her if she could remember anything more about the Sunloc Company to please call me then I wished her good luck on the sale of the houses and left.

The commute traffic was still at its peak so I just relaxed and went with the flow; from the back of my mind the question pushed its way through who would want me dead and I knew it had to be Johnny Peresci. I finally got to the Bay Bridge and it thinned out so I was home in fifteen minutes still a little shook by my thoughts that I could have been leaving in my truck when that killer could have shot me and not David Farrell. It was later than the normal dinner hour and there were no kitchen aroma's spicing the air then it occurred to me it was left over night. I limped into the kitchen from the pantry to a note on the table definitely in Anne's hand, "You're on your own." I called out Anne's name and she responded telling me she was in the front room. I moved through the hall to the front room and sat or rather plopped into my corduroy wing chair.

"How was your trip to the East Bay"?

"How did you know I went to the East Bay"?

"Baite told me. She said you left for the East Bay late in the afternoon so you might be late getting home plus you didn't look happy".

"Actually it didn't go bad I meet Johnny's Father and then gave Anne everything that went on in a nutshell then asked what was in the frig for left overs".

"Do you want to eat first or after I tell you who called and wanted you to call him after you had your dinner". A brief staring contest ended when Anne told him Mr. Travillian called and left a his number it's a local number so he's in town. Before you call him I was told by a little bird that you might be in more danger then you let on can I ask you what you intend to do. Yeah I'm going to increase my life insurance. Why do you always clown when things get serious? I thought to change the subject and It dawned on me Gina wasn't home so I asked Anne where she was and she told me with her parents buying her ice cream at Ghirardelli's. I said I thought it was a little late to take her to Ghirardelli Square. When she answered I couldn't tell if she was smiling or ready to cry she just said, "It's the Grandparents privilege to spoil their grandchildren". I raised an eye brow and facially nodded then was about to agree when I saw she was welling up and a tear dropped from the corner of one eye when she said, "I do hope we have the same chance to enjoy our grandchildren please be careful I can never replace you". This paused me for a sober moment then I took her in my arms kiss her and asked if she could make me a quick sandwich. She didn't answer she just gave me the evil eye look and punched me in the arm that hurt. I tried to hug her again and this time I got it in the stomach. I decided to make the sandwich myself and then I called Mr. Travillian. He answered on the second ring so I thought I caught him leaving for dinner and I started to apologize when he said, "I'm on central standard time and I actual eat on the plane. The reason I'm calling and interrupting your evening is I just found out that fellow that was murdered in the building garage was supposed to be you; is that so"?

"It looks that way at least that's what the police think".

"It's a stupid question to ask you how do you feel, but I was also told it's being investigated as a professional murder for hire. This has to be unimaginably upsetting for you and your family. I talked to Dick a few hours ago in Palm Springs and he'll be down in that area for a week or so dealing with a problem of some questionable paper from Hemet and I'll try to fill in for him here. Meanwhile I'm sure the police here are doing all they can to protect you, but with your permission I've contacted a company here that specializes in client protection they want to meet with you and set up schedule".

"I'm not sure if that will interfere with the FBI investigation you see the Bureau is involved now because they found a connection to the bank failure and money laundering that they and the IRS has been involved with since the bank failed".

"How is this connected"?

"They have a connection between the failed bank and a gangster type character in Oakland and they see a tie to the developer Johnny Peresci who we are financing in the housing development in Union City. It is now evident he was skimming from the construction draws and I was asking too many question. They think he was the one who paid for the hit that went so badly, well so to speak. There was bad blood between us from the start and with me probing his books and his volatile nature he's a prime suspect and I'm sure it's him. He's now missing and on the run so I don't think he's any threat". Peter was quiet and I literally could hear him thinking when he said, "I'll be in the office early tomorrow we should go over our financial position at the development and hopefully we won't have the feds close it down for investigation I also called Myra we got a preliminary accounting report on the Cordy S & L". When he got off the phone I asked Anne if there was any brandy left. She kind of chuckled and headed for the pantry.

Chapter 25

In the morning I headed for the office with this uneasiness about the entire situation with the Hillcrest Housing Development. I never really thought seriously that the feds would close down the sales of the houses for their investigation, but now it seemed a possibility. Peter was there before me and Baite and he hit the ground running. He was in the conference room with the Hillcrest files and the appraisal of the Oakland apartments for Alex Albononi. He invited me in and pointed to a file of a few pages and said it was the preliminary report on the S & L and it's not bad, but Myra's in court this morning so we'll go over it when she's here. He asked if I had Mace's records on the first housing development for the Blackstone Corporation. I told him I didn't and they were confiscated by the Feds when Mace was murdered. Recently I asked Agent Clark if I could take a look at the files because I had something bothering me about something in the files but couldn't remember and I thought if I could take a peek it would bring it back. I was intentionally vague about what file I was looking for because if I told him he would look it up himself and I'd never see it; this way he might let me take a look and he would make note of what I was interested in and then scrutinize that particular file. He gave me the usual dodge about the files being hard to find and he'd get back to me.

"What were you looking for"?

"A mystery company called Sunloc Building Materials. We found a few blank invoices with the company heading and a void check made out to the same company. In talking to the person head of the sales she told me she remembered that name from the first housing development and Mace was involved with that company, but nothing since then. So Dick told me to see if I could get a hold of Mace's files and I'm still waiting". Peter looked at me strangely and said, "When you did that appraisal for Alex Albononi and you pointed out the disparity between the extensive upgrade of the building complex and the lack of money spent to do it. I thought of what you said about him not handing you the cost sheet of the renovations, but it was the manager that did. I recalled that is how he beat it the last time he claimed his hands were clean because he never touched any money or money records he was just a consultant; It smacked of illicit cash and started me thinking because it brought to mind the same thing Albononi was accused of in Pittsburg money laundering. I looked up the tax rolls on that particular property and the owner is a corporation so I looked up the corporation and it's a quickie out of Delaware, "Truckers of Limitation Real Estate Investments LLC" and the president is a Margo Cannelli, wife of Freddy Beans Cannelli. It's all set up with Limited liability for all of the corporate officers and the property has been refinanced for seven hundred and eighty thousand dollars with all profit tax deferred until the property is sold or changes hands; it would be interesting to find out how many other properties are under that umbrella. If the feds were told where to look they would see the finger prints of money laundering all over the paper work. I can't help feeling there is some connection between this Corporation and the Hillcrest

Development and it's definitely shady, the question is what do we do now; do we tell the Feds or let them catch up. I want to secure our loan and be fully paid back, but there is a risk of looking or being complicit in this money laundering scheme".

"I've had a thought for a while about that appraisal for Albononi it was so blatant they may have thought I was going to pick up where Mace left off and be a financial conduit for their money laundering".

"You couldn't be more right". Peter said.

"Let me get back to the Hillcrest question why not let me see where this Sunloc Company is and how it is connected to the Hillcrest Development and more importantly if Johnny was sending them bogus payments".

"How do you propose to do that"?

"I'll call Agent Clark about John Mace's files and tell him I'm interested in the file on the Housing Development four years ago in Union City where Mace was doing some extra curricula financing with a bogus Company and we think Johnny was using the same company in the Hillcrest

Development, but it's unclear which. It's possible he'll need us to identify the bogus company and just asking for the search would clear us of any complicity and it might tell us where the money went".

Peter remarked. "That's good thinking why not go with that and see where it leads and let's get Myra in on this".

I was leaving the conference room heading for my office when Baite waved a message memo at me I took a quick peek at it and it was from Detective Norman asking me to call him as soon as I got the message. I did just that when I got to my office. His partner Medwin answered on the second ring when I told him I was returning Oscar's call he said, "How timely we just got word Johnny Peresci paid Ponzine two thousand dollars to hit the wrong man it must feel bitter sweet you were not the guy, but then again you should be feeling upset that the price was so cheap. He said hold on he just left the Lieutenant's office and he's walking funny I believe he just got an ass chewing". I took that as Medwin's weird sense of humor. When Oscar got on the phone he told me his Lieutenant was just filling him in on the latest development in the Farrell murder. "We've been told Ponzine has turned and said Johnny Peresci was the one who paid him to find a hitman to murder you and why. That was the interesting part of his statement he said Johnny told him you were a pain in the ass and wouldn't stop interfering in his housing project. It sounds like he's pretty touchy what the hell did you do"?

"To be honest with you I'm not sure why he would try and kill me. There was a late advisory from the State to add a special valve to the water supply to all the houses Johnny either ignored it or forgot it, but the plumbing inspector was on site asking when the valves were going to be installed. Of course, the Plumbing contractor didn't know what he was talking about so I stepped in and told the inspector they were on back order that seemed to smooth things over, but Johnny was in ear shot and later threatened me then told me to mind my own business".

Oscar sounded almost lamenting as he said, "He's a weird duck how do you understand someone like him and his cousin they're given the best possible business situation from their fathers and they destroy it with ineptitude and greed; by the way I saw Tom the other night at the Jolly Friars and he told me Allen, Mary Mace's friend is in bad shape they're giving him only a short time to live".

"I knew he was in some stages of AIDS when Mary left Las Vegas to come here and help his partner Jean Le Beau care for him and help at their boutique so I'm not shocked, but I don't wish that on anybody".

"I know what you mean and an irony in all this is I always thought he had something to do with John Mace's murder". I was taken back by the timing of his remark and could only say "Really"?

"You must think it sounds heartless but I'm a cop and there was too much circumstantial evidence to think he wasn't, but I'm not saying this is some sort of divine retribution it's more like you're responsible for your own actions. Aside from that you can relax a bit Johnny is on the run and everyone is looking for him I'll try to keep you posted".

I got up from my desk returned to the conference room to tell Peter what I had just been told by a S.F. Detective that it was confirmed Johnny Peresci paid for my attempted murder. Let me say from the past experience with the Bureau they can be relentless and they have been after this guy Cannelli for years and they'll be looking for a connection between Johnny, the Hillcrest Development and Cannelli and I'm afraid we're in the middle. I think we better tell Clark or Brophy about the Sunloc Building Material Company".

"That changes things completely I'll call Myra and as soon as she is free we'll get together and see what her approach would be to this situation with the Hillcrest Development. We may have to orbit the S & L deal until this is settled let's see what she says".

"What do I say to Brophy or Clark when they call about the Mace files"?

"Tell them the truth we think we have a lead for them, but we want our lawyer present when we explain the course of events".

Myra met us at our office two days later it gave us time to adjust to all that had happened and fill Myra in on the latest developments in the Hillcrest mess. Dick had returned from Hemet and he had Baite set up a meeting in our conference room for Myra, Peter, Dick and myself with plenty of coffee, pastry and all the essentials for a long siege. I kicked it off with the news that the Feds had not returned our call, but I was contacted by Joan Kitmer from the Blackstone Corporation letting me know that Brophy and Clark are going over the finances of the Hillcrest Housing Development and when I get a chance please call her.

I called her right back and I wasn't quite sure what to expect, but she told me she found an envelope from the first housing development from three or four years ago with a receipt for a bank check made out to John Mace for fifteen hundred dollars. The interesting part it was from Sunloc Building Materials and Supplies and the check was issued by Drays Savings and Trust. She told me they never dealt with that Savings Company because it was privet and wasn't federally insured and along with the check receipt were invoices from

Sunloc Building Materials and Supplies. I asked her if she told the Feds about the envelope and she said they had already left. I was about to ask what they thought I should do when Dick's voice seething with anger said, "The son of a bitch was taking kickbacks". Peter appeared more introspective when he said, "That could be but he also could have been the brains behind this embezzlement. I wouldn't mind looking into that Sunloc Company; I wouldn't be surprised if it's a shell company and he set it up; this would give Johnny the opportunity to skim profits from his father and the IRS, I think it's safe to say his father is his mysterious silent partner. Peter told me I'd better call Joan Kitmer back and make sure she notifies the FBI about the envelope with the invoices and check stub from John Mace. If they find out we knew about evidence and didn't tell them we'd be in their cross-hairs".

Myra wanted to get everyone back on target when she said, "Let the Feds handle the Hillcrest mess and Johnny Peresci when it all plays out we'll have a better idea what went on and how to handle it. Meanwhile we have the S & L acquisition on our agenda and the accounting firm has finished their audit. I believe you all have a copy on the table in front of you. However before we get started I have to ask Peter if he is still adamant about retaining the company name Cordy and being included as part of the offer".

"Not necessarily I take it the old man is ego-centric and he would be especially sensitive to who and how he's name would be used so It's nothing more than a bargaining chip".

"So you wouldn't be opposed to seeding the name and logo back to Cordy".

"No, but I want him to sweat a little it will make it easier to deal with him on other points of contention. Don't take it out of the offer yet we'll let him bring it up then we'll give in; it will puff up his ego so we can win on more important issues on a quid pro quo basis". Myra just smiled and asked the rest of us if we wanted to add anything to that. I had to put my two cents in so I said, "You all know about his son Bryan calling me in a panic about the loss of the company name so if we could delay negotiating on that point for a while so we can get him to do some digging into this Drays Trust company in its relationship to the Sunloc Company as Peter said it would be on a quid pro quo bases it might help us on any legal and financial problems with our Hillcrest loan". Dick asked, "What would that get us".

"We would know what the Feds know and it might help in the Feds decision to either hold up the sales of the houses while they complete their investigation or not. After all they will start investigating the Blackstone Development from four years ago and progress to the present Hillcrest Development that could take forever and mean while freeze all the assets during their investigation". You could tell Dick was still angry about Mace and his fifteen hundred dollar kick back when he blurted out, "They can't do that without a court order and Myra can stop it with an injunction". That got Myra almost out of her seat, "That's not always the case Dick you have to remember the Feds by definition means the FBI, IRS and the Treasury not to mention the two police departments involved in the murder that is now connected to a bank fraud case and if it got that far I guarantee they know which judges would be sympathetic to them and try to steer it their way". We discussed the problem from different angles then everyone agreed I was on the right track and to go ahead with my scheme. Myra said if it was o.k. with everyone she would arrange a meeting with the group representing the Cordy S & L a week from Wednesday. She made a point of looking at Peter for a yes or no and he told her he was here until this is done one way or another; besides I'm shopping for a Condo or a decent apartment here in the city so I'll be living here part time between here and Pittsburg. Then almost as an afterthought, "By the way Jim how are we doing with the new office space"?

Dick answered for me. "Baite took over that job, the management here offered to add on to our existing space or there is available space on the tenth floor".

"What's the advantage in moving to the tenth floor"?

"Not much it's a few cents more a square foot unless you like altitude the view will be still Montgomery Street however we won't have to suffer the construction noise and dirt while they reconfigure the space to our specifications".

"That sounds like we're moving to the tenth floor".

I asked Peter if he wanted me to look into the Dray outfit and Sunloc building Supplies. He started to hesitate then said yeah, but be careful and don't get your nose broken. That got everyone laughing, but I wasn't sure if he was serious or not so I let it go at that. He put his finger in the air and said, "Wait, one more thing check on Dr. Yee's credibility in the Oakland neighborhood

I already talked to the AMA and checked his liability insurance and he looks clean, but I'm interested if he has had any problems locally".

Oscar Norman was on his phone talking to someone in the Las Vegas Metro Police and it seemed forever. Medwin was sitting at his desk across from him asking silently half in sign language and half in mouthing who was it. Oscar just waved him off then gave him the wait a minute sign. Medwin sat back in his chair until Oscar was finished and hung up and said, "Who was that".

"That was a detective named Slough from Las Vegas he's in the joint investigation with the FBI on the Corsey death and the Addlemann murder he had some questions about the John Mace murder".

"What do you mean the Corsey death don't you mean murder".

"Well this is the story I get from Slough it seems Brophy and Clark are assisting the local Bureau in both investigations because they have a scenario that connects the murders of John Mace with these two deaths to the Mob. He said one finding has become controversial and it is really how you want to interpret it; the cocaine used in the Addlemann murder was pure and everyone agrees it would have been cut five times before a hooker got her hands on it. The Feds say that proves it was a Mob hit because they had the connections to get pure cocaine. The other argument is that in the Las Vegas night life it is not unusual to buy pure cocaine. The thing that got pushed aside is the Laboratory Mary Mace worked at, Goslar Labs, had a contract to liquefy cocaine for medical use, but they claim their records show no cocaine missing. To further slow up the investigation is the insurance company they're going along with the accidental death of Corsey because they made a deal with the Casino to forgo payment of the policy by just replacing the KEY MAN with a fellow by the name of Morgan; this was some caveat attached to the policy with this stipulation. But what Slough told me was even more interesting there's an elevator security guard at the Casino in Jean told him he thought the woman with Addlemann was a guy in drag or more likely a hooker posing as a guy in drag because she made a project out of lighting a cigarette by cupping her hands around the match to insure a light and after holding the cigarette between her thumb and index finger like a man would, he said it even looked rehearsed".

"Did he say if he could get anybody else to corroborate the security guard's story"? Medwin asked.

"No, but he found out Corsey was very interested in what Mary Mace did at her job at the Goslar Laboratory so much so the owner told Mary to have him stop annoying her co-workers with all his questions and yeah Slough said she worked in their formulating pesticides department and one of the pesticides contained arsenic".

Medwin chimed in with the comment, "This whole investigation points to a pretty sophisticated plan and execution to me the Mob would sent two guys with baseball bats to do the job".

"So you think Mary Mace was a good candidate for this Hooker that was the last person to see Addlemann alive"?

"Well she knew Addlemann and in theory had access to the means to kill him also how to contact him in San Francisco. Corsey went way back with her they were once in the same show in Las Vegas and they all were trying to find her husband's hidden cash. I'll bet Corsey found out something about her she would do anything to keep quiet; and by the way did anyone connect Addlemann to Corsey's death or is that part guess work"?

"Funny you should ask Brophy and Clark are part of the joint investigation with the Las Vegas Metro and controlling the information so evidently Detective Slough is now in the same position as we were in the John Mace murder".

Medwin was sitting in thought then looked up at Oscar who was grinning.

"You're grinning because you're thinking the same thing I am"?

"You bet; The Feds are going to make this a Mob hit if kills every one".

I was sitting in my office fiddling with my roller-dex trying to figure out how best to approach Bryan Cordy about any information on this Dray Savings and Trust and giving him the impression I'm helping him keep his company name without being specific. I finally gave up and just called him. He wasn't in so I left a message to call me. Baite buzzed me on the intercom to tell me the building management and their architect was on the tenth floor and wanted to see me to finalize the office plans. When I got to the future office space I was surprised they had already gutted the old offices and

I must have looked it. Because Mister Neuhaus, the building manager, smiled and said you're surprised we are moving as fast as we are? I just nodded my approval. He then turned to the man with him and introduced him as the architect J. V. Prince. We shook hands and made our way to a plywood table with the drawings for the new offices. We went over them and I saw they were the same as the proposed drawings with a few minor changes so I initialed them and left them to their work and returned to my office. While I was gone Bryan called so I called right back we said our helloes and he asked what's new. I told him I was calling about a favor and if he could give me any information at all about an outfit over in Oakland named Dray Saving & Trust. He told me he knew of them and the head man was a guy named Vince Kerrigan, but that was all he could tell me. Then he said the person you should be talking to is Larry Armorson he knows everyone in the business. He then asked me if I was making any head way in helping him keeping their company name. I told him yes and no it seems Mr. Travillian likes your company name because it co-insides with a company he owns in Pittsburg with the same letters and it's an acronym, he likes acronyms. We'll have to see where this goes, but I'm not the only one in our mix that thinks it's a weak condition of sale. He bought that even though I thought it was a lame answer. I was just hanging up when Baite put a note in front of me it was Mary Mace called and would please call her a.s.a.p. then she told me she had an errand to run and if I would watch the phones. I said sure and called Mary Mace.

The phone rang six or seven times and I was about to hang up when Jean answered with his formal business greeting. I told him who I was and asked if Mary was available. He told me to hang on and I could hear him calling her. When she got to the phone she sounded out of breath, she thanked me for calling right back and said she was outside having a cigarette. I mentioned that I didn't know she smoked and she quickly said on and off when I'm stressed. She said she called to make sure the situation was the same with Union Street and nothing had changed. I assured her it was and she told me she heard from the probate lawyer in San Diego and the total inheritance is over three hundred thousand dollars and I could deposit it into my bank of choice and wanted to know what she should do. I told her not to do anything at the moment and that I would get back to her with all the information she needed on the disposition of the property and where to transfer the money. I started to thumb through my roller-dex for the Hanaford S & L number when it dawned on me that young man at the S & L never called me back about the existing mortgage. As I dialed their number I could feel my resentment building when I got the young man that I originally talked to, to my surprise he remembered me and my question about the mortgage on the Union Street property his courtesy completely disarmed me. When I asked why no one called me back he seemed surprised then told me he gave my message to Mr. Byrd and just assumed he would call me. I then asked if I could talk to someone on the same matter. He was hesitant for a moment or two then told me there was a flag in my account and Mr. Byrd was the only one to handle that account. I asked if he would transfer me to Mr. Byrd's number. He said he would try and in a few seconds I got Byrd's answering machine I left my name and a brief message and a thinly veiled threat to take my account higher to get it resolved. Amazingly Harry Byrd called me back with in a half an hour with a sappy apology telling me his secretary misplaced the original message and he was only too happy to answer any questions pertaining to the mortgage on the Union Street property. I repeated the first message that his secretary misplaced and my primary question was about the prepayment penalty. He seemed to have a pat answer but then said he would reduce the prepayment by half if there was a substantial deduction in the Mortgage. I thought of something John Mace would often say, "Prepayment penalty is like being pregnant you are or you're not there's no half way". I felt something was wrong mostly because Byrd had lost his condescending tone and his unconvincing attempt at friendliness. I thank him and told him I would get back to him. Without much thought I just dialed Larry Armorson's number at Cordy S & L and got him directly and realized it was lunch time so I told him I didn't pay attention to the time and was sorry if I interrupted his lunch. He said, "No big deal I'm manning the fort every-body's out to lunch so what up"? I explained to him the situation at the Hanaford S & L and the peculiar offer from Harry Byrd and was he familiar with this discounting of the prepayment penalty.

"Now you're asking me to rat out a brother Savings & loan officer especially since he was my boss at the

Hanaford S & L and block my advancement, in said S & L".

The matter of fact way he said it made me laugh and then I asked if he was serious. "He said he most certainly was, but of course, he held no ill will. However Mr. Byrd has his ass in a sling he personally formulated the wording in the mortgage refinancing documents for the Hanaford S & L someone took them to task on that prepayment issue and the California Department of Business Oversight ruled against them voiding all original contracts. It wasn't in the papers, but half the lawyers in the state know so let us say they are amenable to any reasonable solution. I know they are very interested in getting these types of refi's off their books so I could probably make a deal with them on a refi and get you the same deal no prepay and keep the second".

I told him the new buyer wants to reduce the principal so she has more positive income and probably would like to get rid of the second mortgage.

"That makes it juicier. I'll dangle it in front of Byrd I know he'll go for it and after he wiggles and squirms enough to my liking I'll mention the Lady has an inheritance and might be interested in depositing some of it in their S&L.

I stopped him in mid-sentence with a question about Dray Savings & Trust and asked what he could tell me about them.

"What do you want to know"?

"Everything you know".

"That's a lot why don't you give me your clients name and let me take care of her and I'll call you back".

"Sure, her name is Mary Mace and I'll have her call you today".

I called Mary and told her to have the inheritance transferred to the Cordy Saving & Loan here in San Francisco. I gave her Larry's phone number and told her to call him and he would set everything up for her.

Of course, she had a million questions about ownership and when could she have the top flat vacated so she could move in and ten more questions. I told her to call Anne she knows all about the ins and outs of tenant landlord legalities.

In an hour or so Larry called me back and asked what I want to know about Dray Savings & Trust. I asked him if he got Mary Mace and he said yeah and she's all straightened out so what about the S & T? I told him it might be going under a microscope by the Feds and I'm hoping we're not going to be dragged into some messy financial transaction by way of a third party.

"Well let me say I always thought it was a little shaky mainly because it was in the hands of Vince Kerrigan. Originally he was an escrow officer in a title company over in the East Bay that was involved in a co-mingling of company and client's funds; when the dust settled there was a short fall of over one hundred thousand dollars which the partners made good and they accused Vince of embezzling, but the DA couldn't get enough evidence to even indict so the blame was spread around the company as general incompetence and the head man was fired. Vince left the company by popular demand and hook up with the Teamster Local putting together their version of a credit union. My main concern is it is privet and can avoid a lot of official scrutiny. Now that

I've bared my soul to you; you owe me a confidential answer to my question. What would be my position in the S & L if your company buys it, can you tell me where I would stand"?

I told him the truth, "You are one of the reasons Travillian was interest in buying the company rather than just doing business with it".

The FBI contracted Myra and wanted to know what this revelation was that I had that would put them on the right track in their investigation. She told me it was Clark that called and she told him she didn't like his choice of words and if this was the Bureau's attitude we might be better off going to the Press with the story. I also will write a letter to the Bureau explaining our position and the heading won't be "To whom it may concern" it will be addressed to your boss. She said she could hear him swallow his tongue and it almost gaged him, but he apologized and they got on with a normal conversation and to put everyone into the correct pecking order Myra insisted on the meeting be at her office. Myra arranged the meeting in the evening for everyone's convenience. We settled in her office seated around her desk with Brophy next to me on my left and Clark on his left. Myra kick it off by stating if everyone agreed this meeting would be off the record and held strictly to Mr. Kerry's information he has on the Mace files on the Developments of the two Blackstone housing projects in Union City. Everyone nodded in the affirmative and when I mentioned the Sunloc Building Material Company Clark interrupted and said that's old news I hope you didn't drag us down here for that?

I glanced at Myra and she looked annoyed, but said nothing. I thought maybe it was a bad idea to have this off the record and I said so. I noticed Brophy slowly put his hand on Clark's arm to silence him when he said let's start over again. Then Brophy continued; we've been down this road before and it don't work; I'll give you what we have and see if that jives with what you know. I didn't believe him, but we had nothing to lose by telling them what we knew so I told them what we found out and was pretty sure it was the same information they had. Their blank looks confirmed I was right so I pressed on with the information Larry Armorson gave me about Vince Kerrigan and his connection with the Teamsters Local in the East Bay and the Dray Saving & Trust and I emphasized the privet status of the company. This is probably old news to you but what you might not know is Sunloc had a business account there and the administrator of all its accounts is Mr. Kerrigan. I've been lead to believe that one of the major borrowers is a real estate investment company called "Truckers Limitation LLC" and the president is Margo Cannelli. I thought their reaction was predictable there was a short and thoughtful silence as if it was a courtesy then Clark wanted to know if that was it and I replied yes. He thanked us for our information and got up and left with Brophy trailing behind.

As soon as they were out of ear shot Myra said, "Clark couldn't wait to get out of here so he could write down what you told them before he forgot the name of the real estate company and a detail or two".

"You really think so"? I said.

"You can bet on it that's why I wanted anything said off the record they would have to rely on their memory and chances are they won't remember everything so they'll have to call you. Quote, "Just to refresh their memory on a few finer points" unquote. It's a lesson in unpretentiousness which I think will do Clark some good".

Chapter 26

Myra informed all concerned she heard from Mr. Cordy and he was pressing for a final meeting with Mr. Travillian on the sale of his Savings & Loan. We all met at Myra's office and when Peter sat down he had a smirk on his face when he looked at Myra and remarked Cordy has realized you're not a stenographer. She said, "Oh yeah he's quite professional he now calls me counselor". That got a rise out of everyone however Dick looked lost and we all realized Dick had not met Mr. Cordy yet so Peter filled him in on the stenographer joke. Dick just raised an eye brow and said, "I can't wait". Everyone had the paper work from the last meeting so Myra got right to it. She started with the audit pointing out a few weak points in the loan portfolio which she said was probably made simply to close real estate loans from his Real Estate Company, but all their payments were currant so it's a moot point, but they were low interest and already ten years into a thirty year mortgage. He owns the building the business is in so we want it part of the deal. But of course, his appraised evaluation is astronomical so I think this is the biggest negotiating point. The rest is furniture, stationary inventory, good will and of course, the Cordy name. She asked Peter if he had any particular part of this sale he wanted to use as a foil in negotiating over the name Cordy for a logo. He answered promptly, "Oh yeah, we'll start with the price of the building and see where it goes from there". Peter looked around like he was looking for conformation from everyone when Dick said, "You're the boss".

"Well that maybe, but I'm looking for some input does anyone have any ideas or suggestions anything at all? Dick sort of sat back in a comfortable chair and looked distant and that told me he and Peter had kicked this around until their ideas started to contradict one another so motor mouth me jumped in with a suggestion that we just go simple. Take the list of priorities that Myra laid out and present them to Mr. Cordy and see what he comes back with. Peter said, "Why not".

The meeting with Cordy and Company was held in the conference room of the law firm of Sloan, Pacemann & Associates the following Monday at nine A.M. sharp. We all met outside the conference room and greeted each other then entered together. The scene was impressive with law books covering one wall from a few feet from the floor to the ceiling. An oblong oak table split the middle of the room and twelve high back chairs positioned at comfortable intervals with one at each end of the table. There were legal pads, pencils and empty water glasses in front of each chair with several pitchers of ice water strategically positioned within reach of everyone. Without being lead to our seats we all picked chairs on the same side of the table as our colleagues and opposite the Cordy Group. I noticed how everyone picked their seats and wondered if it was by pecking order or natural comfort selection. Mr. Cordy swaggered into the room first spewing confidence and took the first chair from the door and, of course, it was the head of the table; Peter sort of ambled in talking to Dick and settling for the other end of the table. As everyone else filtered in I found my-self sitting opposite Terry Munoz with Dick to my left and Myra to the right of Peter conversely Larry Armorson was to the right of Mr. Cordy and Bryan between Terry and Larry. Peter didn't sit right away he half stood and said, "For anyone who hasn't been introduced to the young man next to Myra he is my partner, major investor Dick Somers the Managing Partner of Scranton & Associates here in San Francisco. A consummate professional he acknowledged humor with an appropriate half smile half grin as he nodded to the other side of the table. Not to be out done Mr. Cordy took the opportunity to introduce Terry Munoz to everyone as his stenographer as he grinned at Myra. At this point it was pointed out by a perky young lady from Myra's office that there was coffee, tea, mineral water and appetizer size pastries on the side board on the opposite wall. Everyone was waiting for someone to move when Peter and Dick headed for the side board it prompted a simultaneous controlled assault on the pastries. Some took their pastry and drinks back to their seats and others stood and drank their coffee while perusing the book shelves. Mr. Cordy took his coffee and cornered Dick and Peter at Peter's end of the table and they chattered until Myra called everyone back to the business at hand. Peter interrupted Myra and told everyone he apologized for creating a stock holders meeting atmosphere rather than an S & L acquisition and it's my fault. I asked Myra for the breakfast buffet because I can't seem to look at food in the morning until nine o'clock. No one seemed to be put off by the buffet however I was sure Mr. Cordy had something to say about it when he talked with Peter and Dick just minutes ago. I felt Mr. Cordy was starting right out of the gate to take control of the negotiations. He confirmed my thoughts when he jumped right in while everyone was still getting settled and asked, "How did we come up with the appraisal of the building the S & L occupied". Without taking a breath he informed everyone he was in the real estate business for over forty years and he never saw such a distorted evaluation. My eyes immediately went down the table to Peter and I didn't have to wait long for a response. He now had his business face on he looked directly down the table at Mr. Cordy as he replied, "The appraisal was done in accordance with the accepted appraisal practices of cost of replacement per square foot, condition of the building, income and expense and other like property comparison sales".

"That is exactly what I'm talking about the numbers and the property used in the comparison".

"Could you elaborate"? Peter replied.

"To start with where did you get the square foot replacement cost at thirty dollar per square foot from"?

"Our appraiser is also a general contractor and is keenly aware of those costs, it's his business, of course, and you're entitled to a second opinion".

I knew Cordy knew I was the appraiser, but I'm not sure he knew I was a general contractor, but Peter's answer definitely side tracked him so he jumped on to the income and expense for the building and told us our figure were wrong and were off by three hundred and fifty dollars per month. Peter's expression never changed when he said, "We took our figures from the accountant that did the audit; you used projected numbers that can only be thought of as out of the thin air". Things were definitely getting tense that's when Larry Armorson interrupted Mr. Cordy and said he thought it might be a good time to take a break. No one answered immediately so Larry stood and stretched like he had been sitting for hours, but the meeting was only forty five minutes old. He asked Cordy if he would like a cup of coffee. He shook his head no and reached for the pitcher of ice water and while pouring he missed and half got on the table. Terry dropped her pen and moved to the end where the water was spilled with some paper towels. Mr. Cordy looked more mad then embarrassed and he moved out of the way and followed Larry to the buffet table. The silence was palpable. I glanced down the table to Peter and he and Dick had their business faces on but Myra had a slight grin on her face like she was enjoying every minute of it. I looked over at Bryant mainly because he was the only one left on that side of the table and he looked stoic his eyes seemed riveted to the buffet table at Larry and his father. It took almost fifteen minutes for Larry to calm Cordy down and by this time everyone was on edge and fidgety. In a more controlled way Cordy asked Peter how the appraiser came to his choice of buildings and locations for his comparisons. Peter's head was down looking at the appraisal he was obviously on the list of comparisons when he looked up and said, "The buildings used for comparison were in the Mission close to the same size as your property with two one bedroom apartments above the commercial businesses and yours were mostly in other areas like the Sunset District, which have higher property values and yours had bigger or more apartments above their commercial businesses. I hardly see how you can use them as a comparison and question ours". Larry again headed Cordy off from saying anything more about the comparisons and brought up business good will. Then reminded everyone of the property's location in a major commercial area and with its well know name and logo which adds to its obvious curb appeal. Peter said, "I absolutely agreed with you and that is why I included your S & L name and logo in our offer". I looked quickly at Bryan he still was stoic and expressionless. Cordy put his hand on Larry's arm to hold him from saying anything and then in an impassioned voice said, "How can you expect me to give up the name and logo I have worked for forty years to earn the respect and admiration here in the Mission Community".

"That is not the case I said from the beginning everything is negotiable".

"So you're telling me I have to negotiate to keep my company name and logo".

"Yes it is, we noted that in our first preliminary offer and as item #7 in our final offer. If you missed it or misinterpreted item #7 we will certainly give you time to review it, but it's on the table to negotiate".

At this point I thought the whole deal was going down the tubes. Mr. Cordy was flustered and his face was red as a beet. Larry Armorson again jumped in and suggested Mr. Travillian might be right and they should take time out to review the final offer. But before anyone could respond Mr. Cordy asked Peter why did he discount the S & L's loan portfolio by thirty percent. Peter's attitude got sterner and his voice followed in kind when he said, "The loans in your portfolio are quoted as the face value at the time they were funded, their average age of their thirty year amortization has twenty years left that leaves eighty percent of their original face value. You can't expect us to assume those loans at their original cost".

"I certainly do, that is the price of doing business in California."

"Mr. Cordy the price of doing business in California is no different than any other part of the country; if you doubt that I will personal fly you to my home town Pittsburg Pennsylvania and introduce you to any number of business organizations and you can present the same case and I guarantee the outcome will be the same as here and now". Mr. Cordy stood and said he didn't think there was anything else to discuss and informed his people they were leaving and they left. Now I was sure the deal was dead. To my left everyone was quiet I sat waiting for a response and it was Dick that asked everyone in general what we thought. I thought the deal was dead, but I didn't say so, Myra hemmed and hawed then said, "I'm sure he wants to retire and when he calms down he'll realize he couldn't bulldoze Peter and swallow his pride then get back to the table with a more realistic counter offer". Dick then asked Peter what he thought. "He tried to sell a pig in a poke his whole counter offer was ridiculous I'm banking on him wanting those loans in his portfolio. He has already made his money on them up front and the remainder will give him an income for twenty years. Conversely they are a stagnant investment for us the payments and interest will never change and because of their age and interest rate they're unsaleable. I believe we can use the loans and his company name and logo as leverage to have him be more realistic on the worth of the business property and his idea of the price of good will. The only thing of value to us is the property it is the only tangible item that will appreciate". Myra asked' "So you want this deal to go through".

"If at all possible, yes, hopefully that was all bluster on his part and if he's sincere in negotiating in a quid pro quo atmosphere I think it can be done. I feel I must bring up one important thing in all these negotiation with Mr. Cordy he is selling his life's work he is bound to inflate himself and the fruits of forty years of work and toil, however I feel we must bring him back down to earth to a more realistic price for his company".

When I got back to the office Baite told me the office space was completed on the tenth floor except for the carpet and the manager wanted to know if I had time to approve of the layout. I asked her if she had a chance to go up and see the new digs. She said she did and asked if I changed the reception area. I told her it was Peter's idea to cut down on the reception area and add an office just to its right. She wanted to know why. I told her Peter wants the office for you and we'll get someone else to answer the phones and take messages. If that means my job description is changed do I still have to make coffee. I told her I had it on good authority only on rainy days. She laughed and said Dick has already told her of her new job, but not about my own office I must be getting up in the world. "I heard the S & L meeting didn't go well".

"It was a disaster I don't know why Mr. Cordy didn't just turn down our final offer and not bother coming to a meeting because he wasn't happy with one point of the offer".

"Because he wants to sell and retire and I'm sure Dick and Peter know this so that's the reason for the give and take approach, I'm sure he'll be back".

"You really think so"?

"Yes I do".

"Well when I left the meeting I'd bet the farm the deal was dead".

"Give it about a week or two and I think you'll hear from them probably Larry Armorson will break the ice by phoning you to test the waters".

"Why are you so sure"?

"I'm not a 100 % sure, but Mr. Cordy has let it be known to anyone who would listen in the Mission, especially a lady that he has been seeing for ten years or better, that he was being courted by a large corporation from back East to buy his business and he had them on the hook for a half a million dollars. If this didn't go through rumors would fly that the offer wasn't near that amount and the buyers backed out then his credibility and not to mention his ego would be tarnish, he couldn't stand to have that happen".

"Did you mention this to Dick and Peter"?

"No I'm sure I don't have to if I'm right Mr. Cordy telegraphed his punches with his behavior at the meeting".

"Thanks for those comments I think they are insightful it makes me think more of what went on at the meeting. By the way before I go and see the Manager did you compile those rent comparisons"?

"Yeah why"?

"They were unquestionably accurate and I'm sure they made the point that Mr. Cordy's rent schedule was a flight of fancy. I have to tell you I stole your thunder everyone assumed they were from my appraisal and I didn't tell them any different".

"Don't get too full of your-self I gave them directly to Dick and he was the one who slid them into your appraisal so your plagiarism is no longer a secret".

"Oh now I can die happy knowing my sin is forgiven".

"Not yet young man I'll be silent if you get me deep pile carpet in my new office".

Without missing a beat I answered, "What color"?

I met Mr. Neuhaus on the tenth floor of our new officers. I reviewed the plans for the office layout and thought they were what we were looking for and I approved them. I then took a number of carpet swatches and when I returned to our office I put them on Baite's desk with a note, "This is the best I could do just remember a deal is a deal so mum's the word".

I no sooner got through the pantry when I could tell things were not right. I opened the kitchen door and glance around, the baby was in her usual place sitting in the high chair playing with her dry cereal there was something on the stove perking away and smelling good, but no Anne. I called out and she answered telling me she would be right out. I went to the frig got a beer and sat down at the kitchen table. Anne came out of the bath room and asked how was my day and I had to ask her what's wrong because it was obvious she had been crying. She took a deep breath and in the most casual tone said it's just a woman's thing however her bottom lip betrayed her, it started to tremble and the tears started flowing. I took her into my arms and knew enough not to try to be funny; Anne doesn't just cry it had to be something deep and of course, I thought of her mother. She squeezed me extra tight then released me and asked if I was hungry she almost immediately changed into my Anne. She said get a couple of plates, knives and forks we got baked eggplant with Romano cheese in a tomato casserole. I chanced a little humor, "Your wish is my command" it didn't quite pass muster. She raised the corner of her lip which wrinkled her nose in mock annoyance then said this looks like a Chianti night. "I love it when you talk like that you look Ava Gardner beautiful".

"If you don't get a move on with the plates and the wine it might be the last thing you get around here". She knew how threats worked on me so I almost stumble getting to the pantry for the wine. We settled down to dinner and were halfway through the Chianti when I ventured the question if her mother was here today. The initial response was slow and deliberate then the rest was an almost incoherent diatribe on her mother's insensitivity, self-centered and self-serving gestures of help. She finally collected her-self and looked at me with those beautiful brown eyes all wet with emotion and then began to explain why her mother is the way she is in her defense, but today it all came to a head. She said it started when her mother was complaining that her father's family was so ungrateful no matter what she did for them she would have to squeeze a thank you out of them. "I thought I was being diplomatic when I told her there were times when they didn't appreciate whatever you did for them to be brought up often enough to be irritating so when you say you help people you sometimes do it for the wrong reasons".

"That's when my mother attacked, as she often does, you think I would be smart enough to avoid getting into these conversations, but no there I was defenseless as she berated me as one of those in her in-law's family and that I didn't appreciate anything she did for me. I don't know why I try to explain to her how other people see her because she's as thick as a log you can't seem to penetrate. And of course, I lost my temper and I told her I thought it was time she should leave and that started another round of accusation and reliving ancient family history according to my mother's version".

The leasing company scheduled to have my car serviced so I notified the office I'd be a little late in the morning. So I was surprised by the reaction of our receptionist Carrol when I walked in because she looked surprised. My in box was empty so I headed for my office. I was intercepted by Dick who asked me to step into his office and Peter was already there and asked me if I wanted coffee. I just knew something was wrong Peter was not a coffee gofer so I told him no and asked what's up. Dick asked me if I read the morning paper. I told him no; so he handed me the Chronical. In bold headlines "The missing East Bay developer found beaten to death in the Delta then left on the side of the road". Peter asked me if I knew this reporter Edmond

Dailey. I immediately glanced at the buy line to see the reporter's name and it was Dailey. I told him no; I never met him. Well you might want to read the article he mentions your name more than once. I didn't get two sentences when I read Johnny Peresci was the East Bay developer that was beaten to death. I froze the rest of the article was a blur I just stood there looking at a mass of print I must have looked catatonic. It probably registered with Dick first that I was unable to decipher the print because he started to explain what was in the article.

"After the splashy headlines this fellow Dailey claims to have been on this story ever since the John Mace murder which he refers to as a "professional mob hit". Peter and I talked about that remark, a mob hit; we agree it had to be leaked to Dailey by the Feds because the local police believe the murder was someone he knew. He weaves you in and out of his article by claiming your connection to Johnny Peresci as quote a money lender and that he paid to have you killed, but of course, his hitman hit the wrong man and he infers by using the term, "He'd been told" that his information came from you. He goes on to rehash the Mace murder and his connection to the failed bank in the East Bay and money laundering than a gory account of Johnny's murder. It's reported he was beaten to death with a baseball bat and the weapon was left next to the body. Dailey believes he was left on the side of the road with the weapon as a warning to others not to do anything without first clearing it with the powers that be. He rationalizes that Johnny was a loose cannon and acted on his own when he hired the two men to kill you and he paid for it with his life". Dick's last sentence was probably the most accurate of the whole article. I slowly came around as Dick was talking and I stared to get a clear picture of what Johnny did and why he was murdered, but a thought passed me and I couldn't quite remember who said it. "That you are responsibly for your own actions". I thought without malice that in Johnny's case he asked for it. I was stuck on my last thought when Dick brought me around with, "Do you think you should call your wife"? I went to my office and called her at home and she was with her father still going over inventory so she hadn't seen the paper. The timing of my call and the tenor of my voice gave away any casual segue into the Chronical story. She immediately asked what was wrong. I started to tell her the news story from the middle of the story then realized I hadn't organized it in my mind so the story got ass backwards. I gave up and told her Johnny Peresci was murdered.

"Well from all accounts he was skating on thin ice for quite a while and it seems it all caught up with him. I know it sounds cruel, but it makes for a safer atmosphere for you." We talked for a while longer about trivial things to normalize the news and I hung up. I sat at my desk and the feeling of relief was creeping into my mind to a point I felt relaxed and normal Anne was right with Johnny dead I felt safer.

Chapter 27

Myra called to tell me she heard from Larry Armorson asking for a meeting to work out the differences between our Companies on the acquisition of the S&L. I told him I would have to check with you so are you free to sit down with them soon or let me know when and I'll put it on my calendar. But keep in mind we have to go over the Savings and Loan's history and it depends on how you look at it the history is shaky.

"What do you mean shaky"?

"We'll go over those points when we meet."

"Give me a hint what points are you talking about"?

"Government Regulators have an acronym "CAMELS" it stands for six topics to insure safety and soundness of banks and S&L's; Mister Cordy's S&L was in trouble in all six categories especially C for capital adequacy and E for earnings. It was about that time Larry Armorson jointed the S&L and I'm sure with his savvy of these regulations he got the S&L back on track. The regulating agency at that time was lax and I could find no follow up by any of the agents; that might give us some leverage in the negotiations by asking Mr. Cordy what was the final disposition by the Regulatory Agency"?

"My God you have that framed in a way that only a lawyer could handle it".

"That's why I'm here".

"We better make it sooner than later how about Wednesday next week"?

"My calendar is clear you're on, but make sure you leave time to go over those Government Regulations".

"See you this Wednesday".

When I got back from lunch there was a message from a Mrs. Wright it took me a minute or two to recall who she was and it dawned on me she was involved in the property appraisal in Berkeley for Mr. Albononi. I gave her a call and she told me their financial adviser moved and in doing so lost or misplaced the appraisal for the property in Berkeley. She was wondering if I kept a copy at my office and if so; would I send her a copy. She sounded young and to my recollection the woman I talked to at the property was older so I got vague and told her I would check our files and I would get back to her. She asked if it would take long and I gave her my standard answer, "I'll see what I can do". I told Dick of the phone call and my suspicions and he said to make copies sent her one keep one in our files and send one to Myra for safe keeping. I asked Baite to make three copies of the appraisal and then called Myra back and told her of the situation and she just said good thinking I'll keep them in a special file. I called the woman back and asked for her address and I would have a copy sent by currier at the end of the week. She thanked me and hung up. I just sat at my desk for a few minutes and I thought what was Albononi in all this didn't he keep a copy of the appraisal so I gave him a call but no one answered. I thought that was strange no answering service or may be the girl was on brake. I decided to call back later.

Baite casually dropped by my office to inform me they have set a moving date for Tuesday of next week so maybe you should start packing whatever breakables you have; she had collapsed boxes in the file room.

Tuesday rolled around faster than I expected so I threw all my personal paraphernalia into one of Baite's collapsible boxes along with the appraisal books and some notes than put the Berkeley Property appraisal into my attaché case for tomorrow. I was planning on taking it to Myra's office tomorrow for a meeting on the Government Regulations on savings and loans that would kill two birds with one stone. I stacked the boxes on my desk and was heading for the door when I was intercepted by Baite she told me I got a call first thing this morning from Larry Armorson. He left his number and asked if you would call him as soon as you got in. She told me she and Carrol were with the movers all morning and didn't get a chance to tell me. She told me all the new furniture had arrived and Carrol was tied up on the phones so if I could spare twenty minutes to help her to arrange the file room.

"Let me call Larry Armorson and see what he wants and then I'll give you a hand". As I started to dial Larry's number I realized it was not the S&L number it gave me a reason to pause so I temporally stopped dialing and realized it was a residential number and he was probably at home so I continued to dial. When he answered he thanked me for calling back so soon and then told me he had some critical information on that Drays Savings and Trust that might make it a little scary for us. I said, "Please continue". "I have it on good authority that the feds are already there".

"We know that what else you got"?

"I'll bet you were told it was the IRS and the Bureau however the Treasury Department and the DEA are now involved. It seems there were counterfeit government securities involved".

"Do you know what kind of Government Securities was involved"?

"No, but the Bank in Fremont that the Feds closed was involved with Drays; I heard Drays used counterfeit government securities as collateral. Now the Treasury boys are involved and it is serious and with the DEA involved it has to be drugs and laundering drug profits".

"Do you have time after the meeting tomorrow for coffee and conversation"? I asked.

"That's the other thing I wanted to tell you I no longer am involved with the Cordy S&L, but I'll make time when and where"?

I had a feeling he had left Cordy so I asked him if he knew the Luncheonette on Pine Street it's right across the street from the Pacific Coast Stock Exchange.

"I've heard of it; isn't it the place that has an old lady chopping vegetables in the window and a street guy mimicking her from the street"?

"Yeah they pull it off a couple times a week; I think it's entertaining even if you've seen it before".

"Just let me know when and I'll be there".

When I hung up I thought of what Larry just told me about the Treasury and DEA now involved with the Drays mess and especially the Government Securities scheme. I knew I had to get the word to Dick, Peter and Myra, but I couldn't see how we were involved especially me.

I caught up with Baite and we took the elevator to the tenth floor. She unlocked the office door and when I saw Carol handling the phones behind her desk in the finished product I was duly impressed. The reception area was smaller with furniture in it, but inviting. The receptionist desk was on a slight angle as you entered and very Danish Modern the carpet was neutral tweed and the desk was glass and fruitwood. There were two matching chairs and a magazine table. The wall covering was a commercial rice paper with picture posters of San Francisco buildings in very modern leanings. Then she took me to her office and it was all Baite. The door to the office opened just to the right of the partition wall of the other office which I knew was my office, the carpet was the same tweed, but the walls were jazzed up with the Swedish national colors Blue and Yellow. The blue representing a boarder of a wainscoting and the yellow the bottom half; the top half and ceiling were off while. The first picture you saw was a three mast schooner. It was in great detail like a photograph drawn over in ink. It was so different from the rest of her motif I had the impression it had special personal meaning. The rest was splashy colors of modern arts except behind her desk there was a replica of impressionist Edvard Munch's of the "Scream". To make it more authentic it had the original inscription in German on the bottom "Der Shrie dur Natur". "Scream of Nature". Being frugal she just moved her old desk to her new office with two wood and leather chairs at thirty degree angles to her desk. We moved on to my office the carpet was the same tweed and for some reason I couldn't remember picking out that lighter tweed and of course, I found out later Baite changed it to the lighter color naturally it blinded a lot better than my choice. I knew I was moving all my furniture and wall coverings to my new office some time later so I was surprised when I saw two large Norman Rockwell's prints looking right at me as we entered. Baite was behind me when she said, "Anne told me these are your favorites".

"Where did you find them"?

"The "100 years of Baseball" was easy that's pretty much in circulation, but the "Breaking home ties" was rare I contacted the Literary Digest and they pointed me in the right direction". I was staring at the prints when Baite said the best is yet to come so come on I've got to show you Peter's office. On the way she mentioned Dick's office will be the same he's just moving his furniture from his old office to his new. But Peter's is definitely different. You might call it eclectic or shipwreck depends on your sensibilities. I said I didn't understand her last remark and ask her what is eclectic she said wait and see. When we entered I immediately understood what Baite meant. Of course, the carpet was the same as all the other offices, but the furniture was not; this is what Baite meant by eclectic or shipwreck and there was only one thing on the walls it was a large tapestry depicting some ancient Greek battle. The furniture itself was so unusual I inspected them individually with a running commentary and description supplied by Baite. I went straight to his desk it was an oversize ships captain's sea trunk with legs. The rounded top was cut horizontally with the iron stays cut and hinged and when opened it made a two sided desk, but with all the draws on one side. The joints were Tenon and Mortise so tight you couldn't tell even running your finger over them. The finish was a dark oak and froth with age and deep in depth. Baite said that I might have guessed the desk is English and very old. There was a high back chair behind the desk with hand carvings on the rails and upholstered in padded black material. The side wall had a Chinese Chest standing six feet tall with five main draws and five smaller draws on the side of each main draw. It was a fine grained wood stained similar to the English desk with black iron corners and pulls. The chest matched the two Chinese stick chairs in front of the desk. Actually so far the furniture kind of matched with the sea chest desk and the Chinese furniture, but the Egyptian divan and coffee table with hieroglyphics on its legs was what Baite referred to as eclectic or even shipwreck motif. I was inspecting the divan when Baite said, "It's been claimed this is an original divan belonging to Cleopatra it is said that Mark Anthony preferred this divan for their love making; if you look close you can see the imprint of Cleopatra's derriere as a result of Mark Anthony's impetuous nature". It took me a minute to realize it was a joke because I would never expect that kind of humor from Baite. She saw me blushing so she vowed no more bad jokes then she said just a note on the tapestry it's very old and very good one that Peter had sent from back East. It depicts the "Battle of Thermopylae" where three hundred Spartans held off the whole Persian Army for a number of days only to be betrayed. Baite said she thought every piece of furniture in here was museum quality and I had to agree. Then she suddenly volunteered she thought Peter's taste was inconsistent; she went on to mention she put together his new condo and all the furniture was very traditional and bought right off the showroom floor. We finally got to organize the files, but it didn't take long Baite had half the work done before I got there. I thought of the Berkeley Property and Albononi and went back to the six floor office before they disconnected the phones; when I dialed Albononi's office number I got an intercept operator informing me the number has been disconnected. I was half expecting something like this and was thinking the best way to handle the situation when the movers arrived and moved me.

The next day I dropped off the appraisal for the Berkeley Property with Myra then we started going over the Government Regulation referred to as "CAMELS". I thought they were straight forward, but Myra felt it necessary to spell out all the categories by letter.

C, capital adequacy, A, asset quality, M, management, E, earnings, L, liquidity, S, sensitivity to market risk.

She stressed the two regulations that Cordy's S&L had missed. As she was driving this point home I couldn't help but thinking these were the exact points Peter and Dick were questioning Mr. Cordy at the last meeting and not getting an answer. I was now convinced this was a lost cause with Mr. Cordy's unrealistic property values and his distorted profit and loss statements and his complete misinterpretation of "Good Will". I couldn't see any day light at the end of the tunnel. I had to ask Myra why was Peter having the two of us pursue this S&L acquisition when to me he had already washed his hands of it.

"It was your idea and both Dick and he thought it had merit and I'm sure they want to see where it goes".

"Do you mean it is some sort of a learning curve for me and they've soured from the beginning on the whole project"?

"That's putting it a little strong, I'm sure they want you to pursue this deal to its conclusion one way or the other".

"So what you're telling me is this whole project is a deal for me to get my teeth into; like a negotiating teething ring".

"Whatever your perception is let me remind you they are paying the freight and I don't come cheap and I can't see them spending money on some sort of kindergarten for you so take this serious we have a meeting in the very near future". I apologized and we got back to business. She wanted to know if I have a date to set a meeting with the Cordy people so she can call Larry Armorson. I told her I just talked with Larry and he is no longer involved with the Cordy S&L. She lifted her eyes off the paper on Regulations then kind of stared at me then mused "interesting". I told her I was available anytime, but where do we go from here? She said she would call the S&L and schedule a meeting then see what happens. I took this gap in the meeting to tell Myra what Larry told me about the Treasury and the DEA now involved in the Drays investigation and the counterfeit securities. Her only reaction was the same as a few minutes before she said, "Interesting".

Myra scheduled the meeting for nine o'clock at her office because she said there were only going to be four people. Dick and Peter were unavailable so that left Myra and me. Subsequently she was told by Terry Cordy's receptionist that Mr. Cordy and his son Bryant would be the only two attending from the Savings and Loan. By prearrangement I meet Myra at eight o'clock to get ready for the nine o'clock meeting. Myra was busy with another case for a few minutes so it gave me time to look around at length I had never bothered to take in the size and how elegantly furnished it was mainly because we would always go on to the deck for meetings. The office was quite large, but a little cluttered she obviously like figurines. There was a small conference table at the far end of the office set for four people with legal pads pencils and bottled water at each chair. On the back wall was another Georgia O'Keefe Print of what looked like tropical flower that complimented the one on the opposite wall in back of her desk. The table was blond wood to match the wainscoting and paneling circling the office. There was a small secretary desk with an extension phone just off to the right of the conference table. As an accent she had a small oriental runner on top of a dark colored Berber carpet ostensibly dividing the office from personal and business. I was still checking out the office when the intercom buzzed. I instinctively looked at the six button phone, but none of the incoming lines were lit and when I looked at Myra she had a quizzical look on her face then said, "They're early". She answered her intercom and just said, "Send them up but tell them to use the staircase". When she hung up I asked her why not the elevator. She said, "The view from the staircase is more impressive it will put another chink in Mr. Cody's armor". We both left Myra's office to greet the Cordy's at the top of the staircase, but with Myra looking down at them ascending the stairs it was obvious she was more intent on establishing a dominant negotiating position then greeting them. Mr. Cordy and Bryant were looking at the impressive dome like structure as they climbed the stairs, but Mr. Cordy's body language told the story he knew what Myra was doing. With professional curtesy Myra led the way back to her office. As soon as we entered Myra invited everyone to the conference table. She excused herself and said she had to finish a brief and it would only take a few minutes then went back to her desk. Her attitude signaled their early arrival disrupted her work. I was a little slow but it was now obvious there was a game going on that I didn't know how to handle so I settled in at the conference table and keep my mouth shut it was obvious Bryan came to the same conclusion. I started a friendly conversation with Bryan while Mr. Cordy circled the room taking in the office ambiance then stopped at the sliding glass doors and looked at the garden deck admiringly when the intercom rang. I glanced at the six button set on the secretary desk and saw the first button flashing I thought it odd to get a call before nine o'clock in the morning. Myra answered her intercom and then told Mr. Cordy the call was for him. He began to circle around Myra's desk to take the call when Myra hung up the intercom and pointed to the phone on the secretary desk while he still had his hand reaching for her phone. He clasped his fingers into the ball of his hand like sensing some- thing hot and then headed for the phone on the secretary desk. He picked up the phone then pressed the flashing button and stood facing the picture of the tropical flower with his back to Myra, and almost on top of Bryan, but at an oblique angle to me. His conversation went on for close to a minute with him saying no more than a few uh-huh and a few yeses. When he hung up he looked at me with suspicion like I could see right through his ploy. He turned to Myra and apologized and said an important matter arose at his office it sounded bogus and planned. I was now catching on to the game Mr. Cordy thought he was losing the battle for dominance but he was making mistakes in the game of leverage. Myra had already scored points by scheduling the meeting at her office with its location and professional ambiance. Now his puny attempt with the bogus phone call to get back some of his negotiating leverage hurt more than helped his cause. With these procedural blunders by him it gave me confidence I didn't know I had; so I called everyone to the table including Myra to start the meeting. As we were getting organized I looked over to Bryan and he had his head down and was writing on his legal pad it gave me pause to wonder if he was going to actively participate in the negotiations. That was soon dispelled when Mr. Cordy took their file on the sale of their S&L from Bryan's hands with almost a dismissive gesture. He started off with the tired old argument that our proposal was unrealistic, but he said, "For the sake of discussion let's say we can agree on most points the one I must dispute is Good Will. Your final proposal does everything but discount it all together". I let it sort of hang in the air for a few uncomfortable seconds then said, "It is your arbitrary financial figures with no hard proof attributed to the name of the business that translates into hard money. Let me give you an example along with curb appeal you mention the S&L's logo appearing all over the Mission but you don't give a time line in your monthly P&L statements when this increase in business started or if it was the same before the advertising of the logo for the S&L. Plus what you claim as an increase in revenue doesn't appear in you profit and loss statement for the year. The only conclusion is the advertising with the logo did little if anything in the way of revenue therefore; we discounted your figures on "Good Will" all together".

"Well let me say I wouldn't recommend you as an accountant because it's in plain view for anyone to see".

"Could you show me where in any of these documents these figures appear"?

"It would be a waste of time obviously you wouldn't understand them".

"Try me". I waited for an answer while I reached for my bottle water and caught Myra staring at me with an unsmiling approval. He was moving a few papers then thumbed through a few more so I brought up the government inspection a year or so ago that rejected their savings and loan Capital adequacy and their Earnings as faulty and inadequate. He grabbed his bottle of water and as he was opening it he told me those were recommendation by the regulator to further comply with the government regulation they were not viewed as anything like a violation. Could you give us any documentation of the final disposition from the Regulatory Agency to that effect? He was making a project out of opening then drinking and closing his water bottle while we all waited for his answer. He finally claimed Larry Armorson handled that and he said he would confer with Larry and get back to us with that information. It was apparent to everyone this meeting was going downhill and we weren't forty minutes into it. Bryant finally lifted his head from his legal pad then said, "We have a proposition that might solve this apparent impasse. We are offering to sell thirty percent of the Cordy Saves and Loan for fifty percent of our last selling price".

"And what else"?

"And Mr. Cordy is to continue his Presidency and the power to approve or disapprove all loans summited by all junior partners".

"So he's offering thirty percent of his business for the selling price he original put on the market for which was two hundred percent more than our offer. Did I get that right"?

"Yes, but I have it all spelled out in a counter offer form and, of course, feel free to make any minor changes that does not change the essence of the contract".

"What in essence I see is the blind strike of a dying predator. I'm sorry, but on behalf of my Company Scranton & Ass. I feel I must withdraw every and all offers to purchase Cordy Savings and Loan; needless to say, this meeting is at an end".

Mr. Cordy was siting staring at his pad while raising his pencil between his thumb and forefinger and let it drop on to the pad he did this several times while Bryan was spelling out their new offer. When he heard my reply he fumed. He said, "Who the hell are you "an office flunky" to arbitrarily reject our offer without giving it to someone in authority to read and evaluate the offer". The force of his reply gave me pause to think I might have overstepped my bounds, but I knew he was a bully so I stood my ground by ignoring his bluster. I forced myself not to look at Myra for any support so as not to give Mr. Cordy cause to think he was right; when I heard Myra let into him. "You best temper your tongue Mr. Cordy. Mr. Kerry is the negotiator representing Scranton & Ass. And he has ended this meeting and I have to ask you both to leave".

We all stood and as they were leaving Mr. Cordy made a few snide comments about me so I made a point to ignore him until I heard a reference to my wife. I let drop a file I had in my hand back on to the table and looked quickly at Mr. Cordy but by this time he was at the door and to my surprise both Bryan and Myra got between me and him in a defensive posture, but he had already slid through the door. I was seething and it showed so I just continued to organize my paper work and prepared to leave. I glanced at Myra and ask her, "What's the matter"?

She said, "Nothing now, but I thought for a moment you were going to administer some street justice at the expense of Mr. Cordy".

"Now wouldn't that look great me beating up on a seventy year old man". "That was why I made that attempt to distract you and I'm certain Bryan was thinking of stopping you because you had that look".

"What look"?

"The one that a few of my clients had that sent them to prison".

"I wasn't really listening because I was looking at the legal pad that Bryan was writing on; after a few notes he started doodling and it was quite revealing it was a stick figure of a beat up old dog with band aids all over its body which the rest of the pack discarded by the wayside. Then an odd stick sketch of an army tank with the word "Tanks" in quotes. I showed the legal pad to Myra and she said, "That young man must be in agony".

I got back to the office around eleven o'clock and it raised eye brows they knew I was meeting with the Cordy people on the acquisition on their Savings and Loan and expected the meeting to go most of the day. Dick was the first to ask what happened. I told him I withdrew our offer to buy the S&L and as soon as I organized my notes I'll have a report in detail typed up. He smiled that knowing smile of his then told me to go ahead and he would look forward to my synopsis. I noticed Peter was among the missing so I continued to my office to start on my report. I really didn't have much to write I just rewrote my notes and Mr. Cordy's final offer with his statement of continuing his presidency with total control over approving or denying all loan applications. I made no personal comments and initialed the paper. I asked Baite to type up the report and then called Larry Armorson. When he answered he said, "I was waiting for your call because I already heard the news you rejected Mussolini's benevolent offer to participate in his floundering business at a ridiculous cost. What's wrong with you? You just missed a golden opportunity to experience bankruptcy and avoid all the taxes you're paying now". I laughed at his joke and it helped relax me because of those decisions you make even though you know they're right, but make you uneasy with anxiety because you think, "What if"? I asked him how did he find out so soon because the meeting ended no more than an hour ago?

"His partner Muñoz called me with the news; we'd been working on the counter offer from you and we both vetoed Cordy's counter proposal and it cost me my job and Muñoz is upset with him-self for getting into this situation because he knows he's at the mercy of Cordy and can't see a way out".

"I take it he is the junior partner who has nothing to say about running the S&L".

"You got it".

"Larry if you have time today how about lunch, I'm buying".

"You bet cha what time and where"?

"How about the Luncheonette on Pine at 1 o'clock".

"It's a date".

I wanted to get out of the office so I left at noon and decided to take my time and walk to Pine Street. The weekly show was going on at the front window of the Luncheonette, but I skirted it and went right in passed the counter to the back table sort of out of the way. As soon as I was seated the young waitress asked if I wanted the usual. And as usual she was over made up and under dressed with her skirt two inches from the bottom of her ass. I told her no; just a menu I was meeting a friend for lunch. She asked if it was male or female. I told her one of each and she would have to guess which one was the male. She gave me a long smirk then said, "You got me again; what do you won't to drink".

"I'll have coffee and bring the milk". She returned with the coffee and tiny pitcher of milk and a plate of six slices of Italian bread and butter. She turned to leave and bumped into a customer it was Detective Norman.

He held her with both of this arms to steady her then in the most perfect sounding Italian said "scusi" then a sentence or two in Italian that must have been flattering because her answer was fluttering and she blushed.

"What is this; you keeping tabs on me".

"Not quite I was leaving the Bank of America across from your office and saw you heading down Montgomery and thought I catch up and maybe have lunch so here I am".

"I had no idea you were a linguist where did you learn Italian"?

"Here in San Francisco the family that sponsored us was Italian. They lived here and I was young enough that I pick up the language like a sponge. I had dinner with Tom and Nancy last night and Nancy told me Allen died". It took me a second or two to realize who Oscar was talking about; then it hit me Mary's friend. "I would guess it was aids".

"You would guess correctly he just melted away".

"Did Nancy say what Mary was going to do; if she was going to continue helping Jean at his Boutique or is he going to sell it"?

"She didn't say. Why are you curious"?

"As you know I just transferred that property on Union Street to her and the deal took some doing; as you can imagine it took a favor or two and if she gets it into her head to sell it and move on she'll be looking for another favor". I looked up and Larry was standing next to the young waitress with a grin on his face. She had her hand cupped around his elbow like leading the blind when she said, "I'm guessing you're sitting with the real deal and here is your other guest". Her remark set me off into a fit of laughing with both Oscar and Larry looking at me in bewilderment. I quickly gained control and said to her, "Touché". She smiled placed another menu on the table then asked if anyone wanted something to drink. We ordered and she left with her usual prance, but with a little more prance. I quickly explained the game that the waitress and I play of one-upmanship and the crack about the other guest which got a brief snicker from both of them and I cut it short when I introduced Larry to Oscar and their professions. "What irony I just told Jim about the cops and the gangster escapade, over in the East Bay." Oscar looked at Larry quizzically then said, "You peaked my curiosity what escapade in the East Bay"? He went on to explain the connection between the bank failure in Fremont and the counterfeit government securities used by the Drays Savings and Trust to borrow enough money to finance a Real Estate scheme for local Teamsters which brought in every government agency this side of Denver. Oscar said, "Tell me more". "It will be in tomorrow's newspapers in detail, but essentially Drays used some counterfeit government securities along with some legitimate securities to finance their financial footings with the failed Union Commercial Bank in Fremont and Mr. Kerrigan has disappeared".

"Disappeared like he flew the coop". I asked.

"That's the phrase I was looking for".

Oscar chimed in with, "Can I ask you how you know all this before it even hits the news-stands".

"Jim mentioned I'm in the banking and Savings and loan business and I have friends and associates in the business; we keep each other informed on the nitty gritty rumors and scandals in California and especially here in the Bay Area".

"You're a good man to know. Do you have a business card"? They exchanged cards, had a little shop talk then dropped a few names and our lunch came. The conversation through lunch was chummy mostly talking sports and the crazy antics in the luncheonette; Larry did most of the talking it was obvious he was taken with the luncheonette's characters and raved about the food. When the lunch was over Oscar started to excuse himself by remarking we probably had business to discuss. Larry chimed in with, "Not really just gossip from the world of finance no secrets". The waitress filled our coffee cups as Larry told us one of the big guys in the S&L business was in trouble and scrambling to unload a very bad loan he initiated. I wasn't overly interested because I didn't know any big guys in the industry until Larry mentioned Harry Byrd. He was smiling at me because he knew that would wake me up. "If he calls you beware of Byrd's bearing gifts".

"What's with this cryptic pitch? ; just tell me what he's selling".

"Three continuous properties one has a red tagged hotel on it another is vacant and the third has an old rooming house now occupied by a women's shelter".

"So why was it a bad loan"?

"It's complicated, but in a nut shell Harry combined all three properties into a startup loan to refurbish the hotel; however the developer didn't own the women shelter property he only had an option for one year to buy at a set price. Now the option year is coming due and the hotel has been hardly worked on and the women's shelter is claiming the developer promised he would relocate the shelter and to complete the picture the developer has disappeared and so has all the startup money". "You're right it doesn't sound like anything we would want to take on".

"If the original note was discounted enough and you could rezone the three parcels to a higher density it could be a real sleeper it would make a ton of money". Oscar said he had to get going we all shook hands and after Oscar left Larry told me he was starting his own consulting business and wanted to know if I thought our company would do business with him? I told him one of main reasons Peter and Dick were interested in the Cordy S&L was you they knew you was running the show and the old man was the millstone around your neck. Larry thanked me and in parting said, "Expect a call from Mr. Byrd and tread lightly he's going to approach you with the offer on the South of Mission Street project with a glowing outlook on its potential. If you think at any point your company would be interested I'd like to be involved".

"I'll certainly recommend you. One more thing before you go I need one of your profiles on a Doctor Chester Yee over in Oakland. He's in Geriatric's and is looking for finance for a residential care facility; could you use your grape vine to see if he is legit"?

"I know just the man to call and I'll get back to you, but remember I need work".

"I know, I know one hand will wash the other".

Chapter 28

When I got in Monday morning Baite was in a fit she said some body went through all the files over the weekend. At this point the only file missing was the Berkeley appraisal, but she told me to check my desk files and see that they are intact. As I was checking my desk files I heard Dick come in and Baite tell him the same thing to check his desk files. I heard Dick tell Baite to call the building management and the police. I checked my desk and it seemed o.k. but when I looked into my credenza I was furious all my appraisal books, Elwood financial books, notes and statistical tables were gone; everything cleaned out. When Mr. Neuhaus the building manager came he asked if Baite could get a list of anything taken, but the only thing she could say was missing was some files all the type writers the large copy machine and the postage stamp machine were left. When police arrived they wanted to know if the door was forced open; when they were told no they asked if we had any work done at the office over the weekend Baite told them no. Mr. Neuhaus said wait there was some telephone company men here Friday night they told me Friday they had to add a cable from the equipment room in the garage to the tenth floor for Scranton & Associates. I informed the night watchman that there would be telephone men working at these locations. The Officer asked Mr. Neuhaus if he could give a description of these phone men. He said they had identification tags with pictures and Bell System printed in bold letters so I didn't look to close because they had large safety glassed on. He then asked if the watchman was still in the building. Mr. Neuhaus said he would check and called the front desk in the lobby. He was told he was still here and he was on his way up. When the watchman arrived he told the Police Officer there were two telephone men and they were working in the hall terminal and asked to get into the Scranton office to check the phones so he let one in, but he was with him the whole time and they were in the office no more than ten minutes he was interested in the receptionist phone so he never went to any other office. The Officer asked if he was interested in the main door especially the lock.

"As a matter of fact he did admire the brass lock and mentioned it was a Yale. I was surprised he knew that because you couldn't see the logo". "After you left the office you locked it right"?

"Of course, that's building procedure".

"Then what"?

"The other fellow had to get into the equipment room in the garage and the other fellow had set up the cable at the hall terminal to be pulled down into the equipment room".

"So you took him down to the garage".

"That's right".

"How long were you down there"?

"I don't know maybe forty minutes to an hour".

"Then what"?

"What do you mean"?

"Did you go back up to the tenth floor"?

"Oh yeah, I controlled the elevator so I took the guy back up to the tenth floor. By that time his partner had finished and they cleaned up and they pushed their tool catty to the elevator and I took them back down to the garage and let them out".

"Did they have a truck"?

"No they work out of a storeroom on Sacramento Street".

"Did they tell you that"?

"No, but that's where all the phone men work out of in this area".

I thought the Officer was going to run out of pages in his little note book. He thanked the night watchman and told him he could go home then went to the door to look and inspected it. He never actual touch it, but remarked to his partner that everyone in the office had probably touched the door and the lock so don't get your hopes up. By this time we had all listened to the entire conversation with the Police Officer and the night watchman and were waiting to hear what their conclusion was how they got into the office to steal the files. Dick had his arms folded seeming pondering a dilemma when he said to the Officer, who questioned the watchman, one of them took him to the garage to get him out of the way while the other guy who had been in the office to check the phones picked the lock and stole the files. The Officer just said, "It sure looks like it". When the Police and Mr. Neuhaus left Dick made an effort to get things back to normal, but everyone's thoughts were elsewhere. I was standing next to the doorway to my office when Dick came over and told me to step inside and close the door. Neither one of us sat then he said, "Peter is due in this evening from Pittsburg and wants to have a meeting with Mr. Peresci, but to tell the truth I think we better find out more about this sudden interest in the Berkeley appraisal and why we haven't heard from Mr. Albononi? This somehow feels like it is all connected with the Hillcrest housing development and that phony Savings and Trust over in the East Bay".

"I called Mr. Albononi a few days ago and his phone was disconnected. I got sidetracked on the S&L acquisition meeting and didn't get a chance to follow up on what happened to him. Now I believe you're right this is getting very scary. I can't believe that all this is a coincidence. This Mrs. Wright asks for a copy of the Berkeley Appraisal then the office break-in and the only things taken are our file on the same appraisal and anything pertaining to it and now Albononi is missing". Dick left and I sat at my desk trying to focus on my work schedule that's when I felt my hands sweating I dried them off and continued arranging my work schedule. The longer I looked at my work schedule the blurrier the work and numbers got; I felt panicked. I buzzed Dick and asked if he had a minute and asked him if he had the privet protection agency's number that Peter had offered.

"I'll ask Peter to call them tonight". Dick offered.

When I arrived at the office the following day I could feel my subdued anxiety starting to bubble to the surface. Carrol was on the phone getting the messages from the answering service and put her hand in the air to stop me while she was still writing the message down. Baite came out of the stationary room with two cups of coffee heading for Peter's office. She stopped momentarily to ask how I was feeling in a concerned way and I told her fine. Carrol handed me two messages and I headed for my office without looking at them. As soon as I sat at my desk I got a call on the intercom from Peter to come to his office. Dutifully I trudged into his office and was introduced to a gentleman named Mr. Bekkvelt the owner of the, "Coast to Coast Protection Agency". I was offered a seat and took it, but declined coffee and felt like a child that did something wrong. I kind of twitched around in my chair until Mr. Bekkvelt spoke. He asked me about my hours of business and if I kept to a ridged schedule. I told him not at all I sometime work in the evenings moving around the City doing appraisals and may not get to the office the next day until ten or eleven o'clock. Then at times I might go straight to a job site to check on progress and leave my house at six thirty or seven so I don't have a set schedule. He then asked about friends and relatives and when I gave him a short list and he asked me to write down their names. I did and as he was going over the list I put my full focus on him. He seemed very attentive his facial features were very ordinary and spoke with a slight Northern European accent. His hair was once fair, but now turning grey. His eyes were grey and piercing you could feel them when he prolonged looking at you. That would be the only thing that made him different from any one you meet on the street. Without preamble he went into an explanation of how best to set up a plan to protect me in case of any attempt to hurt or injure me or my family. It sounded to me he was just going to assign a series of bodyguards pretty much around the clock then asked if I knew if the Bureau was still tapping my phone. I told him I wasn't sure so he told me to just be aware of what I discuss on the phone. Peter interrupted by telling me Mr. Bekkvelt is going to accompany us to the Hillcrest development we have a meeting with Mr. Peresci and while we are in the East Bay we should check out Albononi's office and see if anyone knows where he is. I got my attaché case and the Hillcrest file and we went to the garage for my car then left for the East Bay. Peter sat next to me in the front and Mr. Bekkvelt sat in the back with his brief case on his lap going over some papers.

During the drive Peter's conversation was all small talk nothing to do with business and when we arrived at the housing development there was a line of cars parked in front of the construction trailer. Peter raised an eye brow and told me to find a spot to park and let's see what all this is about. Mr. Bekkvelt remained in the car and we entered the trailer without knocking and it appeared we were interrupting a meeting. Mr. Peresci was sitting behind the desk with Jake Peavy and Joan Kitmer sitting on folding chairs facing him and a gentleman standing behind the desk next to Mr. Peresci with papers in his hands in a lecturing posture. Mr. Peresci told us it was perfect timing they just finished their meeting. He introduced the man standing as his lawyer Albie Meyer. After the introductions counselor Meyer began to expound on Contract and Real Estate Law and that the Hillcrest Housing development and its parent company Black Stone Corporation would be held harmless in the embezzlement of funds by a junior partner. Because he was being regulated by construction draws and supervised by an Escrow

Company engaged by the lending institution Reliance industries.

"I didn't know what, in the hell, he was talking about, but Peter's response was "Bullshit". It was short on eloquence but it got every body's attention.

"If you think I took time out of my day to attend this meeting to defend my company's participation in this development you're terribly mistaken. Counselor Meyer if you would surrender one of your business cards I will have our Law firm contact you to address this matter". The response was immediate Meyer came from behind the desk with both hands out in an imploring manner striking a phony court room pose saying, "I merely wanted to give Mr. Travillian a picture of what could happen if the two parties didn't work together to solve the problems". It was clear Peter was hot and not cooling down from being blindsided by this meeting planned to intimidate.

"Well you may think that, but this contrived ambush has all the ear marks of a default in the construction loan therefore I'll have our attorney contact you. I see no further reason to be here so we are leaving". You could hear a pin drop when we left. When we got back into the car Peter mused I'll bet Albononi has flown the coop but we'll check to see if anyone knows where he went. Let's stop at his office. As we were leaving the parking lot Mr. Bekkvelt remarked "That was a short meeting". "Yeah well our principal had this idiot lawyer giving him terrible advice I'm sure Mr. Peresci eventually will see the light and give us a call". In a matter of fact way Mr. Bekkvelt asked Peter if he wanted him to check on the lawyer. Peter told him it wouldn't be necessary and then told me to head for the Oakland Airport. While we were driving to the Airport, Peter remarked that we were way ahead of schedule so maybe we could stop in Oakland to look at Dr. Yee's project which he had planned on doing tomorrow. We drove around the Airport circle and Peter told me to stop at a building mark Civilian Aviation. I parked and he went into the office for no more than fifteen minutes and when he returned he had a fist full of brochures and said, "On James". I continued to the industrial area and pulled up in front of Albononi's office which to no one's surprise was vacant even the name of his company was removed. Mr. Bekkvelt pointed to the vehicles parked in front and remarked they look familiar then asked Peter if he wanted him to put a trace on this fellow Albononi. Peter thought we could get more information on Albononi's whereabouts right here; so we started to the front door of the main building. I stood back and looked at the name over the front door and was momentarily stunned in bold letters "Truckers of Limitation" and under in smaller letters "Real Estate Investors". The first time I was here I never heard of the Truckers of Limitation so I thought it was a trucking company. I saw immediately Peter recognized the name when he looked back at me with a questioning frown. He opened up the front door and we were confronted by Brophy and Clark with a small army of agents packing files, office supplies, check books and phone records literally everything moveable. It was Clark who spoke first when he said, "Bekkvelt what are you doing here"?

And before he could answer Brophy grabbed his hand with both of his in a clasp of comradery; "Luke you old Pirate what brings you here and especially today"?

"Well I don't think it's a secret now so I'll tell you I've been sent to make sure you people do this right". Brophy laughed, but Clark in a whisper heard around the room said, "You mean like the way you secretly entered Polk Street Diplomatic Mission and exited leaving your undiplomatic foot prints all over their building's sanctuary". Bekkvelt ignored Clark's jibe and without missing a beat asked if the young lady would be more comfortable sitting. All eyes went to the young lady standing next to Clark. It was the receptionist that worked for Albononi and she was in a state of shock and actually trembling. Bekkvelt took her by the arm and as he was steering her to a chair told me to get her glass of water. I looked around quickly and one of the agents pointed to a side room and I found a water cooler and paper cups. When I returned Clark was almost shouting that this was a Bureau's case and any interference from Bekkvelt would be dealt with at the highest level. Needless to say I was so confused I didn't know whether to stand, sit or go back to the car, when I looked at Peter he seemed unconcerned like a neutral bystander. So after I gave the cup of water to the young lady I stood back and tried to melt into the background. There was something going here that I obviously knew nothing about, but I had the feeling Peter did which bolstered my confidence so I played the neutral bystander. Brophy approached and informed us we couldn't be here because they had a warrant to remove all pertinent evidence so there is a possibility we could be viewed later as obstructing or contaminating the evidence. Peter told him they understood, but we just wanted to know if anyone knew where Albononi had gone. The young lady started to answer when Clark stopped her and answered for her with what sounded like a pat answer, "That's what we would like to know". We rallied outside around the car and Peter asked Mr. Bekkvelt if this was going to cause a problem for him. He answered, "Not really, but I expect I'll hear about it; this guy Clark and I have history and I don't think he'll pass up an opportunity to try and do me damage". I was standing there like a bump on a log when Mr. Bekkvelt told me he once worked in the diplomatic corps and had a run in with the Bureau over procedures. I guess he thought that was enough of an explanation so we got into the car and headed for Oakland. On the way Peter told me he thought it would now be a good idea to call Myra and you both go to the Bureau with Albononi's Appraisal it now has to be evidence. Than the conversation was about Albononi and where he might be and Peter was convinced he would head back to Pittsburg so much so he told us he has called people back there to stay on the lookout for him. I exited at 7th street and maneuvered around to Broadway then gave Peter and Mr. Bekkvelt a tour of China Town complete with commentary. Mr. Bekkvelt seemed to be familiar with the area so I told Peter China Town here compared to San Francisco China Town was tiny maybe two square blocks. However it is the shopping hub for the entire Chines community in the East Bay and a perfect area for a Residential Care Facility. Residents could shop for their needs and for their children to visit while doing their shopping. Just a block away from the shopping center was the property Dr. Yee wanted to develop into a Care facility so I circled the block to give them a good Idea of it location then parked almost in front. Peter got out of the car to do a sidewalk inspection. The building was all boarded up with signs warning of their unsafe condition and of course, graffiti spray paint all over the front. Mr. Bekkvelt seemed totally uninterested until Peter got back into the car then asked if anybody was hungry. Peter said he could eat something and I was all for it. Mr. Bekkvelt said to continue down the street then make a left then another left and there is a delicatessen right on the corner it's small, but you can't miss it he has Smoked Peking duck hanging in the window and it has the best dim-sum in China town. It was pretty clear Mr. Bekkvelt had been here before so I just follow his directions. We all decided on the dim-sum and it was all he said it would be and then headed back to San Francisco. When we pulled into the garage at Montgomery Street Mr. Bekkvelt asked me if I had time right now to go home to my house and start on a planned schedule for the security for me and my family. He said it so forcefully and professionally I felt I had to say yes. Peter slide out of the car and Mr. Bekkvelt replaced him in the front then Peter told me he'd see me tomorrow. There was little conversation until we got to Hyde Street then he told me there was one of his men there since his morning and he has laid out how the team will cover the street and your parking area. I pulled into the alley and parked in my space. I was waiting for some sort of instructions from Mr. Bekkvelt when a man appeared at his window. He rolled it down and said something to him, but I couldn't hear then the man answered, "They'll be here at five o'clock". He then turned to me and told me it was evident the Bureau was on this and he would make a few calls to confirm what we saw today at the Truckers of Limitation and Albononi's vacant office was being done with a legal warrant. He went on to say, "I would guess it wouldn't take them long to get indictments and our security probably won't be necessary, but until then my men will be with you and your family around the clock". When I got out of the car I was introduced to his man named Arnold. He was average size but well put together with fair complexion and light eyes and flaxen hair cut short in military stile. He made it obvious there would be no last names. Bekkvelt told me there would be two men to cover the entire night and Arnold would be here at 6:30 tomorrow morning. It was obvious that was the extent of the explanations so I wished them a good night and went into the house. It was too early for Anne to be home so I got a can of beer and headed for the front room. The day had been nothing that I had expected. From the beginning of a normal business meeting to this cloak and dagger ending I felt like a wimpy character in a pulp fiction novel with other people controlling my destiny. The more I thought about it the more real it became. I went and got another beer and on the way back to the front room I heard the front door open. I stopped in the hall and saw Anne with packages standing in the threshold. She looked surprised then said, "Your home early, great. You can help me with these packages". She left two in the front entrance so I picked them up and followed her into the kitchen to the dumping ground for all packages.

"I got so much to tell you but first Esperanza called me first thing this morning and we made a date for lunch because she wanted me to meet a friend of Peter's. We meet at the Palace Hotel for a tea lunch with Peter's friend. Her name is Deidre Manly and one of the most attractive women I've ever met; she exudes elegance". At this point she took a deep breath and spurted on. "She has led a fascinating life, although born in England she married an American Diplomate now deceased and settled in Pennsylvania. She has traveled extensively and she met Peter through her son; he's one of Peter's investors. She also has a great sense of humor she told us Peter insisted she stay at the Fairmont Hotel for appearance sake and she thinks it's a waste of money when all of her luggage is at his condominium".

"Well when did you have time to do all this shopping"?

"It was actually Esperanza she and Deidre picked up somethings for Gina in the morning and I promised to have them over to dress up little Gina and take her out to lunch".

"I don't think Gina will appreciate the tea lunch at the Palace". I couldn't resist an easy sit-com joke and it sounded like one but Anne bit.

"Don't be silly we'll go to Mama's Restaurant where Gina can move around without disturbing anyone".

"I'm glad you told me because it saves me from making a call to the Palace hotel to see if they allow children for tea lunches".

"Now you're being a jerk can't you see I'm excited so let me babble on I'm still enjoying the day and I'm looking forward to dressing Gina up and taking her to Mama's to show her off".

"I'm sorry I had an adventurous day and I'm still adjusting give me a little time to catch up". I said.

"That's fine I've got to pick up Gina so do you want me to get anything for dinner"?

"I don't know if it's only going to be me and you surprise me".

"I'll tell you what why don't you put together a salad from the veggie bin in the frig and I'll pick up some cheese raviolis at Basta Pasta and we'll have some of mom's marinara sauce".

"Perfect, don't forget the bread".

As advertised Arnold was waiting for me at my car first thing in the morning. He got into the passenger's seat and we were off to the office. He said good morning, but was quiet for the rest of the ride except for a remark about Hyde Street having a lot of traffic in the evening. Of course, Baite was first in and Carrol was right behind me. Baite told Arnold he could use the conference room while he was here so I headed for my office. I opened the file that I had put together piece meal on Byrd's deal South of Market quoting Larry's account, but I wasn't sure of the actual loan figures so I left them out. In about a half an hour I heard Dick come in so I let him settle down and after he had a cup of coffee I buzzed him on the intercom. I asked if he had time to discuss a proposal I came across; he said absolutely come on in. I gathered up my make shift file and went to his office. I retold Dick the deal as Larry had explained it and what Larry thought the possibilities were and that it could be a sleeper. Dick seemed to be giving the idea a lot of thought when he said to me, "Mr. Armorson appears to have quite a few contacts in the med-management world of finance, is that not so"?

"Without question; he's the one who gave me all the information on that character Kerrigan in the Drays scam".

"I think he would be a great asset to have here why don't we talk to Peter about him because I know Peter mentioned him as being a prime candidate in running the Cordy S&L if we actual bought it".

"That was going to be my next question I wanted him to work with me on this South of Market proposal on a consultant bases".

"It sounds good let's get Peter in on this and see what he thinks"?

Dick started to move papers around his desk so I knew it was time to leave. When I got back to my office I looked at my notes on my calendar and realized I hadn't called Myra about the break in and the missing Albononi appraisal and its probable evidence value to the FBI so I picked up the phone and called. Her receptionist told me she would be in court most of the week, but if I wanted to leave a message on her answering machine she could pick up your call any time even in the evening. I told her please transfer me over to her machine and I left a message about the break in and Peter thought it was time to tell the Bureau you have a copy of the Albononi appraisal.

I was pretty sure I could find this property over in the South of Market that was a mill-stone around the neck of the Hanaford S&L. So I collected Arnold from the conference room and headed over to the South of Market. I was right as we drove down the other side of Market Street I saw a small hotel with the entrance cordon off and the building red tagged and the building next to it had a sign on it "Women's Sanctuary". I circled around back to an alley that paralleled Market Street where there was a large vacant lot contiguous to both buildings along Market Street. I parked in the alley and got out followed by Arnold when I started for the back of the condemned hotel Arnold stopped me. He told me it could be dangerous you don't know if pushers are using it as a place to sell drugs. "Let me check it out stay here and I'll give you the high sign if it's OK". I shrugged OK and he left. It was then that I realized he carried a gun when he instinctively felt for it behind his back. He entered through the back door and was gone for twenty or thirty minutes then reappeared at the back door and signaled me the OK. There wasn't much to look at the place was old and the staircase railing was missing there were no upgrades at all so no repairs were done except for the front entrance there was a new glass door and tiled threshold. It looked like Larry was right the developer took the money and ran. We retraced our steps out the back and around the other building to the front of the Women's Sanctuary. I started to do an eyeball appraisal of the two story building as I walked in front of the both buildings. The Women's Sanctuary was interesting I banged on one of the pillars of the façade it was cast iron probability built right after the 06 quake. I turned to see where Arnold was and saw a woman heading right for me. She was smiling in a know it all way then said, "Its cast Iron built in 1918 right after the war. It's in the National Register of Historic places and a San Francisco landmark". I nodded my approval and she put her hand out and introduced herself as Miriam Frost Chairperson of the "Battered Women's Sanctuary". I extended my hand and shook hers and introduced myself then told her I was doing an appraisal for the Savings and Loan currently holding the note on the property. She gave me an all knowing nod then went into a history of cast iron buildings dating back to the 18th century in England. I waited for a lull in what amounted to an Oxford tutorial on preserving these buildings and asked her what was the original use for the building. She didn't like being interrupted, but she sucked it up and said manufacturing of some sort. In one sense because of the openness on each floor it made it easier to partition off each space for the client's privacy however the bath rooms are limited that's why we need a better building with adequate bathroom facilities. I asked how many women were in the Sanctuary house and she replied twelve, but there is only two bathrooms. If the City father's would OK a few more bathrooms the Health Department would allow us to increase our clients to twenty. Have you applied for permits to add on bathrooms? There is a problem with the landlord and the City. He just wants to sell the building and the city wants us to move to a smaller place because they feel they're paying too much to house too few here. I thought any other information I would get from her would be more like complaints rather than real information so I thanked her and started for the car. Arnold caught up with me then we headed for the office.

As I passed Carrol she waved a phone message at me I snagged it and gave it a quick look. It was from Myra I palmed it to get a better look and she wanted me to call her after six tonight. I called Larry as soon as I got to my desk. He answered on the second ring with his familiar greeting "Yellow". "Larry its Kerry; I looked at the property on South of Market and I think it's flirting with becoming prime property. I paced it off and roughly its three acres. Admittedly there are problems, but I'd like to get together with you, on a consulting bases, for the refinancing or financing with Hanaford S&L".

"Your place or mine sweet heart"?

"You better make it here I don't want people talking it would give my mother-law a field of questions". Larry started laughing then said he'd like to meet my mother-law.

"No you wouldn't". I said. In between his laughing he asked what day and time. I told him tomorrow at say 9:30 and he thought that was fine.

Chapter 29

I called Tom Valance to find out if he knew this Miriam Frost and got Nancy and asked if she knew anything about Miriam Frost and the Battered Women's Sanctuary. "In deed I do. She's a self-appointed chairperson of the Sanctuary, but not without a following in fact a "Cause Celeb" by the name of Sheryl Sims has joined the fight for the BWS as it is now known".

"Who is Sheryl Sims"?

"I see you don't watch soap operas; she plays a wronged woman in a very popular series. As you can imagine her part in the soap opera is tailor made for the cause". What Nancy just told me made me pause for a second or two then Nancy asked if I was still there. I apologized and told her I was just thinking of what she just told me and the obvious complications.

"Listen Tom knows both women in fact he did a lay out for the soap opera series and worked with this Sims gal so he can give you a better picture of the BWS and this Miriam Frost. I'll tell him you called and he'll get back to you". When I hung up I wrote down two things that were potentially problems the move of the Battered Women's Sanctuary and the Cast Iron Building Landmark. I called the Contractor Guild in San Francisco for information on cast Iron construction. I got a very knowledgeable young man who pointed me in the right direction by telling me I could contact a foundry in Walla Walla Washington that had new and old catalogues on prefabrication of anything from major buildings to store front facades. I thank him and before I could hang up he volunteered I was the second one to call on cast iron building in the last month and before that he couldn't remember anyone calling for that information. I naturally had to ask if he remembered who it was that inquired about the Iron cast buildings. He said he couldn't remember the guy's name, but he called from the Hanaford S&L and said he remembered because he had a mortgage with them. I contacted the foundry and they were more than happy to send me a catalogue at a reasonable price and of course I had to ask if they had any requests for information on Cast Iron construction recently from California. He told me not that he was aware of and he would know because he handled all the advertising and information dissemination for the company. I thanked him and put the phone receiver down slowly while I was thinking Byrd didn't follow through and has no idea of what it would cost to save the BWS's Cast Iron façade. I took a half hour or so to think through what Byrd would likely do either ignore the building Landmark status or try to cover it up in hopes we don't find out until after the fact.

I turned my attention to the Health and Human Service's problem of the Women's Sanctuary moving them to a new facility. I called and again lucked out the man handling the Women's Sanctuary move answered the phone a Mr. Pace. I explained who I was and asked him, "Could you tell me the disposition of the Office of the Health and Human Services in the case of the Battered Women's Sanctuary"?

He was very forthright, "I take it you are referring to their present location and our proposed new location".

"Yes, I hope you can enlighten me because I'm getting mixed messages and it's very confusing".

"Well to me personally I feel it's political we have converted an old hotel into twelve apartments with individual baths and a play yard in the back for children. There is a Lady by the name of Miriam Frost who has taken up the cause of the Battered Women and made it her cause. Then made it a sensitive issue by calling it reverse discrimination because the Agency wants to use the hotel for all women in need not just battered women that she says trivializes the cause she represents. Needless to say she found help from a TV personality and one or two politicians looking for votes".

"Has she laid out her own plan so you might come to some kind of agreement"?

"Sort of; she said the Hotel is inadequate and the building they are in now could be remolded into at least twenty apartments with baths".

"Do you think that is a viable solution"?

"It could be if the owner agreed to refurbishing the building and now would be accessible to all women not just battered women; however Ms. Frost is of the opinion the most pressing problem in the City is the Battered Women and everyone else has to take a back seat".

"I will be honest with you I'm appraising the land for a client who is interested in raising it to build a complex of commercial spaces and apartments this social situation turned political will obviously sour the deal. But Mr. Pace; I have a question is there any way my client can help to felicitate there move to a new location that would be beneficial to both sides"?

"Do you mean with some sort of financial help"?

"Yes maybe through a government backed loan to rehab another building".

"We certainly would entertain any help with our budget, as low as it is, we feel hamstringed and unable to move any of our projects along".

"Thank you for being candid with me I am attending a meeting tomorrow on just this proposed land acquisition and the main money man will be there and I will give him all this information to see if we can deal with this problem". Kerry said.

"One other thing before you hang up we had plans drawn up a while back to demolish the building next door to the city owned hotel and increase the apartments by ten that should have satisfied Ms. Frost. It was all approved and then got shelved due to budget constraints. I'll start digging around the files for the plans and if you give me your phone number I'll call you when I find them. I gave him my number than thanked him and told him I would get back to him as soon as possible to let him know where we stand. I wrote down all the conversation I could remember with Mr. Pace so I could tell Larry and maybe he had a solution to this political mess. When the cast iron catalogs got here I was reasonably sure there was a solution in removing the prefab façade and have an architect work it into a new structure that would satisfy the people at the National Register of Historic landmarks.

Larry showed up bright and early in the morning and I met him in the reception area at Carrol's desk.

She was laughing so I knew Larry had a few funning quips in introducing himself. Dick was in but his door was closed; Peter wasn't so I escorted him directly to my office minus the grand tour. As we were getting comfortable Baite appeared in my doorway and asked if we needed coffee at this point I introduced Larry but we both declined the coffee. We were both in a very business mood so I got right to it. I broke out my legal pad that I wrote down the conversation I had with Mr. Pace at the health and human Services. In a mechanical voice I read my notes on the conversation with no other comments except at the end I asked him "What do you think".

"Well it sounds like we could be dealing with a very receptive Agency willing to work with us to help out both of us".

"That's the way this fellow Pace sounded to me; so where do we go from here".

"Good question, did any one talk to the owner of the property at South of Market"?

"About what"?

"About executing the option and buying the property at South of Market"?

"The option doesn't run out for seven more weeks and Hanaford S&L has acquired the option from the developer who quit claimed the property back to the S&L.". I replied.

"Time is money and sitting on your hands is spending money. Your company should make a deal with Hanaford S&L and as I told you Byrd is on the hook and wants it off their books as soon as possible. You could buy the South of Market property at fire sale prices then transact a land swap with the city for their land and after the Real Estate transaction is completed the city agencies have an excuse to relocate the BWS to more habitable apartments at their renovated hotel. After that is completed buy the South of Market property back from the City then go ahead with your plans for your project".

"How would that work"?

"The parties of both properties agree to swop their respective parcels for equal value or if one is worth more than the other a "boot" is established that would be the difference in hard money. It sounds to me the South of Market property is worth more so the City would have to come up with the difference. Here's the piece that makes the deal your company takes back the boot in the form of a second deed of trust that makes it a no cash transaction everyone in the city would love that".

"That might be tricky because it might take forever if one or both of the parties can't agree on a price; it sounds like too many moving parts".

"Not really the owner of the South of Market property has already agreed on a selling price at the end of the option so that cuts the problem in half.

Once the swop was completed we could approach HUD for a government backed low interest loan to rehab the city property then have it turned into a long term mortgage under the auspicious of the Department of Health and Human Services".

The word threw me so I had to ask, "What the hell does auspicious mean"?

"Sort of giving approval and direction and if possible renting the apartments under a long term lease to house people in need. Politically it would be a smart move for the Agency it would help to blunt Ms. Frost's argument of discrimination. Then when the dust settles your company buys the South of Market property back from the City at a price that eliminates the second deed of trust that leaves you with both properties for little more than the original price of the first".

"Why go through that entire rigger mare roll and just buy both properties it seems to me less complicated".

"You told me the situation has turned political having the City own the South of Market property will give them more leverage to counter Ms. Frost's allegations of discrimination and also for them to deal with the National Register of Historical Landmarks. I think it would remove some political obstacles and expedite the start of the development process".

I cut Larry off abruptly when I told him, "It just occurred to me I've never even seen the City property".

Larry mused, "Why don't we call Mr. Pace and get the address of the property and see if he'll meet us there"?

That night I made a point of calling Myra after 6 o'clock; when she answered I apologized for not calling sooner and before I could make an excuse she told me she already talked to Peter and wanted to know when I was available to meet with the FBI. I told her the sooner the better and I'll keep my schedule flexible. We agreed on any time at the beginning of the next week. Before she hung up I asked her if she ever dealt with the city on buying or selling property. She told me she hadn't so I left it at that. When we finished dinner I gave Anne a hand dressing the baby for bed and I mean that literally Gina played with my fingers while Anne changed her diaper and put her into her pajamas. Anne had a glass of wine and suggested we go to the front room and relax so I followed with my coffee. We sat in our usual chairs the Anne said she had coffee today with Esperanza and Deidre. I nodded my head in acknowledgement. "I noticed the same man and woman in two different locations while I was shopping this morning then this afternoon while having coffee with Esperanza and Deidre the same woman was sitting alone having coffee right across from us. When I mentioned it to Esperanza and Deidre they got quiet and I had the feeling they knew something I didn't so I pressed the issue and Deidre said she thought I knew they were security people that were assigned to me. I smiled my idiot smile and had to admit I wasn't told". Deidre went on to explain that the Security was hired by Peter and that she knew the company well in fact they were often hired by the government as security in Diplomatic Missions. "Now my question; why am I being followed and why do I need protection"? I told her I didn't realize they were going to put her under their protection, but I should have realized Peter doesn't do anything halfway.

"The reason there was a break-in at the office and they were after an appraisal I did for a man named Albononi. It turns out the FBI is investigating him for money laundering and Peter may have over reacted by hiring this protection Agency. I wasn't sure I believed what I just said and apparently Anne didn't either.

Consequently there was an atmosphere of doubt for the rest of the evening. Just when I was sure Anne was going to ask more questions the phone rang breaking her train of thought and it was Tom asking me if I wanted to go to the Giant game because the Mets were coming to town. It took me a minute to understand he wanted to talk but not on my phone so I told him I'd have to check with my schedule and I'd call him tomorrow.

When I started out in the morning I was interrupted by a flat tire as soon as I left the back door I could see the car listing in the back. Arnold was leaning on the front fender with folded arms. I turned around and went back into the house and call AAA. When I reemerged Arnold told me changing tires was not in his job description. I told him fear not help is on the way I called AAA. We were the last into the office and Carrol told me Larry was waiting in my office. Arnold went to the library with a pocket book and I went to my office. Dick's door was open so I could hear what business was going on in a one way conversation; I heard Tacoma mention so I assumed he was talking to Oregon. Larry was sitting with his legs crossed and papers in his lap writing in their margins little notes or comments. I walked around my desk and sat in my chair without saying a word because Larry seemed to be engrossed in his work. I gave him another minute then I asked him what's in your lap. He took a deep breath and I thought he was going to yawn, but he excused himself saying his ears feel clogged and they've been driving him crazy all morning aside from that I've been putting some final touches on the proposal we talked about yesterday. I asked him if he thought it was final enough to bring it to Dick and see what the thinks.

"Yeah I do can you ask him if he has time to look at it".

"Well there is no time like the present".

Chapter 30

I called Tom later that morning and we agreed to meet at his studio that afternoon when I got there Oscar was in Tom's office and sitting in Nancy's chair and Nancy was among the missing. Tom came out of his studio and told me he would man the phone while Oscar and I used the studio for privacy so I knew something was up. Oscar almost ritually led me into the studio and we each of us grabbed a director chair facing the mural of the San Francisco Transamerica building used by Tom for photo back ground. He got right to it when he said, "Of course, you know Allen is dead, but some questions have surfaced about what killed him". He paused to let me catch up to the statement then continued. "His partner Jean insisted the body be medically examined before embalming and because of his AIDS condition it was assumed that was the cause of death; as it turned out it was helped along by arsenic, metallic arsenic which in Allen's death is highly suspect. Most arsenic that the average person would encounter would be from ground water or food this arsenic was from smelted metal sometimes used as a weed killer. There was no garden, no flower bed and no place would you use weed killer so I brought the case to the assistant DA and he is dragging his feet and not too enthused about pursuing this as a murder and at this point neither is my Lieutenant. Jean; Allen's old partner is claiming Allen was symptomatically poisoned and it was not a mercy killing somebody wanted him dead. When he was asked who would do such a thing, "He didn't replied he got emotional and started crying; if he's right the only two people I know of is Jean, of course, and Mary Mace it would have to be one of them because they had access to him on a daily bases".

"Of course, he would have to have meant Mary Mace, but when Jean was asked if he meant Mary he got vague and evasive so that leads me to believe he has something to hide".

"Oscar it's pretty apparent to me you still are convinced Mary had something to do with her husband's death".

"I do and I believe Allen was also involved and that might give Mary a reason to eliminate someone who could tie her into the murder of her husband. If I were Jean I would be leery of Mary because she might think Allen told him what went on the night her husband was murdered it might make him next on her list".

"Her list; what list"?

"Think of the people in her life that either have been murdered or died suspiciously and somehow she benefited".

"Could it be your policeman's suspicious nature that drives your conclusions"?

"That could be, but that isn't the main reason I asked Tom to contact you. It has to do with this security company that has been hired as your bodyguard and that reporter Dailey the guy that reported on the attempt on your life in the Chronicle. I got a call from the Captain of your local police station he told me this guy Dailey has been hanging around the station asking a lot of questions about you and your protection agency. Also the Captain has been contacted by someone from the Justice Department and asked to cooperate with this company and its owner by name. With-in a matter of minutes he got a call from a man named Bekkvelt informing the Captain that his guards are armed and on a twenty four hour watch on you and your family. This, of course, was more than just a curtesy call the FBI will do a similar procedures so there is no confusion that would lead to an unintentional physical confrontation between the men guarding you and the police. Are you aware of the guards carrying guns and do you know if the FBI Agents were also informed?

"Yeah I was with my boss and this fellow Bekkvelt when we ran into both Agents Brophy and Clark at an office that they were removing the files under a warrant that covered that office and the one of our clients. Both Brophy and Clark knew Bekkvelt in fact Brophy greeted him like an old friend but Clark not so much".

"I got to say the Justice Department being involved at this level is highly unusual and raises a lot of curiosity the Captain is aware of the bungled attempt on your life so he is running a patrol car by your house twice a night".

I thanked him for the update and then proposed lunch at his convenience at the Pine Street Luncheonette on me.

He said, "You're on; how about Tuesday around 1 o'clock"?

"See you there".

Arnold and I met Myra at her office a day or two later and we took a cab over to the Federal Building. On the way I had the opportunity to tell Arnold about the

Justice Department calling the local police station to inform them of the twenty four hour watch on my house and asked him if this was a usual occurrence. Arnold stayed to form by not answering the question in very few words. The lobby was almost empty and Arnold told us he would wait there so we breezed through the security then took the now familiar route to the floor occupied by the FBI. We were buzzed in by the receptionist then escorted by a lesser agent to Brophy's cubical. Clark was already there and they took us to a large conference room which seemed over kill it was like sitting in a gymnasium. No one remarked about the space so I said nothing and sat at the end of the conference table. I glanced down the table and I had the image of a bowling alley. Clark broke out his tape recorded and announced, "This conversation is going to be recorded so we are going on the recorder". I thought it sounded redundant, but I kept my mouth shut. He continued with almost a pained look on his face, "Now what is all this about a real estate appraisal"? Myra and I were used to Clark's attitude so she took the full appraisal and separated it from her yellow legal pad then slid it across the table in between Brophy and Clark along with my comments about the disparity in the reported money spent on the rehab of the units and the apparent cost of the actual work done. Clark spoke into the tape recorder very officiously describing Myra sliding the appraisal over to them and assigning it "item number one". At this point I knew this meeting was going to take longer than necessary so I decided not to answer any questions without Myra's approval; mainly because it was being taped and who knows what they would interpret from anything I said. Brophy started off with a lot of general questions like my name, where I worked, how I met Alexander Albononi and when did he hire me to do this appraisal? I glanced at Myra and she nodded her head to go ahead and answer. Both Brophy and Clark were interested in my encounter with Johnny Peresci and Albononi's part in reconciling our differences. They spent ten or fifteen minutes asking about Albononi's connection to the embezzlement of the construction money in the Hillcrest Development. Myra asked if they were interested in the appraisal and the subsequence break-in at Mr. Kerry's office and events that led up to it or is this going to be another session on Mr. Kerry's general knowledge. Brophy apologized and said they were just trying to clean up some loose ends and yes they were very much interested in the appraisal. He then opened up the appraisal began to read it then asked questions on my figures and how I reconciled the property's stated construction costs to the actual construction costs. I told him what page and paragraph to turn to for the construction cost for labor and material published for the Bay Area by the Building Contractors Association. Clark stopped fiddling with the tape recorder long enough to state this would be more of an IRS investigation then ours. Brophy gave him a steely look and an awkward moment was avoided when Myra said she thought it would be more than just of interest to them because the property is owned by the Truckers of Limitation Real Estate Investment Company owned by the Cannelli family. It was also brought to our attention that they refinanced the property for over six hundred thousand dollars; a profit, by our math, of three hundred thousand dollars tax deferred. I thought it would be of interest how they could explain where the money came from that was the difference between what they say they spent and what the actual cost was. And to us it looks like this all ties into the Drays S&T that is your ongoing investigation on money laundering. I nudged Myra by the arm to look at the recorder because the light was out; Clark had turned it off. Myra composed herself as coolly as possible then said, "I think we have given you enough information to digest and we could continue this at another time. I am sure you both realize as attorney for my client I am entitled to a copy of the tape recorded interview in its entirety". Clark immediately came alive with all kinds of apologies explaining the recorder malfunctioned destroying the tape. Myra said she would save them any trouble then told Clark to just give her the tape and the case is closed. Brophy and Clark looked at each other several times then informed Myra it would be their responsibility to dispose of it. Myra said, "That's fine I've been taking notes and I will kept this as a document and a record of our releasing a copy of the property appraisal owned by the Truckers of Limitations Real Estate Investments along with all costs compiled by Mr. Kerry". She then started to organize her papers to signal our leaving when Brophy apologized by saying he was sorry this interview got so far afield, but if we would be a little patient for a few more minutes and fill us in on some finer points of Albononi's relationship with Johnny Peresci and the Hillcrest housing development. Myra sat back in her chair and looked over at me with her make it quick expression and let's get out of here. Myra set the mood so I ran with it I told Brophy Albononi was some kind of disciplinarian used by the silent partner, who we suspected was his father, to kept Johnny in line. He also had a relationship with the Truckers of Limitations Investment Company and the Drays S&T. that was the extent of what I know of Mr. Albononi. We left with the usual thanks for coming parting words from the Agents. On our way back we picked up Arnold in the lobby and took a cab to Myra's office. On the way I told her I didn't think the recorder malfunctioned I think Clark turned it off on purpose.

"You can bet our life he did as soon as he realized what he said about the IRS. He knew it would be viewed as a statement of an idiot. Brophy let it out that they found a letter in Mace's files from Welsh laying out exactly how to rehab property with dirty money and then refinance it to recover the cash as a legally deferred tax business transaction".

We got back to my office after lunch and Carrol had a stack of phone messages. I was thumbing through them and told Arnold I was going to ask Carrol to order us sandwiches and if he would like one; he told me he grabbed something at the snack bar in the Federal Building while he was waiting for us. I changed my mind and thought I'd get something later. I took a quick look at my messages and right on top was a phone call from Harry Byrd with the please call back box checked. I thought I'd call Larry first and I was just about to lift the phone when Dick buzzed me on the intercom and asked me to come to his office. He looked busy his usually clean desk was covered with papers separated into piles. He asked me how the meeting with the Bureau went and I gave him a quick rundown on the conversation. He moved a pile of papers and at the bottom was Larry's proposal on the South of Market. He opened up the file folder and pulled out a hand written sheet of paper with his notes and question. I watched him look down his nose through his new reading glasses familiarizing himself with what he wrote then without changing his posture or position looked over his glasses and asked me if this was all Larry's proposal or did I have a hand in it. Just the way Dick phrased the last sentence I knew he didn't like it. I told him Larry wrote the proposal, but I did most of the leg work with an eyeball appraisal of the building and properties. I talked to the gentleman at the City about their building that would be in the swop and he thought HUD would be an avenue of finance to rehab the property with the City leasing it back. I then told him Larry had worked on the original proposal the one you have in your hand and is updating it to further explain why he suggests this complicated procedure.

"I see the Hanaford S&L has the option to buy the property at the South of Market have you contacted them to get a price on the Hotel and see if they're willing to reassign or sell the option"?

"Not yet, Harry Byrd who sits on the loan committee has been offering the property to us, but there has been no price discussed; however I know he is under the gun to get the property off their books and I just got a message to call him".

"Well there's progress give him a call and let me know what happens".

I went back to my office and called Mr. Byrd. I realized it was his privet number because he picked it up on the second ring without it going through his secretary. I told him I was returning his call and he was business-like but friendly. He got right to the South of Market property asking me if I had a chance to look it over. I told him I gave it a basic inspection and an eye ball appraisal. He sounded anxious and asked me what my impressions were. I told him I walked around the inside of the Hotel and apparently the developer did nothing accept install a new entrance door. When I walked the perimeter of the both properties I stopped to inspect the cast iron façade of the other building where I was approached by a woman named Ms. Frost. She informed me the building was in the National Register of Historic Buildings and also a Historic Landmark here in San Francisco and the home of the Battered Women's Sanctuary. I asked him if he could tell me what she is talking about.

"She is a self-appointed do-gooder who at times sounds delusional; I wouldn't pay too much attention to her. She presents herself as a champion of all battered women, but the City's Health and Human Services is the Agency that takes care of the Battered Women".

"That may be but I checked and that particular building is classified as a Historic Landmark which means we'd have a hell of a time getting approval to tear it down to build apartments".

"I do understand your concern, but that is what your company does; take the property out of the Historic Landmark classification and get it rezoned to build apartments. That would be the reason you could acquire both properties at a very reasonable price".

"Let me do some more research on it and I'll get back to you. I'm not putting you off I have to get more information on it so I can present a more viable proposal to my Bosses".

He asked if I had any idea of time I needed before I could get back to him.

I told him I didn't because both Partners were working on their projects and I didn't know how much time they had to spare to go over the proposal and make a decision. He thanked me and hung up.

I sat at my desk for a minute to catch my breath then pick up the phone and called Larry. I filled him in on Dick's reaction to his proposal and my conversation with Harry Byrd. He told me he extended the South of Market paper with more detailed explanations in the proposal and he talked with Mr. Price at City Hall and made an appointment to see the property to be swopped this Wednesday at ten o'clock and if I could make it. I said I would have to get back to him and then he asked me if Byrd quoted a price on the South of Market deal. I told him he seemed over anxious so I was playing coy not even asking the price to give the impression I was dealing with the feasibility of whether the property was worth pursuing. Larry said that was one way of dealing with Byrd, but he would get a price now and start knocking it down. Before he hung up he said he had sent the newer and greater revised proposal today by messenger and should be at our office on the hour. I couldn't resist a jab so I replied, "We're waiting with bated breath". He had to do me one better, "Please relax and breath normal and buy some breath freshener". After we hung up I thought of what Larry just said about getting a price from Byrd now and start knocking it down so I called Byrd back. I told him I was sorry because my mind had been elsewhere, but you never quoted a price and I'll obviously need it to present it as a proposal. He started off with a sales pitch on the Hotel saying it was underpriced because the land alone was worth more without the building. I cut in and asked the price before he got carried away with more bullshit. I still had to squeeze him to quote a price and he finally said, "With almost one hundred and fifty feet of commercial frontage on South of Market and the property close to an acre the going price would have to be $320,000.00". I said nothing and let it hang in the air for an uncomfortable moment or two then told him that was close to the price of prim property in the business district. His response was that this property is prim property in walking distance of all major bank branches, the stock exchange and the main financial district. I bit my tongue before I said something really sarcastic and just said, "I wouldn't want to walk it in the rain". What about the other property"?

"To buy the option its $15,000 if you exercise the option the property is $220,000".

"I'll have to ask the obvious question why is the property, with the Cast Iron Building and twice the acreage, a $100,000.00 less"?

"Two things first the obvious one is the problems getting it out of the Land Preservation to rezone it and second the owners inherited it from a relative who died and left it to them, however its free and clear of any debt, but he put it in the National Register to save taxes and it will be some work clearing title. They're just interested in selling it; any price is pure profit".

"I'll take this to a meeting as soon as I can arrange it with Mr. Somers and Travillian along with some comparative sales in the neighborhood".

"I can help you there; we have five properties that were recently sold and all in the close proximity". I thanked him, but told him I would have to do it impartially.

Chapter 31

Things were relatively quiet through the following week except for the meeting Larry and I had with Mr. Pace from the City and a gentleman he brought along from the Human Welfare & Neighborhood Development by the name of Lester Morris. We were told he had great influence in rents and concessions considered by the Welfare Department. Mr. Morris was quite helpful in fact he laid out how and who to get in touch with at HUD. He told us they had already approved the plans for the restoration of the building involved in the swop, of course, that was before they ran out of money. He said he was in favor of the tentative plan to solve the problem with the BWS. That coincided with Dick asking if Larry and I had the finished proposal on the South of Market deal. We told him we had; so he told us he would set the meeting for Tuesday of the following week.

Larry and I went into the meeting totally prepared and confident the proposal not only had merit, but the City and Byrd were on board to start negotiations. So Tuesday we met with Dick and Peter in Dick's office at nine sharp. I sat across from Larry and Dick across from Peter at his small conference table. It took on the air of a normal conference with a pitcher of ice water and glasses with pens and pencils at each sitting, but the joking comments about the morning news especially a weatherman who couldn't get it right and Baite circling the table with a tray asking if anyone wanted coffee with their pastries took some starch out of the meeting. Peter kicked it off with a vote of approval on the succinctness of the final proposal. He mentioned it was easy to read and understand and brief which is always appreciated. However Dick and I have decided there will be no debate I for one am in favor of going ahead with the deal of buying the two properties on South of Market whether or not the City lives up to their verbal commitment and push for rezoning. Dick on the other hand is not and he'll give you his reasons. Dick started off asking me why I was programing the properties for light commercial and apartments of fifty units he didn't think it could be justified because there was nothing close to that many or style within a mile of the area to warrant the rents needed to make the project viable.

"I agree with you it is out of the way that's why it has to be a destination. The front will be the original cast iron façade in the 19th century motif and the rest of structure has to fit into that motif with a top of the line general store featuring gourmet groceries and a restaurant owned and operated by a locally popular chief that has a following. Parking has to be also a feature with enough for the residents and the commercial businesses. I know it will be expensive to build but I feel if we do it right the first time it will prove out over the long run".

"What kind of rents are you talking about"?

"Maybe a tad less than the middle to high side of the better places in town but we give them extras they wouldn't get anywhere else like valet parking for the residence at the elevator in the main garage. Offer car service for a fee on premise such as oil changes and a gas pump to top off their cars. You could even have a grocery delivery from the general store on premise.

I believe if it is run right with good people it will gain a reputation and when the first wave of tenants cycle through in a year or two you can start adjusting the rents".

"Why didn't you put those reasons in the proposal"?

"I thought they were getting ahead of the basic proposal; we really haven't gotten into the architecture and I just got the catalogue from the Foundry that makes the Cast Iron facades. They cast the iron in Walla-Walla up in Washington then ship it down here in pieces to be assembled on the job site so the cost hasn't been established especially if we decide to extend the facade to the third, fourth or even the fifth floor".

"Dick looked over at Peter and said, "Sounds good". Then back to me and said, "Start negotiating".

I was on my way home and on high octane it now looked for sure this project will get off the ground. Arnold was driving when he turned to me and asked, "What's got you so stoked that you're humming "Hail to the Chief".

"Was I? I didn't think anyone could recognize the tune when I hum it so far off key".

"I heard it in all the keys imaginable standing at attention for twenty years".

"I take it then you were in the military".

"Semper Fi".

"That was the longest conversation he spoke since he started as my bodyguard and it turned out it would be the longest up until his job ended". I wished him a good night and went into the house the backway. As I was going through the pantry I could smell what could only be my Mother-in-Law's cooking. As I entered the kitchen she turned abruptly from the stove and bellowed out "You hit the headlines again". Before I could answer Carl my Father-in-Law as he was coming from the hall said, "I thought we were going to let Jim get relaxed before we showed him the evening paper".

"Well what's the big deal show him the paper".

As Carl was pushing the evening paper across the table I saw the headlines. "Justice Department protecting Jim Kerry their star witness". I squared the paper up on the table to read it and I scanned a few sentences ahead to something that caught my eye. It was the name of Mariam Frost and this guy Dailey the reporter was claiming her as his source and went on to quote her. "This man Kerry is using the Justice Department to pressure the City Agencies here in San Francisco to condemn the building the Battered Women's Sanctuary now occupies to move to a building owned by the City so his company can tear it down and build apartments instead of up grading this building". The next two sentences were just filler, but then he reports there was a brake-in at the office of Scranton & Associates on Montgomery Street Mr. Kerry's employer. On the police report the only thing taken was an appraisal done by Mr. Kerry for the Truckers of Limitation. It's a Real Estate investment group owned by the wife of the notorious Freddy "Beans" Cannelli now embroiled in an investigation of the Drays Savings and Trust for extortion, money laundering and counterfeiting government securities. It appears this now mysterious appraisal has disappeared so the Justice Department has placed security around the clock to protect their only witness to the contents of the appraisal". He reminds the readers of the attempt on my life and the gory details of how they mistook the garage attendant for me and it cost him his life and then on to the murder of Johnny Peresci the one suspected accused of ordering my murder. He then tied Johnny Peresci into the Drays S&T investigation for money laundering and his connection with Freddy "Beans Cannelli". When I thought about it he made a lot of editorial leaps in his story but I could see he had some inside information and wondered where and who gave him the information.

When Anne arrived with the bread for dinner and little Gina under her arm my mother-in-law, out did the town crier, informing Anne and most of our neighbors of the newspaper headlines. It took more than an hour to get Anne back to normal and get my mother-in-law off the subject of the newspaper article. I asked her what smelled so good and that did the trick, she went into detail on how she made the cannelloni. I told her it sounded great, but in a dead serious tone I asked her, "Isn't that the same as Rollitini"? She adamantly defended the difference by telling me that Rollitini has chicken livers in the stuffing and cannelloni had just chicken. I couldn't resist the opening so I got my jab in, "Well if you just add some chicken livers to your cannelloni we would have Rollitini".

At this point she started into an elaborate explanation in detail of the difference between in preparing the two recipes. She stopped when she realized from the grins on everyone's face I was putting her on. That put her into a defensive attitude with a reply that could only come from her, "anyone who couldn't pick a decent color for a car couldn't possible understand a recipe".

No one said a word, but you could tell we were all having trouble digesting the last statement. She was glowing in the wake of her last remark then said, "Dinner is ready". She was smug through the rest of dinner, but quiet which suited everyone.

Arnold was waiting in the morning as usual leaning against my car in the back of the house. There was nothing cryptic about his expression it was his everyday disapproving look and is all he said was did you see the evening paper. I told him I did and we were off to the office without a further word. Likewise nothing was said at the office except good morning so I trolled off to my sanctuary and began to set up the phone calls to get the property negotiations started. My first call was to Harry Byrd he wasn't in so I left a message to call me back. My second was to Mr. Pace at the Health and Human Serves at the City. He also wasn't in so I left a message to call back. I sat at my desk with a hollow feeling with the papers for negotiating set in order on my console to my right, but no one to discuss it with it was a frustrating feeling. The intercom buzzed to snap me out of it; it was Peter and he asked me to come to his office. When I entered I could tell he was going over the construction stages of the Residential Care Facility in Oakland and he looked a little distant. He looked up when I entered his office and I thought it took him a second to recognize me and his face went from a question mark to smile when he said, "Jim good come in and sit down".

"As you can see I'm trying to decipher the stages of this construction schedule for paying the contractors as you know we are directly financing the actual construction. Normally a bank would do this but we're the bank so I need some help. I should have had you in on this right from the start, I thought you had a lot going at the time but now I need help".

"Of course, let me see what you got? And one question if you don't mind"?

"Shoot".

"Why are you financing this project out of your packet"?

"That's one of the secrets Dick and I thought we would ease the information to you a bit at a time looking back we should have clued you in right from the start. We don't actually use our money we have investors back in the East that put money into our projects on a case by case bases. We put together a quick Corporation of limited liability and pool the money in an account in a local bank here in California. The investors get the interest rather than a bank and when we finish and mortgage the property the short turn around on their construction money makes their yield higher. At this point we give the investors the option to assume the mortgage or take the pay out on their construction loan. Our track record has been very good and so there is never a shortage of investors".

"Well that's great but what do you want me to do"?

"They're done with the demolition and of course, you know Peavy he's taking over as superintend of construction and I'd like you to coordinate stages for payment pretty much what you were doing at the Hillcrest Project".

"Is Peavy on the job site today? If he is I can run over there today and get started".

"I assume so but you can call him on the job site he's taken over the construction trailer. While you're here can you tell me what's your take on the article in the evening paper on you by this reporter Dailey"?

"I never met this guy and the only thing I heard was he hangs around the police stations for drips of information. Maybe you could ask your friend Bekkvelt he seems to have a lot of influence with the Justice Department".

"It's probably not that important it will be old news by this afternoon and forgotten". I took the file from Peter and retreated to my office to look through the file. Looking through the file I saw four Polaroid photos each from a different position showing the façade with the stone face supported with steel I-beams and the rest of the building demolished. I picked up the phone and called Joe Peavy over in Oakland to tell him I'd be by today and he told me that would work great because they've started on the foundations and I'd be great working together again. By the time I got there the concrete contractor had half the foundation dug and Peavy had taken new Polaroids in the same four directions. We chatted for an hour or so while Arnold scoped out the site and talked to the construction workers. I laid out the scheme of things as far as the construction draws and to expect me a couple of times a week. I took the photos and put the dates on their backs then said good-bye and we headed for the office. It was now past noon so I stopped and picked up a sandwich to go and again Arnold passed on lunch I was wondering when the hell does this guy eat? When I ask him he said he'd get something later. I cruised past Carrol as she held my messages in her hand at the level of my waist and I snared them without breaking stride. I had my hands full so I had to wait until I got to my office before I could see who they were from. I thought they felt a little light there was just two messages one from my wife and one from Larry. I was a little disappointed I'd expected an answer from Harry Byrd and Mr. Pace. I called Anne first at the pre-kindergarten school where Anne was keeping their books she wanted to know if I liked the idea of going to Mendocino Coast for a weekend in September. She explained the owner of the school owned a house near the town of Mendocino and was offering to rent it for the weekend but there are other people interested and we'd have to tell her now.

"Absolutely, how many bedrooms and baths"?

"Three bedroom and two baths and it's on the cliffs over-looking the Pacific Ocean one of the girls here stayed there once and told me the sunsets are magnificent and says it's a perfect get away".

"How much"?

"We're still talking price because that's the height of the season".

"That means you're afraid to tell me the price".

"Don't be a cheap-skate I'll tell you when I get home tonight it's not that expensive".

"Then that means it's expensive".

"I'll get a hold of Nancy and see if she and Tom would like to go that will cut the price in half".

"You're going to rent it whether I agree or not so just go ahead and tell her yes".

"I knew you'd understand". And then she hung up.

I hung up and laughed to myself because I knew how her mind worked she already rented the house in Mendocino and then called me to tell me the decision had to be made immediately or the house would be gone forever. Somehow that makes me part of the decision good or bad. I got back to business and called Larry I could tell by his voice things aren't going well. So I asked the obvious question "how's it going"?

"I wish I knew I've been calling Mr. Pace all morning and I know he's dodging me so I called the other fellow Mr. Morris and he was more forth-coming. He told me because of that article in the paper about you and your company the City Fathers have put a hold on the swop because it is too politically charged".

"Just give me a few minutes I'm going to try and get Harry Byrd I think he's avoiding me also one way or the other I'll call you back". I dialed Harry's privet number and he answered not realizing it was me and it was obvious when he started fumbling around the issue of the South of Market property. I pushed the issue and he finally told me the Savings and Loan Directors have soured on the sale of the property and decided to put it on the books as inventory. I knew what was coming, but I asked anyway. "You and I know that is bullshit S&L's don't voluntarily take bad loans into inventory so what's going on"?

"I'm afraid it's you they feel you have a history of associating with questionable characters and it would somehow reflect on the Savings and Loan".

"I don't know how much you had to do with this decision, but my company and me by extension have the money and the plan to get you and your S&L out of this very bad loan YOU made and I think it will come back to bit you in the ass". I called Larry back told him what Byrd said and we agreed to meet tomorrow to try and sort things out.

I could hear Dick and Peter in the outer office coming back from lunch so I figured no sense waiting to give them the news that the South of Market deal was falling apart so I got up and intercepted them before they got to their offices. Peter didn't seem to be surprised when I told them we had trouble with the deal, but Dick was frowning and I had no idea what was going through his mind. Peter waved us both into his office I sat as Peter skirted around his desk to his seat, but Dick remained standing with his arms folded. Peter said, "Let's hear it". I went through the morning's events step by step trying not to have my involvement the sole reason for the deal to fall apart with no success. I finally apologized in around about way and saw Dick smiling. "Peter and I talked about this very thing this afternoon at lunch. We thought this could be an eventuality so not to worry we'll go ahead with the purchase of the Cast Iron Building property when the option expires assuming the price is still within bounds. You would have to believe the S&L would not exercise the option they're in deep enough and another $220,000.00 would be throwing good money after bad. I believe Mr. Byrd knows first- hand about throwing good money away. He has to be under a lot of pressure to do something about that hotel loan he made and if we buy the property next door it would have to occur to him we would be an obvious buyer who would be interested in the property. Peter told me he checked with the original

Realtor who wrote up the option contract on the Cast Iron property and said the owners are very anxious to sell so we'll deal with this Mariam Frost and the relocation of the Battered Women's Sanctuary. As far as the National Register of Historic places and it being a purported San Francisco landmark that can be handled politically most of these titles were for tax purposes and the City would love to get them back on the tax rolls. That leaves the City property that they would like to develop to ease the pressure to houses the homeless and or Battered Women but they lack the funds. That was the other property in the swop if it made economic sense to buy it rehab it then lease it back to the City over a long term bases that would also be on the table". I left Peter's office a little numb I went back to my office and sat thinking; it was slow in coming but I finally realized Dick and Peter were ahead of Larry and I the whole time. They had formulated plan "B" before Larry and I had put together the original deal.

After I organized my file by inserting Dick and Peter's changes I called Larry and told him how Dick and Peter had a plan "B" that would change the deal and we probably do nothing until the option on the Cast Iron Building property expires. I asked him what he thought about plan "B" and his response was interesting he said, "When you got money and experience all else follows". After I hung up I couldn't understand if he was being funny or he was serious with some quote from some half-baked philosophy major from psychology class 101. At any rate we were back to square one. I decided to leave everything in my office for the night so Arnold and I headed for the elevator. When we got to the garage and the attendant was getting my car Arnold told me there was going to be trouble at the Oakland job site. He waited until the attendant brought the car and left then asked if I wanted him to drive. I told him I would and as soon as we got in he told me the construction workers on the job site told him there was going to be a job action and a picket line by the Teamsters Union because there are nonunion workers on the job. That would mean no concrete deliveries.

"What's the first I heard of it are you sure the information is accurate"?

"They all said they were told that morning so I called Mr. Bekkvelt and he said he would look into it today. He has experience in this sort of thing so if I were you I would wait to hear from him". Nothing more was said so it was a quiet ride home. I was moody all evening and Anne asked me a few times if anything was wrong and when I was evasive or didn't answer she decided I was a lost cause and ignored the mood I was in and let me stew in my self-imposed dilemma. The morning brought little relief and Arnold was no help he told me he hadn't heard from Mr. Bekkvelt so the situation was Status Quo. On the way to the office I was trying to figure a way around a Teamster's strike if there was one and what Bekkvelt could possibly do. When I got to the office my mind was a fuzz-ball. Dick and Peter were not in yet so I called Joe Peavy at his construction trailer hoping for some good news. When he answered "Peavy" his voice was high and sounded strained. I started to ask him what was going on when he interrupted me by stating, "There was a job action going on right now with a picket line and he had no warning yesterday this was going to happen. Then no more than ten minutes ago I got a call from someone with no name stating if you forgot what was in your missing appraisal and couldn't remember being on the Berkeley property site the job action would go away. If this is agreeable tell your construction superintendent to tell the picket line leader that the incident has been resolved and the concrete trucks will roll".

"Did you recognize the caller"?

"No but he called from a public phone because he took too long to get me the message and the operator interrupted telling his time was up and to deposit another twenty five cents".

"Alright try and keep some kind of normal progress going on the job site and I'll get back to you as soon as I can with how we'll handle this". In less than a half-hour I heard Peter in the reception area talking to some-one. Before I could get from behind my desk Peter was at my doorway with Mr. Bekkvelt I stood and invited them in Mr. Bekkvelt entered first and then Peter as he closed the door. Mr. Bekkvelt sat with Peter to follow and both had that teacher to student look so I knew I was in for a lesson in an informational format. Mr. Bekkvelt broke into a smile when he said Arnold thinks you're the most cooperative client he has been associated with since he started in this business and I have to commend you it makes for a much safer situation for everyone. Peter had the same expression he had when he sat down then said Mr. Bekkvelt had an explanation of how to handle the job action over in Oakland and then motioned for him to start. "I talked last night with an Agent JB Kliner from the Bureau I'll just say she's in communications.

She told me they intercepted that call that Joe Peavy got yesterday for you and identified the caller. Brophy called me this morning to recommend you do as the caller suggests just play along. From past experience I believe the Bureau has this under control and this is just another piece of evidence they're putting together in building their case against Cannelli and the Drays Savings and Trust here in Oakland. Let me tell you why I think Brophy's opinion is a compelling one. Your project over in Oakland will conservatively take one year and the concrete structure itself along with all the sidewalks and walkways will take a lot of concrete enough that you can't afford any disruptions and the length of the trial will fall with in that year more or less insulating you against any strikes. On the Bureau's side they like the idea that Cannelli and company will be under the false belief that the bureau knows nothing about your damming Appraisal". I was riveted to Bekkvelt's every word when he finished I found myself sitting straight in my chair and my hands knotted in my lap like I was back in the principal's office in grammar school. I tried to regain my adult posture by unknotting my hands and using them to smooth out an imaginary wrinkle or two on my slacks. Peter saw that I was embarrassed by my own uncomfortable behavior so he went at great lengths to try to persuade me that he hadn't thought of this approach to this problem and he was sure Luke's solution makes sense. His little pep talk helped and I got a grip on myself to a point where I could ask a few meaningless questions about the Bureau's involvement which were answered by Bekkvelt in a tone of tolerance. The rest of the meeting was a discussion of the loose ends which Peter tied up in a hurry and they left. I called Joe Peavy at the job site. He answered on the second ring and I told him to go ahead with the caller's advice from yesterday and tell the picket-line leader the problem has been resolved. Joe asked if I was sure about this and told me if you give into these people once they'll be back more and more with demands. If I were you I'd go to the City of Oakland because they have an agreement with the Federal government on this sort of thing where local contractors can be hired by the City belonging to the union or not to help employment of the local labor force. I knew he had the best interests of the company in mind but I couldn't tell him the real reason for this decision so I told him I agreed with him but the decision was made at the top. He said, "O.k. I can see the loud mouth on a bull horn right now so I'll go tell him now". I knew Joe felt defeated but so did I. I changed to another outside line and called Larry hoping to bare my soul on the situation over in Oakland when instinctively stopped. I heard Peter and Bekkvelt in the hall and when Peter said I'll talk to him which gave me pause so I put the phone down and waited for Peter to call me into his office instead he appeared at my door entrance. "I'd like to explain what's going on and Luke Bekkvelt's involvement in all this". He seemed to realize he could be heard in the outer office so he took a cautious step in and closed the door. He didn't sit so I knew this would be a short talk and in turn I leaned forward with my arms folded and my elbows on my desk with a look of complete attention. What he told me I had half guessed that Bekkvelt was a contractor that has worked for the State Department from time to time and therefore had connections to the federal law enforcement agencies and sometimes there ongoing investigations. "Through happenstance your Appraisal of the Berkeley property is a nail into this man Cannelli's coffin. So for all the reasons we discussed before in my office I think it would be a prudent move to go along with his suggestion". I told him I had already called Peavy and I was sure the picket line would be gone tomorrow. He nodded uncomfortably and returned to his office. When I thought I had all I wanted to deal with Carrol buzzed me on the intercom to tell me a Mrs. Mace was on line two. I ran my eyes around the room and took a deep breath than lifted the receiver and punched line two. "Mary what's shaken"? My street talk caught her off guard so her response was a little slow but very Mary, "If I showed you; you might leave your wife". I was always unsure where flirting crossed over to seduction with Mary so I laughed it off and asked what I could do for her. She wanted to ask me about investing some of her money from her inheritance. I told her that really wasn't my field, but I could recommend several good investment counselors. She said she had already talked to a few and they just confused her so if I had time maybe we could meet at my office and help her understand her options and then I could take her to lunch. The lunch part was said tongue in cheek so she could say she was only kidding if I declined with an excuse of pressing business, but I didn't. We made a date for the following day at 10:30.

That night I asked Anne if she knew how much Mary had inherited and she said only what I told her "a few hundred thousand enough to pay down the Union

Street Flats to a positive cash flow with about one hundred thousand to put into a bank CD". I told Anne about Mary's phone call and she told me she thinks she has something else on her mind if she got investment counseling she is being cagey money never confused her. One thing about Mary that Nancy said, "Most men see her as beautiful and helpless however she is the epitome of the femme fatal". I thought about that but I knew Nancy disliked Mary for an unknown reason and I was sure that played into her opinion.

Ten thirty the next morning Mary arrived. The office was in full swing. Dick had a meeting with two men from Oregon and Peter was in conference with Dr. Yee. Carrol buzzed me to tell me Mrs. Mace was here to see me so I popped out of my office and headed for the reception area. My movements locked up just a hair as I saw Mary; she looked devastating. Of course, she was standing half turned in my direction to help her to create a magazine photo. She was dressed in form fitted man tailored light grey pin stripped suit with patch pockets and a small silver flower pin in her lapel. She was accessorized in black two inch pumps that showed gracefully under the cuffs of the sewn increases of her suit pants along with her matching leather shoulder bag and attaché case. To top off her ensemble she wore a white man tailored Oxford pointed collared shirt opened at the neck with a black onyx neckless close to her throat and matching earrings. Her dark hair was parted in the middle and flowed in natural waves to her shoulders with what looked like natural grey streaks, of course they weren't; if she had on make-up it was a touch of lip stick the rest was all natural. I remarked how handsome she looked in her business attire. She just nodded with a smile and we headed for my office. I offered her a chair and by the time I got around my desk to my chair she was seated with both her shoulder bag and attaché case on the floor. She had her legs crossed and was removing a pair of black skin tight leather gloves. I sat in mine and we got to her questions about her investments. She said she saw two different counselors and their advice was pretty much the same kind of standard approach to the stock market they recommended brokerage houses and safe types of investments you know widow and orphans stocks. I'm looking for something a little more tangible maybe a business or real estate something I can see. I could see where this was going and I would avoid being her business advisor at all cost. She brought up Jean Le Beau's boutique as a possible investment she said she could buy Allen's piece of the business. So I countered with she would have a very good idea how well the business was doing and what Allen's end would be worth. She appeared to be thinking it over but I knew she had thought all this out way before hand and somehow she was trying to hook me into this business with her. She sort of coyly said that she needed someone to organize things to set up the business on financially sound bases. Again I countered with she could get a lawyer who specialized in setting businesses on a strong financial bases and I could certainly recommend one. She got quiet for a few heart beats then said you're suggesting Myra Pacemann's law firm. I told her that was exactly who I was thinking of, but there are plenty other lawyers who could handle the job. She seemed to lose interest and changed the subject by asking what restaurant I had in mind for lunch. I told her Le Central it's in walking distance only a few blocks on Bush Street. She started to snicker then told me John use to say they only served beans there. I said, "Yah the cassoulet it's my favorite, but they have a great Nicoise salad". I thought we were ready to leave when she said, "I have something to show you it's a file that John had hidden that the Feds missed". She opened her attaché case and took out a manila envelope and started to hand it to me. Without making any attempt to take it I asked what was in it. "She said a seven inch reel of a whole bunch of separate recordings of conversations and a print out of a column of numbers and names I didn't recognize".

"Why didn't you give it to the Feds when they were searching his effects"?

"Well I didn't find them until later so I got nosey and rented a tape recorder to listen to the type, but I didn't understand what everyone was talking about so I put it back in the envelope and forgot about it till now. So I was hoping you would give them to the Feds to save me the embarrassment of explaining the time lapse".

"Well how do I explain to Brophy and Clark where and how I got them"?

"You're clever you'll think of something".

"No I'm not clever: I'm not going to look at them and I'll give them to the Feds and tell them just what you told me". She seemed a little miffed. she toyed with her shoulder bag strap as though she was thinking of an answer, but I felt this was all part of her script; she was an excellent actress and I was sure she had a plan B. I had a sneaking suspicion all this was her plan B, but I couldn't figure out what was her objective.

When we left my office at around eleven forty five we encounter a gauntlet of people leaving at the same time. Dick stepped out of his office with his clients and when he saw Mary he light up with a surprised hello then introduced her to his two clients. Peter and Dr. Yee were next and Dick introduced her to them and Baite was at the receptionist desk with Arnold so I did the honors before we left. Arnold was at the elevator before us and when the doors opened he ushered us in. Mary gave him a questioning look so I explained Arnold was my security man and would accompany us to the restaurant that seemed to satisfy her and she asked no more questions, but I could see her jaw locked in scrutiny. When we got to the restaurant Arnold surprised me by speaking to the mater-de in French obviously about our reservation and we were shown to a table in a corner that seemed made for privacy while Arnold stayed at the bar in our direct line of sight. Mary was obviously impressed and asked, "How many languages did your security man speak". I told her I didn't know he spoke French in fact he spoke so little I wasn't sure he spoke English. She frowned at my joke then danced around the issue of the manila envelope during lunch except she asked if I recognized any of the numbers on the print out. I said, "How could I; I didn't see them so I don't have a clue". That's when she slid a note over to me with numbers on it I looked surprised when she said those are the numbers that are in the envelope see if you can make heads or tails of them. I automatically slipped them into my pocket. When we finished Arnold had a cab waiting for Mary at the curb. As we left the restaurant she got all the attention and I was all but invisible this was to be expected. When we got outside she asked Arold what if she had made other arrangements and didn't need a cab. He answered he would simple tell the cab to go. Mary looked at me and said, "He's not only security but a Major-domo". Mary got into the cab and left. Arnold and I walked back to 300 Montgomery and when we got into the elevator I asked Arnold, "How many languages do you speak"? He casually said, "Just a little French, you know ordering from a restaurant menu and getting direction to move around a French speaking country". He was too casual about it so I was sure he was understating his language skills after all he worked for Bekkvelt who probably worked at American Embassies' all over the world. I began to feel even more secure under his protection. There were no messages so I called Joe Peavy to see what if anything was going on at the Oakland job site. He told me nothing was new and the work was going along smoothly and then mentioned there was a construction draw due. I told him I would be out in the morning with the check book so have all the bills to be paid. I sat back and looked at the manila envelope thinking of how best to get it to the FBI. I was sort of spaced out when I realized Peter was in my office door way he said, "A very pretty lady is she a client of ours"?

"I will do my best to not have her as a client". With that Peter stepped into my office and closed the door then said, "Dick tells me she is John Mace's widow. You sound like it's complicated is there a problem"?

"I'm afraid it is her real reason for coming here was to give me an envelope of her husband's full of evidence that the Feds missed when they tossed their apartment a few years back and I'm trying to figure out how to get it to the Feds with as little involvement as possible".

"Go through Myra and let her handle it". I looked up at Peter and said, "Problem solved".

"There has been another problem solved, Cannelli, Kerrigan, Albononi and four others were found guilty by a grand jury on a number of counts and are being held over for trial. Of course, they posted bail and are hunkered down with their attorneys over in Oakland awaiting the trial date".

"I thought Kerrigan had run and was not found yet"?

"That's true but I imagine he was found guilty in absentereo, but Bekkvelt told me one of the principals is willing to testify against the others for considerations probably a reduced sentence or they might cut him loose. He thinks it's Albononi".

"Now that you mentioned Bekkvelt; I wonder if you could ask him a favor. Mary slid a note to me at lunch with numbers on it and told me they were the numbers on the print out in the envelope. I have no idea what they are and I bet Bekkvelt could find out on the QT".

Peter put his hand out and said he'd run it passed him and see what he says.

I called Myra and told her the situation with Mary Mace and the envelope. She asked if I looked at it. I told her sort of and that Mary slid a note with the print out numbers on it to me at lunch. "But you didn't open it and it's sealed".

"No I didn't it is sealed". Then she told me to bring it over personally. When I did she gave me a receipt then she told me she'd let the Feds know about it and see how they wanted to handle it. I put the envelope into my attaché case along with the check register and checks for the Oakland project for tomorrow and then corralled Arnold and he drove me over to Myra's office where I dropped off the envelope then we headed home. Arnold was not only talkative on the way home but informative. He said he saw Mary tell me what was in the envelope at lunch and that the Feds missed it when they initially searched their home. He told me to treat her with caution because she has all the ear marks of someone working on her own agenda and could possibly be using me to channel information to the Feds for her own purposes. I thought for a minute what he just said, "You said you saw her tell me". Then you must read lips. He froze for a spit second then smiled and said, "You once said I didn't talk much you just got an example why". Almost spontaneously we both started laughing. When we got to my house he asked me to please keep the conversation to ourselves I nodded an OK. As I was getting out of the car I asked if he could read lips in French. He said, "Now you're pushing it".

My mother-law was in the kitchen chopping vegetables and preparing her famous marinara sauce. When I asked her where Carl was she all most bit my head off. "What the hell do you think I got nothing else to do all day but to keep tabs on my husband". I thought, oh-oh the honey moon is over. I took a beer out of the frig then headed for our bedroom. I put my case on a little work table I used to go over paper work in privet then went to the front room to stay clear of my Mother-law. It didn't work she caught up with me in the front room. She was in her uniform with the tools of her trade, an apron and a wooden spoon. She wagged the spoon at me while she wanted to know why I was home so early. The mood she was in it wasn't hard to figure Carl was incommunicado at his club. I made the mistake of answering her. I told her I had to get an early start tomorrow so I left the office early today. "Yeah you sit around drinking beer while your wife is working you men are all the same sitting around while the women do all the work". I had enough of her snide remarks and smug comments she finally hit my exasperation button. I told her outside of the kitchen she didn't know what a day's work was and for thirty years you went through an average of two cleaning ladies per year that alone says volumes. I've been told that's a neighborhood record. As far as making dinner here to my knowledge you invite your self no one asks you to cook so why don't you just shut the stove off and leave. The color red started at her neck and rushed to the top of her head getting darker with rage then she exploded. "You don't even belong here this is my house I gave it to Anne so you can't tell me to go; especially from someone who can't even pick a decent color for a car". The car thing made me laugh and took the steam out of the moment so I told her to go back to the kitchen and finish the marinara sauce. She mumbled something about not being appreciated and headed back to the kitchen to finish her marinara sauce. I realized she was impenetrable and will deal with only what she wants to. It wasn't long before I heard Anne's car coming through the alley. When she came into the kitchen I heard her ask her mother what she was doing hear. Her mother immediately started into a rant about me and not being appreciated. I heard Anne ask where her father was and she got the same answer I got about drinking beer when all the women are out working. Little Gina came running down the hall followed by Anne. She jumped into my lap and Anne headed for her chair. She sat with a heavy sigh and asked what's going on. I told her I think the honey moon is over. Her face drifted with a forlorn look to the front window and through the wavy rain glass to a cable car passing by, "Well it was fun while it lasted".

It was raining hard when we left my house and let up substantially by the time we were over the bridge and on the job site in Oakland, but still coming down. We parked right in front of the construction trailer where I could get a good view of the site. It was coming along nicely all the foundations were poured and the forms were in place to pour the first floor walls. There were only two or three men in raingear tying up rebar other than that the job was at a standstill. Arnold had driven over so he stayed in the car listening to the news on radio while I lugged myself into the construction trailer. Joe Peavy was at a desk pushing around bills and payroll. He heard me coming so when I entered he just pointed to a table next to his desk and started moving the paperwork to the table as he said good morning. He had everything arranged to be paid, but before that I asked him are there any problems. He told me no just the weather we're pouring high strength concrete and this rain can dilute it or otherwise contaminate it so the weather is controlling the pace of the work. "I take it then there's no problem with the Unions"?

"No; so far so good".

"If you can I'd like a time line on the progress here. I'll tell you why the obvious one is we'd like to know when you expect to finish, but more important the construction money is being drawn down from an escrow account in Pittsburg and the longer the job takes the more interest we pay".

"I'll have it by the end of next week". We went over the bills and the payroll; I wrote out the checks posted them and I was on my way. When I got back in the car I told Arnold thank god for Joe because this job could be a heart attack maker". When we got back to the office the only message was from Myra so I gave her a call. She said she was in contact with the FBI ever since she gave them the envelope and they've been bitchy and persistent about who gave the envelope to her.

"They're threatening to get a judge to do a number of things to put me through a ringer if I don't comply, but they're blowing smoke they really can't do a hell of a lot because of the Lawyer client relationship. I have to ask you now do you know what was in the envelope"?

"Not for sure I gave you the print out with the numbers Mary gave me at the restaurant and she told me there was a seven inch tape recording reel with different conversation and she couldn't understand what they were talking about".

"Did she mention if she recognized any of the voices maybe even her husband's"?

"You know I didn't occur to me to ask, but if it was John's tape it stands to reason she recognized some of the voices. I'll bet she's panicking that who-ever is on it will find out she listen to the tape so there must be something on that tape that is incriminating or the FBI wouldn't be jumping through hoops".

"Listen to me Jim; don't talk to anyone about this until this plays out and the content is made public".

"Well it's a little late I told Peter and asked him to check with Bekkvelt on the QT on the numbers on the print out".

"Well they're responsible men ask them to keep it under their hats until it's made public".

Carol buzzed me and asked if I wanted something from the Deli for lunch and also Larry called while I was on the phone with Myra. I told her a turkey on rye with mayo only then switched to an outside line and dialed Larry number. The first thing he asked if there was anything knew on the plan B decision to go ahead and buy the Cast Iron Building property. "As far as I know it is still in the works as soon as I find anything out I'll call you. The place has been real busy and I've inherited the Oakland Residential Facility construction project and there has been a few bumps, but it looks all straightened out now so I'll have more time to look at the Cast Iron Building deal. I'll call you and we'll have lunch and I'll fill you in on what's new and exciting". As soon as I hung up Carrol buzzed me to tell me Anne was on the other line. I punched the blinking button and just said, "What's up"?

"You were on the money last night; the honey moon is over my father called this morning to tell me he's filing for a legal separation".

"He said he's filing does that mean your mother doesn't know yet"?

"No not yet but I'm sure she'll know before the day is out so I'm calling you to warn you about tonight I'm sure she'll be over the house but I don't know if she'll be the martyr or the scorned woman either way she'll be targeting you".

"So what do you want me to do"?

"Work tonight don't come home until 9:30 or 10 by that time she should be ready to go home".

"Where's Carl".

"Evidently he's been staying at the club so this has been coming".

"OK I'll see you around 10".

Chapter 32

My sandwich arrived so I dug right in. I had two bits when Arnold excused himself as he came into my office apologizing for interrupting my lunch then saying Mr. Bekkvelt would like to talk to me then handed me a telephone number on a piece of paper. He left with no other explanation. I finished one half of the sandwich washed it down with a half of a cup of coffee then called the number. When he answered he knew it was me because without even a hello he told me the numbers Peter gave him were off shore accounts to be more specific three were numbered accounts in a bank in Liechtenstein called the LGT Group. "The other four were probably also off-shore accounts but they would take a while to tract down. The LGT Group is a bit unique in one sense; the individual print out numbers will get you in their door because the numbers represent a trust within the bank set up by the investor when he opens an account. To put money in an investor sets up a trust account. To take it out you need a corresponding number for each set of numbers for each trust account then the trust reverts immediately back to the investor avoiding taxes. It is not as complicated as it sounds and along with the Secrecy Banking Act in Liechtenstein they have the German Federal intelligence Service[Bundesnachrichtendients] it's a tongue twisting German compound word you'll see it referred to as BND they've been frustrated and chasing their own tail trying to crack this tax shelter so far no one has. The numbers on the print out are only half the sequence without the other sequence they're useless. I understand Myra is handling this with the Bureau. Is that true"?

"Yes it is".

"Very well let her deal with the Bureau they're privy to the information I just told you, but keep this conversation we're having between us and strictly confidential".

"Yes of course". I hung up and was flabbergasted I sat back in my chair and realized it was more information than I really wanted to know. I started thinking about the situation and it occurred to me I could be a prime witness in any East Bay investigation by the FBI that involved Cannelli and the Teamsters local because of that envelope. It also occurred to me something Arnold mentioned about Mary being sneaky getting me to do her dirty work by giving the envelope to the FBI. I finally realized I'd been staring at the wall for over an hour. Now I had to figure out how to kill time until 10 o'clock to avoid my mother-in-law. At this point she was more of a threat then Cannelli so I thumbed through the newspaper to the movie section and an old movie of Clint Eastwood "Play Misty for me" was playing at a theater in the Mission. I missed it the first time around so it's perfect. I'll stop at El Faro for some Mex then head for the movie. I told Arnold I had something personal to do tonight and he could take the night off. I got no reaction from him so that was that. It was like being a kid again I got a humongous pork burrito at El Faro's two large candy bars and headed for the movie. I lost my self in my teenage years in the backseat section of the theater. The inside was a real old Movie House with Corinthian columns and fresco painted ceilings a through back to another age it brought on some nostalgia and I reveled in it by the time the movie was over it was safe to go home. I found my car on the side street where I left it however Arnold with his arms folded on his chest was half sitting on the street side front fender waiting for me. I didn't know if I was surprised or annoyed so I said nothing I just got in the car and he got into the passenger seat. I put the radio on to catch the news so nothing was said until we were turning into the alley of my house it was then he said, "I am sorry but it is my job". And me being a wise ass I asked him if he liked the movie. That was the first time he actually laughed at the same time he was saying I was OK. The baby sitter was waiting for me and told me Anne was driving her mother home but wasn't sure when she would be back. I paid the baby sitter and when she left I checked on Gina who was sound asleep. It was now near 10:30 so I decided to wait up for Anne not because I wanted to know what the situation was between her mother and father, but guilt. When we first married we agreed that all family problem would be handled by who's ever family had the problem; in that way we would avoid interfering in each other's family, but with my family thousands of miles away I was told of few if any problems. But Anne was constantly in the line of fire with an eccentric mother a father who relied on Anne to handle her mother essentially Anne was the parent and they acted like her children she was constantly dealing with their problems. I heard her drive into the alley and I wanted to console her so I moved into a position near the pantry to give her a hug as soon as she came in. She went right passed me saying tell me about your four hours of freedom in the morning I'm going to bed. I figure all bets were off so I got a beer from the frig and headed for the front room and decided to go to bed after she fell asleep. The next morning I was pussy footing around the kitchen while Anne dressed the baby and had her in her high chair feeding her. Finally Anne said, "Stop the soft shoe sit down and have your coffee". I said, "Yes mommy". "Don't you start I had enough of that last night". I nodded in the affirmative hoping that got me off the hook. There was an immeasurable short silence then like a deluge the words came spewing out. "It's not her logic that befuddles me because it's nothing new it's the prolonged manipulation of a situation turning not once but twice and at times three or more times to accuse everyone else of fault by distorting facts or ignoring them. If you bring them to her attention then you're siding against your mother. You remember I told you I thought of cutting her out of our life completely I came very close last night, but you know what stopped me". I obediently rocked my head no. "I knew she would sit on the front steps bemoaning to the neighbors what a lousy daughter I was for keeping her from seeing her Granddaughter". She took a breath and looked at me accusingly then said, "I would make a lousy Psychiatrist because I never said anything for or against and never took a position". In my best Psychiatrist's voice I told her a good Psychiatrist doesn't take sides he takes money. She said shut up and go to work. I knew when the getten was good so I blew air kisses round and left.

The next three days went smooth with no problems at the East Bay construction site and it was Friday and pay day for the boys in Oakland. I called Joe to confirm all the pay roll checks arrived this morning from the pay roll accounting firm. He said they did then asked why I called every Friday about the payroll because if anything is wrong he would call the payroll people and they fix it.

"The reason is simple and not simple; there is no bank involved in the construction loan it's all privet. Peter and Dick have raised the money through a group of investors essentially they're the bank. A bank would control the loan by construction draws I'm taking it one step further by paying everything as we're billed especially the payroll. I get the payroll cost in advance because everyone is paid one week in the rears I transfer the exact amount to the accounting firm on Thursday so the control is tight. It's a little more book keeping for Baite, but it's easier to stay on top of the money. "Boy that's a hell of a lot better than Hillcrest Development no one knew where any of the money was going and I don't know how you got that development out of the red and salvage any profit".

I said, "Mirrors Joe mirrors". He laughed and said, "Speaking of bills I got a dozy from the concrete company, but it's thirty days so there is plenty of time".

"How much"?

"Fifteen hundred yards, but the interesting thing is they billed five dollars less per yard then in the bid should I mention their mistake or will you handle it".

"NO I'll handle it". When I thought about it I was sure it is part of the deal to forget about the Berkeley Appraisal this was obviously a bribe. I considered it a perk for being a witness for the FBI. The rest of the day was uneventful so Arnold got me home just after six in the evening. Anne was in the kitchen feeding the baby and her body language was screaming something was wrong; I immediately asked if her parents were ok. Without answering my question she told me Nancy called and told her I was in the evening paper. She told me I'd better go get a copy of the Examiner there's a news stand in front of the Buena Vista at the end of the block. I walked out the front door and the evening shift wasn't expecting me to leave so soon because I just got home. One of the security people had to scramble out of the van across the street so I slowed down so he could catch up I was feeling a bit paranoid so I welcomed the company. I got down to Beach Street where six or seven news-stands were lined up in front of the Buena Vista Cafe. I found the one with the Examiner in it, but there was someone already there and blocking the stand while reading his Examiner. I was really getting antsy to see the article about me in the paper so I said excuse me and almost pushed the man out of the way to get at the news-stand. My heart jumped when I saw the name of Dailey the reporter on the by-line through the glass door of the newsstand. My first thought was the son of a bitch is writing about me again. I put in some coins and opened the newsstand and took out the paper then I could see his article was in the left hand column on the front page this alone worried me. I unfolded the paper to see if the story was continued on anther page and it was which also worried me so I folded the paper back put it under my arm and started to headed back home. When I turned I was directly in front of the cafe window I saw a neighbor enjoying a before dinner cocktail. He gave me the high sign and motioned me to come in, I lip synced "I can't dinner is on the table". He smile and moved his hands in a, "What are you going to do sign". On the way back I apologized to the security guard for not giving him a heads up when I was leaving the house. He gave me a head nod and it's not a problem comment and we both trudged up the hill to the house. Anne was waiting for me in the front room. The baby was on the floor in blissful play. Anne was building tension by not saying anything so I broke the ice before I open the paper by asking if she heard what's in the article. "Just a few things I think you better read the article and read it aloud to me". I opened the paper read a few lines to myself to get an idea where it was going then got comfortable and started to read.

Edmond Dailey
Investigative Reporter

There has been a new development in the Treasury Department and FBI investigation of the Drays Savings and Trust in Oakland. It's a mystery envelope that the FBI says it received while the trial was in progress and wonts to enter it as evidence. The Defense counsel, of the law firm of Morrison and Tate are objecting to the so called evidence being submitted half way through the trial.

Here we are again over in the East Bay where the FBI had the grand Jury indict Freddy "Beans" Cannelli a former Local Teamster official and Vincent Kerrigan the president of the now defunct Drays Saving and Trust of money laundering, intent to defraud the government and other assorted crimes. Mr. Kerrigan has flown the coop so consequently has been indicted in absentereo. The investigation has been long and exhaustingly thorough and the FBI said the envelope had just come to light when it was sent to them by Mr. James Kerry through his attorney Myra Pacemann of the firm of Sloan and Pacemann. Mr. Kerry is the same Jim Kerry who was the intended victim of a mob hit when the hitman mistakenly shot and killed the garage attendant where Mr. Kerry kept his car. The trigger man was shot and killed by the police but the murder for hire was traced back to the developer of the Hillcrest Housing project a Johnny Peresci who was later found murdered and dumped on a road in the delta. Mr. Kerry is now being treated as a witness for the prosecution and has around the clock FBI protection. It all started when an associate of Mr. Kerry, John Mace was murdered in gangland stile, in their office at 300 Montgomery Street. Mr. Kerry found the body when arriving for a schedule meeting and the case is still unsolved. Mace was the reputed financial brains of the local bad boys over in the East Bay. Mace had a long history of being involved in Teamster loans of a number of casinos in Las Vegas along with financial dealings with the Union Commercial Bank in Fremont which has been closed and under a separate indictment of its officers. Their financial world started to crumble when it was unearthed that a housing project Hillcrest Development, which was being financed by a Bank loan brokered by Mr. Mace and his associate Mr. Kerry, was found to be skimming money from its construction draws to a fictitious company Sunloc Building Materials LLC and reporting little or no profit to the IRS. The financial institution handling all these transactions was Drays Savings and Trust.

Jim stopped to take a breath and Anne asked him if he was OK. "He said yeah the rest of the article is all blah, blah, blah. This article is long on wind and short on accuracy and some juggling of facts to leave it open to a defamation suit against the Examiner. Of course I'm personally mentioned so I'm prejudice, but it's just a rehash of the original police report with a few new facts and a lot of superstition".

"At least he didn't mention Dick Somers or Scranton and Associates in his column". Anne said.

"Yeah well he has John Mace brokering loans when he was dead that says something for his lack of investigating; that works for us".

"The thing about the envelope was not generally known so who leaked it to him"? Anne said.

"Could come from a lot of sources once it is put into evidence, but you're right who would know I gave it to Myra to give to the FBI"?

"I think we could narrow it down by the process of elimination".

"You know it could be the FBI themselves using this character to leak whatever information they want out to the public and you know at this point I really don't care. You know when I got home I thought I asked you about your parents; has things settled down"?

Anne picked up the baby to put on her lap as she looked at me and said, "Same old same old".

"Did I smell Chinese when I came in"?

"Yes you did it's in the oven just waiting for us".

"Did I ever tell you how much I love you"?

"Yes every time I sent out for Chinese".

"Not every time".

"Yes every time".

The weekend should have been more distracting because of the article in the paper and Anne's problems with her family, but the thing that kept recurring to me was the Envelope and who leaked its existence.

Like Anne said we could make a list of possible people who are candidates for someone who would leak that kind of information, but of course they would have to know about it and have a reason to leak it. Every time I thought of someone who knew about it I couldn't think of a reason they would leak it and conversely when I thought of someone who would leak it I couldn't figure out how they would know about it. So that's how the weekend went Anne concerned if not worried about her parents and me spending my time on an unsolvable solution.

I couldn't get myself organized Monday morning and got to the office at 9:30. Carol greeted me with a prolonged hello seemingly to gage my demeanor obviously everyone in the office had read or heard about the article in the Examiner. My response to her was I'm fine then I asked if Peter or Dick was in. She told me both so I stopped first at Peter's office his door was opened so I hit his door jamb with a warning knock then stuck my head in and asked if he had a minute. He said, "Of course, is this about that guy Dailey and his article in the Examiner"?

"Yeah".

"You mind if I call Dick in we talked about this over the weekend and decided to wait until today to discuss it with you".

"No not at all Dick was my next stop". Peter buzzed Dick and within a minute he came into Peter's office and closed the door. He asked me how my family especially Anne was coping. I told him all and all not bad they're very supportive especially Anne she gave me her solution it was to give Mr. Dailey a 38 caliber vasectomy. The remark put Peter into a series of chuckles but Dick broke out into a belly laugh then stopped and asked if she really said that, of course, I told him she did and that put him into another belly laugh. He stopped laughing and got very serious when he said, "I've already call Myra and she's aware of the article and I told her we should sue the Examiner and this bastard Dailey".

Peter asked me what I thought.

"I'd rather wait at this point I'm more interested who leaked the information about the envelope. Obviously once it gets to the court a lot of people get to know about it, but not its contents so that's a possibility and it's also a possibility it was the FBI for their own reasons. My concern is if we move on this guy Dailey and the Examiner without the complete or wrong information they could get away with a retraction and a printed apology in the back of the Examiner's food page upside down in Latin". My joke took a beat or two to sink in and their reaction was a tolerating smile so we ended the meeting and I retreated to my office. Carrol had put my messages on my desk and I saw Joe Peavy had called twice so I called him with the feeling the news had to be bad. And it wasn't bad but not great. He told me some of the workmen were on the job but that loud mouth picket line leader was back in action and holding up concrete trucks from delivering concrete to the pumpers and that makes it impossible to pour concrete above ground level. I asked him if it was possible to pour concrete anywhere at ground level until we resolve this mix up. He told me no because it would take too long to organize the finishing team and by that time the truck mixers would start to break down the concrete consistency and strength. In any case the building inspector is already taking sump tests of the first few truck loads and if they don't pass the test the trucks are turned away. In my frustration I asked Joe, "what could we do"? Joe told me he didn't know but this can get nasty the loud mouth picket line leader is a hired gun he's a professional picket organizer he's white and not from Oakland the General Contractor supplying all the carpenters is Black from Oakland and along with his men are not in agreement with this stoppage they see it as a personal problem between the Developer and the Union and money out of their pockets. I asked him if there was enough work to keep the men on the job working on other jobs until we settle this situation. Probably until the end of the week then if I have to lay-off any body there will be fireworks. I told Joe I'm rapping up the work on my desk and I'll be there by this afternoon. Because of the possibility of the situation getting out of hand at the job site I filled Arnold in on what Joe told me on the way over to Oakland. Arnold was driving, but not his usual overly alert-self he was not checking the rear and side view mirror in a disciplined sequence he seemed to be concentrating on the road. About half way across the Bay Bridge he asked me if anyone had called Mr. Bekkvelt. I told him I didn't know and I didn't think so and why would Mr. Bekkvelt have anything to do with a job action in Oakland? He said it was his belief that the City of Oakland Development Agreement by and between the City and Prologis CCIG and a U. S. Government agency to have Unions and local contractors work together to help bolster the local labor market so it doesn't make sense that the Union has ordered a localized strike or job action. I personally never heard of the agreement so I thought about it all the way to the job site. The street to the entrance to the job site was lined with strikers all being kept on the side walk by the police. As we passed many of them yelled distorted labor chants and of course the jerk with the bull horn got right in our face and pointed me out by name. We passed through the gate and parked in our usual visitors spot. We were facing the gate and we could see the picketers and three quarters down the street and the guy with the bull horn was now shaking his fist at us in defiance. I went into the construction trailer and Arnold filtered into the workers on the job site. Joe was on the phone when I entered; whoever he was talking to it sounded official. When he finished with the conversation he hung up in frustration then told me that was the Redevelopment Agency here in Oakland and they don't know what this job action is all about and according to the National Union they don't know either. I told Joe to call the Oakland Tribune and maybe the local TV Station they'll get someone on it and get answers faster than any government agency. He gave me that "Eureka" look and started dialing information. I sat back and listen to Joe talk to a number of people at the Paper and the TV Station mainly because I didn't know what else to do when Arnold came into the trailer. He obviously wanted to say something so I asked what's up. He said Joe's right if this isn't straightened out and soon there's going to be trouble. The picket line stopped pipe being delivered and the plumbers that are on the job have no material so they'll be sent home. They're talking about pushing the picket line off the street so they can get their pipe delivered and the carpenters say they're with them. I looked at Arnold and said you mentioned Mr. Bekkvelt do you think he could help. There is no harm in asking, but I have already took the liberty in calling him and he is aware of the problem and is at this time calling the people involved in the government to expedite a solution. Joe looked up from his desk and asked, "What the hell does that mean".

Arnold said it will be resolved by the end of the day or the Union Local will be fined five thousand dollars a day until they stop this illegal work stoppage. So you're saying we just sit back and wait until the end of the day to see if the crew can work tomorrow. You could do that, but if I were you I'd start talking to the contractor out there and try and calm down the situation and let him know it should be resolved by tomorrow. We all thought that was a good idea so we left the trailer and caught up with the men on the job site and told them that the problem should be resolved by tomorrow, however the plumbers wanted to know what if it isn't then what? So I told them if it isn't I'll have them paid to work with the carpenters until it is resolved. That did the trick all but a few thought that was a solution. When Arnold and I were leaving the picket line I heard my name in a very unflattering description by the leader and along with a few of his bully boys leaned on our car to slow us down but the policemen tunneled our way through the gauntlet. When we got to the Bay Bridge I asked Arnold how sure was he Mr. Bekkvelt can resolve the labor dispute. His reply was a bit terse; "Did you notice that the placards were well worn and the slogans were generic and could fit any situation or cause". I just mumbled no.

"They were professional strikers paid by and at the beckon call of the Local Union when Mr. Bekkvelt says he'll do something it's done". I sort of chewed on that on the way back to the office.

Chapter 33

Peter and Dick were waiting for us to return with the full story from the surprise work stoppage at the Oakland job site. I told them what Arnold had told me about the agreement between the Oakland Redevelopment Agency and some privet company and the U. S. Government to insure jobs for local residents from Oakland. Then he said he was told if the local Union persisted in the work stoppage they could be fined five thousand dollars a day until they removed the illegal picket line. "Where did Arnold get this information"? Dick asked.

"Why don't you ask Arnold he's in the library"? Jim replied.

Peter cut into the conversation when he told us he got it from Mr. Bekkvelt because Bekkvelt mentioned it to him a few months back. This might be in retaliation by Cannelli for the revelation in the paper by our friend Dailey that you were not going along with his scheme and actually going to be a witness against him at his trial. Of course, if it is Cannelli's doing it looks like it is back-firing on him I'm sure the International Brotherhood of Teamsters will come down on him if for nothing else then for the publicity. I think Arnold is correct and the stoppage will be ending tomorrow. There were more discussions pro and con until after five o'clock when we broke up and headed home. On the way home the warm weather was brought up and we both agreed to forget about a jacket and tie for tomorrow so when Arnold showed in the morning he was warring dark colored slacks a short sleeved dress shirt, but no tie or jacket. I had an instant thought that this was as informal as he would get.

I, of course, had on jeans and a polo shirt. I told him I would drive today to give him a break. He told me it was not necessary it was all part of his job. I told him I needed some windshield time to keep my feel for driving. He acquiesced with a nod and opened the driver's door for me and I noticed a tattoo on his forearm "Semper Fi" it didn't surprise me. On the way over the Bay Bridge he was leaning on the arm rest between the seats with a mirror in his hand positioned so he could monitor the rear view traffic behind us. Originally I would see this as corny or needless dramatics, but not by Arnold. It made me uneasy but I said nothing until we got off the bridge and on to the city streets. When I asked him what the mirror was for. He told me just a precaution. The way he said it had a calming effect and I eased back into my normal driving posture. We turned into the street entrance to the construction site and I saw a patrolman and no picket line and breathed a long sign of relief. We were passing the patrolman who looked marooned in this valley of four story buildings when he interrupted the scene with a wave and a smile. We went through the open gate and I sung the car into our usual parking space. Before I could turn the ignition off the front windshield erupted with a loud thud followed by an eerie cracking sound in the air. I saw the bullet hole surrounded by a spider web of fracture glass at the same moment I was hit by Arnold and pushed to my side of the car and in the same motion he unlocked my door and I was outside the car on the ground and he was on top of me. In a calm voice he said get under the car and then sort of slithered to the back of the car and I could hear him yelling to the policeman to check the rooves for a sniper. I felt sticky blood on my shoulder and I could see blood on my arm, but when I checked everything out I wasn't bleeding. All this happened so fast I couldn't get my wits about me, but it was apparent someone was trying to kill us. The next thing I knew Joe Peavy was yelling to Arnold an ambulance was on its way. I was in a state of shock when I yelled to Joe that I was ok and I didn't need an ambulance. His reply was abrupt, "Not you its Arnold he's bleeding badly". In my half stupid state I realized the blood on me was Arnold's. The workmen from the site came to see if they could help and were told by the police to stay out of sight but two ignored them and along with Joe brought the emergency first aid kit from the trailer and began putting gauges into the wound trying to stop the bleeding. I was still floundering around the car hiding behind the driver's side door and when I looked at the windshield it all got into prospective. The bullet hole was on the passenger's side of the windshield where I normally sat. It was another case of mistaken identity and I was the intended victim and out of stupidity another person shot when mistaken for me. I made my way back to the rear of the car where Arnold was being helped by Joe and two of his men. Arnold was conscious and directing Joe how to position the gauges and bandages to stop the bleeding. I couldn't tell if the wound was in the lower neck or the shoulder, but it was obvious his right arm was not working and his hand gun was lying idly by on the concrete where obviously it fell.

This was the first time I was involved in anything like this so I had no way of knowing the seriousness of the wound but there was a lot of blood and the helplessness we all felt led to an anxiety that was palpable; then the beautiful sound of the ambulance heralding Arnold's rescue. The paramedics were fast they had a heads up from the police of Arnold's wound and his general condition so they had him in the ambulance and on an IV and ready to roll in record time. They told us there was no room for any of us in the ambulance and they were heading for the emergency room at Kaiser Hospital. Now there were two more patrol cars from the Oakland P.D. blocking the entrance to the job site and placing crime scene tape around the area. I could see two or three officers on the roof of a four story building just one hundred feet or so from the crime scene. One of the officers held up both arms and yelled "rifle with scope" then pointed to the area next to his feet. The sergeant told them to secure the area and for all to get off of the roof until the Lab boys got there. He then turned and began questioning everyone to get a sense of what happened. I told him who I was and quickly my story then asked if I could leave to go the hospital. He told me to wait until he interviewed everybody and then turned to Joe Peavy and started to ask him the same question when I asked if I could call my boss and he nodded yes. I called Peter from the trailer and told him what happened and that Arnold was shot and taken to Kaiser Hospital and I was heading there as soon as the police were through with me. It was typical Peter; he calmly asked where Arnold was wounded. I told him I wasn't sure there was so much blood I couldn't tell if it was his neck or his shoulder. In a controlled information seeking tone he said, "I meant was it on the job site or was it on the way there"? Now I was feeling foolish so I apologized and told him the job site. He asked if the picket line was there when we got to the job site. I told him no just a patrol car and two policemen who were obviously getting ready to leave because there was no picket line. Then a sniper shot Arnold just as we were parking at the job site. As soon as you can get away go to the hospital and I'll meet you there after I contact Luke Bekkvelt and give him the news.

When I left the trailer the site was full of cops. There was now a Lieutenant from the Oakland P.D. and two detectives. They were talking to a man in protective garb and while taking off a pair of latex gloves told them it was a M1 army rifle with a scope and still had three 30-06 rounds in the clip. The rim markings on the shell casings don't look like military probably commercially manufactured I didn't recognize the markings, but that should give us a good start. The Sergeant who was first on the scene said he had to get to the hospital and offered me a lift. Thankfully there was little said on the way to the hospital, but when we got there I followed the Sergeant through the information and security screen then listened to the prognosis from a nurse in emergency surgery. I couldn't understand very much except he had a broken shoulder and he lost a lot of blood and that he still was in surgery. The Sergeant told me there was nothing really to do so I should go to the waiting lounge until he's out of surgery however he said they recovered the bullet it was lodged in the car seat that could be a good sign it meant the bullet went straight through. I thought he said it to make me feel better and it did. It was an hour before Peter got there and Arnold was still in surgery. He said let's go find a cafeteria and I want you to go over the entire incident from start to finish. Over a cup of coffee I did just that he didn't interrupt once and at the end asked a few questions about the rifle the police found. I told him it was a M1 with a scope he seemed to think that over, but then just said well we'll have to wait this out and hope the surgery goes well. We went back to the waiting room and settled in for the results of the surgery when Peter suggested I clean up I still had blood on my arm and my polo shirt was stained from the shoulder to the waist, but the dark color of my polo made it less obvious. The policeman that was on duty when we first got to the job site came into the waiting room. I gave him the high sign and he came over then asked if we heard anything about Arnold's condition. I told him he was still in surgery and then asked him how the investigation was going at the crime scene. He didn't hesitate he told us the general consensus was the murder attempt was poorly planned and probably decided in a hurry. The first responders that searched the roof found the shooters only means of entering and leaving the roof. Four buildings down was a pigeon coup someone had for sport and was obviously being used by more than one sportsman. You could step over the two foot parapets separating the building rooves to a staircase door in front of the coup that lead to the street. Someone disabled the lock on the door to the stair case to easily enter or exit the building. They found a fresh thumb and palm print on the door pull they're sure the last person on the roof was the shooter and this staircase was his only means of escape. As the policeman was finishing up on the murder site evidence a Suit and Tie appeared just off to the left of the patrolman. He was holding his credential at shoulder level when he said his name, which we didn't get, and he was from the FBI, that we got. He asked the patrolman to step out into the corridor and within a few minute returned alone. He first asked how my security guard was doing we told him we didn't know he was still in surgery. He nodded in a half sympathy and half acknowledgement then told us this attempted murder was all part of an ongoing investigation and all information and evidence is confidential and that it was now a joint investigation between the Oakland P.D. and the FBI. I looked at Peter and said, "This all sounds familiar". It was two more hours before we were told he was out of surgery and the prognosis was good and it would be tomorrow before he could see anyone so that was our cue to leave. My car was now a crime scene so Peter offered me a ride home and of course I accepted. When we were leaving the Hospital the Press had the FBI agent cornered at the emergency entrance peppering him with questions as the patrolman stood by smiling looking as innocent as possible. As we passed he turned to us and nodded with his head at the Agent with a vindictive smile. We continued on but I saw that all knowing look from one of the Press that picked up the body language from the Patrolman. We were followed to Peter's car but escaped before answering any questions. When we got to the Bay Bridge he asked me how I was feeling my response was kind of weak when I said OK. He told me he checked with the Bekkvelt people and there are two security people at our house right now so I'll drop you off and keep you posted on Arnold's condition.

"You didn't talk to Bekkvelt"?

"No I was told he's out of the country, but he was told of Arnold's wounds and would be kept updated on his surgery plus he'll be back by tomorrow evening". Peter dropped me off in front of the house when I realized my keys for the front door were in my car at the crime scene so I headed down the alley to the back door. I was met in the back by one of the security guards; the talkative one who told me my mother-in-law was in the kitchen with my wife than rolled his eyes as in comment. When I walked through the pantry and into the kitchen all talking stopped. Baby Gina was happily chewing on the railing of her playpen and Anne interrupted her argument with her mother to ask me where my car was because she didn't hear me drive through the alley. I made up a story about Peter and I being in Oakland and on the way home it was easier for Peter to drop me off here and I would get my car at the office in the morning. That seemed to satisfy them and they resumed their heated discussion while I went to change. After I showered and changed I could hear the argument was getting loader even from our bedroom. Discretion being the better part of valor I thought I'd hide here until things calmed down when I heard the front door bell ring. I peek out of the bedroom to see Anne and her mother still engrossed in their argument so I went to the front door and it was a cab driver with a pickup order. I told him to pull half way into the alley and I'd get his fare. I got my mother-in-law kicking and screaming into the cab and off to her own house. When I got to the kitchen I asked what that was all about and Anne replied, "This is going to be a wine night so break out a good Chianti". I dutifully went to the pantry where Anne was now hiding any alcohol of value from her father and retrieved a bottle of Tuscan Chianti. By the time I returned from the pantry opened the wine got two glasses and headed for the front room Anne was in her favorite chair and the baby was exploring the floor. I didn't know where to begin so I poured us a glass of wine and went to the front window. I could hear Anne talking but I had tuned her out and was more or less inspecting the distorted design of the leaded glass that blurred the images in the street. I was brought back to the moment when Anne asked me if I was listening to her.

"I was shot at this morning, but they missed me and hit Arnold. He was out of surgery when we left the hospital in Oakland and the prognosis was good and we'll find out the results tomorrow".

Anne was stunned it took a full 30 seconds for her to respond and when she did it was condemnation of her stupid argument she had with her mother for side tracking her thoughts when she knew as soon as I entered the kitchen something was very wrong her eyes began to well-up with tears when she said, "This job with Dick and Peter's Company isn't worth this violence and danger we could easily go back to buying and selling houses".

"That exact thought struck me while I was waiting in the hospital, but I think given it time it will seem more like a reaction then a thought out decision however it is certainly an option. The obvious situation I'm in and by extension you and the family unfortunately we are already in it; the Cannelli Trial, the FBI investigation of everything Mace was involved in here and Las Vegas and these connections with the murders in Las Vegas and now I'm on the witness list for the prosecution in the Cannelli trial. I think we better stay as close to the Feds as needed and especially this Security Company of Mr. Bekkvelt. We both had a long pull on our wine then called it a night.

Peter called first thing in the morning and told me he'd pick me up when I was ready. I told him right now I'm ready when you are. Anne was understandably not right from the shock last night and said she'd hang out at the house today with the baby. I left by the back door and my new security man was waiting and leaning on Anne's car talking on his radio. He ended his conversation and nudged himself off of the car with a few body jerks and introduced himself as Joe my new security man the talkative guy that was there when I got home from the hospital. He put his hand out in greeting and I noticed the same tattoo on his forearm that Arnold had, "Semper Fi". The impression I got was irrational but I felt safe and secure with just a hand shake. When Peter came to pick me up Joe asked if I wanted him to follow us in a separate car or should he go with Peter and me. I looked at Peter and he told him to jump in and let's go. On the way to the office he told me we had an appointment at Kaiser to see Arnold at 11 o'clock and Luke Bekkvelt will meet us there. When we get to the office Baite has ordered you a new car and I understand there is a joke about the color so you sort it out with her. We'll try to settle down to business as soon as Arnold is out of the woods because the Feds are going to tie this murder attempt to the Cannelli trial and that means you're going to be called as a witness or at least they'll try. That will make your life distracting to say the least with balancing work, home and keeping the family safe. We will do all we can to help you especially keeping the family safe and we do have assets Mr. Bekkvelt and his people have been protecting Embassy personal for a decade and Joe in the back seat will attest to that. When we got to the office Baite settled Joe into the conference room and I told her I wanted a green car. She said, "Your mother-in-law won't be happy".

"Good it will be something to complain about and get her off Anne's back". Baite didn't crack a smile because she knew I wasn't joking. Carrol had no messages for me so I was off to my office to call Joe Peavy. Joan Kitmer answered and in my surprised I said "What are you doing there"? "When the need is the greatest it's Joan Kitmer who responds to the call, but to answer your question Joe called me last night with the news of the shooting and asked if I could fill in today in the office because he was sure he'd be on the work site making sure everything is progressing at a normal rate".

"I hope I didn't sound to rude when I asked what you were doing there".

"Not at all if I took offence every time someone was rude I'd spend half the day in the waiting room in some psychiatrist's office".

"Well I called to see if all was back to normal".

"From what I understand it is; your car was towed away yesterday and all the crime tapes are gone but they're still searching the building where the shots came from, but everything hear in on schedule".

I told her she could tell Joe that Arnold survived surgery and his prognosis was good and I'm going to see him this morning and I'll give him and up-date by this afternoon. She thanked me and hung up. I could hear someone coming toward my office and it had to be Dick; he would get antsy sitting behind his desk so he did a lot of walking around the office.

Of course, I was right he appeared at the door jamb to my office and asked, "How is Anne handling all this".

"You know Dick I'm not sure there were family distractions by the time I got home last night so when I gave her the news of the shooting I don't think it registered that I was the intended victim not Arnold".

"Well I dropped in to tell you that Esperanza and Deirdre are going to try and get Anne out to lunch maybe that will help. And we're going to finalize the Cast Iron Building and the adjoining hotel property some-time today so it's a heads up it's going to be your baby". I didn't even have time to think about it when the intercom buzzed and Peter told me it was time to leave for the Hospital. Joe was at Carrol's desk and asked for Peter's car keys. When Peter looked surprised Joe said, "Just procedure I'll check out the garage and your car". We gave Joe a head start but everybody was startled by the new procedure even Peter. All went well and it was a smooth ride over the bridge and we were at the hospital fifteen minutes early and waiting for us was Luke Bekkvelt and now a three some of Brophy, Clark and the agent we meet yesterday his name is Greg Ostlander. After we were formerly introduced to agent Ostlander Brophy explained they were here early to talk with Arnold step by step on yesterday's event especially just before the shot was fired. Brophy then asked us to accompany them to a small office the hospital provided for their information gathering; that was a euphemism for interrogation. I was asked to give them an account of everything I could think of before, during and after the shot was fired. We spent the better part of an hour going over the previous day's events with Clark sporting a miniature tape recorder and the new guy Ostlander taking notes. The whole time Bekkvelt was in stone silence. I told them the previous day was really uneventful until the shot was fired so the questions were few and we left the little office for Arnold's ward. He was sitting in bed on an angle facing us when we entered his room. His right side looked like it was all in a cast. He had a trapeze just above his head so he could reposition himself with his left hand around the bed for more comfort. The room looked sterile not only hospital sterile, but comfort sterile. There were no flowers, get well cards, empty candy boxes or even candy wrappers the water pitcher and glass with a flexible straw were in perfect alignment. I knew he had a weakness for candy so I made a mental note to get some before we leave today. We all said high and he smiled but was looking past us to the hall then asked me to close the door. After I did I was ready to say how sorry I was when he beat me to it by cutting me off and asking what the feds told us. I looked at Peter and then Bekkvelt when Bekkvelt said, "Not much in fact nothing". Arnold wanted to know what kind of a rifle was used. Bekkvelt told him a M1 Garand with a scope.

Arnold wanted to know if it was a MC52 Marine snipper and what size scope? When I looked at Peter I could tell he was also at a lost to what all this was about; we both thought this was a hospital visit to cheer Arnold up not a military debriefing. But, of course, that's what it was and what little I knew about Arnold this all made sense. The rest of the conversation was between Mr. Bekkvelt and Arnold with Peter and I watching a ping pong match between Arnold and Bekkvelt. Bekkvelt told Arnold he talked to some one at the Feds Lab and they have a trace on the serial numbers on the rifle but they expect that to take time. The ammo was not military and the rim markings were commercial with the letter "H". They traced it to a Winchester Repeating Arms Company in New Haven Connecticut. However they have sold 30-06 cartridges to the military in particular the National Guard here in California. The most promising news was the scope was a civilian a Leupold VX and had to be mounted by someone who knew what they were doing so they're checking all the gunsmiths in California and surrounding States for anyone who remembers working on this unusual job. Bekkvelt finally got around to asking Arnold what was the feds so interested in the sequence of the day leading up to the shooting. "They have a theory they're working on and it's typical FBI when Jim pulled into the parking place at the job site, remember we switched places from the day before, they can't believe anyone could miss putting a round through my head, believing I was Jim, from that short of a distance and with a scope unless it was meant as some sort of a warning and not meant to kill me or as they believed I was Jim Kerry. I told them when Jim pulled into the parking space the car hit the space curb just as he turned off the ignition the car lurched forward and so did I; that's why the shooter missed my head and hit me in the shoulder". I excused myself and told them I had a nature call but I went down to the news stand and bought a hand full of candy bars and headed back to Arnold's room. The timing was right Arnold was tired and going down-hill when a nurse showed up to tell us it was time to go. I was the last to leave so I dumped the candy on the bed his face light up like a child and in an embarrassing tone said thanks. Bekkvelt waited until we were on the side walk in front of the hospital entrance to just repeat what Peter had already told me about the security and my family was their primary concern when I saw a familiar face heading in our direction. I cut Mr. Bekkvelt short and said we have a visitor from the press heading our way with a purpose. He just calmly smiled and told us to head for Peter's car and he would handle him. We said our good byes like parting friends and while heading for the car I caught a reflection in a parked car window of Bekkvelt stopping and engaging the newsman; it was long enough for us to escape.

Chapter 34

Joe was leaning on the car but alerted to the situation he opened the doors and started the engine. We each picked a door and slid in just as Joe got behind the wheel and put the car in gear then drove normally out of the parking lot and on toward the bridge. Peter was in the passenger's seat up front and turned to me and asked how I knew that guy was a newsman. I told him he was the same guy that was at the emergency entrance yesterday asking questions from that agent Ostlander. We were half way across the Bay Bridge when Peter mentioned my car was ready so why not pick it up on the way to the office. We did just that and Peter took over the wheel of his car and Joe and I drove to the office in a New Green Ford. I called Joe Peavy as soon as I got to my desk I got Joan Kitmer again she asked how Arnold was doing and I told her that was one of the reasons I called Arnold is doing very well. He was sitting up talking and seems to be more intent on catching who shot him more than just getting better. Would you pass that on to Joe and tell him if there is any problems at all call me. I was in kind of a haze the rest of the day so I welcomed Carrol's intercom message that it was five o'clock and if I had nothing for her she was leaving I decided I was too. The ride home in the new car was uneventful. When I entered the kitchen Anne was in an upbeat mood which I was grateful because I still didn't know how she was taking this shock. I could see the debris left from a prolonged lunch and when I rolled my eyes over the remains she explained Esperanza and Deirdre came over with a ton of stuff from a Russian Deli out in the Avenues. Of course Esperanza had to dress up Gina and we went to Ghirardelli for an hour or two to show her off then back here for lunch. There's plenty of left overs so you can have a gourmet dinner with smoked salmon, pickled herring and potatoes and even pelmeni in chicken broth. I asked Anne to put it aside for now and I'll pick at it later is all I could think of was the last glass of wine from the bottle of Chianti left from the night before. So I scrounged around the kitchen until I found it and headed for the front room with a glass and the bottle. On my way Anne told me Tom Valance called and asked to give him a call when you get a chance. So I took three steps back to the kitchen and dialed Tom from the kitchen table while swinging the wall phone cord around Anne as she was sprucing up the lunch remains. As I was waiting for Tom to pick up his phone I grabbed a fork and speared a pelmeni and I was half way into pouring a glass of wine when Tom came on the phone. I mumbled through an apology and told him I was picking on the remains of Anne's lunch and asked him to hold on while I wash it down with a glass of wine. He had this great forced cackle he would give you to counter any bad joke or ridiculous situation and he gave it to me in spades. "I understand they missed you again, but more importantly how is your security guard"?

"He's apparently out of the woods, but they're talking about another operation to put a plate and screws into his shoulder".

"There was just a sketchy account of a shooting in Oakland in the paper this morning with no names, but

Oscar called me and told me you were involved and your security guard was shot".

"How is Oscar so well informed after all this was Oakland"?

"He's following the Cannelli trial through his contacts in the Oakland P.D. he still has his theory of who killed John Mace and It was not a mob hit".

"Man you talk about a bull dog the guy never gives up".

"That's the best description of his detective instincts I've ever heard, but to a fault; his superiors are on him to stay with their own investigations and let the FBI do theirs. He tends to stay on cases that are taken over by another departments or agencies. When he gets the bit in his mouth he can't seem to spit it out".

"That's good for the victim and bad for the D.A. and Homicide's batting average".

"You got it he's their stallion with blinders. You know come to think about it Father Gorman remarked once that Oscar has an acute sense of justice and thought it came from his time in the D.P. Camps as a child. I guess we could go on and on so let me tell you my main reason for calling Oscar is interested in the nuts and bolts of the shooting and would like to talk to you. If there are no objections could you meet him this evening at Mecco's in the Cannery"?

"Tom are you and Nancy free tonight"?

"We could be what do you have in mind"?

"A buffet type dinner here and bring Oscar".

"I know Nancy will be all for that what time"?

"I'll get back to you in a minute or two as soon as I clear it with Anne; I'm a little concerned about

Anne she is sporting a thin veneer of confidence and moral strength that I know is fragile because of the attempted murders and compounded by finding herself in the middle of her mother and father's dysfunctional marriage".

When I asked her if she felt like having Tom and Nancy over tonight for some Tuscan Chianti and left overs she was genuinely enthusiasts and she said sure I'll worm up the pelmenies. I called Tom back and told him come over any time it's just a buffet. Tom, Nancy and Oscar used the front entrance and as they entered the hall Oscar noticed the front room bay window to his left as Tom and Nancy headed down the hall to the kitchen. Oscar motioned to the window and mentioned it's a very handsome window and asked if he could take a closer look. I told him, of course, and we both went to the window. He ran his fingers over the glass in an endearing way then turned to me and asked if I could tell him about acquiring the now famous envelope. I told him it has to be a matter of recorded evidence; now didn't you get that information from the court records? He said he wanted to hear it from the horse's mouth. I was trying to think if I was braking some rule or law by discussing the would be evidence of the trial. Oscar read my mind when he said, "There's no gag order and it looks like the judge isn't going to allow the envelope or any thing that came with it into evidence. I'm interested in how and when Mary contacted you about the envelope".

"I told him she called me we had lunch and she gave me the envelope with a printout of numbers then told me to give them to Feds because she was embarrassed about the time lapse between the time her husband was murdered and then".

"Did she say where she found them"?

"Not exactly some place in his belongings".

"Did anyone else see this transfer happen I mean when she gave you the envelope"?

"That's funny you ask that because we had lunch at a French restaurant and Arnold accompanied us and I found out he spoke French and read lips because he sat at the bar a good thirty feet from our table and he later gave me a verbatim account of her side of the conversation after she left".

"Why did he tell you what she said"?

"I don't know, but he told me to give them to the Feds a.s.a.p. So I gave them to my attorney and she passed them on".

"Did Mary know you had a security guard with you all the time"?

"I suppose so; yeah I'm sure she did".

"And she physical gave you the envelope in the restaurant where Arnold could see you accept it"?

"I didn't answer for a few moments then said I see where you're going you think she used me as a patsy".

"I'm afraid so".

"You still haven't given up on your belief she had something to do with her husband's murder have you?

"No I haven't and I'm starting to upset you so let's go and see if there is any smoked salmon left".

"Wait I thought you were interested in the nuts and bolts of the attempted murder in Oakland"?

"I am, but I have an account of the attempt from the police report what I need is your account from the day before until you pulled into the parking space at the construction site. However there is time for that later let's go eat". It dawned on me Oscar didn't ask about the numbers on the print out sheet I realized he probably guessed what they were. By the time we finished the buffet, which took two hours, I was glade Oscar decided it was too late to continue the questions on the time frame of the Oakland attempted murder. We said our good byes then we thought it was late so we'd clean up in the morning and turned in.

I beat the 9 o'clock starting time at the office by an hour and change to call Joe Peavy at the job site before 8 o'clock. He asked me, in sort of gallows humor, "How y'a hangen". I had to laugh for once I had no come back. He asked about Arnold and if he could have visitors. I told him as far as I know yeah we saw him yesterday and he was kind of doped up but sitting up and talking about the shooting. If you like I'm going to see him today and I could pick you up and we can make it a party. That will work fine things are chugging along here as normal as you could expect and Joan is a life saver she's handling all the pestering calls from the news people so she'll be here after 9 o'clock and any time after that I'm free. That's great I'll give you a call when we are leaving. Peter was in a little early and told me he would take over the leg work on the Oakland job and with Peavy in charge he could see no major problems so I could get started on the Cast Iron Building project. I thumbed through my files in my credenza and found my notes on the Cast Iron building then called Larry Armorson with the news the Cast Iron building was back on. He asked

485

all kinds of questions which I couldn't answer so I told him is all I know is the both properties are in escrow and should close soon. One reason I called I just dug out my notes on these properties and I'm looking at a catalogue from a company called Walla Walla Foundry up in Washington with a slew of Cast Iron facade designs you told me you know an architectural engineering company that has worked with these facades. He told me he did and asked if he should give them a call and start the ball rolling. I told him please do and also ask them about construction companies they've worked with in the past for this kind of project then let me know how busy they are so we can get this plan in motion. Then I asked him if he thought it was too early to nose around for long term financing he told me it was never too early and he would make a few calls. Meanwhile I mentioned I have a sick friend over in Oakland I have to see today and I'll touch bases with you tomorrow. He casually asked if I saw the byline in the morning paper. I told him no. Then he said the shooting is in the paper and your name is prominent again. It mentions your guard caught a bullet meant for you. Then this guy Dailey goes on about your security guard with many talents one being able to read lips in French and is employed by a security contractor that works for our Diplomatic Corps here in this country. He makes it sound like your security guard is a spook and then infers the next question; what is he doing guarding you? He also sounds like he is back tracking on his last article about the murder of your old boss Mace. He writes he was told "by an unnamed source close to the case" that they're rethinking the theory that it was a mob hit and possibly a murder of revenge by someone in the financial world or someone close to him. For reasons I couldn't understand myself Larry's news didn't bother me in fact I brushed it off as another trashy article written by a wannabe and wasn't interested in even reading it. So I pulled out the surveyor's map of the City's plot plan of both properties and put them together with the catalogue of the cast Iron facades to start a package for the architect. I heard Carrol and Baite talking in the reception area then Peter and Dick joined them and from drips and drabs of the conversation I heard my name and Dailey's so it was obvious they were talking about the article in the morning paper. I decided to get into the act so I moseyed out of my office and into the reception area. Peter and Dick looked surprised to see me but Baite said I thought I saw your privet phone line lit when I came in I'm glad I'm not seeing things. Yeah I have to get an early start today I've got a lot of ground to cover. Dick asked if I saw the morning paper and I told him no but Larry kind of filled me in and to be truthful I'm not interested in reading it because from what little I've heard it's the same old trash. Peter cut in by asking what was on my agenda that I had so much to cover today, but before I could answer Dick said let's continue this conversation in my office. Dick went right to his big black desk chair swiveling it just right for his comfort diagonally from his leg well Peter opted to half lean half sit on the end of Dick's desk facing me and I took the chair at the opposite end of the desk facing Dick forming a talking triangle. As soon as we were settled Dick asked the question I truly couldn't honestly answer, "How do you feel and how is Anne taking all this". "As for the first part of your question I will vacillate between anger and fear, but neither really interfering with my everyday life and as for Anne she is over the shock and is consumed with the question who is leaking all this bogus information to this guy Dailey. Out-side of that we're handling the situation as well as can be expected". Peter mused over my answer then asked, "Have you been sleeping through the night or waking after a few hours then have trouble getting back to sleep. I'm not prying the reason I ask you look a little rough from lack of sleep".

"Yeah I have for the last few days, but I'll get over it as soon as I get my nose into the Cast Iron project. I want to see Arnold today with Joe Peavy I already called Larry Armorson and he's calling some architects to get this thing rolling so I'm sure time cures all".

"That all sounds good however we think you and Anne should take a vacation. Take a few weeks and get away from it all. Baite has some brochures from a tour outfit in Hawaii why don't you show Anne the brochures and let her pick out a tour of an Island or two".

All was well with Arnold. He thanked Joe for as he said, "Pugging up his wound". I thought we were going to distract him with good news of his prognosis and a family size box of milky-ways, but he was intent on discussing the shooting and the process of catching the shooter. He was adamant that the shooting had something to do with the Cannelli trial, but he wouldn't mention me as the intended target. Joe tried kicking around the local sports teams but Arnold wasn't interested so we sat back and listened to his theory of who and why the shooting took place at the construction site. Joe got glued in and listened to Arnold's theory then asked a few questions and that started Arnold off on the long conversation that was more of a discourse on criminal behavior. After I dropped Joe Peavy off at the construction trailer me and my shadow, Joe my bodyguard, started for the bridge that's when I made up my mind that a Hawaiian vacation was a great idea. I took the rest of the day off and headed home. Anne was mopping around the house so I dropped six or seven brochures of Hawaiian tours on the kitchen table and watched her face light up. I told her to pick out a couple of Islands and we'll have Baite make all the arrangements. She asked why Baite she said she could make the calls to the Tour Company. That's when I told her the best part, "The Company is paying for the trip". It only took five days and Anne, Gina and I were aboard a flight to Honolulu. We stayed only two days mostly to see the Pearl Harbor Memorial then on to Maui where we spent most of our vacation about two weeks then on to Kauai's Poipu Beach where we spent our honey moon. It did the trick we both were so loose by the time we were on our way back it was almost like we didn't have a care in the world. While we were in Honolulu for two hours waiting for our connecting flight to the main land I went to a news stand for something to read and right in front was a line of newspapers from the main land and the first one was the Oakland Trib with headlines "Kerrigan caught on the Isle of Jersey off the coast of England". The article went on to explain it is a tax haven centered between main land England and the continent of Europe and more importantly there is a question of extradition between Jersey and the United States. He was traveling with a Canadian Pass Port in the name of Emmanuel Potts. The Feds are searching the financial institutions for any accounts under this name however it is a financial haven so information is privileged. Now it appears the Diplomatic Corps of Canada, England and the United States will have to thrash out the future of Vincent Kerrigan with the Bailiwick of Jersey claiming jurisdiction and autonomy from England. All the way home on the flight I was fascinated by the term Bailiwick I was trying to figure out what the hell it meant and then we landed and put me out of my misery. We were leaving the baggage area through a narrow security check when Joe my security man appeared and asked, "How was our trip". I handed him the Oakland Trib and asked if anything was new on Kerrigan and what the hell is a Bailiwick. He looked away to hide his smile then turn back and said, "I think it is a jurisdiction". He told me he would fill me in later then grabbed one of our bags and said to follow him he was parked in a restricted zone. As we approached I could see a black sedan with diplomatic plates. When we got to the car it was almost surrounded by airport security checking out the car and its plates. Joe approached them dropped our luggage on the side walk and said something as he held up what looked like a badge and the airport security men nodded and slowly dispersed. Without saying a word he opened the trunk and started loading our baggage into it. He closed the trunk then opened the back door for Anne and Gina in a smooth coordinated motion like he obviously had done it many times then headed for the driver's door and that was a cue for me to get into the passenger's seat. As we drove off the remaining airport security guard waved a salute to Joe. When we were on our way I asked him if he could tell me what was that all about and where did you get the diplomatic car. In a monotone he replied, "No I can't". So I said no more until we arrived home then thanked him and told him I'd see him in the morning. He nodded in acknowledgement and said, "Welcome home". Once in the house Anne was more than curious when she asked me, "Could I explain how we rate a diplomatic car from the airport". I told her I wish I knew. We weren't back a full day when Anne was subjected to a tirade by her mother. I could hear most of it when Anne pointed the phone at me with a wicked grin so I could hear her mother's rant about leaving her at the most terribly lonely time in her life to run off with her grandchild to some cockamamie Island just to get a suntan, it didn't faze either one of us. Anne handled the rest of the conversation with a lot of little phrases like I'm sorry it's not possible and no; that's not workable and finally she just hung up. I asked her about her father and if she heard from him her reply was no news is good news so I said no more.

When Joe picked me up in the morning I could tell he was itching to tell me something so I asked, "What's new"? He said he shied away from telling me yesterday in the car so as not to upset my wife. The Feds have a suspect in Arnold's shooting and it all seems to be connected to the Johnny Peresci murder and the first botched attempt on our life. We were still parked in the back of my house so he turned to face me from the driver's seat with the look of a person in a dilemma. I've been told not to discuss any of this with you, but I'm going to do it any way. When you get to the office there will be a message from your attorney to call her. The FBI is having her set up a meeting with them and someone from the Federal Prosecutor's Office to discuss the Cannelli trial and to coach you on how to present your evidence. I know by reputation your lawyer is sharp and she's dealt with the feds before but they have been chasing this group for years and I've heard they have turned one or two of the group so they'll be accusing each other of all the crimes in the indictment. When this gets into full swing it tends to bring in anyone on the sidelines to look like conspirators. Unfortunately you fit the bill here with two attempts on your life and guilt by association some people will think "where there is smoke there's fire". I was stunned I looked out the side window at nothing I could hear Joe talking but nothing registered. Finally I said well we might as well go to the office and see what Myra has to tell me. Joe was right on the money as soon as I got to the office and everyone finished asking about our vacation Carrol told me Myra called and said as soon as you got to the office to call her it was very important. When I got settled at my desk I called Myra. She was upbeat saying she loved the Islands and asked about the flight especially with the baby. I painted her a rosy picture of our vacation then asked what is so important that I have to call you before I even get settled into my office routine. She told me the FBI wants to have a meeting before you have to testify at the Cannelli trial, "That is if you testify at all". "When is this meeting"?

"When are you free"?

"Anytime let's find out what's on their mind".

"I'll call them now and get back to you". She hung up and I gazed at the wall in front of me to more or less make my mind as blank as the wall. It only took twenty minutes and Myra was back with a time and place for the meeting. Now that Joe put me on guard I knew I'd be transfixed on this meeting with the Feds wondering how deep I was in this mess. The meeting wasn't scheduled until 1 o'clock on a Wednesday at the Federal Building. So we met at a coffee shop around the corner at about 10 AM to go over what Myra thought they were going to ask me and go over the chain of events prior, during and after I made Albononi that appraisal. We met Brophy at the FBI office and he took us upstairs to the Federal Prosecutor's Office to meet the man who was going to represent the Government in the Cannelli Trial. We all were introduced to a gentleman by the name of Jeremiah Raushour. He was standing next to his desk obviously waiting for us then put his hand out to everyone in an over done magnanimous gesture. He had big hands for a small man. He stood an inch or two shorter than me and at least four inches shorter then Brophy that put him at eye level with Myra and he concentrated his conversation at her eye level. At first I couldn't tell if it was their mutual height or the fact they were both lawyers. It became apparent it was he who assumed she would understand the legalese jargon to move this meeting along quicker. I thought it odd at the time but he didn't look imposing, outside of his large hands which he used to gesture often, he looked very ordinary with small defined features, short dark hair and eyes I couldn't imagine him in front of a jury. His suit was dark and expensive with a white on white French cuff linked shirt and a deep red power tie all playing to the script of the Napoleonic litigator. I was soon to find out his speech patterns and phraseology didn't necessarily reflect his thoughts and it was intentional because he could dupe you into following the direction he wanted to get the result he wanted. I was getting leery with all the lawyer speak between Myra and Mr. Raushour so I sat back and let them set all the ground rules. I could tell Brophy was of the same opinion, but of course we were in different situations. Mr. Raushour started by asking me where and how I first met Mr. Albononi. I told him in the office of Scranton & Associates here in San Francisco and to arrange for development loan for an East Bay Company named the Blackstone Corporation. I then explained the actual company that was the developer was Hillcrest Housing Development which was owned by Blackstone Corporation. At this point he seemed to cut to the chase and jumped to the appraisal I made for Mr. Albononi and asked how the appraisal came about if you were involved in a different deal arranging a development loan. I explained my boss Dick Sommers was the motor behind procuring the loan I was to make sure they stayed to the letter of the contract and stay on target with the construction schedule. As it turned out the construction schedule fell behind and I attributed it to the developer a Johnny Peresci. Our working relationship deteriorated to a point where Mr. Albononi was brought in to work as a liaison between the developer and me.

"You're referring to Johnny Peresci".

"That is correct".

"OK I got that picture so get to the appraisal over in Berkeley".

"He called me and asked if I would do an appraisal on a piece of property for one of his clients".

"Well moving right along I'm told you became skeptical of the money not reported in the cost of the renovation". Raushour remarked.

"Yeah, that's about it".

"I was also informed Mr. Albononi never physically accepted the cost estimate, I mean he kept his hands in his pockets. Is that right"?

"Yeah I gave it to the manager of the complex a Mrs. Wright".

"Did he tell you who his client was that owned that particular piece of property"?

"No he didn't".

"Then at a point of time later he called you and wanted to know if you had a copy of the appraisal, is that right"?

"Correct, but it was really someone making believe it was Mrs. Wright that called because the voice was too young sounding for the woman I met at the property so I told my boss I thought something was wrong and he said to make a copy and give it to our lawyer Myra Pacemann which I did".

"Then your office was burglarized and they took nothing but your appraisal of the Berkeley property, is that not so"?

"Yes".

"To your knowledge the only copies of the appraisal is in the one in the keeping of you attorney Ms. Pacemann and the one stolen from your office, I'm I correct"?

"Yes that is correct".

The following silence was a relief everyone had heard this story so many times it was like a blessing. Mr. Raushour continued the silence by hand writing his notes in perfect grammar school cursive without asking me to repeat once. He finish writing and asked me if the woman that I thought sounded too young to be the original Mrs. Wright had any accent or any unusual twang from a different part of the country.

I told him I couldn't tell they were short conversations. He seemed to reread my statement then said that will probably do it and just to bring you up on this trial and what's going on and what we can tell you Mr. Albononi is no longer a hostile witness he has agreed to cooperate as a witness for the prosecution. We believe that Margo Cannelli, Freddy Bean's wife was the second Mrs. Wright that called you for the copy of your appraisal and she is on record as owner of the Berkeley Property and Mr. Albononi is willing to testify to that. One last thing I know it is now obvious that Ms. Cannelli doesn't know we have a copy of your appraisal and we assume she had the other copies destroyed so it is important nothing said in this room or about this case leave this room before we go to trial. We all agreed and the interview was ended. Mayra and I left Brophy with Raushour to further plan his strategy and headed for the elevator. There were people in the elevator so we said little if any-thing until we were in the lobby. I stopped Myra before we got to the exit and asked why she was quiet during the meeting. She told me it was all just rehashing your statement you made earlier. I'm really waiting for more information on the progress of this case because

I've heard they have someone for the shooting of Arnold and they're being too quiet about it. You might ask your friendly security guard if he knows anything about this rumor and I'm willing to bet from the way Raushour was asking you about Margo Cannelli she is involved with the shooting. I said it sounds like a good idea.

Chapter 35

When we got outside Joe was waiting at the foot of the steps to the Federal Building and when he saw us he turned to hail a cab. Myra begged off and told me she was going to walk over to Market Street to do some shopping and for me to call her if I hear anything. I hadn't eaten lunch so I told the cab driver to drop us off at the Pine Street Luncheonette. When we got there Joe had the same reaction as everyone else when they first walked in, "Apprehension". It was after two so things were slowing down and the little table in the back was vacant. As we were passing the young waitress she said, "Your table's empty but your late there's no more Italian biscuits". Joe followed me to the table and when he sat he asked, "What was the waitress talking about, what Italian biscuits'? I told him it's a running gag about calling biscotti an Italian biscuit.

"I'm Italian and biscotti is a biscuit only twice baked so what's the joke." Before I could answer he actually flushed pink and sheepishly said, "I just got it it's a privet joke". I told him not to let the waitress hear that because she'll ride you about it unmercifully. "I won't tell if you won't tell". He said.

"I told him mum's the word". He just lifted an eye brow and smiled in a scheming way; then I told him the food was very good Italian home style. He said he was fine he had something while we were at the federal building and moved the menu to the edge of the table without looking at it. The waitress showed up as we finished our conversation on the biscotti and stood a foot from Joe with the bottom of her mini skirt just above the table top. It was distracting to say the least. Joe was facing me but his eyes were on the bottom of her skirt. She asked me what'll I have and I asked if they still had veal and peppers.

"Yeah".

"Great I'll have a hero". Her answer was more of a comment you mean a grinder. I said, "Of course a rose is a rose". She looked at me strangely then turned to Joe and asked him for his order. He asked if they had enough for two orders. "Sure" she replied. Then can I have the veal and peppers on a plate with the bread on the side. She said, of course, and then left with the skirt dancing in rhythm to the swing of her walk. Joe's eyes followed her all the way to the ordering counter. He looked back at me and I said she dresses like that for the tips. He said maybe if she gets enough tips she can afford a longer skirt. I blurted out a laud laugh and she turned from the ordering counter and looked at me with an accusing stare knowing she was the brunt of our humor. I told Joe I was going to pay for that stupid laugh. That triggered a laud laugh from him and I knew we both were in her cross hairs. To change the subject and mood I brought up the rumor that the Feds had a man in custody for the shooting of Arnold and asked Joe if he heard anything. He started rearranging the condiments on the table then his eyes darted around the counter area then said, "You know we shouldn't be talking about this in here".

"Well that's true, but there's no one here and the noise from the front is more than enough to drown out our conversation". He took a quick look around again then told me they did and he looks good for the shooting and possibly the Peresci murder. "That was fast did they have a snitch or an informant to finger this guy"?

"No I've heard it was his stupidity. They got a fix on him from the thumb and palm print from the door pull on the roof where the sniper shot Arnold. He obviously discarded his gloves before he left the roof. They traced the M1 to the National Guard Unit he was in and they reported it stolen four years ago. He bought the scope on a hunting trip to Montana at a swap shop and the guy who sold it to him pointed him to a gunsmith to mount the scope on his M1 and both identified him from his photo. From what I've heard the Feds have all kinds of physical evidence plus this guy is a European auto mechanic with his own shop that works on Margo Cannelli's Maserati and Oldman Peresci's vintage Fiat which could supply the connection. I don't know this but the word is this guy has a record and this could be a murder attempt for hire on the Arnold shooting and if he's hooked into the Johnny Peresci murder and it's a murder for hire he could get the needle. With all this going on the Feds are acting like he's cooperating "quote" with the investigation".

"So who hired him"?

"Nobody knows however at this point it sounds like they're all cooperating which means they're all accusing each other of everything in the indictment and probably then some".

"Why are the feds playing this kind of game why don't they promise immunity to the people who are less guilty then convict those who are the Kingpins"?

"You used the right word "Game" the FBI knew the mob was skimming money from the casinos in Vegas especially the Feline Follies but not where they were laundering it now they're sure the conduit was Freddy "beans" and the Drays Saving and Trust was the laundry. The game is to pit all the players against one and other over the shootings and the murders and they're hoping this will shake out the organized crime guys from Vegas by naming some names and if they can get Kerrigan extradited back here for trial it would be the icing on the cake".

"I asked Joe if he knew the name of the auto mechanic accused of the shooting and I could tell by his suddenly dark expression he thought he already said too much". "He said he didn't get a name, but it will soon be coming out in an indictment". He was saved from further interrogation when the food arrived and the waitress's comment "Enjoy". From that point on everything he said was guarded so we finished a late lunch and headed back to the office. I settled in behind my desk and glanced at the clock. It was a quarter to four so I thought Myra would be back from her shopping so I called. The receptionist put me right through to Myra and I didn't waste any time I told her what Joe said about the FBI having Arnold's shooter and possibly Johnny Peresci's murderer and the connection to the Las Vegas mob. After a lingering moment she said, "Interesting keep me posted on any more info". She hung up before I could respond and when I went looking around the office both Dick and Peter were gone so I followed suite. Joe dropped me off at the house a little early, but Anne was home and conjuring up my old favorite baked ziti.

She had all the ingredients assemble in a baking bowl ready to put into the oven. She was surprised to see me home early and asked if she should put the ziti in now or do you want to wait it will only take twenty minutes. Why don't we wait a while I had a late lunch. I pecked Anne on the cheek as I was heading for the refrigerator for a cold beer. I opened the door and to my pleasant surprise there was a cold bottle of Sauvignon Blanc from Cakebread Cellars always my first choice. I asked what was the occasion and she said nothing really I thought it might be just the ticket to offset the grilling the FBI gave you this afternoon. It wasn't even a grilling I was introduced to the government's prosecutor who is handling the Cannelli trial and he wanted to go over my testimony we were out of there in no more than an hour. Myra thinks they are compiling so much evidence against Cannelli that they don't think it is a good idea to have me testify because of the my connection to Mr. Bekkvelt. "What has Bekkvelt have to do with the government's case with the Cannelli trial"?

"Come on Anne; his man Joe picked us up at the airport with a car with diplomatic plates and when his name is mentioned in the presence of agents or in a conversation about the FBI's investigation they go quiet. He's obviously connected to the government's diplomatic corps at a high level and they don't want him dragged into this trial where a defense lawyer could have a field day putting him through an embarrassing line of questions that have nothing to do with the actual trial".

"You know I'm very worried about this whole situation I'll be happy when it's over with". After Anne said that I decided not to tell her what Joe told me about the evidence that the FBI had for the trial.

Two days later Myra called to tell me the Feds have a very strong case against both Margo and Freddy Cannelli for everything in the Federal indictment along with everybody connected to the Drays Savings and Trust. Arnold's shooter said he was hired by Margo Cannelli and he's telling all because the FBI has unsurmountable physical evidence tying him to the Johnny Peresci murder. By the way the shooter's name is Karl Meiss and it looks like he's been in trouble before because he went right for self-defense plea but settled for a man slaughter plea bargain for the Peresci murder to avoid a murder for hire that could put him on death row. According to Meiss he owed Johnny money and when he was on the run he told Meiss he needed the money but Meiss says he didn't have it and they fought then he claims Johnny pulled a knife and in defense Meiss hit him with the baseball bat. So I doubt if you'll be called as a witness, but don't totally discount it because the Feds have been known to pile on evidence as an abundance of caution. I'll keep abreast of the trial and keep you up to date.

Larry called me while I was on the phone with Myra and after I settled down and digested everything Myra had told me I call him back and he told me he got the ball rolling. He told me he talked to an architectural and engineering firm that was recommended by a construction company, that he knew had experience in this field. I have to tell you I think we should put this on hold until all the problems with the BWS are solved. Then we could go ahead with plans to submit to the city and the National Register of Historic places along with the San Francisco Landmark committee.

I told him I thought he was right I probably jumped the gun I better run this passed Peter and Dick before we spend a ton of money while flying blind. To my surprise Peter was adamant that we get moving ASAP on the Plans for the demolishment of the existing building and the architectural and engineering plans so we can present them to the City and he'll deal with Miriam Frost. I got back on the horn to Larry and told him Peter was insistent we go ahead immediately with the Plans for the South of Market property. "Why is he so insistent"?

"If I had to guess I'd say he already has the group of investors and don't want to have this drag on and chance it turning their enthusiasm sour". "I'll find out when the architect can meet us out at the property and get this going". We left it at that.

For the next month or six weeks Larry and I were reviewing plans submitted by Porcaro & Kiely Architectural and Engineering firm for what would be our concept of a 1890 Art Nouveau building with an 1900 Classical style Cast Iron façade. It wasn't easy and even with the architect's patience and perseverance it wasn't going well. Just when we were getting close to scraping the idea and go with one or the other Mr. Porcaro came up with the concept of an atrium in the center separating the two. The front facing the street would be the Cast Iron 1900 style with commercial space for shopping and amenities for the residence; in the apartment section of the back and sides of the building which would be Art Nouveau. He had the atrium designed with balcony gardens at each apartment overlooking an Art Nouveau fountain surrounded by chairs and tea tables of the nouveau design. Of course, we would have to cut back from fifty to forty apartments to fit this design into the physical dimensions of the property and cut out some parking, but Larry and I thought it solved the problem of the overall design. I kept the rough sketches and asked Mr. Porcaro if he would draw up more detailed drawings so we could bring them to Peter and Dick. I was so taken with the design I took them home to show Anne. She was more enthusiastic then me and started penciling in her ideas on the rough sketches. We talked about the project all through dinner then put on the TV to catch the late night news. As soon as the TV went on there was Peter Travillian being introduced as the new owner of the building that is the home of the Battered Women's Sanctuary? The introduction was being made by the same Supervisor who not long ago was champion in their cause to stay at the original site and the "Cause Celeb" soap opera actress Sherry Sims as they both fought for more of the camera. They were thanking Peter for helping them with their solution by financing a complete refurbishing of a City owned hotel. They were shamefully taking credit, in their words, for addressing the problem head on for the Battered Women's Sanctuary by finding temporary rooms for them at one of the City owned hotels until Mr. Travillian has finished the alterations at the new Location. Peter stepped forward and explained his company had bought the property and is in the process of filing permits to build apartments which everyone knows is a critical issue in the City. However the buildings on the property are in bad physical condition in fact one building has been red tagged and scheduled for demolition by the City and the other is nonfunctional from a practical prospective. However a more immediate concern is the possibility of an incident that could trigger a building collapse. So the City with the urging of these two people on my right Supervisor Melon and Miss Sims is processing the paperwork to demolish both buildings. He thanked everyone and melted into the back ground as the Politician and the Actress fought for the eye of the camera. When the news was over Anne asked "Where was Miriam Frost she was the most vocal"?

I had to say it, I couldn't help it. "It appears they left her out in the cold".

Anne was a second or two slow for my pun to sink in, but her response was sheer Anne. "If the corn gets any higher I'll have to start singing Oklahoma". The next morning the office was nothing but talk of the interview with Peter and the two twits he had them making a complete turnabout from their previous stand on the location of the WBS and helped paved the way for our project on the same property. We were all in the reception area when Peter came in and of course it was Baite who was the first to start clapping then we all joined in. Peter raised his hand in melodramatic fashion then said, "Please, please I don't deserve it, but if you want to through money feel free however I prefer paper coin weigh my pockets down". The ensuing laughter was genuine and we all took turns congratulating him when things got to normal Peter asked me to come to his office. He told me he had an important meeting this afternoon starting at 1 o'clock with a gentleman from the Walla Walla Iron Works and along with Dick he wanted me and Larry to be there. I called Larry and he said he was on his way to drop off a proposal for a client and he'd be there before one. I wasn't very hungry so I hung out at the office sorting out junk mail. About noon time I heard a commotion in the reception area and when I looked it was Peter and a young man lugging in a large projection camera and a box of material. I offered them help but they were already at the door of the conference room so I opened the door for them and tried to look helpful. The young man mounted the camera on the end of the conference table and Peter dropped the box of material on the side of the table with a loud thud. Peter made a gushing sound of relief then turned to me and introduced the young man as Maxwell Toomey from the Walla Walla Cast Iron Foundry in Washington. He's here at our request to show us the Company's promotional film on the cast iron building making from the forging to the finished product. It was a big thirty five millimeter projector and it looked very professional so I didn't want to touch anything so I kept my hands in my pockets. Max opened the material box and took out a pair of speakers than began hooking everything up and by that time it was just about one o'clock and Dick and Larry were coming through the door. Peter made introductions and went on to explain Max was going to run a forty minute film on the making of a cast iron facade. Baite was at the door with bottles of water and asked if anyone wanted coffee or anything else. No one answered so she just put the bottles on the table and left. That signaled Max to begin the film. It went on for the forty minutes and had everyone fascinated in the making and designing a cast iron façade. However the last ten minutes looked added on it even had a different narrator. It was a about dismantling an existing cast iron facade and the subject was our building on South of Market. It was informational without sounding commercial and the narrator delivered the material smoothly and it was very well written. When it was over Max gave a little spiel along with distributing a catalog and reading material for everyone. He asked if we had any questions and said he would appreciate any input then said he knew this was all academic until you actual start building one of the structures and at that point call me anytime and I will gladly help. While Max was giving his spiel Peter had Baite call the building management to send up a couple of men to transport the camera equipment to Max's van in the garage. We all thanked him and he left. The whole time of the film and the subsequent meeting only took one hour and forty five minutes so we were all waiting for Peter to give us an explanation because it was obvious this was not a show and tell meeting. He kind of half sat on the end of the table facing us and asked what we thought of the film and if we thought it was something the local Public TV channel would be interested in running. As a second thought Peter told us not to dismiss Mr. Toomey's offer of help in erecting a cast iron façade or building because of his youthful looks. You will come across his credentials in the reading material he distributed to you; he is a graduate engineer and has a Master's degree in metallurgy. After about ten or fifteen minutes of everyone putting their two cents in

Peter told us he was thinking of having the narration changed to Ms. Frost's voice over and some face time on the film with the Public TV's permission it would make her a de facto spokes-person for Cast Iron Buildings History. Dick was sitting quiet and it was obvious to me he and Peter had talked this all over beforehand so I looked over at Larry and I was sure he was thinking the same thing. If Miriam Frost accepted this offer it would take all the wind out of her sails and show she had no real agenda in the WBS cause except for the Cast Iron Building History. Peter asked if there were any questions so I asked how sure was he that the Public TV station would run the film and how sure are you Ms. Frost would accept the offer. "Not a hundred percent on either but I've made a donation of money and the film itself to the TV station and they let me know they reviewed it and thought it was a sound scientific and historical film on the forging of the Cast Iron. I also let it be known that Miss Sherry Sims will also be offered the job of narrating the film if Ms. Frost declined. He told us the last remark about Miss Sims being involved seemed to create some theatrical buzz at the TV station". There was that moment of silence when everyone expected someone to say something and it was Larry.

"That was shear brilliance the idea in its self to turn their real or imaginary WBS problem around and have it appear they solved it by themselves and if Ms. Frost declines your offer Miss Sims would kill to get in front of the camera." Peter just nodded yes to the obvious then said, "That's all I got". Dick was the first one to move and Larry and I followed and headed for my office. Once there Larry mentioned Mr. Porcaro told him a

Mrs. Mace called about a roof garden job and wanted to thank us for the referral. I just looked at Larry and told him that's the first I heard of it although I did give her his business card. "It sounds like a great idea. I don't remember her mentioning a roof garden, but as long as I'm not involved, she can do as she pleases".

We wound up our day and on the way home Joe gave me an update on the Cannelli trial. "It sounded like it was going to the ordained script of the government's plan. Freddy was being tried separately from Margo. She was getting scared while she was waiting for her trial to begin so true to the governments script she is "quote" cooperating with the Feds to get a better deal from them and the most surprising news was Vince Kerrigan slipped through everyone's fingers and left the Ile of Jersey for Stockholm Sweden. Unbeknown to the authorities he was married to a Swedish woman who accompanied him from Canada when he fled the Americas then when the time was right they both got a plane out of Heathrow to Stockholm where he'll be protected by Sanctuary law. Outside of the laundered money he out and out stole from the Drays Savings and Trust the Feds are more interested in who gave it to him to launder. It's not really a secret who gave him the money to launder and the feds are giving him a choice come back and testify for a reduced sentence or he will be on the run from the people he stole the money from for the rest of his life which might be sooner than later. I'm sure he knows hiding in plain sight in Stockholm is politically safe but not from the people he stole the money from".

When I got home I had an ear full for Anne. She slowed me down saying she keeps track of the trial from the newspapers but she wanted me to go over the meeting with Peter and the man from Walla Walla a second time. She said the same thing Larry said that Peter's strategy was marvelous and couldn't see the Public TV station or Frost or Sims turning the offer down. I asked her if Mary said anything to her about a roof garden she was thinking of installing at Union Street. She told me no, but she did complain about a tenant who parks their second car partially in her driveway. I explained to her for the umpteenth time she owned the building and it was up to her to tell the tenant not to park in her driveway or turn over the running of the property to a management company. I knew what her answer would be but I asked Anne anyway, "What'd she say"? She said because we owned property we would know how to handle people like that. She said it in her little girl's voice and realized she was talking to me and changed to her lost and helpless voice and realized she wasn't getting anywhere then asked if I'd have you give her a ring. I frowned at the last part of her sentence and Anne said, "What can I tell you she's hot for your body".

"You know there are times I can't tell if she is just flirting or actually making a pass at me".

"Be careful young man remember divorce is expensive". I gave Anne the double take and she wasn't smiling. I made a puny attempt to make light of Anne's last remark of course it didn't work so I changed the subject. I asked, "What did she hear from the home front". She graciously let the Mary Mace conversation go and told me it looks like her parents' separation was going to get messy. Her mother now had a lawyer that told her a legal separation is not enough and she should sue for what is legally hers. I said, "That's not good".

"That's the understatement of the mouth she is going to further isolate herself from his family and that leaves me the only one on her side of the family left". I had to respond, "I know we made an agreement when we married not to interfere in each other's family matters, but this has all the earmarks of your mother moving in here and that is out of the question".

"Oh no; that has never even been considered she would disrupt this house hold to a point of disrupting our marriage and I cannot have that".

"What if she brings up the apartment down stairs again she already told the tenant she was moving into their apartment soon and they should start looking for a new place".

"NO no; I already straightened that out with the tenants and my mother I told my mother they have two years left on their lease".

"I didn't know that when did you give them a new lease".

"Tomorrow".

It took me a second for it to register then we both started laughing.

Chapter 36

Larry's consulting business picked up so he couldn't meet me at the architectural firm for about a week. I didn't think it really mattered because Peter liked the plans and we were just about at the point where they would run off the plans to file with the City. I met with Mr. Porcaro to more or less finalize any minor changes and he mentioned Mrs. Mace's roof garden plans were ready for my inspection. I wasn't really surprised I knew Mary would pull something like this so I told Mr. Porcaro that I was sure his architect has covered all the bases so we'll go with his plans. Well there is also a matter of replacing the wooden rear staircase with some sort of metal. We've suggested either wrought iron or a decorative cast iron. She said you should decide. "What's the cheapest"?

"It's the wrought iron".

"Then wrought iron it is".

"You're not interested in seeing the drawings"?

"No I'm not and is it possible to have Mrs. Mace's roof plans ready by tomorrow".

"Certainly but to be safe come by after 4 o'clock and we'll have everything ready for you".

THE END FINISHED HERE

I was still at the bay window in my revere when I heard, my name being called several times somewhere in the distance. When I snapped out of it I realized it was Anne telling me it was Tom on the phone. I retreated to the kitchen and picked up the phone and said, "Hi"."

"Nancy said Anne just told her Mary was murdered today could that be right"?

"I'm afraid that's right and the police are going after Allen's old partner in the Boutique La Beau it seems he was seen leaving by the back staircase right after gun shots were heard. And to add to the irony the investigating detectives are Oscar Norman and Peter Medwin."

"Do you think this has anything to do with Mary's inheritance? You know I was told she was going to help out Allen and Jean with a cash injection into their business,of course, that was before Allen died".

"I truly don't know and at this point I'm a little numb with all the murders and accidental deaths that have happened in the past few years and who knows maybe Allen's Partner Jean can shed a light on all these events. I believe the police certainly think so."

"This is terrible she just got her life in a stable position financially and it appeared in her personal life there must be something that we don't know about that caused this to happen". Tom mused.

"Your probably wright I think the police are going to dig up some of her past not only that we don't know about, but the reasons she took the course she took". We chatted on for a few more minutes when Tom asked me if I knew of any of her relatives. I told him I doubted she had any mainly because she inherited her Aunt's estate uncontested. Then Tom said, "Maybe we should start thinking about her funeral we don't want her buried in an unmarked grave somewhere". That sounded like a sober comment after all the upsetting events so I told him that was something we could address tomorrow or the next day right now I'm not thinking straight. The next morning I called Dick and told him of Mary Mace's murder and pretty much how I found her body and who the police suspect. He was predictably speechless so when he started asking me questions, they were the ones I couldn't answer, I explained I had to go to the police station today to give them a formal statement and I'll be late getting into the office. We left it at that and I headed for the police station.

I was expected so the desk sergeant told me to go ahead to the detective division on the second floor. It was the same set up a rough circle of desks maned by men oblivious to everyone around them while they were on the phone and Oscar was one of them. He was still on the phone when I got to his desk so I was greeted by his partner Medwin seated at his desk that abutted Oscar's. He offered me a seat next to his desk and turned to a small typewriter on a portable table at his left and began loading paper into the carriage of his typewriter. Oscar was still on the phone when Medwin said, "Why don't we get started".

"Where do I start"?

"Why were you at Mrs. Mace's apartment"?

"I told him about the roof plans and picking them up at the architect's office and heading for her apartment at close to six o'clock. Her front door was agar and that was unusual so I was on guard when I entered I called her name twice with no answer then I saw her sitting on the couch with blood seeping from her chest. For reasons I can't explain instead of calling the police immediately I looked over the murder scene and the only thing that struck me as being wrong was the Hummel figurine it was missing from the mantle. It was her prize procession. At that point I went to the neighbor's and called the police and a squad car was there in ten minutes. Medwin asked how to spell Hummel and to describe it. I didn't realize Oscar had finished his conversation on the phone and was listening to my statement. I spelled it out, "HUMMEL" it is a figurine of a boy under an umbrella. I realized Oscar had left his desk without a word. Medwin asked why I was involved in her roof plans and some more question about the arrival time of the first squad car. He then started to ask redundant questions about me first arriving at the murder scene that's when Oscar came back to his desk with a large file. Medwin stopped typing and asked Oscar, "What are you doing with the John Mace murder file". He didn't answer right away he was leafing through the middle of the file then stopped with a gasp of satisfaction and said, "I thought so". He pulled out a page cut from a magazine and handed it across his desk to me and asked is this the figurine. It was and I told him so. Oscar started talking to Medwin like I wasn't there. "She was there when her Aunt died and she must have taken the figurine after her Aunt was dead. This puts her at the scene of crime and why no one ever found her Aunt's will. She must have destroyed it". Medwin finished typing the last sentence then handed it to me to read and sign which I did and then left for my office. It was obvious they thought they talked too much in front of me their abrupt silence while I read my statement proved it and I was just as happy to leave. Back at the office I was treated like a leaper with quiet sympathy so I buried myself behind my desk and mulled over what Oscar had said to Medwin about Mary and the death of her Aunt and especially her inheritance. I couldn't believe Mary would do such a thing, but a nagging thought in the back of my mind kept pushing through that Mary always seemed to be consumed by the quest for money.

Carol buzzed me on the intercom and told me Myra was on line two. I punched the blinking light and asked her, "What's up". "Well that question has irony. I just got a call about Mary Mace's murder and your unfortunate time and place to find her body. I also understand you were at the police station to give your official statement this morning. I'm not sure what they told you about the suspect Jean Le Beau but I would guess not much so I'll fill you in this guy Le Beau has confessed to her murder and being an accomplice in her husband's murder. That would make the FBI's contention that it was a mob hit wrong and maybe a little embarrassing". My mind jumped over a river of possibilities I was thinking about before Myra called with the shocking news that Jean Le Beau was involved with John's murder that meant Allen in all probability killed John. I hardly heard the rest of what Myra was saying and our conversation ended with a let's stay in touch. I finally came to the conclusion I was rationalizing from what Myra just told me it is apparent Mary must have had something to do with these murders. I heard Peter in the reception area talking to Carol I couldn't distinguish what he was saying but I did hear my name. Within a minute I heard him in my doorway so I looked up and said, "What's up"? He gave me a friendly smile and stepped in and closed the door behind him. He asked how did I feel and if I was done with the police, but remained standing so I knew he wouldn't be here long. I told him I'm still a little upset, but otherwise OK and who knows about the police they're always asking questions. "Well I'm assuming you didn't have time to see the morning papers so let me paraphrase the article by our friend Edmond Dailey. In a left handed way he compliments you for actually breaking the case for the FBI. He goes on to say by your doggedness tracing the line of embezzlement by Johnny Peresci to the Drays Saving and Trust you led the Feds to the Vegas dirty money and who was laundering it. The trial for Freddy Cannelli is over and he was found guilty of his part in the laundering of the money skimmed from the Vegas Casino the Feline Follies and now the Nevada Gaming Commission has suspended their license subject to their own investigation. He concludes with, "You were leading the Feds to the Laundry where the Vegas skimmed money was washed and that is why the Feds had tight security on you throughout the investigation".

"That sentence is a little flowery, but I think it is accurate".

"So I'm either a hero or a goat depending on who reads it".

"No neither; we all see you as a gutsy guy who did his job and went beyond the scope of what was expected to get the job done right. If you think you need a few days or more to get back to feeling normal take Anne and the baby to the coast. Baite tells me Anne has a place in mind in Mendocino go there and bill our office. Do you have any questions"? Before I said no Peter was halfway out the door. I called Anne at the Gina's baby school. She mentioned the Cannelli conviction in a tone of finality then asked how the meeting at the Police station went. I gave her the short version then told her the offer from Peter and before I could say another word she said hold on and put me on hold. She came back in five minutes to tell me we had her boss's place in Mendocino for next Wednesday through Thursday of the following week. I told her I had some clothes shopping to do and I'll see her at home. Anne was home and on the phone when I walked through the pantry so I went to Gina sitting at the kitchen table and she told me she was writing her numbers for homework. I told her they were great, but I couldn't tell them from pencil scratches so I kept her amused until Anne was off the phone. She was all excited she was talking with Nancy and Tom and they're going with us to Mendocino. The following week progressed to Wednesday and we were off to Mendocino. Tom and Nancy followed in their car because they could only stay a few days then had to get back to San Francisco. Tom told me the best route would 128 over the coastal mountains rather than route one on the coastal scenic drive it's shorter in time and distance. I was all for it to me route one was a little scary driving around those cliffs and it made my stomach queasy, but of course, I used Gina as the reason we should take the mountain route. The house was fine two bed room two baths, but a view from a magazine ad. The house was perched on a cliff along with a few others but spaced generously with a frontage of forty or fifty yards to a sheer cliff and at least one hundred feet above a natural cove. The view was one hundred and eighty degrees of the Pacific Ocean. We were getting organized when Nancy said she already had dinner for tonight but she wouldn't tell us what it was so I peeked. It was Sauerbraten with potato dumplings and, of course, she bragged it was her mother's old family recipe. We went to the town of Mendocino to shop and nose around and buy a stuffed whale for Gina then returned for some comfort food. Tom produced a loaf of old country dark Rye bread and a bottle of white wine from Napa valley. In almost an apology he said he knew I liked Sauvignon Blanc but the girls asked for this Semillon it's a little less dry and a bit creamier it goes really well with the sauerbraten. Between the ocean air and the long drive everyone was famished and the choice of sauerbraten was perfect for the cooler salty ocean air. We finished dinner just in time to see the sun setting on the horizon the limited clouds just above the horizon gave the sky a band of colors from yellow, red and magenta. We talked over coffee well after sunset and not once was Mary Mace's name brought up not even in passing. We all retired and Anne built a bed for Gina out of pillows and blankets right next to Anne's side of the bed, but in ten minutes Gina was in bed with Anne. The two of them were giggling and tickling one and other while I blissfully fell asleep. I woke up abruptly after midnight and knew I couldn't get back to sleep so I went to the kitchen and wormed up a cup of left over coffee and sat with a view of a full moon reflecting off of the eternal Pacific Ocean. The light from the moon laid a track from the horizon to the shore. It reminded me of and old world war two movie film the wake of a torpedo heading for an unsuspecting ship. I heard a noise and turned to see Tom in his bath robe leaning on the door frame to his room. He asked if there was any coffee left. I told him to help himself. He did a quick heat up of a cup and dropped into a seat next to me. He mentions he saw Peter on the TV with Melon and Sims and thought he did a masterful job wooing those two into his corner.

"I got a call from the TV station to do a few stills of your project Cast Iron building. It's pretty apparent they're going to run that film on Cast Iron building in a mini series of two one hour programs. I thanked them for the business and they told me to thank Mr. Travillian I'm going to thank him when I get back to San Francisco. I understand you saw Oscar and Medwin at the Homicide Division for a formal statement on Mary's murder did they shed any light on why Jean shot her"?

"I got a shocker for you he admitted shooting Mary and also being an accomplice in John's murder".

"John's murder; you mean John Mace"?

"Yes I do and Oscar made a slip and let it out in front of me he thinks Mary murdered her Aunt for the money". Tom looked at me sideways like I was out of focus and said, "You're not kidding".

"No I'm not and like you I can't believe it". They both sat quietly staring out to sea for a few uncomfortable moments when Tom continued to speak in a monotone. "Allen told Nancy he had something on John that would embarrass him socially and would not go well in the business world and if he didn't stop harassing him about the loan payments he would tell the world".

"I would think Oscar probably told you he always thought Allen had something to do with John's murder and if Oscar's theory is right that means Mary was also involved. Anne thought there was a liaison going on between the three of them and I hate to think about it, but hate, threats and a lust for money is a recipe for murder". They both thought they exhausted the subject and decided to go to bed. Tom and Nancy left Saturday morning and Kerry's left the following Thursday morning on the way home Anne told me she would like to make this an annual trip. I thought it over while driving home and told Anne it was a good idea. We took our time driving home and finally pulled into the back of the house late in the afternoon. Anne went to open the back door and I started to get the luggage. I saw Anne take an envelope off of the door knob and quickly open it. When we were settled inside I asked Anne what was on the back door. She told me it was from her mother and I didn't want to read it. I agreed and we left it at that. I got in bright and early Friday morning and raring to go. Baite was talking to Carrol at the receptionist desk and they wanted to know all about the trip to the coast. I gave them a quick story with Nancy bringing sauerbraten mainly to watch Baite's eyes water. Baite said I was lying and only saying that to make her envious. Not really but if I was trying to make you envious I'd tell you how it tasted in the ocean's salty air and how the white semi-dry wine complimented the dark robust sauce and the potato dumplings. Baite was smirking when she asked if I took that from an ad in a cooking magazine. I said yeah partly, but it was great. She told me there was pile of messages from people that couldn't wait for me to get back from your nature's retreat. When I got to my desk she was obviously joking because there was only one and it was from Larry. She followed me into my office and presented me with a four day old newspaper and told me she saved the paper because she knew I was incommunicado in the wilds of Mendocino. There was a featured article about Mary Mace's murder by my friend Dailey against my better judgement I read it. For a change the facts were fairly accurate and he only mentions me a few times, but when he runs out of facts he again quotes a sauce he can't name that Jean and Mary had an affair that ended badly. I threw the paper into the waste basket and called Larry. He asked about the coast and a few questions about Mary's murder but thank heavens he went to the business at hand the cast iron building he told me the engineering and architecture plans and permits were approved and now it was up to the contractor to start dismantling the existing façade. That's great I'm going to go over and see if he's started on the façade you want to meet me there? He told me he couldn't and that's why he left the message he's going to be tied up for a couple of weeks on a job that's taking all his time. I was getting ready to leave when Baite stuck her head in the door and said she forgot to mention the contractor is going to be delayed on the dismantling of the Cast Iron Building because the TV station want to film it and the film company is not ready.

"Did they say how long"?

"They didn't give a time it's something technical".

I called Tom at his studio to see if he and Nancy had any trouble getting home. Nancy answered and we chatted about Mendocino and then I got Tom. He told me while we were still up in Mendocino they had Mary's remains cremated. "She's interned at a cemetery in Colma. I was thinking we could visit her at the cemetery like a small memorial service. She has no relatives and her friends are few especially now so maybe you, me, the girls and Oscar said he'd go. What do you think?

"Yeah Tom I'm in; even under the circumstances I think you're right. Do you have a day and time in mind"?

"Next Tuesday 10 o'clock we can pick you two up and go in one car".

Tuesday morning it was drizzling and cold and we all huddled around the Crematory Wall housing the remains of the departed. Oscar was the only one without an umbrella and tried to get under Tom's, but his shoulders couldn't make it and were getting soaked. Tom read a passage from a Gospel according to Mark about crossing the Jordin, which I thought was part of a parable and it was short and to the point. The girls looked uncomfortable during the, would be, service and not because of the weather Anne and Nancy were reluctant to go and pay homage to Mary after the revelations of what she did.

But they told us they decide to go along on the notion of a basic propriety. Tom and I had no idea of what they were talking about but it had the effect of us all going together. We were there a bit more than a half an hour and Tom invited us to his house for something warm to drink. Oscar was the first to respond saying he was soaked and needed a brandy and coffee. Nancy had a buffet all laid out when we got to their house and the freshly ground coffee's aroma was wafting through the kitchen. We all settled in the family room and immediately the deeds and misinformation on Mary's life circled the room until Oscar stopped the speculation and offered the story of Jean's confession. "Jean confessed to helping Mary and Allen kill John". From this point on everybody was spellbound. "According to Jean Mary planned the murder and Allen went along enthusiastically. He supplied the gun which he bought at a gun show it was a two shot derringer then modified the barrel and breech to firer twenty two ammo. Mary went to San Diego a day before to see her Aunt to give her an alibi and after having lunch with her Aunt went straight to the airport for the hourly flight to SF. He picked her up at SF airport and drove her to John's office building. She went into the building through the garage killed Mace and at a prearranged time he picked her up outside the building's garage and drove her to the SF Airport for a flight back to San Diego. She tucked the gun under her seat of the car and told him to throw the gun in the Bay. He didn't; he told us he wrapped the gun in plastic from one of his swearers and hid it. Allen voided the nine thousand dollar check he gave Mace the next morning and according to Jean when Mary found out she was furious because it could be viewed as suspicious. Allen didn't actually trust Mary with money and especially the part of the plan that when Mary inherited all of John's money he would get the check back and then Mace's wealth turned out to be all smoke and mirrors with no cash. Jean said this is when the seeds of mistrust started. Mary claimed John had buried money and she would find it, but Allen was skeptical. Jean asked Mary for financial help for his business and when she turned him down he threaten her telling her he never threw the gun away and her finger prints are all over it. He said she wired him five hundred with a promise of more. Her Aunt died shortly after and the promise of more when they settled her inheritance. When Allen got sick Mary volunteered to help out and brought this salve with her to help ease Allen's sore and stiff joints. The salve turned out to be DMSO a skin penetrating gel used for the same conditions for race horses and laced with arsenic. It was not detected because of Allen's bout with AIDS it was assumed it was the AIDS that was attacking his immune system. Mary went back to Las Vegas to work until she got her inheritance. Jean would hear from her sporadically then suddenly he gets a phone call from her telling him she just sent him two thousand dollars by wire and one thousand was for him and he was to contact a guy named Micky Addleman and give him the second thousand. He didn't question her what this was about because he needed the money and contacted Addleman at the address she gave him and gave him the money. After Allen died Mary recommended the same salve for Jean. After using it he felt his health deteriorating and feared he had gotten AIDS. He was being cared for in a clinic and a visiting doctor was skeptical of the diagnosis because of the type of symptoms and ran a toxicology test and it came up positive for arsenic. The rest, of course, you know, but the last irony in all this is he shot her with the same gun that she used to shot her husband.

Oscar gave us a ride home and on the way he asked about Larry and our project over in Oakland then asked Anne how was little Gina doing and seemed to avoid asking about her parents. We talked about everything but Mary and the murders, but I had these nagging thoughts that maybe I mentioned DMSO to Mary and that gave her the idea to use it on Allen and Jean. I put it aside as ridiculous. Oscar dropped us off and we spent the rest of evening avoiding the obvious question "why".

It didn't take long for Dailey to get his last story on Mary Mace into the paper. Anne called me at the office to tell me she read the article by Dailey in the morning paper and something is in it that I might be interested in so I should read the article and she'd like to know what I thought of it when I got home. I asked Baite if we had a copy of the newspaper and she showed up at my office with the paper and Dailey's article all circled in red. I looked at her questioningly and she said Carrol did it first thing this morning and don't throw it away Dick hasn't read it yet. I sat back and read the article. His by-line was, "Five person memorial for Mary Mace at a Colma Cemetery". He went on to describe the half hour service in the rain and mentioned all who attended by name and I read a brief excerpt from the Gospel according to Mark. I started laughing to myself and thought he couldn't get anything wright because it was Tom that read the excerpt from the Gospel not me. The rest of the article was all filler about Jean La Beau's alleged confession, then the landscape, the weather, the drive from San Francisco to the cemetery in Colma and the melancholia of a cemetery. No one else mentioned the article or the newspaper so I went about my business with a dull memory of the day before. I had an emerging feeling this was all going to be behind me and I lost this lethargic feeling of semi-helplessness and was eager to turn a new page. The rest of the day was all short meetings with Dick on work pending and positive calls from Joe Peavy on the Oakland project. Before I left I called Anne and ask if I should stop at Macaluso's and get some bread. She said why not; so I did and drove home. When I got to the pantry I could smell the food on the kitchen stove. The table was set for three Gina had graduated from her high chair to the table.

There was an opened bottle of wine breathing on the table, but some- thing was wrong. Anne was moving around mechanically even our greeting kiss was off the mark. My first thoughts were her mother had called or was here and upset Anne so I fished around with a few question about her day. She was sort of noncommittal then asked if I read Daley's article in the morning newspaper. I tried to rethink what was in the article because it was obvious this was what was bothering her. I replied I did. She said, "Don't you think it was odd that Daley knew who was at Mary's memorial service by name and that there was a reading from the Gospel according to Mark"?

"Well yeah and true to form he got the person reading the Gospel wrong he mentioned me not Tom".

"Fine; just think a minute it was raining there was no one insight just the five of us how did he know the Gospel according to Mark was read at all"? I vaguely knew where she was going so I said nothing and let it hang in the air until she continued. "We talked away back about the leaks to this guy Dailey and we couldn't match up any one with both a motive and the knowledge to leak the information to him. Who of the five people at the Memorial Service had both and now in less than a day Dailey comes up with this bit of information in his article".

"Yeah well he didn't get the story right he had me giving the Gospel and not Tom so who ever gave him the information wasn't there".

"That's where we differ he was there and he is clever enough to just give Dailey the story and let him fill in the details by himself that's where the inaccuracies come in. These leaks were thought out in advance to make sure he wouldn't be recognized as the source". I was looking at her dumb founded she now let the conversation stop with a facial expression of smugness making me say his name.

"Oscar".

"Yes".

"But why"?

"To keep his belief alive that it was not a mob hit".

CPSIA information can be obtained
at www.ICGtesting.com
Printed in the USA
BVHW031044070219
539718BV00004B/21/P

9 781984 574091